# Veil of Embers

## The Threadfire Series
## Karla Molina

Karla Molina

First edition

Cover art by Llysaan

Illustrations by Llysaan

Editing by Donna Hillyer

# CONTENTS


Prologue                                    2

1.  Hunters Watch                           5

2.  Commander                              13

3.  Look to the Forest                     18

4.  Merciful End                           27

5.  Spreading Sickness                     30

6.  Willful Blindness                      34

7.  Whispers in the Library               40

8.  Into the Mist                          45

9.  Divine Intervention                    49

10.  Reckless Encounter                    54

11.  Vaelric's Mark                        59

12.  Fragile                               65

13.  What a Pleasant Surprise              70

14.  Run Away Scarf                        74

15.  A Storm is Coming                     80

16.  The Gathering                         87

17.  Kelpie's Song                         91

18. Slán Agat                          105

19. Unspoken Truth                     108

20. A Night of Terrors                 113

21. Morning Light                      116

22. Seeds of Doubt                     121

23. A Watcher's Duty                   124

24. Glimmer Before the Dark            127

25. Festival                           136

26. The Weight of Loss                 146

27. The City                           149

28. A New Member                       154

29. The Elk                            162

30. A Council of Fools                 168

31. The Truth                          174

32. An Unlikely Companion              181

33. A Terrible Influence               186

34. The Full Story                     192

35. Hard Truths                        196

36. Silent Sorrow                      201

37. A Desperate Plan                   205

38. A Glimpse of the Void              213

39. An Urgent Plea                     225

40. The Bridge of the Forgotten        231

| | |
|---|---|
| 41. Part 2 | 240 |
| 42. A Bitter Homecoming | 241 |
| 43. New Beginnings | 243 |
| 44. Uneasy Reunion | 249 |
| 45. Dinner with a Monster | 256 |
| 46. At The Cliff's Edge | 261 |
| 47. Dangerous Paths | 266 |
| 48. Unlocking Potential | 271 |
| 49. Power Has a Cost | 276 |
| 50. The Fall | 288 |
| 51. Meanwhile in Lumora | 294 |
| 52. The Moment Ruined | 307 |
| 53. Training | 320 |
| 54. A Race Against Time | 330 |
| 55. Samhain | 338 |
| 56. Home | 348 |

INNISGLEN
CAILLEACHS KEEP
LUMORA
GLENTHAR
RIVER BOANN
COILL DORCHA
THRACIAN
FROSTFIRE
MEADOWRUN
AONACH
MARA SCATH
BAELMERE
THE HOLLOW
DRAOI
CLUAINARA
IRONRIDGE
WHISPER PINES
GLEN NA MARA
LIRS HAVEN
DUNMARA
DRUMNEACH

# PROLOGUE

Sweat glistened off Sorcha's skin as she pulled the bowstring tight, releasing a deep exhale.

"We haven't got all day princess," Drystan cupped his hands around his mouth as he yelled across the field. "Some of us still have battle exams."

Riona elbowed Drystan, he winced as he playfully shoved her back, both laughing. Sorcha watched Lumora's cadets, soon to be field officers, watch her. All eyes locked onto her as she steadied herself and aimed at the targets ahead. Druid elders stood nearby, whispering among themselves.

Commander Nethran pointed toward the field and called out, "Ready?"

Sorcha inhaled and focused on the Commander. "Ready."

Runes flared along Commander Nethran's skin as a sudden rush of air circled around the targets, setting them in motion. Erratic and fast as lightning, they flew across the field as one charged toward her. Sorcha ducked into a roll and loosened an arrow. It struck the target dead center, dropping it instantly.

"Lucky shot" Eirin called out, his black hair falling across his face.

"Do it again," Drystan hollered.

Riona cheered as the others whopped and shouted, "You've got this!" Her frost white hair catching in the breeze.

Sorcha rolled her eyes. "Thanks, guys. I've got it."

Another target she didn't notice slammed into the side of her head, wood splintering on impact. The world blurred, ringing filling her ears, but she fired another arrow and hit her mark. Crimson dripped onto her hand as she wiped her nose, her vision slowly coming back into focus. In front of her, Rhosyn, Eirin, Riona and the others shouted and pointed behind her, but she couldn't make out the words when another blow struck the back of her head, sending her stumbling forward. Targets buzzed overhead when a loud snarl cut through the ringing in her ears. Her eyes followed the sound to canine teeth gleaming in the sunlight as it crept close. Large paws vibrated the ground as it stalked forward, a loose rendering of a wolf was in front of her. Its skin stretched too tight over a frame that was decayed and falling apart. It was at some point a living creature but now its reanimated form was glowing a faint blue as an elder flicked her hand.

Suddenly, the runes on her arms glowed faintly, pulsing with an unfamiliar golden light. The animal lunged and Sorcha let her arrows fly. Lodging themselves deep into the animal's skull and chest, the creature falling just short of her feet. She pivoted firing again and again without a single glance, each target falling from the sky in a perfect circle around her.

Commander Nethran stood before her now, arm outstretched. Sorcha grabbed his hand as he pulled her upright.

"Did I pass?" she asked, smiling as he met her gaze.

"I'd say you more than passed." He laughed, clapping her on the back. "Welcome to the Circle of Light. Let's get you your runes."

The Elders approached, congratulating Sorcha as they placed their hands on her arms.

"Welcome to the Circle of Light, Ranger."

They began to whisper, and fire erupted across Sorcha's skin. Her teeth clenched as she held her breath, the runes burning into her flesh. The magic felt like pins and needles spreading through her when suddenly light surged outward. The elders gasped as they stepped back. For just a moment Sorcha was nothing but light. Then it vanished, leaving gold flecks dancing across her skin. Sorcha looked to the Commander, the Elders and the silent cadets. An elder stepped forward, resting a hand on her shoulder.

"It was just an unexpected magic outburst. Magic can be unpredictable at times." She smiled gently and returned to the elders, walking away toward town.

# Chapter 1
## HUNTERS WATCH

Crouching low, Sorcha steadied her bow as she inhaled the scent of damp earth and wild roses. On the exhale her gaze scanned the trees as loud cracks split the limbs.

At first, each snap was separated by a breath, a moment in the brittle stillness. Then the sounds began to quicken, splintering closer together, until they echoed the rapid beat of her heart.

The brush in front of her began to tremble.

Leaves shivering in endless motion before a white rabbit leapt out. It sat curiously as it examined her, its silver-threaded eyes catching the last of the daylight. Light seemed to gather within them, swirling like liquid starlight as it tilted its head with a slow, deliberate twitch of its ear.

Before Sorcha could react, it turned and vanished back into the trees.

"For Lugh's sake," she muttered, relief loosening her grip.

She slid the bow across her back, rubbing at her temples since the sleepless nights had left her painfully on edge. A chuckle escaped her lips, half anxiousness and half exhaustion.

"It would have made a wonderful dinner."

As she stood there, her gaze drifted to the horizon, where the sun sank in its slow, enchanting ballet.

The hum of insects and distant calls of owls had vanished. The smell of burning pine choked her as a sinister mist drifted in.

A sudden gargling snarl ripped through the forest.

Shadows danced across the forest floor, twisting into the illusion of hands reaching from beyond the trees. The mist curled in thicker, blanketing the forest in darkness. Her eyes darted from one obscured corner to the next.

Sorcha backed away slowly as two creatures crept from the shadows. Her heart hammered in her chest as beads of sweat slid down her face. Their movements were jerky and unnatural, like puppets on frayed strings. At first glance, she mistook them for ordinary wolves but as they stepped into the dying light, she saw they were the size of horses. Their heads snapping violently from side to side as they bit at the air, revealing teeth like jagged glass. Deep scarlet hues dripped from their maws, glistening like droplets of dew.

Patches of peeling flesh slid from their frame, their limbs bent at odd angles. The smell of decay hit her hard, sending her stomach lurching. Her fingers curled around the dagger, muscles coiled as she tried to steady her aim. She hesitated though, because they didn't attack. Instead, they circled her, burning ember eyes tracking her movements. The larger one stepped closer. Its growl softened to almost a whimper as its eyes locked with hers. The smaller one lunged as claws sunk into decaying flesh. Their snarls shattered the stillness as they collided, clawing and snapping in a frenzy that sent blood misting through the air. She watched the two tear into one another, waiting for an opportunity to strike. As soon as the beast exposed its chest, she hurled the dagger at it. A strangled cry tore from its throat as the blade struck hard, sinking in to the hilt. Its howl was almost human as it slumped to the ground. The remaining wolf turned its molten gaze onto her, letting a screeching wail escape its throat before it bolted into the trees. Instinct kicked in as she reached for her bow and fired without hesitation.

The twang from the string echoed in her ear before the distant scream told her she'd hit her mark.

She stood steady with her bow still raised, another arrow notched and waiting. At her feet, the beast lay grotesque, twisted in death. Horror churned in her stomach. Its eyes were human.

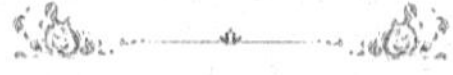

She never forgot that night; the memory haunted her every time she walked this path. Tonight was no different.

Months had passed, but the overgrowth hadn't changed, nor had the hush of twilight. Nothing exciting had taken place this evening as she finished up her patrol.

Stepping into the clearing just beyond the forest's reach, she paused and closed her eyes. The night felt cool against her skin. The crickets chirped softly as the breeze stirred the leaves. Opening her eyes, she looked at the stars above and the moon's silver glow upon the field. The moment was lost to the crunch of leaves underfoot, jolting her to attention. Sorcha tensed as her hand moved to her bow. Her eyes swept the tree line until she spotted a shadow shifting at the edge of the meadow. It was tall and cloaked in a hood that dipped just above the eyes.

"Who's there?" she called, her voice cutting through the night. *"Sorcha."* Whispers filled the air, her name carried on the wind swirling around her. She looked to the hooded shadow, its burning eyes meeting hers.

A wave of heat surged through her chest, crawling beneath her skin. Her runes glowed with flames, dim at the start, then surging with a strength she wasn't able to restrain. Her knees buckled, and the forest spun violently, her veins boiled and her vision fractured, she dropped to a crouch.

*Something inside her was trying to escape.*

Everything was so hot it felt like she was bathing in flames. The fire violently rose in her throat; her nails bit into her skin as she tried to fight away the pain. She let out a scream, arching back, clawing at her throat as a stream of swirling light and fire ripped free and into the sky, bursting into small droplets of starlight.

Stardust rained down all around her. As it kissed her pale skin, the runes faintly glowed but the pain and fire had dissipated. Auburn hair clung to her cheeks, as the golden threads stuck to her forehead. She looked to the woods, sweat and hair blurring her vision, but the figure was already long gone. She remembered the symbols' power, which the Tuatha had once gifted her, as she stared at her runes. The gods had long since abandoned this world, leaving mortals like her to hold the line and keep the balance.

Her birthmarks intertwined with the runes, glistening faintly gold, the magic sending a buzzing sensation through her fingertips. She pushed herself back onto her feet. "What just happened?" she whispered, as if the night might answer.

Standing there, she examined her body and then searched the tree line once more before her eyes fell on the city of Lumora, tucked in the valley below. The lights shimmered in a ripple like a reflection on water, its large golden spires a beacon in the night. Her steps were heavy and weighed down, like she was pulling her feet through mud, her throat still slightly aching as she entered through the city's gates.

Lumora pulsed beneath the moon's glow. Lanterns filled with star sap lined the streets, casting golden light across the cobblestones. The scent of spiced ale and warm bread mingled with the sweetness of night-blooming flowers. Laughter drifted through the air, softened by the low voices of merchants closing up their stalls. In the distance, Skyfall Waters roared, a cascade tumbling from the clouds into the great circular fountain below, etched with runes that shimmered faintly. As she passed, the falling spray caught the light, scattering faint rainbows beneath the lanterns.

The townsfolk said Skyfall Waters carried healing magic, a sacred link between Lumora and the Veil itself. They whispered that Undines, the water spirits, moved through its depths, and that on quiet nights, the lucky might glimpse their iridescent forms. Some believed the Fae blessed the falls, their laughter sometimes heard in the mist. As her feet dragged

across the stone, Sorcha could hear the local tavern still alive with music and conversation. The tavern doors burst open, and out spilled a young man and woman laughing. The two stood close, lost to passion, and slipped away into the closest alleyway moments later.

Sorcha shook her head and smirked as the familiar cobblestone streets led her home. It was a stone house in the quieter part of town, tucked between the sloping hills. Bundles of dried herbs hung by the door, their earthy scent blending with the cool night air. As she reached for the handle, her fingers brushed against the carved sigil, a protective rune, ancient and unlike any in Lumora, its edges smoothed by time and touch.

Her parents had vanished nearly four years ago. She was told they were patrolling the forest just outside of Lumora and would be back by nightfall. But they never returned. She'd been twenty then. Old enough to keep their home, old enough to know she was foolish to keep such hopes that they'd return, but her heart was too stubborn to let go. She traced the rune again; it flickered with the faintest whisper of light. *Maybe they were still out there.*

Pushing the door open, she leaned her bow against the wall and dropped the rest of her gear beside it. Her body ached from the long day and the sudden explosion of light. There were too many questions spinning through her mind, but it was all too much to decipher in one evening.

As she walked past the hallway mirror, her reflection caught her eye, and she winced. Leaves were tangled in her hair, and dirt streaked across her cheeks and forehead. Her skin was slick with sweat, like she'd just stepped from a shower. She looked like she'd fought the forest instead of walking through it. Running her fingers through her hair, she began pulling the leaves free as she made her way to her room.

Inside, she paused to pull her shirt over her head and shake off her pants. Tossing her clothes into the corner, she grabbed an oversized shirt from her bedpost on her way to the bathroom.

The cool water poured into the tub, rippling as faint runes along the stone glowed to life. The enchantment was old, set generations ago to warm and purify the water. Every home in Lumora held such traces of magic, small blessings left behind from the age of Wild Magic. Lanterns of star sap brightened at dusk without a flame, hearths caught with a whispered word, and doors sealed themselves against the wind. Magic was everywhere, woven into the bones of the city and the rhythm of its people.

Sorcha dipped her hands into the rising water, watching the light shimmer across the surface. To most, it was simply another comfort of life in Lumora. For her, it quietly reminded her how deeply the world connected to the Veil.

Emerging from the bath, she pulled the shirt over her head. Her damp curls fell wild around her shoulders like a tangled mane. Collapsing onto the bed, limbs splayed across the blankets, she exhaled loudly. Her body throbbed with a dull ache as she stared at the ceiling and began counting crows, much like she did as a child when sleep evaded her. She had counted to almost a thousand before she tossed and tossed again. Sleep refused to come. She was hot and uncomfortable as she sprang from the bed.

Opening the windows wide, she breathed in the cool night air. Then, turning back to her bed, she slipped beneath the blankets, wrapping them tightly around herself as the steady rhythm of the waterfall outside murmured through the quiet. Its sound, constant and familiar, worked to lull her toward an uneasy sleep.

As her eyelids grew heavy, the world slipped away, fading into darkness. Shadows curled at her feet, soft fog shifting in and out of focus. The faint glow of the Veil hovered in the distance. She knew what came next as the whispers began curling around her ears. Ahead, the vision wavered, lights humming like distant stars. It was the *wisps*. They hovered ahead, their lights pulsing with a strange urgency. They weren't leading her deeper into the unknown, no woods or winding paths. Instead, they circled her, frenzied and chaotic, darting back and forth as though running from something. Their whispers were loud and frantic as a man stepped from the shadows. Just beyond the glow of the wisps, his figure was half concealed in darkness. Sorcha's chest tightened as his eyes met hers.

The wisps faltered, their lights dimming as if his presence alone drained the life from them. Their soft whispers escalated into desperate, shrieking cries: "Wake up!"

But she couldn't move. The world around her rippled, his figure blurring like a heat mirage. She knew without a doubt that this was the figure from the meadow. Her chest still ached as if seared by fire, the scent of pine lingering in her nose. It felt like she'd been standing there in the stillness for hours when suddenly the fog pulled away. Darkness plunged over her as she gasped awake.

The blankets tangled around her. Her heart pounded as loud as the steady rush of the waterfall that broke through the birdsong. Sunlight was bleeding into the room.

# Chapter 2
## COMMANDER

Sorcha rubbed her eyes, clutching the blankets until her knuckles whitened. Cool air brushed her skin, raising goosebumps as sunlight crept across the floor, chasing away the remnants of night.

The room was its usual contradiction of order and chaos. Shelves bowed beneath the weight of bestiaries, spell books, and old star charts. Trays of drying herbs crowded the vanity. Half-folded clothes draped from the dresser like surrendering flags. She dragged a hand through her hair, wincing as her fingers snagged in the tangles.

"It was nothing," she whispered, as if saying it aloud might make it so. Swinging her legs over the bed, she stretched, her toes tapping against the cool stone. The dream still clung to her; the gold runes, the forest's decay, the twisted creatures. She'd seen too much to pretend it meant nothing.

Shaking off the thought, Sorcha crossed the room and grabbed a shirt draped over a chair. She sniffed it, squinting toward the light. "Clean enough."

She pulled on yesterday's trousers, tying her hair back as she tore a hunk of bread from a loaf on the counter. Moving quickly, she shoved it between her teeth, bow and quiver slung over her shoulder in one practiced motion.

Casting one last glance at her room, she kicked the door shut behind her.

The morning sunlight caught the gold stitching on her sleeves. Her boots clacked against the cobblestones as she hurried through town. She nodded to a few early risers and waved to children hurrying to school, but she didn't slow down. Commander Nethran had made his opinion of her lateness very clear already, many times.

By the time she reached the square, the city was fully awake. Market stalls creaked open, vendors called greetings across the courtyard, and Circle members were already gathering. They checked their gear, adjusted armor, and spoke in quiet, focused tones. The rising sun gleamed on metal and rune marked leather, a low hum of enchantment weaving through the air as protective wards settled over each piece.

Commander Nethran stood near a carved stone post. The sun caught strands of his dark-violet hair, which looked almost black until he shifted after he had tied it back. His lilac eyes looked over the movement around him as he rolled his broad shoulders, the muscles rippling as he moved.

Nethran was built for the battlefield. The ink that marked him from wrist to throat pulsed faintly under his skin. He earned each rune, which recorded rank and mastery. More runes meant more power. Nethran had more than most.

His eyes were sweeping across the group once more when his sight landed on her. He pushed away from the post and straightened, his stance shifting from relaxed to what seemed like irritation. "Glad to see you've joined us on time, Sorcha."

Sorcha paused and offered a faint smile, trying to keep her tone even. "Commander," she nodded, "ready for the day."

His eyes swept across the other Circle members before returning to her. "Thrilled to hear it." A few hushed laughs and scoffs escaped the other lips. "There's a patrol briefing at Skyfall. We move in two minutes." He pointed his finger at Sorcha. "Except you. A word."

The others moved toward the falls, murmuring as they passed. Sorcha stayed put, watching as they gave her weary glances. Her expression tightened.

"Yes, Commander?" she said as she stood at attention.

"We've talked about this." His voice was low but firm. "You're my lead ranger. That means you set the tone and expectations. You don't trail in late."

"I know." Her shoulders sagged slightly. "I'm trying. It's the dreams; last night's were worse than usual."

Just as Nethran's gaze landed on Sorcha, a flicker of shimmering light zipped past his shoulder. Sorcha's eyes widened as the silvery blur buzzed around them, no one else seemed to notice as she watched it dart beyond sight but not before she caught the faint scent of wildflowers and heard the tiniest giggle in her ear as it disappeared.

Nethran didn't flinch, but his brow twitched. "Something amusing?"

"No, Commander." She clenched her jaw. Of all moments for something else strange to happen, this wasn't it.

Nethran studied her for a few moments. "Trying isn't good enough. You'll have to do better." Without another word, he turned toward Skyfall.

As they approached the falls, the roar of the water greeted them as the Circle stepped into the square. Mist caught the light, scattering it across the carved stones and moss lined path. Runes shimmered faintly overhead, forming a barrier of protection that hummed just beneath hearing.

The Circle of Light gathered in a loose semicircle.

Mason, who had been standing off to the side with Eirin, exchanged looks. Riona checked her belt as Drystan shifted uncomfortably. Emry pulled a worn notebook from his satchel, ready to write notes.

A Druid elder, hair braided in silver coils, cleared his throat as he approached.

"Members of the Light, let's not worry the townspeople or surrounding communities with talk of creatures or odd plants. I've read the reports, and I hear your concern. Keep up with your finding and send them directly to us. We will decide what needs attention and what is necessary for our people to know."

Rhosyn's honey-gold eyes met the Elder's. Her voice was soft but confident. "If there aren't any issues, I'll gather samples. We'll know soon enough if what's happening."

She stepped forward slightly; the sun caught the black waves of her hair. A few strands had slipped free from her braid, brushing against skin that was rich, the warm brown of a polished garnet. Her freckles stretched across her nose and cheeks like flecks of gold dust. She moved with quiet certainty, unhurried, but purposeful.

Sorcha watched her for a moment, then checked her gear again. The elder took a final bow and, one by one, the Circle turned and moved out, their steps quiet on the stone.

Sorcha lingered. Above, the runic ward flickered faintly, pulsing once before settling back into stillness. She turned to face the waterfall. Droplets shimmered in the sunlight, veiling the falls like threads of glass. For a moment, the roar of water seemed to dull everything else when she saw a pair of iridescent sparkling eyes peeking through the falls. Sorcha moved closer to see what it was when a faint giggle echoed, followed by the delicate splash of water. A beautiful, luminous face appeared from inside the waterfall. Somehow it remained within the falls, its body shimmering like millions of scattered diamonds on water. Curiosity pulled her a step closer; the cold mist brushing her toes as she leaned toward that glimmering face.

The creature tilted its head, watching her with a mischievous smile as it lifted one hand to its lips and blew a kiss.

A burst of water arced toward Sorcha, like a handful of rain tossed through the air. She flinched, blinking against the spray. When she looked again, the creature was gone. Only ripples remained, dissolving into the rush of the falls. It had to be the Undines. Elemental water spirits, like nymphs, but they blessed their waters with healing powers. Sorcha had never seen one before; no one had that she knew. She had a rising sense that the realm was shifting. She would keep this to herself for now because Lumora still felt safe.

She adjusted the straps of her quiver and headed for the center of town. There was still a patrol ahead and a growing sense she'd need to be more vigilant than ever.

# Chapter 3
## Look to the Forest

**M**orning light spilled over the rooftops, the sky was still waking as beams of pale-gold threaded through the clouds. Sorcha crossed the town's edge, her boots clicking on the worn paths. Her task was simple: check in with townsfolk, gather word from the nearby farms, keep her eyes open.

Just a routine patrol, but the tension in her steps hadn't eased since the meeting at Skyfall. A cool breeze carried the scents of cinnamon sugar that kissed her nose, and her stomach grumbled in response.

"I suppose the bakery is the first stop this morning." Looking towards the stone and wood buildings, smoke puffed from one peculiar chimney. It was as though it was trying to create stairs to the heavens but strayed too far right, sat her favorite bakery. Loaves of bread, biscuits, honeyed buns and other sweets lined the shelves in the window. "Milis Bakery" gold lettering hung over the open door as a tall, stocky older gentleman walked out, clapping flour into the air from his hands. Milo. He had a strong yet gentle face with the most joyful smile. He dusted flour from his arms, his sea-foam eyes crinkling as he waved Sorcha inside.

"Here," he said, pressing a honeyed roll into her hand. The pastry was still warm, the glaze sticky on her fingertips. "Those damn deer will be the death of me. I'll be out of business, and you'll be out of honey rolls. Wee devils need to be controlled."

The buttery sweetness melted across her tongue, and she nearly choked trying to hold in her laugh. Soon she was snorting, and Milo doubled over too, shaking his head.

"I'm serious, Sorcha!" he said, wagging a flour-dusted finger at her. "Stop laughing. They're conspiring against me."

"Milo," she said between chuckles, "I highly doubt the deer are holding secret gatherings to discuss your downfall."

"You just wait, missy. You'll see." His grin lingered, though his tone softened. "In the meantime, could you do something about it?"

Sorcha licked a smear of honey from her thumb and nodded. "I'll help reinforce your cellar door and leave food out to draw them off."

"Good girl," Milo muttered, already stuffing extra rolls into a paper bag. He shoved it into her hands, the warmth of the bread seeping through the paper. "Take these before the deer do."

Sorcha shook her head, smiling as she stepped back into the morning light, the comfort of sugar and laughter clinging to her even as she turned toward the rest of town. By the gossip well, where the older women always gathered to talk, two muttered about squirrels tearing through dried herbs and the forest feeling "off." Sorcha made a note of it as she thanked them and kept moving. Since her last encounter had nearly ended with her throwing herself into the well to escape their questions, she had learned to keep conversations short. She knew that if she lingered too long, they would corner her about whether she was seeing anyone or planning to marry, which was the last thing she wanted to discuss. She'd rather face wolves than the village gossips.

By midmorning, she had made her way through most of the inner paths, looping out now toward the distant fields.

One last stop before circling back was a small farm on the outermost edge, where crops thinned and the woods crept closer with every season. She knew the place; the apple trees were her favorite. The sweet smell of apples carried on the breeze when they ripened. They were a quiet and lovely family. They had sheep, a few chickens, a sweet dog who would bark happily, and they were always generous with apples in the fall.

But the moment she stepped past the gate, she felt it. The quiet that welcomed her was anything but normal, the absence of the barking dogs or clucking from the coop. A heavy, sour sweet stench drifted on the breeze, strong enough to sting the back of her throat. The house ahead was quiet, but as she stepped closer, she saw blood trailed along the ground to the barn.

The barn door was ajar, its edge splintered as if it had been forced open. She drew her blade before stepping inside. The smell of blood and decay crashed into her.

Three sheep torn open in brutal, careless slashes. A small pile of decapitated chickens lay nearby, sliced up and gutted. Entrails spewed across the barn floor as flies buzzed in lazy spirals above the carnage. Dried drag marks streaked the floorboards, leading toward the back pasture.

A man stood in the shadows, shoulders hunched, his face pale. He stood over a mound as tears streamed down his face as he turned to her.

"We didn't hear it come," he said, voice rasping like he'd swallowed gravel.

She knelt down, studying the ground. Wide claw marks scored the floor, deep and uneven gouges. Claws that had broken off were submerged in the blood. Next to it, almost lost in the gore, were boot prints.

"Which way does the trail lead?"

The man pointed silently towards the woods. She'd followed the blood through the fields, slipping into the trees, boots silent as she moved. The sun had just disappeared below the horizon, giving way to a darkening velvet sky. The faint trail of fresh footprints leading deeper into the trees.

Fog rolled low, swallowing her boots. A shape formed ahead; she crouched instinctively behind a fallen log. Branches cracked in different directions, snapping her aim between shadow and sound.

Her eyes locked onto a shape materializing in the haze. It was a figure, tall and strong. For a moment, she wondered if it was the injured beast. But as he stepped closer, his face came into view, outlined by moonlight filtering through the trees.

His coppery-blond hair had just brushed the tops of his broad shoulders, and slate-blue eyes stood in stark contrast against the dark. His jaw was powerful and square, softened only by the faint shadow of stubble that traced its clean lines. Sorcha watched him closely, her attention locked onto the man in front of her. He appeared to be searching for something when a sudden crack behind them startled both to attention. Branches continued to break under the weight of the unseen.

When out of the undergrowth, the wounded creature lunged. Its snarls tore through the stillness. Sorcha spun, bow rising in one fluid motion. Her runes flared beneath her skin, heat racing along her arms. But before she could release the string, the man stepped forward and raised his hands. His tunic caught the wind, the fabric clinging just long enough to outline the strength of his arms, the long stretch of his torso. Sorcha's gaze snapped between him and the approaching creature.

Mist coiled around the forest floor, curling between tree roots and twisting through the air as if it had a will of its own. As the creature charged, the haze snaked toward it, wrapping around its limbs, constricting as it struggled forward. Its snarls turned to screams when the mist curled around its legs, it thrashed against the force overtaking it.

The man turned pale, staring wide eyed as he whispered.

His hands moved, and the mist responded. It surged around the beast, tightening its grip until the creature's struggles faltered. A final, pitiful whine slipped from its throat before it dropped, panting and still. Sorcha watched, her arrow remained notched, her eyes locked on the man. Her heart was still drumming in her ears. She hadn't decided if he'd just saved them or if things just became more dangerous.

The creature, stunned, stared at him with a mix of terror and sorrow. As the fog receded, Sorcha thought she saw compassion flicker across the man's face. He turned to her, holding her gaze, rooting her to the spot.

"I mean you no harm, Sorcha," he whispered. His voice was low and edged with a rasp, yet it slid through her like silk, sweet and unsettling all at once.

Her grip on the bow loosened slightly. The shimmer in her hair caught the moonlight, gold threads glowing under the moon's gaze, and his eyes lingered there for a moment before returning to hers.

"How do you know my name? Who are you?" Her voice wavered despite her best efforts to keep it steady.

He hesitated, listening to leaves rustle in the treetops above.

"Kyron."

Her gaze shot to the subdued creature slumped on the forest floor.

The creature whimpered as Kyron knelt beside it. The gray clouds curling gently around them as he placed his hand over its face and the creature went limp beside him.

"It's safer if you leave this part of the forest," he warned, his voice was filled with frustration but also strained. Before she could speak, he stepped back into the shadows. His figure dissolved into the haze with the creature, leaving her alone in the clearing. The forest was suddenly so quiet, as if neither he nor the creature had ever been there.

Doubt crept in. Had she imagined it? She searched the area twice over. At first, there was nothing. There was not a trace of them to be seen. Then, as if the moon were illuminating the path for her, light poured onto faint tracks, revealing small splatters of decayed flesh. Subtle signs, nearly hidden by fog, but enough to confirm what she'd seen. Unease twisted in her chest as she turned toward Lumora. Kyron's warning wrapped around her thoughts, constricting all others from her mind.

By the time she reached town, the night was well past midnight. Torchlights swayed in the breeze. Their flickering glow lit the tall golden gates and guided her to the central guard post. Her boots tapped on the cobblestones in slow rhythm as she began to gather her thoughts. She quickened her pace, trying to think of what she would tell the Commander.

Inside, Commander Nethran stood at his desk, poring over a stack of reports. The lantern's glow lit the dark amethyst strands of his hair. He looked up suddenly as she entered, his eyes narrowing.

"Everything all right, Ranger?"

Sorcha hesitated. The surreal events clung to her thoughts. She hadn't had time to process them, but she knew she couldn't keep them to herself.

"I followed the beast that attacked the small farm outside Lumora," she began, voice steadying. "But I ran into someone while tracking it in the woods." She tried to collect herself for a moment before continuing. "He subdued the creature and then vanished."

Nethran's expression darkened.

"You found it, but it got away?" Nethran's face changed from calm to irritated within moments. "I'm not following. What do you mean, they vanished?"

She shook her head.

"Respectfully, sir, I mean they disappeared. One moment they were there. The next, gone into the mist." She waved her hands in the air, trying to illustrate what she meant.

"I know how it sounds, Commander. But all I have is a name Kyron."

His name settled heavily in the room. Nethran's eyebrow raised, and he tapped his fingers on the desk for a moment, lost in thought. "You did the right thing, reporting this. I'll alert the Circle. For now, head home. We'll figure out what it all means tomorrow."

Sorcha nodded. Relief and confusion tugged at her in equal measure. Giving a brief salute, she turned to leave. She could go home and crawl into bed, pretend the day hadn't happened, but her nerves refused to settle.

Her boots carried her, almost without thought, toward the low amber glow of the tavern windows. Inside, the familiar hum of clinking mugs and quiet voices wrapped around her like an old cloak.

Drystan looked up from his corner table, one brow raised. The color of Scots pine lingered in his hair, a burnished brown touched by the sun, which was half pulled up in a neat knot. The rest falling over his shoulders stopping short of his collarbone. A few stray pieces fell across his cheekbones, framing his face.

"You look like you've seen a ghost," he murmured, sliding a mug across the table without waiting for her to ask.

She dropped into the seat across from him; the wood creaked beneath her weight.

"Something like that," she mumbled, lifting the ale and gulping down a few mouthfuls. Then she leaned back in the chair with a sigh.

Drystan chuckled, slipping an arm around her shoulder. Those bluebell eyes, adorned with long eyelashes, stared into hers.

"Let's have it," he teased. "What's going on?"

Sorcha looked at his devilishly handsome face and exhaled, letting herself lean into the comfort of his arm.

"You know that quiet family on the edge of the fields? The ones who always give out apples at harvest?"

Drystan nodded. "How could I forget? Those apples alone kept me alive all last season. Why?" Then his smile faltered. "Did something happen to them?"

Sorcha let the words fall freely as her hands trembled slightly. "Many of the livestock perished along with their dog being severely injured. Their barn is also damaged."

She shook her head, teeth clenched. "Whatever did it didn't kill to eat. It tore them apart and just... left the bodies." Her thoughts went back to the beast in the woods as her voice trailed off. She reached for the mug again, gulping more down.

Drystan was quiet for a beat, his fingers drumming against the mug, watching her stare into hers. Then he gave a small nod.

"I'll head over there tomorrow, lend a hand with the barn door. I'll have Mason come with me."

Sorcha turned to him, her expression softening. "Thank you."

He waved it off. "Don't. It's the least I can do."

He flagged the barkeep for another round, then gave her a grin full of trouble.

"So... how many drinks till you come home with me?"

Sorcha chuckled into her mug. "I came out to drink, not to carry your sorry ass home."

Drystan winked. "That's one way to get you into my bed."

Sorcha laughed again, raising her mug. "To surviving another day."

Drystan shook his head and smiled. "Another day."

# Chapter 4
## MERCIFUL END

As the fog thinned, the golden city blurred behind him; his knees hit the soil before he'd realized he'd dropped.

The fog carried Kyron and the creature on a storm cloud of mist, landing them into a grove just beyond the sanctity of the Tuatha Dé Danann. The city shimmered behind him, fading into the distance as he turned to the figure slumped by his side. Gnarled bark and twisted limbs wrapped around a body blackened like ash. Crimson veins pulsed beneath the skin like molten sap, crawling through the bark that veiled what was left of a face.

His gaze caught on a faint star-shaped mark etched into its shoulder, and his breath hitched.

Alenia.

She had vanished from the Tuatha court two weeks earlier, a witch and a scry gifted with healing and foresight. Kind and soft spoken, her eyes had been the color of primrose petals, and a small star birthmark had rested above her heart. Whispers had always followed her, saying she came from the stars themselves.

Kyron had come to these woods on a different mission entirely, but that no longer mattered. As he knelt in the ash and ruin, staring at the twisted remains before him, he knew it was her.

The darkness had taken hold and there was no coming back from it now.

The creature's body jerked suddenly, bones snapping, limbs twitching in violent spasms. Kyron flinched, then steadied himself as its jaw unhinged in a snarl, revealing jagged teeth slick with black saliva. He stepped forward, forcing calm into his voice, and spoke her name.

"Alenia."

For a moment, the thrashing stopped. The creature's eyes, wild and blood fogged, found his. They shimmered faintly pink, like spring blossoms steeped in starlight. Tears welled and cut pale tracks through the soot on her cheeks. She shook her head in a silent plea.

Kyron's throat tightened as he reached for his blade, her eyes watching closely as his sword cleared its sheath. He hovered it over her chest, just above the star mark he had once kissed as flashes of young love flickered behind his eyes.

The memories of kisses stolen under the ancient yew trees, flower picking in his mother's gardens and how she'd smell of sweet clover for days after, the sunsets they watched from the golden fields of the Tuatha.

His gaze held hers as he watched her struggle to remain in control of what little was left of herself and he knew that this was better than damnation.

"I'm sorry," he whispered, the words breaking apart in his throat.

The blade drove down and ribs snapped beneath the force of it. The sound was sharp and splintering like tree branches cracking in winter as a soft cry tore from her throat and then fell away into silence. Her body shuddered once before it stilled and in that moment, her face seemed almost peaceful. Her eyes lifted toward the violet hues of the sky, to the faint shimmer of stars dancing between the clouds.

Kyron felt a hollow relief that he had found her, that he had been the one to say goodbye. Yet the truth ached in his heart. It wasn't peace he felt, only the sharp grief of farewell. If he had found her sooner, there might have been a way to heal her. To save her from the darkness that had taken hold. Now all he could do was make sure she hadn't died alone.

Kyron stayed on his knees beside her body, his hand still resting on the hilt as he bowed his head and whispered into the stillness.

"May the Dagda show you the light. May the Don take your hand and lead you through the rivers that run steady and true, and guide you home to Tír na nÓg."

# Chapter 5
## SPREADING SICKNESS

**M**orning broke with the relentless chirping of birds, dragging Sorcha from a restless sleep. She groaned, stretching the ache from her limbs. After too much ale and too little rest, she'd finally drifted off and now the birds refused to let her keep it.

Then a sharp knock rattled the door. "Sorcha! Grab your gear, let's go!"

Commander Nethran's voice thundered through the morning air. She blinked hard, heart leaping awake faster than her thoughts. Still half dressed, she stumbled toward her boots, tugged them on, and snatched her cloak from the chair. The second knock came just as she yanked the latch open.

Nethran stood waiting with Circle members at his back, all already armed and alert.

"What's happened?" she asked, rubbing the sleep from her face.

"A hunter reported a strange plant with a sickness in the woods," Nethran said, eyes scanning her to make sure she was ready. "It might be connected to last night. We need to check it out."

Sorcha grabbed her bow and quiver, throwing them over her shoulder. "I'm ready."

They set out at once, moving through the waking streets as pale light climbed the rooftops. A town scout led them to the trees, and the city's warmth fell away behind them. Early sun spread thin across the forest floor.

The deeper they walked, the quieter the woods became, until only the soft thud of their steps remained.

She knew the clearing the moment she saw it. The trees stood lifeless, gray and brittle, bark peeling in flakes that crumbled at the lightest touch. At the center, something pulsed. A massive black flower rose from the earth, slick and glistening, its petals curled inward like a clenched fist. Pale dust drifted from its core and settled over the dying ground.

Mason hovered closer. "That's not normal."

No," Nethran said, careful but intent as he studied the thing.

Rhosyn crouched by a patch of shriveled grass. She brushed the blades and pulled back as they powdered beneath her fingers. "The soil is dying. Don't touch it, whatever it is; it burns." Her gaze followed the falling dust. "Look, it's spreading."

As more dust settled, a dark seep rose from the earth beneath the bloom, thick as tar, slithered outward. Sorcha felt her pulse climb. This was no natural blight.

"Stay back," Nethran said. "We don't know what it is." He looked at Sorcha. "You said the creature fell here."

"Exactly here," she answered, and had to swallow before the words would come.

A whisper brushed her ear, faint and singsong like. She stilled, looking to the others; none reacted. The whispers curled around her name.

Sorcha.

She turned around, scanning the clearing, but there was nothing there. Just wind shifting through the dead trees. Then the whisper came again.

Sorcha. She slowly moved away from the group until the voice was closer. The whispers laced with laughter like splintering glass, cracking and cackling.

A slow chill crept up her spine. She turned slowly toward the laughter, but her knees locked in place. Rooted to the spot, she forced herself to look back. The others remained focused on the flower, oblivious to the whispers clawing at her ears. Movement beyond the trees caught her eye as she watched the figure run between the trees, too fast to pin down. At first, she thought it was a small child as it ran, but when it crouched low behind a tree, she could tell it was no child. A tail curled behind it, thin and bristled like a pig's. Hooves pressed into the dirt where small feet should have been. Its hands, narrow and ended in talon-like claws. The head was almost human. Its sunken face gleamed with liquid silver eyes that refused to blink.

Sorcha froze when the thing shifted, its gaze still on her. In a sickening motion, its body snapped forward. Bones cracked and limbs twisted as its skin shed away. Fur rippled over the new skin formed as it hunched down onto all fours. In the space where the figure had stood, a rabbit now remained. She stepped back, steadying herself against a tree.

Of all the cursed things to come across, a Pooka. The rabbit didn't move as it watched her and the others. After a pause and a twitch of its ears, it sped across the clearing and vanished. Sorcha stood motionless. Nearby, Nethran continued his examination of the area. He gave a quick nod to Emry, who immediately pulled out his notebook, sketching the twisted flower in precise, methodical strokes. Riona lifted a cloth to her face, shielding herself from the strange dust still lingering in the air.

Mason's fingers drummed against the hilt of his sword, a restless habit he had never broken. Sweat beaded on his sun-kissed skin, sandy hair curling in the damp air. Amber eyes tracked the treeline as his foot tapped out a steady rhythm. Eirin leaned against the tree, his cleaver resting across his shoulders. His obsidian hair falling into his eyes, forcing him to slide a hand through his hair.

Sorcha stood still, her eyes lingering on the spot where the rabbit had vanished, when a hand settled on her shoulder. She flinched before recognizing Eirin's voice.

"You alright?"

She drew in a breath and forced a smile. "Sorry, yeah. I'm good."

"It doesn't seem that way. You're awfully pale." "Really, I'm fine. Just tired."

Eirin studied her for a moment, his brow furrowing. "Is this about the Hudson family?"

The image of the barn flickered behind her eyes. Torn animal bodies, the blood. The smell of decay. Her throat tightened.

"Yeah. It's been a long week already."

Nethran's voice cut through the thick air. "We'll need samples quickly but carefully. Rhosyn, Emry, take what you can from the plant and soil. We're heading back to Lumora. The Druid Council has requested our presence."

Sorcha nodded, her fingers tightening around the curve of her bow. She had faced countless threats before, but this was different.

The trees whispered behind her as they started back toward Lumora. By the time the city's gates came into view, the towering spires of the library rose against the fading light, pale and watchful beneath the evening sky.

# Chapter 6
## WILLFUL BLINDNESS

The library of Verdant Light stood in the late-morning sun, the light reflecting off the shelves reaching towards the skylights. A large oak grew at its center, branches twisting and reaching to hold up the floors above. Two large black iron staircases sat on either side of it. They spun between the branches to the second and third floors of the library.

In an alcove at the very top, housed a full-length mirror. At a glance, it looked like any other mirror. Its edges adorned with Celtic knot-work that weaved their way to a triple knot at the top center, each of its points bejeweled in emerald. Its surface rippled and shimmered at a whispered incantation and Sorcha watched wide eyed as Circle members from all over the continent stepped through. The Circle of Light summoned the other Circles of Eadartha once more.

Sorcha trailed Commander Nethran as he entered the circular dome. Ruby dipped battle scenes splattered the walls, contrasting with rainbow hued Eadarthan landscapes. Lumora City, its golden spires, illuminated the mural's center where a large circular table sat. Magic pulsed in the air thick with an electric catch, like clothes clinging after drying, a tingling shock beneath the skin.

The floor was covered in runic inscriptions, which seemed to hum faintly like distant thunder as they reflected the soft lantern light. Sorcha felt a familiar unease prickle her skin as she joined the assembled warriors, druids, and scouts. She surveyed the Circle members, noticing the nervous expressions they wore. Restless, they exchanged furtive glances, while the council sat stiffly, their faces betraying their mounting irritation. At the chamber's far end, a tall Druid Elder cleared his throat, signaling for the meeting's start. Elder Thalor stepped forward, his hands clasped calmly, his face a mask of practiced patience.

"Thank you for assembling so swiftly," he began, voice composed. "We've received reports from several provinces now and would like to put everybody's minds at ease. The reports show these incidents are isolated, scattered, and unverified. While unfortunate, these occurrences are not entirely outside the natural variance we see during seasonal transitions. Especially with Samhain approaching."

The silence in the chamber stretched for what seemed like an eternity. When a man in burgundy leathers stepped forward, a representative from the Coastal Circle. "Our shore wards have failed. The healing pools are stagnant, and thick with black algae. Whatever this is, it's not seasonal."

Thalor inclined his head, the gesture polite and unwavering.

"We are investigating environmental factors in those regions. Tidal interference, the unseelie, perhaps even residual magic from past conflicts. Let us not jump to conclusions."

Commander Nethran's arms folded across his chest. "We've encountered something this morning. A tar-like bloom spreading through the forest floor, draining the life from everything it touches." He paused, rapping his knuckles on the wood tabletop. "As for the livestock attack, I believe it isn't an isolated incident. There were signs of intent. Something hunted for the sake of it, then left the bodies to rot."

The elder's response was dull, as he picked his nails with the tip of a small blade. "We appreciate your swift reporting, Commander. The Circle of

Light will evaluate all submitted findings, but we must be cautious not to tangle unrelated events."

Sorcha glanced around the room. Most of the Circle members wore practiced expressions, calm to the point of almost dismissive. A few avoided eye contact altogether.

"The Circle of Light will continue to monitor the situation," Thalor continued. "Unusual flora, magical disturbances, unexplained activity, anything of note is to be documented and reported through official channels. Let's be clear, there is no sign of a real threat at this time."

He let the words hang in the air, final and unquestionable. As the meeting adjourned, the chamber emptied in murmurs and rustling cloaks. Nethran lingered at the edge of the platform, addressing the Circle of Light directly.

"I'll be sending cadets on standard patrols," he said. "The rest of us will remain here, combing the archives. If this has happened before, we'll find it."

With that, the Circle dispersed into the aisles.

Sorcha moved toward the nearest shelf, inhaling the scent of aged-wood polish. Her fingers trailed over the spines of tomes until they settled on a worn green volume: *The Creatures of the Wild: A Balance of Magic and Nature.* She pulled it from the shelf and slid into a chair, lantern light casting long shadows over the pages.

From the corner of her eye, Sorcha spotted Drystan sauntering over, a stack of dusty scrolls balanced precariously in one hand. He dropped into the chair next to her with an exaggerated sigh, stretching his legs beneath the table.

"Researching how to save the world, are we?" he teased, his grin almost infectious. "Or just looking for more bedtime stories?"

"Some of us take this seriously, Drystan," Sorcha retorted, though a small smile tugged at her lips. "Maybe you should try it sometime."

"Gods, and here I thought I was contributing, keeping morale up."

Before Sorcha could respond, Commander Nethran's voice cut through the banter like a blade.

"Focus, both of you," he hissed, his voice low and sharp. "We're not here for games. We need to find something useful in these archives."

Drystan leaned towards Sorcha, peering at the open book. His long brown hair fell over his scarred eyebrow, and his lapis eyes gleamed in the library's dim light. His elbow brushed against hers, a familiar distraction. Across from him, Mason mirrored Drystan's actions, batting his eyelashes at Sorcha. Soft thuds echoed on the polished floor as Riona descended the staircase, her long, silvery blonde braid swaying with each step. Her diamond-colored eyes, flecked with frost, scanned the group with amusement.

Crossing her arms, she chimed in, "Oh, good. A battle of egos."

Drystan threw his hands up in mock surrender, while Mason leaned back in his chair, smirking. "Riona, this isn't a competition. He knows I'd win."

"Win what, exactly?" Mason retorted.

Across the table, Eirin spoke loudly enough for everyone to hear. "Can you all just stop? We all know I'm the best looking one here, and, unlike you lot, I'm not making a fool of myself." He grinned at Sorcha, biting his lip slightly, holding her gaze. He was undeniably handsome, and he knew it, his runes shifting over his muscles like a serpent.

Rhosyn, Sorcha, and Riona burst into laughter, while Emry, Drystan, and Mason glared at Eirin. Emry, usually lost in a book, tried to hide behind it, his straw-colored hair and sky-blue eyes giving him away. He couldn't help but crack a smile, and soon everyone else was laughing too. At the head of the table, Commander Nethran gave them a look that could quell a rebellion. He was clearly a father at the end of his rope.

Riona rolled her eyes. "Enough, you lot. Take your flirting somewhere else before Sorcha explodes."

Caught between a glare and laughter, Sorcha muttered, "I'm fine, thanks. No need to worry."

Riona leaned in, lowering her voice. "It's almost impressive, really. They've turned flirting into a sport."

Riona straightened, finding a seat beside Emry. As Sorcha picked up some scrolls, she saw Emry wink at Riona as he brushed her hand. Sorcha smiled and returned to her book.

As the night wore on, the chatter died down, replaced by focused silence. The soft light of the lanterns did little to combat the encroaching darkness. Shadows stretched across the towering shelves, and the once inviting smell of parchment now felt stale. The Circle's progress was no better than when they had arrived. Sorcha rubbed her temples, staring at yet another ancient text that evaded the topic of magical corruption, offering no real answers. Across from her, Riona slammed a book shut with a frustrated sigh, pushing her chair back.

"If I have to read one more sentence about balance and the natural order, I'm going to lose my mind." Drystan leaned back, tossing a crumpled piece of parchment onto the table.

"I think I just read the same sentence in three different books, all worded slightly differently. I vote we burn the lot of them."

Emry shook his head, raising an eyebrow. "Pretty sure burning books is a crime, even for us."

Drystan grinned. "Then we'll blame it on the corruption."

Even Emry chuckled at that, though his tired expression mirrored the rest of them. He turned to Commander Nethran, who was still skimming a massive tome. "Commander, I think it's time we admitted defeat. For now, anyway."

"We're all running on fumes," Riona added. "We could use a break. Food, maybe a drink or several. Then we can come back and keep going."

Drystan sat up, a mischievous glint in his eyes. "Now that's a plan I can get behind. Who's buying the first round?"

Sorcha half expected Nethran to dismiss the idea outright, but he closed the book in front of him with deliberate care and leaned back in his chair, surveying the group.

"Fine. We'll take an hour. Eat, drink, clear your heads, but we return here tonight. This doesn't wait until morning."

They exchanged relieved glances around the table.

Even in Nethran's rare moments of leniency, they came with boundaries, but it was better than nothing. Everyone began moving at once, stretching and lifting themselves up as if they weighed as much as boulders. Sluggish, they all began to file out as Sorcha finished stacking books, scrolls and tomes. She grabbed her cloak from the back of a chair when a loud bang echoed through the library. She froze, listening for the sound. Then it came again. As her eyes slid over the library, she spotted books scattered across the floor, some open, others torn or askew. Sorcha took another step forward to further examine, but a hand tugged at her arm. She turned to see Rhosyn smiling at her as she pulled her toward the door. "Come on, we've only got an hour!" Sorcha smirked. "Alright, you're right. Let's go." But Sorcha kept her eyes on the shadow moving between the aisles of books.

# Chapter 7
# WHISPERS IN THE LIBRARY

The tavern doors swung open, warm air chasing away the chill. Mason and Drystan were already bickering over the first drink. Commander Nethran took his usual seat, ignoring the bunch. The rest of the Circle trickled in, visibly relieved.

Rhosyn greeted them with a knowing look. "I see you've started without us."

Drystan replied dryly, "Time is ticking."

Emry shot Drystan a look before raising his glass in a mocking toast. Drystan winked and blew a kiss at Emry, who pretended to dodge it. "No way, philanderer! Gods know what company you've been keeping." Another round of laughter erupted, the day's tension melting into shared humor. Eirin smirked. "At least this place is quieter

than the library. Fewer chances for Drystan and Mason to trip over themselves."

With drinks in hand, the Circle settled into simple conversation. Riona glanced around, shaking her head. She lifted her drink. "To ancient texts that say absolutely nothing."

Drystan raised his in response. "And to the brilliant fools who read them, anyway."

Mason muttered into his glass, "Speak for yourself."

Rhosyn laughed. "We're all fools." She raised her glass higher, and Eirin smiled as he reluctantly lifted his in return. Sorcha leaned back, watching the surrounding faces. They weren't just colleagues. They were her friends.

A serving girl passed by with trays of bread and roasted roots, the scents of rosemary and garlic chasing away the old must of scrolls and ink. Emry hardly looked up, his charcoal scratching quick strokes across the page. He angled his notebook toward Rhosyn, murmuring something about the strange twist of the flower's petals. She leaned closer, her dark braid sliding over her shoulder, debating whether the curl of its stem was natural. Their quiet talk pulled in Mason, who offered a dry remark that set Riona snorting into her cup.

The hour slipped by in shared laughter and debate, food dwindling to crumbs between them. By the time they returned to the library, the exhaustion had settled deep.

Scrolls and books lay scattered across the tables. The occasional rustle of pages or the sigh of frustration broke the quiet hum of the room only.

By midnight, fatigue had gripped them all.

Drystan had fallen asleep with his head on a pile of ancient texts, a faint snore escaping him. Across the table, Riona blinked heavily, chin propped on her hand. Emry sat beside her, already dozing, his charcoal still clutched between his fingers. Eirin, ever diligent, worked through his stack of scrolls, though even his focus wavered. Mason had his head in a book as well, literally, drooling.

At the hearth, Sorcha flipped through yet another book. This one was different. With its edges worn, it had no title, no author, no dates, the inside a guide to flowers and herbs. But as she turned the pages, an odd hum began to resonate from it. She looked around, checking if anybody else noticed, but no one stirred. The words that had filled the pages began disappearing, replaced by script she had never seen before.

She rubbed her eyes, certain exhaustion was blurring the words, when Eirin leaned over her chair, his voice low, breath warm against her skin.

"Find anything useful, Sorcha?"

She looked down at the book, but it had returned to its original state, and before she could process it, his lips brushed the curve of her ear. The sudden contact sent an unexpected shiver down her spine as she turned her head toward his touch. Eirin was smirking as he placed his hands on her shoulders and pulled her gently back into the chair. She exhaled, leaning back in the chair as Eirin's hands began to work. His thumbs pressed into the knots of tension, tracing slow, deliberate circles. The weight of the day faded beneath his touch.

A book snapped shut.

Commander Nethran stood at the table, his presence cutting through the quiet. The faint glow of the runes on his forearms flickered in the firelight; his expression unreadable.

"That's enough for now. There's no sense in running ourselves into the ground. We'll regroup after breakfast and split into teams for rounds."

The Circle stirred, and Eirin returned to his seat, stacking the books he had in front of him. Drystan mumbled something incoherent, earning a jab from Riona.

"Wake up, Drystan. Lumora needs its heroes. It won't save itself."

Riona winked at Emry. He smiled in return, grabbing her books as he passed. Riona followed behind him, leaving Drystan slumped over the table.

Drystan groaned, refusing to lift his head. "Give it a few hours. Maybe it'll sort itself out," he muttered. Then louder, "Mason, get up."

"After you, princess," Mason mumbled. Ignoring the banter, Nethran continued. "Sorcha, you'll patrol the woods near the Hollow. Take someone with you. Drystan or Riona. The rest of you will cover the surrounding areas."

Sorcha nodded. "I'll take Riona, sir. She needs more field time."

Riona grinned, barely containing her excitement.

She shot Sorcha a quick smile.

The Circle dispersed, but Sorcha lingered, drawn by an odd pull toward the shelves. She groaned and stretched, rolling her shoulders to ease the tension.

Reaching for the books she had gathered, she began returning them to their places, her fingers hesitating on the last one. It was the book that had shifted at her touch, its pages alive with changing text before Eirin had arrived. The moment his presence settled beside her, the words disappeared. Now, she opened it again, but the pages remained stubbornly still. Footsteps murmured in the background as the others said their goodnights, their voices fading toward the doors.

Sorcha flipped through the pages again, finding nothing. With a sigh, she closed it firmly. As she turned, a movement at the edge of her vision caught her eye: a shadow reaching for the shelf. Instinctively, she spun around, but the aisle was empty, devoid of anything but scrolls. Expecting to find that everything was still in its rightful place, she turned back, only to find the book was gone. She shoved through the stack, pushing pages and tomes aside and searching under the desk and beneath the shelves. There was no sign that the book had ever been there.

Then, slow, creeping footsteps echoed behind her, followed by a scrape that dragged along the wooden shelves, eerily like nails raking against them. The footsteps stopped just beyond the nearest shelf. Carefully, she crept toward the shelves, peering through the gaps in the books, searching for hands, feet, or eyes – anything. Only shifting shadows met her gaze. Suddenly, a sharp pain shot through her temple, causing her to jolt back and knock her head against the corner of the shelf. The sudden ache blurred her vision for a moment. The footsteps had stopped, and breathing curled around her ears.

No, she wouldn't entertain this tonight; whatever it was, it could keep its shadows. "Goodnight," she whispered, not waiting for a response. Turning on her heel, she strode toward the front doors, resisting the urge to look over her shoulder.

Outside, the crisp night air hit her, and she exhaled loudly, tapping her feet on the cobblestones. Pulling her cloak tighter, she began walking through the empty streets, her thoughts tangled with the strange encounter in the library.

# Chapter 8
## INTO THE MIST

Sorcha awoke and hastened to gather her things as she threw on yesterday's pants and a shirt she recovered from the depths of her dresser. She was practically sprinting towards the tavern.

Drystan was the first to notice her arrival, flashing that ever annoying grin.

"Looks like you're off to the Hollow," he teased. "Don't get lost in all that haze. If you do, call for me. I'm great at rescuing damsels in distress."

Sorcha rolled her eyes as she strode toward their usual table. "Good thing *I'm not a damsel.* But I'll let you know if the woods need rescuing."

Across the room, Riona's voice sang over the conversations. "Drystan, stop flirting and eat something before you collapse."

Riona had already perfectly retied her snowy braid, making sure every strand was in place, as she sat. Her eyes followed Sorcha as she approached.

"About time," Riona remarked, a faint smirk tugging at her lips. "I was starting to think I'd have to eat alone."

Sliding into the seat across from her, Sorcha let the warm smell of bread and herbal tea soothe her nerves. The spread was simple, fresh butter, honeyed fruit, and steaming cups of tea.

"So," Riona said, "we're heading into the Hollow." Sorcha's hand hovered over her tea for a brief moment. The name alone stirred unease. The

Hollow wasn't just another part of the woods—it was old, untouched, a place even seasoned trackers hesitated to tread.

"Not exactly how I pictured starting the day," Riona added, her tone light.

Sorcha leaned back, forcing a wry smile. "You mean you didn't wake up hoping to wander into a cursed forest covered in unnatural mist?"

After breakfast, Commander Nethran summoned them to Skyfall Waters. A new recruit wearing an eager smile, delivered the message before darting off to the horse stalls. The Circle then gathered together, collecting their cloaks and weapons, and headed toward the square.

The morning air was crisp, and sunlight warm as they gathered beneath the towering falls.

Nethran stood tall, speaking sternly, "Here are your assignments," he announced, holding a journal aloft. "Remember, I need your reports at the end of each shift." He then split them into groups, assigning each to different forest regions. Mason and Emry were tasked with tracking creatures and cleaning up any carcasses, meticulously noting their locations. Rhosyn and Drystan were to collect forest samples and document any observed changes. Eirin was to interview hunters, take their statements, and record details about regions and towns. Sorcha and Riona were assigned to patrol the outer edges of the hollow, where they inevitably had to venture. As they began loading the horses, Mason and Emry approached.

Mason handed Sorcha the reins as she mounted. "Try not to hog all the excitement, alright?"

"What? And wait for you to catch up? Not likely," she retorted.

Mason laughed. "Fair enough."

As she was about to move her horse, Mason placed a hand on her leg. "Seriously, be careful out there; things have been different lately."

Sorcha covered his hand with her own, nodding. "You too, okay?"

He stepped back as she urged her horse forward. Emry was whispering something to Riona, his voice low and close to her ear. Sorcha saw a faint blush creep onto Riona's face before Emry stepped back. Riona swung into the stirrup and mounted Briar. Mason and Emry turned and rode off, their horses at an easy trot. The rhythmic clopping of hooves echoed against the stone paths, mingling with the distant sounds of Lumora waking. As Sorcha and Riona rode out, the familiar warmth of the fields gave way to dense woodland. The open blue sky narrowed under a thick canopy of towering trees, the path twisting like a serpent through the underbrush. Vibrant greens faded to muted hues, shadows stretching unnaturally beneath the branches. A sudden chill permeated the air as sunlight struggled to pierce the dense fog that clung to the ground.

Riona rode beside Sorcha, but as the darkness crept in, Riona struggled to hide her nerves. Sorcha spoke in a whisper. "Stay alert. The Hollow is known for its illusions." Riona shifted in her saddle, gripping the reins tighter. The horses' hooves softened against the forest floor, muffled by the thick moss below them. The further they rode, the more muted the world became.

At long last they reached the Hollow's threshold. Sorcha pulled the reins back to halt her horse. Shadow let out a huff through his nostrils followed by a loud whinny. The horses refused to settle down, nervously pacing as Sorcha dismounted, then Riona. Sorcha led the horses to the sturdy branch of a hawthorn tree, tying them with just enough slack to allow them to escape if necessary. Side by side, they stepped toward the woods. The ground felt soft beneath their boots, muffled like everything else in the Hollow. The silence stretched for a moment before the whisper of steps reached their ears. A rustling sound ahead, not from wind but something unseen that stirred just beyond the trees.

# Chapter 9
## DIVINE INTERVENTION

A light haze gave the woods an ethereal quality. But as they traveled, the fog shifted; tendrils that slithered through the trees thickened as they pressed further into the center of the forest. Shadows danced between the spaces unseen. A cold touch on Sorcha's shoulder sent heat coiling beneath her skin. The runes flickered beneath her clothes. It wasn't just the warmth; it was a vibration that sent a warning. She rubbed her arm, shrugging off the sensation. Her eyes drifted to the trees. They grew taller the further they went. Their branches tangled together like lovers' hands. Sunlight struggled to reach through their grasp. Forcing her eyes away from the forest, she looked to Riona. She didn't seem concerned yet, and her runes didn't glow as they pushed through the thickening gray.

"I can barely see two feet ahead. Is this normal in the Hollow?" Riona murmured, her voice taut with unease.

Sorcha, ever composed, tightened her grip on her bow. "No, it's not. Something isn't right."

Riona's fingers brushed her knife hilt, nerves prickling. They crept slowly, carving marks into the trees; but the marks kept vanishing.

"Are we going in circles?" Sorcha asked, her voice barely above a whisper.

Riona crouched, brushing her fingers over the damp earth, her expression unsettled.

"Sorcha, look here." Riona pointed to the ground, tracing the trail of black tar crawling around the trees.

They were in the middle of decay. Obsidian vines twisted around the ground, tangling with brush. They clawed their way up the trees and branches, dripping with a darkness that choked the life from them. Just then, Riona rose abruptly, her head snapping toward the distance. A low, haunting sound cut through the emptiness, a single howl that sent a chill racing down Sorcha's spine.

Another howl followed, then another. Each one closer than the last. The eerie chorus echoed from all directions, amplified by the emptiness of the forest.

"By the gods," Riona muttered. "It's the Wolves of the Wild Hunt."

Sorcha's skin was now ablaze, its glow a beacon in the shadows. Riona's own runes were now glowing softly, flickering in acknowledgment. The Spectral wolves, harbingers of death and imbalance. She swallowed hard. "What if they're sick...like the others?"

Riona's jaw clenched, her knuckles white around the grip of her daggers. The thought of facing the already lethal wolves that may be twisted in sickness made her sweat and dread knot in her stomach. The howls grew louder, the sound wrapping around them like a tightening noose. Sorcha turned slowly, runes glimmering beneath her skin. Shapes flickered at the edges of the trees. Humanoid silhouettes with eyes like burning rubies. The wolves prowled at their feet, snarls low, some snapping their teeth.

"Bocanachs," Sorcha hissed. "Ready your daggers." Sorcha remembered that the bocanach got pleasure from causing fear and despair, often lingering near spaces of pain or death to feed on the negative emotions. That they were in the middle of decay and dead animals made it a perfect hunting ground. Sorcha didn't hesitate, now knowing what she was up against.

Her fingers flew to the string, notching an arrow in a practiced motion. The first specter lunged, its form flickering like smoke, and she loosed her shot. The arrow struck true, shattering the figure into vapor. But no sooner had it vanished than two more emerged, gliding toward them with eerie, weightless grace. Sorcha fired again. And again. Each shot dissolved another shadow, yet more kept coming.

"Keep moving!" she barked.

The wolves surged forward, red glowing eyes locked onto their targets. Sorcha spun, heart pounding, loosing an arrow into the nearest one. It let out a piercing howl as its form flickered and dissipated, but there were more. They now we're surrounded.

"We need to climb," she called, voice strained. "We'll have a better vantage point!"

Riona nodded, sheathing her daggers before launching herself up the nearest tree. Sorcha followed, her quiver bouncing against her back as she climbed. Fingers slick with sweat made the climb harder. From their perch, the specters prowled. Sorcha loosed arrow after arrow. Each hit sent another enemy dissolving, but for every one that fell, two more emerged. The runes surged, heat racing through her veins like liquid fire. It gathered at her fingertips, coiling around each arrow like unseen threads of light, ensuring she never missed. With every pull of the string carrying more force than the last, the power inside her rose, demanding to be unleashed.

"We can't hold them off forever!" Sorcha shouted.

Riona pulled a rune stone from her belt, her lips moving swiftly in an incantation. She held it aloft, its faint glow slicing through the air. For a moment, the Bocanachs hesitated, their flickering forms wavering. Her own runes flickered, like lightning bugs in the night.

"Buy me some time!" Riona yelled.

Sorcha fired faster, her shots striking true, even as wolves clawed at the base of the tree. One managed to climb, spectral claws digging into the bark. Sorcha grabbed her dagger, slashing at its face until it lost its grip and tumbled back to the ground. Her vision blurred. For a moment, she saw flashes of shadowy figures writhing in agony, voices rising in a chorus of screams. She clenched her teeth, shaking her head to clear it, fingers tightening around her bow.

"Riona, whatever you're doing, hurry!"

Just as she turned her back to face what was below, a snarl split the air, and jaws clamped onto her calf, teeth sinking deep. Fire and ice shot up her leg, and she screamed as she was yanked violently from her perch.

The world tilted down, and her perspective spun as her back slammed against the ground; her bow flung across the ground. The wolf began dragging her. Dirt filled her mouth as she clawed at the earth. Kicking wildly, her free leg smashed into the wolf's ribs. It only growled, dragging her faster. The sky churned above, the last shreds of light coiling around the treetops. Her vision blurred, flickering between the present and somewhere else. The figures writhed as they came in close. Their voices squealing in delight, drinking in her pain. She could see them swarming like bees around a honeycomb. Each one diving in to take an invisible bite, she clenched her teeth trying to focus, but suddenly the wolf let her go, as the other wolves whimpered. Lowering themselves as they backed away. The shadows twisted, disintegrating as the fog started to part. A shadow took shape in the mist as it stepped forward; a towering horse. Twice the size of any mortal steed. Its mane flowed like liquid silver. A body carved from the night sky streaked with fallen stars. Its eyes burned an icy blue white, haze curling from its nostrils with every breath. Vapor pooled around its hooves, swirling like water stirred by unseen currents. Sorcha's breath caught. Her voice was barely a whisper. "The Ceffyl Dŵr..."

The horse let out a deep, resonant whinny—a sound that rumbled through the clearing. It raised onto its hind legs as it reared back with its hooves striking the air. A wave of silver erupted outward, cascading through the clearing like a tsunami. The wolves recoiled, their howls turned to frantic yelps as they scattered into the shadows. When the Ceffyl Dŵr landed, it was with an earth-quaking crash; the ground beneath it rippled like water. A deep hum reverberated through her body. The aura surrounding it was ancient. Possibly older than the forest itself. Her pulse thundered as fear rooted her to the spot. The horse locked eyes with Sorcha, looking her over as it slowly approached. The horse snorted, releasing a shimmering cloud that cloaked the clearing in its dusting of glittery silver. Slowly and carefully, the Ceffyl Dŵr halted mid step and turned away, vanishing into the shadows. Sorcha's breath came in shallow, uneven gasps. Her fingers dug into the ground beneath her, knuckles white.

The divine presence of the Ceffyl Dŵr wasn't a coincidence in Sorcha's mind; it couldn't have been. She stood slowly, balancing on one leg as she looked for Riona. Riona appeared beneath the tree they perched in, her eyes wide and hands slightly trembling. Sorcha reached for her bow, meeting Riona's eyes.

"We need to move." Her voice was steady now. "That thing wasn't here by chance."

Riona nodded, her expression grim but determined. Without a word, she looped an arm under Sorcha's, steadying her as they moved. The mist slowly dissipated as they retraced their steps.

# Chapter 10
## RECKLESS ENCOUNTER

As Sorcha and Riona stepped beyond the fringes of the Hollow, the tight coil of tension in Sorcha's chest finally began to unwind. Riona had just glanced at Sorcha, who trudged beside her in silence, when things shifted abruptly. A sudden gust carrying a strange chill sent a shiver racing down Sorcha's spine. "Not again," she thought as the air began to thicken. This wasn't the same dense, oppressive fog from before but something else entirely. It was lighter and held an iridescent shimmer as the glow curled around their legs, rising higher with each breath. Sorcha halted, her hands became sweaty, and a slight heat wave washed over her. "Riona," she murmured, her voice strained.

The mist deepened, swallowing the light, muffling all sound. Sorcha turned, reaching into the fog trying to feel for her.

"Riona!" she called, panic lacing her voice. "Where are you?"

A figure emerged from the haze, its silhouette sharp against the swirling clouds. Sorcha's breathing was labored as Kyron stepped forward. His hair caught the faintest glimmer of light like smoldering embers. She let out a long exhale and met his gaze.

"What are you doing here?" he demanded, annoyance clear in his face. She gripped her dagger's hilt tighter. The sudden urge to throw it at him flared, and she struggled to stay calm.

"Just taking a stroll through the forest."

A smirk played across Kyron's lips, the kind Sorcha wanted to wipe off. "You and Riona, wandering into the Hollow with only arrows and a dagger? That's either incredibly brave or incredibly foolish." Distant howls echoed through the trees. Sorcha's pulse quickened as Kyron glanced at the shadows, then back at her. "Honestly, I'm betting on foolish, considering the look of your leg." He stopped pacing and leaned against a tree, arms crossed, gaze dropping to her leg.

Sorcha's eyes narrowed. "Why do you care?" she snapped. "You're the one who keeps vanishing and reappearing like a ghost."

Kyron inhaled deeply, taking another step. "Just blindly walking—sorry—limping into danger," he continued, ignoring her question, his voice softer. "You have no idea what you're getting into."

Sorcha set her jaw, refusing to back down. "Avoiding the question, I see. I can handle myself."

Kyron tilted his head, studying her. He was close enough now that she had to look up to meet his eyes. "Can you?" he asked softly. Something in his tone made her breath catch. "You were lucky today." He stepped closer, mere inches away. "Your birthright saved you." The words chilled her.

She forced a scoff, shaking her head. "What?"

Kyron gave a low laugh, quiet and mocking. "You really don't know?" His gaze held hers, unwavering. "Your runes aren't just ink bound by laws, limits, Sorcha. They're different, without limits. The kind of power that doesn't need to be given. I know you feel it."

Sorcha grew more frustrated with each word. "What are you talking about?"

Kyron took another step. "You'll find out soon enough," he murmured. Something in his voice unsettled her, making her feel as if the ground had shifted. Before she could demand more, the clouds swirled around him, twisting and swallowing him. And then, just like before, he was gone.

Loud singing cut through the fog. "Sorcha!"

Riona's figure emerged from the haze, waving her arms as she called out.

Sorcha blinked, her mind still caught in the moment that had just vanished with Kyron.

Riona raced toward hers, grabbed her arm and practically shouted at her. "What happened?"

Sorcha hesitated, her throat dry. "I... lost sight of you for a second. It must have happened when I looked back." Her voice trailed off as she tried to sound convincing. Riona studied her for a moment before clicking her tongue. "Come on," she said, whistling for Briar to lead the way back to Lumora.

The ride back was silent. The rhythmic clatter of hooves was the only sound between them. By the time they reached Lumora, the sky had deepened to indigo, with the warm glow of sap lanterns lining the streets. The familiar sight of the Circle's Heart came into view, and as they dismounted, Commander Nethran was already waiting at his desk. The runes on his forearms flickered faintly in the dim lighting, casting patterns on the stone walls.

"You're late," he said, but then his eyes snapped to Sorcha's leg. "What happened out there?"

Riona hesitated, glancing at Sorcha before answering. "The Wolves of the Wild Hunt is what, but then..."

Sorcha inhaled, then finished for her. "We think the Ceffyl Dŵr appeared... it was a massive horse made of water. It drove the wolves away."

Unease crossed Nethran's face. "A horse," he repeated flatly. "A water horse. You must have been near a river."

Sorcha nodded, shifting on her feet. "You definitely saw the Ceffyl Dŵr," he said, exhaling through his nose. "Or at least, it let you see it."

At her frown, he pushed off the table and started pacing. "It's not a guardian. Not the way you're probably thinking. The Ceffyl Dŵr isn't here to help us. It doesn't take sides." He glanced at her. "But it is territorial."

Riona, arms hanging beside her, raised a brow. "And it doesn't like wolves in its territory?"

"Exactly. It doesn't like anything in its territory." Nethran stopped near the map, fingers tapping absentmindedly against the edge. "The old stories say the Ceffyl Dŵr belongs to the rivers and the mists, neither living nor dead. It doesn't seek battles, but if something wanders too close into what it considers its own—it will act. Sometimes violently."

Sorcha's stomach tightened. "So we weren't saved. We were just in the right place at the right time?"

He nodded. "Or the wrong place, depending on how you look at it." He fixed her with a steady gaze. "You were lucky. If that thing had decided *you* were the intruders, you'd be at the bottom of the river right now."

Riona scoffed. "Comforting."

"Don't mistake it for an ally," Nethran warned. "It's a force, not a friend. It moves with the river and shifts with the fog. And if you see it again, be sure you know which side of its waters you stand on."

Neither Sorcha nor Riona had an answer. "We'll discuss this further in the morning," he

decided. "For now, let's get that cleaned up."

Sorcha gave a stiff nod as Commander Nethran had gently guided her to a chair. Grabbing medical supplies and rune-stones, he tended to the wound on her leg.

"Ow!" Sorcha yelped as Nethran cleaned the wound.

He chuckled. "Don't be such a baby. It's just a scratch."

Sorcha shot him a glare. "Hell's teeth, Commander! It hurts."

He shook his head and finished bandaging it up as he tapped her leg. "All better. Riona, if you would help her out the door"

# Chapter 11
## VAELRIC'S MARK

As they stepped out onto the streets of Lumora, the soft lights and chatter were music to her ears. She smiled to herself and began walking, limping her way through the winding city. Passing by the falls, a faint giggle sang through the air. Turning toward the sound, she saw a shimmering pair of violet eyes emerging from the circular basin.

The Undine whispered, her lips moving, but the words were lost beneath the rush of water. As Sorcha limped closer, the spirit blew a kiss of water that splashed against her leg. The droplets soaked through the fabric, and a strange warmth began to bloom beneath her skin.

Lifting the edge of her pant leg, she pulled away the bandages. The cut was gone. So was the Undine.

Sorcha stood at the falls for what felt like hours, staring at the spot where the spirit had been. Finally, she whispered, "Thank you."

She walked home in a daze, her thoughts tangled and unsteady. The encounter replayed again and again in her mind, each time slipping further from reason until she could no longer tell if it had truly happened.

Inside, she crumbled. The familiar scent of herbs and wood wrapped around her like an old friend as she slumped against the door. Her fingers traced the runes etched into her arms. *Kyron.* They tingled faintly under her skin, like old kindling reigniting. The runes shimmered beneath her flesh, glowing softly like liquid sunlight.

*Who was he? And why did her runes react to his name?*

The questions tangled in her mind as she climbed into bed. Her eyes tracing patterns in the ceiling shadows, but her thoughts kept pulling her toward the things unsaid. She reached for her journal near the bed and began sketching Kyron's face and writing everything that she could remember. She wrote well into the evening until her hands grew heavy. Eventually the world slipped away, and the dream unfolded like a tapestry of beauty.

The trees rustled gently as she moved; the wisps guided her deeper into the woods. Her steps made no sound upon the frost-kissed ground as the trees thickened, their canopies closing in. Suddenly the ground rumbled, and the forest thinned, revealing a vast frozen expanse.

She now stood at the base of a towering mountain range. Its jagged peaks sliced through the sky like blades. The air was colder here, the heat from her lip curling in soft puffs. She scanned the mountain range, spotting a narrow path stretching before her, winding upward into the mountains.

Emerging from the shadows were large stone golems. Massive figures carved from rock, their eyes glowing blue. Despite their imposing size, they paid her no mind, Moving through the paths as if she weren't there at all. The wisps circled her briefly before darting ahead, disappearing toward the path.

"Where are you leading me?" she whispered.

But the wisps only pressed on, slipping into the darkness of the mouth at the mountain's base. The cavern seemed ordinary—cold stone walls, the faint drip of water echoing in the dark. She kept pushing forward as she ventured deeper. The air thickened, growing heavy with an oppressive weight. A sickly scent curled in her nostrils, clinging to her senses. Then she stepped into the open expanse. What should have been a thriving underground forest was a nightmare. The trees, once majestic, had twisted their branches into unnatural shapes and were blackened and rotting. The ground was littered with the remains of creatures, beasts that had once been beautiful but were now grotesque, their bodies warped and decayed. A shiver ran down her spine. The river cut through the land, dividing it in two. One side, clear as glass. The other was black, writhing, fighting the current. Twisted creatures clawed their way from the depths, their mouths gaping, silent, until the screams came.

Sorcha backed away, but movement at the edge of her vision caught her attention. She turned fully, focusing on the group of men gathered in a tight semicircle, their tattered hooded cloaks barely disguising the figures beneath. All eyes were locked on the man standing at the center.

He was taller than the rest, a figure both beautiful and monstrous. His sharp features reminded her of shattered glass; elegant but dangerous. His eyes, like ember fragments, burned with steady ferocity. The runes carved into his skin glowed a deep, pulsing crimson, veins of molten power threading through the markings like living fire. Suddenly his gaze snapped upward and locked onto hers. All the air fled her lungs. The scream clawing its way up her throat died before it could escape.

"Interesting," he mused, tilting his head as though examining a rare specimen. "I wonder which gods dropped you at my steps."

Sorcha barely had time to process the words before he moved. He was a blur before he was on her, the odd familiar scent of pine hitting her face. His grip closed around her arm, twisting it fiercely behind her. White hot pain shot through her shoulder as a cry tore from her lips.

Within seconds, he was back in front of her, still holding her arm in his iron grip, a twisted smile tugging at his lips. The surrounding wisps darted frantically, their glow flickering as they dimmed. She could hear them now, their voices almost like whispers on the wind.

*"Wake up."*

The blade of a dagger gleamed as he brought it up to her arm, the cold metal biting into her skin before she could even react. He leaned in, his breath warm against her ear. "You're mine."

The dagger pushed deep into her arm, ruby staining her skin as blood spilled from the cut.

Sorcha bolted upright, gasping for breath. The dream still clung to her, suffocating as she clawed for air. Moonlight bled through the window, painting the room silver.

"It was just a dream."

She repeated the words like a mantra, willing her body to still. But then she saw it; the dark wet streaks trickled down her arm, soaking the bed sheets. Panic surged through her, forcing her onto her feet. She stumbled toward the vanity, hands moving on instinct. Her mind reeled, but her fingers worked with steady precision as she pressed herbs to the wound, tracing the edges with cleansing rune stones and finally securing strips of linen in place. The bleeding slowed, but the unease gripping her did not. As she tied the last bandage, her stare fell on the mirror. Her hair was tousled from sleep, shimmered faintly in the moonlight, catching the glow like the sun had kissed stardust. Freckles dusted her skin like scattered constellations upon an impossibly pale sky, but it was her eyes. They once held a vibrant green that looked foreign to her, dull and sunken in. She turned away and stepped into the living room, toward the small reading nook nestled beside the main space. Bookshelves lined the walls, packed with well-worn tomes of varying sizes, their spines softened by years of use.

A steady fire crackled in the hearth, its warmth casting flickering shadows across the room.

At the center sat a small oak table, its legs carved with intricate curling leaves that held a glass top. Beside it, a worn leather chair stood waiting, its surface creased with age and softened by time. Sorcha sank into the chair with a heavy sigh, her eyes fixed on the flames as they twisted and danced to a rhythm only they knew. Her fingers instinctively reached for the notebook lying on the table. Pulling it onto her lap, she uncapped her pen and began to write. Every detail of the dream—the landscapes, the creatures—flowed onto the pages, her hurried words accompanied by quick sketches.

As a scout for the Circle, it was her duty to notice every shift in the land, every detail, and record them. The familiar routine brought her a small measure of comfort. A fragile sense of control in an otherwise chaotic world. Time slipped away as Sorcha wrote tirelessly, her thoughts pouring onto the pages until her hand cramped and her eyes burned from the strain.

When she finally set the notebook and pen aside, she stretched her arms overhead, wincing as her stiff muscles protested. She rolled her ankles to ease the tension and sighed. Placing the notebook back on the table, she rose and made her way to the kitchen. The space was simple yet elegant, much like the rest of her home. Stone floors etched with faint runes pulsed gently as she stepped inside. Sorcha muttered a soft incantation, and a ripple of blue light flowed across the runes, spreading warmth that reached her toes and traveled upward. She retrieved her kettle, an intricate yet understated piece, little etchings of the sun phases, one of her favorites and set it on the stovetop.

As the water began to heat, she paced the kitchen, her thoughts circling back to the nightmare and the blood. Small crystal jars lined the shelves, each filled with carefully preserved herbs and flowers. Sorcha reached for chamomile, lavender, and star flower, crumbling the dried petals into her cup. Their delicate aroma filled the air, soothing her nerves, if only slightly. Tea in hand, she settled onto the wooden bench by the window. She cupped her hands around the warm mug, staring out into the predawn darkness. The thought of sleep felt distant now, unattainable. Instead, she watched the sunrise, hoping its light would bring clarity to the chaos lingering in her mind.

# Chapter 12

## FRAGILE

In the early morning hours, Sorcha poured herself another cup of tea before dressing for the day. Choosing a fitted black shirt to conceal the bandages and keep the steadily bleeding cut out of sight. To secure the fabric, she fastened an intricate floral arm cuff. Then, pulling her hair into a tight ponytail, she slid into a pair of black riding slacks and her worn boots. As she stepped outside, she tried to reason with herself.

I still have responsibilities, she mentally reminded herself. As she shook her head. "I scratched it, or I cut it on something. Maybe the bedpost while thrashing around."

The memory of the man's wicked grin as he slashed her arm flickered through her. Clenching her jaw, she shook her head more firmly as if to banish the image.

Then quickened her pace toward the city center. By the time she reached the square, people were readying for their day, voices lively as they greeted one another. The scent of freshly cooked oats and herbs filled the air, mingling with the crisp scent of morning dew.

Whatever happened last night can wait until after patrols, she told herself as she squared her shoulders before entering the square. Near the center, Circle members had already gathered. Drystan gestured animatedly as he spoke to Eirin, whose all too serious expression seemed glued to his face. Sorcha looked over the members looking for Riona. Riona slipped in beside her a few moments later, nudging her with an elbow. "It's about time you showed up. Thought you might have overslept."

Sorcha rolled her eyes. "I was here before you."

"Doesn't mean I can't mess with you." Riona

grinned, clearly enjoying herself.

Sorcha let out a huff of annoyance as she focused back on Nethran, who had begun outlining their assignments.

"Everyone clear on their assignments?" The commander glanced around. "Good. Dismissed."

Eirin and Drystan were sent to check on a missing Druid who had been scouting the river's edge along Baelmere. The town lay far east of Lumora, past Meadowrun and the Whisperwood Pines, nestled between two large hills known as Aonach and Draoi. Rhosyn was assigned to the woods of Lumora to monitor the spread of the black blooms. Her talent and intuition with nature were unparalleled. Lethal in her craft, she worked her runes in a way that made nature itself seem to whisper, a force all her own. Mason was tasked with testing cadets in training, ensuring they were combat ready while overseeing the school's progression. The Circle members scattered, each heading toward their designated tasks. Sorcha lingered for a moment, watching them depart, when Riona fell into step beside her, glancing over with quiet curiosity.

"You've been awfully quiet this morning. Something on your mind?"

Her tone was light, but curiosity gleamed in her gaze. Sorcha wanted to tell her about the dream. About the whispers still echoing in the back of her mind. About the creatures calling to her from beyond. Her own runes ached to be read, to be understood, to be shared. But she wouldn't. She couldn't burden Riona with the nightmares that had seeped into her waking life.

"Just tired," she insisted.

Riona raised an eyebrow but didn't press further.

The morning dew clung to the forest, the scent of damp earth thick in the air. Sorcha and Riona stood at their posts, the woods stretching endlessly before them. Riona leaned in slightly, fingers idly twirling one of the twin knives at her hips.

"So tell me again. How do we run into the Wolves of the Wild Hunt, almost die, a god shows up, and now we're supposed to act like it's all business as usual?"

Riona was spinning her daggers in her hands before she threw one into a tree. "And no one is talking about it, why?"

Sorcha adjusted the strap of her sling bag. She didn't meet Riona's gaze, keeping her expression neutral, but Kyron's words rang through her mind.

*"Your runes saved you, Sorcha."*

She kept replaying it over and over, rubbing her arm as if it would somehow answer the questions she had.

"I don't know, Riona. We were lucky. Whether or not it is a god, it didn't attack us. It helped. That's more than we can say for most things in these woods these days."

Sorcha's fingers brushed over the bandage beneath her sleeve, wincing. The cut still stung.

"We had a job to do. That's why we're here, isn't it? To monitor things, figure out what's going on before it gets worse."

Riona straightened, her grin returning.

"And if it gets worse, at least we'll get a second chance at a fight. Prove we can hold our own."

Sorcha let out a harsh laugh. "Let's hope you don't get your fight. We have enough to deal with as it is, and I do not need to save your ass too."

Riona shot her a look. "You know it was exciting, fighting back in the Hollow. Don't pretend it wasn't."

Sorcha turned to her horse, a wide smile spreading across her face as she tightened the

"Riona, the day I find fighting for my life fun, you can assume I've had brain damage," she chuckled.

Riona grinned. "So, where are you off to this time? Whisperwood Pines? Meadowrun?"

Sorcha mounted her horse, pulling herself into the saddle. "Patrolling the usual routes in Meadowrun. Checking in, making sure no one has disappeared."

Riona, still smiling, looked at the knife she was turning over in her fingers. "Sounds thrilling. Meanwhile, I'll be here, guarding the post." She sighed dramatically. "Try not to have too much fun without me."

"Never." Sorcha meant it. Riona was like the sister she never had, the closest thing to family.

Riona's smirk softened, her tone turning more serious. "Watch your back, yeah?"

Sorcha paused, her fingers brushing the reins of her horse.

"I'll be fine. You just make sure nothing sneaks past you."

Riona saluted with her knife, her grin returning. "Nothing gets past me. You know that."

With a final nod, Sorcha turned toward the path ahead. Behind her, Riona leaned back, her knives gleaming faintly in the morning light. Sorcha rode off, watching as Riona's silhouette blended into the background, the sight of Lumora slowly bleeding into the morning sun. The neighboring town of Meadowrun was not a far ride, an hour at most. The path ahead was paved with cobblestones, the rhythmic clatter of Shadow's hooves meeting the stones blending with the soft rustling of leaves. It was a simple journey, but it allowed Sorcha to take in the countryside's beauty. As she neared Meadowrun, the road lined with wildflowers, their vibrant colors painting the landscape like a living canvas. The air carried a faint, sweet fragrance.

# Chapter 13
## WHAT A PLEASANT SURPRISE

Meadowrun was renowned for its riches; not in gold or jewels, but in fields of flowers that stretched endlessly toward the horizon. At night they glowed with a brilliance that rivaled the stars, every hue of the rainbow shimmering against the dark sky. Those who thought Meadowrun beautiful in daylight had never seen it under moonlight. Radiant teals, violets, and bell-shaped blooms scattered across the ground gleamed with a pearlescent sheen, while amber petals flickered like fire. Their vibrant petals were cultivated into teas and perfumes sought after by travelers from all regions. The town itself felt like stepping into a painting, with cobbled streets winding through quaint buildings adorned with ivy and blooms spilling from window boxes. As Sorcha entered the village, she tied her horse at the stables and slipped into the market. Casually leaning into a stall, she lowered her voice. "Anything unusual? Any sightings?"

The vendor, a wiry woman with a weathered face, shook her head. "Not much here, lass. Just the usual: fish are scarce; the river acting funny. Folks have been whispering about odd blooms further downstream, but not here yet."

Sorcha thanked her and moved on, her thought caught on the mention of the odd blooms. As she passed through the square, a young boy darted toward her, clutching a small toy bow.

"Are you one of the Circle? Did you come to fight the monsters?" His wide eyes brimmed with awe.

Sorcha crouched slightly to meet his gaze and smiled, ruffling his hair. "Just checking in. No monsters today, I promise."

The boy grinned, clutching his bow tightly before running back to his friends. Sorcha's smile lingered before fading. *No monsters yet*, she thought grimly.

Turning down a quieter street near the edge of the market, where the noise of the crowd gave way to quieter conversation. Her steps slowed, then halted entirely. Her gaze locked on a man standing at a vendor's stall, his back partially turned as he inspected something in his hands. His strawberry-kissed hair was loose, slightly tousled, his profile unmistakable.

He held an intricately etched crystal rune, its surface shimmering faintly with gold light. The vendor gestured animatedly to a collection of other runes displayed on the table, but Kyron barely acknowledged them. His focus was entirely on the rune in his hand.

"What was he doing in Meadowrun?" Sorcha's heartbeat quickened. Kyron turned, slipping into a small tea shop at the market's edge. Sorcha followed at a distance, curiosity pulling her forward. The small gold bell chimed softly as he stepped inside. The shop's cozy interior was steeped in spices and dried flowers.

Kyron sat at a small table near the window, his long fingers delicately tracing the edge of the rune before slipping it into his pocket. He leaned back in his chair, his gaze scanning the street outside as if waiting for someone.

Sorcha hesitated in the doorway a moment, took a steadying breath, and walked towards him. Her boots barely made a sound on the wooden floor, but Kyron's eyes flicked to her before she even reached the table.

"Following me already, Sorcha? I'm flattered." His voice was low, teasing, and entirely too self-assured.

"You're not exactly easy to miss. What are you doing in Meadowrun?"

Kyron tilted his head and gestured to the cup of tea in front of him. "Having tea. Care to join me?" His smirk dared her to.

Sorcha narrowed her eyes. "You know that's not what I meant. You're in a town under the Circle of Lights watch. I don't think that's a coincidence."

Kyron chuckled softly. "Ah, always so sharp. You'd make an excellent tracker, you know." He sipped his tea before continuing. "But no, I didn't come here for you if that's what you're thinking." His gaze falling on her for a long moment. "Though it's a pleasant surprise."

She ignored the way her heart skipped at his tone keeping her composure. "Then why are you here?"

For a moment, Kyron's teasing demeanor faded. "There are things stirring in the water, Sorcha. Things that shouldn't be." His voice was quieter now. "I'm following a trail."

A chill skated down her spine. "And the rune?"

His smirk returned as he leaned back in his chair.

"A trinket." His thumb rubbed over the rune as he held it "Beautiful, isn't it? But harmless. You're welcome to inspect it if you like."

Sorcha didn't reach for it. Her eyes remained steady. "You know I don't trust you, right?"

His smile widened, slow and deliberate, but it didn't quite reach his eyes. "I'd be disappointed if you did."

Kyron stood then, stepping closer. His fingertips skimmed her cheek, light as a feather, tucking a stray lock of hair behind her ear. Before she could react, he pressed something into her palm. Then, just as smoothly, he turned and walked away.

Sorcha stood frozen in the tea shop, skin burning in the wake of his touch. She glanced down at what he had left her. A crystal unlike any she had ever seen.

Its blue and orange hues shimmered and swirled, shifting like liquid fire as she tilted it in her hand. She ran her fingers over its smooth edges, and the instant she touched the rune's markings, a jolt of energy surged through her. Her fingers tightened around it briefly before she slipped the rune into her pocket. She let out a slow breath, her gaze lingering on the place where Kyron had stood only moments before.

# Chapter 14
## RUN AWAY SCARF

Sorcha left the little tea shop after Kyron. He had already entered the bustling market square, weaving through the crowd with effortless grace. Sorcha tried to follow, but she couldn't navigate the crowd as smoothly. Before long, she lost sight of him. By the time she managed to push through, he was gone.

She sighed, lingering for a moment, her thoughts still on him. But a merchant's voice quickly broke her reverie, shouting above the noise for help. A child had darted off, clutching a silk scarf stolen from the stall.

"Another day in Meadowrun," Sorcha muttered to herself as she sprinted after the boy. He weaved through the streets like a seasoned thief. His small size giving him an advantage. Sorcha chased him around corners, down narrow alleys, and through busy lanes. For a kid, he was fast. Finally, she turned onto a quieter street at the town's edge, panting. The child had vanished. Instead, she found herself standing at the outskirts of Meadowrun, where vibrant flower gardens stretched out before her. The fields were a tapestry of color, alive with the sweet fragrance of late blooms.

She took a moment to appreciate the view, the heady scent reminding her that these were likely the last flowers of the season before winter's frost claimed them. A strange pull urged her forward, to walk along the carefully laid stone paths. Her runes tingled beneath her clothes, a soft, almost imperceptible warmth. She followed the sensation until the vibrant beauty of the gardens began to fade. The air grew heavier and a volatile stench hit her nose. Her steps faltered as she reached the brook at the far edge of the field. She heard scurrying feet and paused for a moment.

In the field, two white rabbits with glowing gold eyes stared back at her. Her thoughts rushed back to the forest. It was here again. They leapt toward the flowers. Wilting bright petals curling and browning. The trees along the brook were withering as well. Their bark split and oozed black sludge that pooled in foul smelling puddles. It reminded her of the decay they had found in the forest earlier that week. The rabbits watched her as they scurried toward the brook and paused. Their bodies unnaturally still. One thumped the ground with its foot hard. The other only stared at her before tilting its head toward the water, its gaze shifting. Sorcha followed its eyes to the brook. The brook seemed ordinary enough, its surface smooth and reflecting the dull light above. But at the bottom, an odd darkness swelled, slow and curling like ink dissolving in water. The harder she tried to make out the blur, the more it blurred, slipping from her grasp as if resisting her stare. She turned back to see that the rabbits were still staring, frozen mid motion as if caught in time. After a lingering moment, they bolted. Bounding across the brook in a flurry of panicked movement before disappearing into the woods beyond. A shiver crawled up Sorcha's spine. She narrowed her eyes, scanning the tree line, and that's when she saw it.

A shadow, shifting between the trees. It moved as if it belonged to the forest, slipping between the trunks, its form barely solid.

The moment its eyes met hers, her runes flared, heat pulsing across her skin, sharp enough to sting. The markings built into a slow burn, spreading up her arms, curling around her ribs. Its figure shifted as the shadows swallowed it whole. As it disappeared, the pressure in the air lifted.

The world snapped back into motion as if unseen hands had loosened their grip as the trees whispered with the wind once more. She stood still as fear and anger clawed their way up her throat. She didn't understand what was happening, and the urge to scream into the ether and curse the gods was unstoppable. Her head ripped back as the anger, frustration and exhaustion clawed free. Her scream filled the air, startling the crows, caws screeching as they took to the sky. She screamed until the air left her lungs. Her throat was raw and ached, but she felt a little lighter. Her fists began to uncurl as she drew in a slow breath before reaching for her journal. She began to write.

She documented everything—the appearance of the decay, the foul stench that clung to the air, the eerie stillness that had settled over the land. Every detail she could because getting lost in work was better than trying to piece together whatever was happening to her. She wrote and sketched until her hands ached. That's when she decided it was time to turn back towards town.

By the time she returned to Meadowrun's square, the sun had dipped lower in the sky, casting long shadows across the cobblestones. She approached the merchant whose scarf had been stolen. She felt guilty as she admitted she had lost the child and the scarf. Without hesitation, she reached into her own coin pouch and offered compensation on behalf of the Circle. The merchant hesitated for a long breath before taking the money; her withered fingers curled around the coins with a slow nod.

"A shame," the merchant murmured, tucking the coins into her apron. She wore a smile that didn't quite match her eyes. The emptiness in her stare was cold and harsh. Sorcha leaned in a little closer to her as she looked at the odd black liquid oozing from her ear. "But you tried," she whispered as she held Sorcha's stare. Eventually, Sorcha forced a smile. The woman didn't press the matter further, sparing her from the headache of paperwork and a reprimand she wasn't in the mood to endure. But she took back out her journal to make a note of the black liquid coming from women before strolling through the market square.

She decided a quick bite to eat might help ease the unsettling feeling in her stomach as she passed a merchant selling fresh berries and dried salmon. Exchanging coin for her meal, she sat in the shadow of the stables. Sorcha fiddled with her charcoal pencil, unable to shake the thought of the old woman, so she drew her with her teeth sunk into salmon jerky. The salty brine and sweet smoked cherry paired perfectly with the raspberries. Crouched in the corner, jerky hanging from her mouth and hands stained with coal, she finished the last details in her drawing before shoving it back into her pack. Wiping her hands on her pants, she fed the last of her berries to Shadow before they rode back. As she mounted Shadow, she stole one last glance at the lively town before turning toward the road, townsfolk waving as she passed. The sounds of laughter and conversation faded behind her, replaced by the rising whistle of the wind as she neared the wooded path ahead. Nothing seemed out of place, yet she could swear she heard her name. It wasn't just the wind. The woods were whispering to her. A strange pull tightened around her like an invisible thread tethering her to something just beyond reach. Pressing forward, a creeping unease gripped her. Her hands trembled slightly as she tightened her hold on the reins, eyes locked on the trees long after Meadowrun had disappeared from view.

When the distant rumbling of the falls reached her ears did relief finally break through. The sight of Lumora ahead felt like a beacon. When she arrived at the outpost, she found Riona throwing daggers at a makeshift target, each blade hitting its mark with effortless precision. The thud of steel against wood echoed through the quiet early evening air. Sorcha leaned against the door frame with her arms crossed. A smirk tugging at her lips as she watched.

Riona finished her practice and turned, wiping sweat from her brow. She caught sight of Sorcha's smirk and raised an eyebrow.

"What's that look for? Lose another thief?"

"It only happened twice," Sorcha replied, stepping forward, tilting her head slightly as she walked, hands behind her back. "But... yes. I spent a lovely afternoon chasing a child halfway to the next town. Didn't catch him, though." She let out a long sigh.

"Impressive," Riona said dryly. "What's next? Letting squirrels rob the fruit stalls?"

"Careful," Sorcha teased. "I might just leave you to patrol alone next time."

Riona rolled her eyes, grabbing her water flask. "Fine, but at least I'm not chasing children and losing them."

"Touché," Sorcha admitted with a laugh, now talking with her arms moving around wildly. "But in my defense, the kid was fast. Besides, it's not like Meadowrun is brimming with excitement."

Riona snorted. "Well, at least you made it back in one piece. Anything else happen?"

"Not much," Sorcha said, her tone shifting, arms dropping to her sides. "Just found some more of that decay near the brook. It's spreading."

Riona's expression turned serious. "You think it's connected to the woods?"

"Probably," Sorcha replied, but she really wanted to say was, yes, it's all connected, that she could sense it. "I'll report it to Nethran, but, honestly,

I don't know what to make of it." Sorcha felt guilt again for not being completely honest with Riona, but what if she was wrong?

"Anyway, enough about that. The festival's coming up, and I need a new dress. You're coming with me to shop, right?"

Riona groaned, tossing a dagger into the dirt. "Do I have to? You know I hate shopping."

"Yes, you have to," Sorcha insisted smiling and now tugging on Riona's arm. "You always look amazing, and I need your help."

Riona smirked, pulling her arm from Sorcha and crossing them. "Fine. But if my dress outshines yours, don't say I didn't warn you."

"Deal," Sorcha said, grinning. "Now, let's get out of here before we end up stuck on an overnight shift."

As the next patrol arrived to relieve them, Sorcha and Riona walked off together, their laughter ringing out against the quiet evening sky.

# Chapter 15
## A Storm is Coming

Leaving the tea shop and maneuvering through the crowd, Kyron slipped into the forest. Glancing over his shoulder, he scanned for any unwanted eyes. Satisfied that he wasn't being followed, he pressed on until he reached a familiar clearing by the stream. The air was still and the soft murmur of water was the only sound. He inhaled deeply, centering himself before lifting his hands in a series of intricate gestures. Words slipped from his lips in hushed whispers, threading through the air like an unseen current.

Mist danced in, twirling through the trees and unfurling from the stream. It thickened, shifting and swirling faster. Growing taller and expanding outward until it consumed him entirely. The world around him blurred as the forest dissolved into shadow and light.

When he blinked, the Tuatha Court stood before him. The massive golden arches gleamed in the soft glow of the ever burning lanterns. Intricate designs woven into the towering gates that marked the entrance to his homeland. Exhaling as he steadied himself before stepping forward. The gates parted, allowing him passage, and the familiar faces of the Tuatha met his gaze.

Some greeted him with warm smiles while others with a mere nod or nothing at all. He had grown used to fact that he was one of them, yet never fully belonged. It no longer bothered him after all this time. Forcing a smile, he made his way toward the Tuatha Council. He had already begun to walk through what he would do as he approached. In his mind a checklist:

- Hand over his report on Sorcha

- Recount any developments

- Be sent on his way

As Kyron was lost in thought, a thundering behind him echoed off the marble floor in full sprint. He barely had time to turn before he spotted a large white wolf with sapphire eyes mid jump. Bracing himself, he let out a shallow breath just as the wolf slammed into his chest, knocking him back against the wall. Kyron gritted his teeth, annoyance flashing across his face, but there was also a playful glint in his eyes. He shoved the wolf off shaking his head as a smile tugged at his lips.

"You know, Conall, this is getting old, don't you think?"

The wolf snarled, flashing its teeth before its form twisted, muscles shifting beneath pale skin as it began to morph. In seconds Conall stood before him. His silver hair tousled as few strays fell over his cobalt-blue eyes. A long scar ran along his cheek. A stark contrast against his otherwise smooth features. He laughed as he grabbed Kyron by the neck locking him into a tight choke hold. Kyron let out a breathless chuckle, struggling to break free. With a sharp elbow to Conall's ribs, he twisted, slipping a hand between Conall's arm and his own throat, prying himself loose.

Still laughing, Conall nudged him hard. "Where the hell have you been? The council's been talking."

Kyron ran a hand through his hair, sighing. "When doesn't the council have something to say, Conall?"

Conall studied Kyron for a moment before his expression shifted. His voice lowered slightly. "This about the woman you're scouting?"

Kyron didn't respond right away. He held his ground, but the air between them had changed.

Conall's gaze narrowed. "By the Morrigan, I knew it. Damn it." He let out a rough exhale, rolling his shoulders. "Everyone's been so uptight about watching over the gods' messes."

Kyron nodded. "Yeah, it isn't the first time we've had to clean up after them, and it sure as Tech Duinn won't be the last."

Conall's eyes lit up with curiosity. "So what's yours like? I'm watching some pompous ass in the middle of nowhere near Ironridge. He seems to fight with godlike strength, especially with mead. I catch him practicing in the early morning hours by the lake with a massive hammer." He waited a moment before smirking. "So, what's Lugh's daughter like?"

Kyron began speaking when the Dagda entered.

He and Conall immediately stood at attention, their conversation forgotten. They nodded in silent acknowledgment as the Dagda passed his presence commanding yet fleeting.

As his footsteps faded, both let out a breath. Kyron turned to Conall. "Where's everyone else?"

Conall glanced toward a towering domed building, its single spire piercing its center. He nodded toward it. "The council has been pushing the younger members hard in training, making sure we're all battle ready."

Kyron clasped Conall's arm firmly. "Make sure the job gets done?"

An arrogant smirk crossed Conall's face. "Of course I will," he replied, his voice edged with sarcasm.

Kyron strode through the towering doors of the dome, his boots echoing across the polished marble floor. The scent of damp stone and burning incense filled the air, mingling with the faint hum of voices. Rows of young warriors moved in practiced formations, their blades slicing through the stillness with precision. At the center of the hall, overseeing their training was General Aogan. The Tuatha veteran was an imposing figure, broad shouldered, silver streaks threading through his raven black hair. His presence alone commanded obedience. Even the youngest recruits seemed to stiffen as he passed. When his eyes landed on Kyron, there was no warmth. Kyron approached, bowing his head slightly in greeting.

"Report." Aogan's voice was jagged, cutting through the murmurs of the trainees.

Kyron exhaled. "There's a sickness spreading across the land. It's affecting both animals and humans. I've seen it take hold in the villages. Crops are withering, creatures moving strangely, as if driven mad. And it's worsening."

Aogan's expression remained unchanged. "Go on."

Kyron shifted. "As for Sorcha; there have been moments when her magic has surfaced, but she doesn't understand it. It manifests in flashes; it's uncontrolled. She's still struggling to accept that it's part of her. And as of now, she has no idea how to use it."

Aogan folded his arms. "Have you made direct contact with her?"

Kyron didn't hesitate. "No."

Aogan turned, fixing him with a hard stare. "It would be foolish and awfully bold of you to think you can lie to me, Kyron."

Kyron's teeth clenched and he went rigid. He considered doubling down but knew it was pointless. "Yes. I've run into her."

Aogan studied him. "And?"

Kyron clenched his fists. "I've tried to keep her safe. I know what the council expects, but she's vulnerable."

"That is not your decision to make."

"You wanted a report," Kyron spat out. "I gave it to you."

Aogan didn't react. "Your orders have changed. You're staying here for the next few weeks. The council will decide when you're sent out again."

Kyron's anger flared. "You're pulling me out? When the sickness is spreading? When she—"

"This is not up for debate. You've been too close to this. You're thinking like a mortal. And that is a weakness we can't afford."

Kyron's whole body tensed, every fiber of him wanting to argue, but he knew it wouldn't change anything. With a slight bow, he turned on his heel and walked away. The weight of his orders settled over him like the storm clouds above. Flowers swayed along the stone walkway. As the scent of rain and cinnamon mingled in the air, wrapping around him. The trees shimmered in hues of violet and deep blue, their leaves catching the light in a dance with the wind.

He continued to the edge of the Tuatha Court, sitting himself in a field of gold grass. His hands sank in slightly as he faced the sky, watching as the clouds rolled by. The puffs of gray and purple held shimmering veins of silver light, illuminating the sky. The smell of rain grew stronger as the wind began to howl. He sat there for a while, looking out onto the Tuatha Court, listening to the rumbling of the hungry storm ahead. Kyron's thoughts came crashing into a memory with his mother.

The memory was vivid, his mother sitting by the fireplace in a large ornate armchair. He was playing with some books creating structures for his wooden animals when a loud crack filled the air. The tree outside the library window were ablaze in the storm. Watching as ash and smoke floated towards the skies, he dropped everything and ran into his mother's arms as another crack shook the very ground. His mother's soft eyes met his. "Do you remember the stories of Balor?" Kyron shook his head no as he buried deeper into her arms.

"It is said that in the fury of a thunderstorm, Balor himself stirs awake. His stomach rumbles through the dark clouds, hungry for chaos and ruin. That his appetite is insatiable, but trapped beneath us all he can do is drown the earth in his tears. So when a thunderstorm comes, it reminds us he is far gone. Try as he might, the only destruction he can cause is that in which we survive every day."

Kyron looked confused as his mother chuckled. "Think of him like a stinky old troll stuck under a bridge. "

Kyron chuckled to himself, looking up at the clouds, dread slowly filtering in. Maybe something else stirred in those clouds after all as the rumbling grew louder, his thoughts shifted to Sorcha. Her name brought distaste. He was just another watchmen and her the job. Just another forgotten person caught in the game of the gods. Yet Sorcha was different. She didn't loathe herself or flaunt her power, nor did she act like a victim despite her circumstances. Perhaps it was this quiet resilience that drew him closer. She simply didn't know how deeply the gods had meddled in her life, and Kyron knew she deserved the truth about her parents, even if sharing it meant facing dire consequences himself.

Then the sky wept, rain pouring suddenly and fast against Kyron's skin. He pushed himself off the ground and got to his feet, moving toward his home on the hill, his footsteps unhurried as he began his walk. It took a while for Kyron to reach the hill, and by the time he stood at his door, he was soaked to the bone. His clothes clung to him like weights, and his shoes squished with each step as his toes curled in the water filling them. With an exhausted sigh, he pushed the doors open, warmth spilling out along with the familiar scents of summer. The lanterns flickered faintly, and he could hear his mother and others speaking in the library. Quietly, he crept up the stairs, hoping to slip past the multitude of questions he was sure to be asked.

# Chapter 16
## THE GATHERING

Meanwhile, back in Lumora, the meeting room behind the enchanted mirror carried the quiet weight of long standing duty. The glow of runic light reflected off the polished oak table, casting shifting shadows across the faces of those gathered. Leaders of the Circles sat in their usual places, some leaning back, arms crossed, while others rested their elbows on the wood, fingers tapping absently. The air smelled faintly of parchment, old magic, and candle smoke.

Commander Nethran sat at the edge of the table, his arms folded as he scanned the room.

"It's been a while, hasn't it?" His smirk was subtle, even warm. "Some of you I've known since we were barely old enough to wield a sword. Others joined later, but we've fought side by side, broken bread, and despite the years and distance, here we are, still standing, still answering the call, still putting up with each other."

A quiet chuckle rippled through the room. Even Kael, usually the most reserved, smiled.

Nethran exhaled, shifting slightly. "For months, we've listened to the Elders argue, sitting in on their endless debates, and what do we have to show for it? Nothing. The problem isn't getting better. They're getting worse." He tapped the runic map carved into the table, the veins of glowing light dim beneath his hand. "And now, whatever this is, it's reached Lumora."

The room quieted.

"That's why I called this meeting. No Elders. No politics. Just us. So tell me. What the hell is actually happening out there?"

Elara of Ironridge was the first to speak. She leaned forward, hands clasped together on the table.

"You all know Ironridge depends on the mines," she said. "The gems, the metals; we keep the trade alive. But the rivers we use to refine them? They're turning thick,

clogging the tools, ruining the stones. And the creatures in the caverns, the ones we've coexisted with? They're turning hostile. My miners are fighting off cave bats, *clurichauns*, and spirits instead of doing their damn jobs."

Kael of Cailleach's Keep let out a slow breath. "Our glacier rivers were once clean enough to drink from the source," he said. "Now? Animals refuse to go near them. Elk, the foxes, even the vultures won't go near it. The ones that drink it, die. If this keeps up, by spring, the meltwater will poison the entire region. The lowlands won't stand a chance." He hesitated, then added, "And we're seeing more activity. Fairy mounds where they shouldn't be. Creatures slipping through the Veil. With Samhain approaching, it's only getting worse."

Finnian of Glenn na Mara, normally the most laid back of them, rubbed the back of his neck. His blue eyes flickered with worry.

"The ocean's wrong," he muttered. "The trade routes are unpredictable. Algae is spreading fast, and something is moving beneath the waters, too big to be any beast we know of. Sailors whisper about shadows large enough to capsize ships. And then there's the singing." He hesitated. "It happens at night. A melody, it calls to the people. And the ones who follow it don't come back."

Aedon of the Hollow, the youngest among them, finally leaned forward, resting his arms on the table.

"The Hollow's never been safe," he admitted. "But now? It's worse. The mist never lifts. My best scouts, hunters who have lived in those woods their whole lives, are vanishing. We find their tracks leading in, but never out. And the creatures…" He ran a hand through his dark hair. "They aren't the same. The Unseelie Court is riding with the Wild Hunt. Farmers are losing livestock. Hunters come back with wounds that don't heal, if they make it back at all."

Nethran let their words settle, his expression unreadable.

"This isn't just a sickness. It's spreading. It's not stopping."

Elara shook her head. "We can't keep pretending this is something we can handle alone. If we don't start working together, we're going to lose."

Kael gave a curt nod. "If the water goes, everything goes with it. We need a plan. Now."

Finnian's gaze flicked to Nethran. "And what about the elders? What have they told you?"

Nethran's jaw tensed. "Nothing useful." His gaze swept the room. "That's why we're here. We know these lands better than anyone else. If we actually work together, we might figure out what ties all of this together."

Aedon tilted his head slightly. "And how do you expect us to do that?"

Nethran leaned forward, resting his hands flat on the table.

"We stop acting like separate Circles," he said. "We share actual information, weekly reports, direct and unfiltered. No more secrecy. No more politics."

One by one, the leaders nodded. Talk shifted to the festival, only three weeks away. A rare moment of unity, even as unease loomed over them.

Before the meeting ended, Nethran's voice steadied. "Patrols stay tight. I expect officers from every Circle at the festival. And I expect them to keep it safe."

One by one, the leaders rose, murmuring among themselves as they left. Nethran lingered, staring down at the glowing map. Whatever was coming, it was already here.

# Chapter 17

## KELPIE'S SONG

As the Festival of Light approached, unease settled over Lumora. Whispers, carried by merchants and farmers in hushed tones, circulated through the markets and taverns. The townspeople found a goat dead in its pen, with its lips stained as if with soot. Near the forest's edge, a fox lay sprawled, its eyes clouded and leaking a black substance that soaked into the ground. Birds swerved erratically in the sky, some plummeting to the earth lifeless. Though The Circle documented each occurrence, they couldn't determine the cause. The elders attributed the events to illness, even as the air grew heavy with each patrol.

The town continued its preparations. Lanterns adorned the eaves, vibrant silks decorated windows, and the air filled with the scent of perfumes. To bless the celebration and ward off ill fortune, people polished their sacred bowls and carefully etched runes onto their rims. As preparations reached their peak, a few Circle members were dispatched from Lumora. Their mission: to travel to Glenn na Mara, the coastal port a day's ride away, to procure supplies that the town lacked. These included offerings from distant lands, intricately woven silks, and artifacts brought by seafaring ships. Sorcha, Riona, and Rhosyn volunteered readily, their minds equally focused on the mission and the prospect of new festival dresses. Commander Nethran, cautious of their eagerness, assigned Eirin and Emry to join them. Eirin was to ensure the mission's focus, while Emry's expertise in artifacts made him a logical choice for the trip.

"This way," Nethran had told Emry with a pointed look, "there's better odds if anything happens."

The group departed at first light. Soft glow of dawn barely kissed the horizon as they left Lumora's gates behind. The air was crisp and quiet, save for the soft clatter of hooves and the rustling of saddlebags. Sorcha stifled a yawn as she stretched in the early morning sun.

"It feels strange leaving now," she murmured. "The festival's so close."

"It's why we're leaving," Eirin reminded her, his tone brisk. "If we don't bring back what's needed, there won't be much of a festival at all."

"You act like this is a punishment," Riona said, her voice teasing. "Glenn na Mara is practically a treasure trove."

"For you, maybe," Eirin muttered. "Some of us have to work."

"And some of us know how to balance it," Emry said, his tone warm and light as he glanced back at the group. "Besides, she's not wrong. Glenn na Mara's market is famous for a reason. Spices, fabrics, artifacts. It's the kind of place you'd want to visit, even if it's work."

"You're also forgetting the books," Rhosyn said dryly, her lips twitching into the faintest hint of a smile.

"Among other things," Emry replied with a grin.

Riona nudged her horse closer to his, her eyes glinting with amusement. "Just don't let those books bankrupt us."

"Excuse me, I'll have you know I'd use my money," Emry said, his grin widening. "I'm a very discerning spender."

Sorcha leaned toward Rhosyn, lowering her voice. "How long do you think they'll keep pretending they're not together?"

"Too long," Rhosyn replied, smiling and rolling her eyes.

The journey continued for hours, marked by serene landscapes of golden fields, dense forests, and gentle slopes. As the afternoon progressed, the salty air grew stronger, and by the time the sun began to dip, they reached the final hilltop, offering a view of Glenn na Mara. The town below shimmered in the sunset, its bustling harbor filled with activity. Ships gently swayed on the water, their sails decorated with ribbons and charms. The streets were adorned with crushed seashells and pearlescent stones, which scattered the golden light, creating dancing rainbows. Vendors crowded the market square, their stalls overflowing with colorful goods: silks, intricately carved runes, and a blend of spices filled the air. "It's beautiful," Sorcha whispered.

"It is…" Eirin agreed, his gaze encompassing the town. "Let's not get too distracted."

Rhosyn began listing the items they needed: "Sacred bowls, spices, silks, and runes. It shouldn't take long."

"Unless you let Riona shop," Emry teased, drawing a glare from Riona.

"We're allowed to shop," Riona stated, gracefully dismounting. "And while we're at it, someone will surely find the perfect book."

Emry replied, "Can't make any promises," though a smile played on his lips.

Eirin feigned disgust, saying, "Could you guys just stop already?" Laughter erupted from Sorcha and Rhosyn.

The group separated to explore the market, planning to meet at the harbor once finished. Sorcha and Rhosyn strolled through the stalls. A gown that shimmered in the fading light caught Sorcha's attention. Its emerald-green fabric appeared to move like water, with gold embroidery adorning the bodice. "That one would suit you," Eirin murmured, having silently joined her.

Surprised by the warmth in his gaze as he admired the gown, Sorcha responded, "It's not practical."

"Not everything has to be." Eirin's lips quirked, but his voice was softer than usual.

"That's the one," Rhosyn said firmly, her voice leaving no room for argument.

Sorcha hesitated, brushing her fingers over the fabric. "It's beautiful, but... isn't it a little much?"

"It's the Festival of Light," Riona said, appearing beside them. "It's one of those nights you can, and should, dress like a goddess."

"She's right," Eirin said as he paced, his arms full of goods.

"And it's more than just a dress," Emry added, stepping closer. His tone was thoughtful. "The designs here reflect the gods' influence. Wearing something like this is honoring their presence."

"Careful, Emry," Riona said with a smirk.

Sorcha flushed, finally relenting. "Fine. But if it's too much trouble to pack—"

"It's not," Eirin interrupted, already signaling to the shopkeeper.

Rhosyn was with Emry and Riona, while Eirin hung back with Sorcha as they walked through the vendors. They needed scraps of clothing for the corn dollies to be made for the children, decorative bowls for the fruit and grains, ingredients for the Lammas loaf, mistletoe, and, last, cleansing runes. The coast hailed many of them as being one with the sea.

Rhosyn stopped at a vendor who displayed many silks and clothes and began bargaining. She eventually walked away with a basket filled with purples, blues, reds, and oranges piled high and neatly.

"I think I did rather well," she stated proudly.

Riona chuckled. "I'd say you robbed them blind with your charm." Her fingers drifted over the fine silks and cottons.

"I did not! It's not my fault the man wanted to take me to dinner." She winked.

That was when Eirin and Emry howled with laughter. Riona smiled and wrapped an arm around Rhosyn.

"See, boys? This is why you let the ladies' shop."

Emry bowed dramatically. Eirin smirked. "Is that a challenge?"

"We accept," Emry answered. "Watch and learn."

Eirin and Emry took the list from Rhosyn and walked toward a younger woman selling baked goods. Sorcha, Riona, and Rhosyn stood far enough back to watch the exchange.

"How much do you want to bet they get talked into buying more than what we need?" Sorcha said to the others.

Riona accepted the challenge with a grin. "I'll buy the first round tonight if they do."

As the late afternoon wore on, the city's music and bright chatter swelled until they could no longer resist joining in. Turning on their heels, they drifted toward the nearest row of vendors, the air rich with spice and laughter.

Sorcha slowed as they passed a stall lined with delicate wind chimes carved from bone and shell. They swayed gently in the breeze, pearls catching the light like drops of moonfire. She reached for one, her fingers brushing the smooth surface as a strange warmth bloomed in her chest.

"My mother had one like this," she murmured. Rhosyn rested a gentle hand on her shoulder.

Sorcha covered it briefly with her own before letting go and moving on.

Eventually, the two rejoined the others. Their arms full, one basket brimming with ingredients for Lammas bread, the other overflowing with sweets.

Sorcha eyed the baskets and laughed. "Looks like you owe us a drink."

Riona turned toward Emry, shaking her head. "What?" Emry said, looking entirely too guilty.

Eirin chimed in, head low. "It all looked good."

Emry declared he could do better, so he walked with Riona to a nearby vendor. He tried to haggle over a satchel of dried figs and wound up paying more than the asking price.

"You're banned from negotiations," Riona said flatly, snatching the figs. "You're a vendor's dream."

After securing the festival goods and packing everything for the return journey, the group settled at a harbor-side tavern for dinner. Plates of roasted fish, buttery crab, and zesty stew were shared over rounds of spiced wine and smooth ale. The air filled with music and laughter as Riona pulled Sorcha onto the dance floor, spinning her with reckless abandon. Even Rhosyn joined, her movements graceful and precise as a flicker of joy lit her features.

Emry lingered at their table, his baby-blue eyes following Riona as she danced. He tried to appear unaffected, but his fingers tightened slightly around his mug as he watched. Her laughter and confident movements drew him in.

"I'll ask her to dance if you don't," Eirin said, looking from Riona back to Emry, a smile playing on his lips.

Eirin then stepped forward, offering his hand to Sorcha. As the music slowed, Eirin pulled her onto the dance floor. His movements were confident and effortless, his soft hair sweeping over his dark eyes as they swayed. "You're good at this," Sorcha chuckled.

"I've had practice," Eirin replied with a roguish smile. "Though I'm starting to think you were born to be twirled around a dance floor."

Sorcha laughed softly. "You're treading dangerous waters."

"I'll try not to let it happen again," he teased. The music shifted again, becoming slower and more haunting. Lantern light flickered across the room, softening the edges and turning everything golden. Sorcha's eyes met a familiar shape in the distance. Blue eyes caught hers, and she paused as she began pushing through the crowd. But when she reached the spot, the figure was gone. At the edge of the floor, Riona brushed a loose lock of hair from her face. She didn't need to look to know Emry was watching her; the awareness pressed against her skin like warmth before a flame. He held out his hand. For a heartbeat, she hesitated, then took it. Together, they moved as if the rest of the world had fallen away, the air between them thick with quiet anticipation. Riona's eyes lifted, her expression softening. "I thought you weren't much of a dancer."

"I make exceptions," Emry said, his voice low. His movements were steady and deliberate, but there was reverence in the way he held her, as if he feared she might vanish if he blinked. Riona let him guide her, her usual wit softening into something quieter, more vulnerable.

"Oh, you must really love me then," Riona teased, her voice barely a whisper. Her gaze lifted to meet his.

Emry didn't hesitate. "I do."

She drew in a breath, the corners of her mouth curving. "Someone might hear you."

"Let them," he said, his tone lighter now, though his eyes didn't waver from hers.

Riona's cheeks flushed, but she held his gaze. The space between them seemed to stretch, filled with unspoken words like the lingering notes of a melody. As the music faded, Riona stepped back, her expression carefully composed as she smoothed her tunic. Emry let her go, his fingers brushing hers one last time before he returned to the table. If anyone noticed, they didn't comment. Along the docks, the waves whispered. Overhead, lanterns swayed, their light flickering on the water. Eirin walked beside Riona, silent and inscrutable. Meanwhile, Sorcha's mind wandered to the blue eyes in the tavern and the night that seemed to cling to her skin.

"Peaceful, isn't it?" Emry murmured, his gaze fixed on the dark horizon. He took a few steps, his hand brushing lightly against Riona's.

"Too peaceful," Rhosyn said from behind them.

Riona gave a soft snort, her unease evident in her glance toward the water. "Don't start with the ominous talk, okay? Not tonight." Silence hung in the air until Eirin abruptly stopped, his body stiffening. He tilted his head slightly, eyes narrowing as if listening for a distant sound.

"Do you hear that?" he asked, his voice quiet, almost hollow. The others paused.

"Hear what?" Rhosyn asked, frowning. Voices, carried on an invisible current, swirled around them. The haunting melody rose from the water, achingly beautiful and laced with sorrow, and enveloped them, its pull undeniable. "It's..." Eirin trailed off, taking a step toward the pier.

"Wait." Emry's voice was urgent, his brow furrowed as he turned to Eirin. But as the hymn swelled, his gaze shifted towards the dark waves, and he hesitated.

"Emry?" Riona's voice cracked slightly as she reached for him, her hand closing around his arm.

"Don't." "It's... calling," he murmured, his voice distant.

"Damn it, no!" Riona snapped, tugging on his arm, her panic barely contained. "Look at me! Stay with me!"

But Emry took a faltering step toward the water, his expression softening into something unrecognizable. Beside him, Eirin moved closer to the edge, his movements slow and unsteady.

"Eirin, stop!" Sorcha's voice cut through the stillness as she stepped in front of him, planting herself firmly in his path. She grabbed his arms, shaking him. "Eirin, look at me!"

The hymn grew louder, its mournful melody weaving through the air. Sorcha glanced back and froze.

A figure swayed just beneath the surface, its form shifting between human and horse. The kelpie moved with an eerie grace, its sleek black coat gleaming like wet obsidian. It resembled a massive horse at first, with a powerful, lean, muscular frame, but something was off. Its mane clung to its neck in long, tangled strands, a mixture of seaweed and bone, dripping briny water. Its webbed hooves shifted into hands, transforming it from beast to almost human. The change should have been clumsy, but it wasn't; the kelpie simply became something else, as if both forms had always belonged to it. Its glowing eyes held an eerie light that reflected off the water. Its sleek, otherworldly form swayed in time with the melody, the song digging into the deepest corners of her mind.

"Emry, stop!" Riona pleaded, her voice breaking as she pulled harder on his arm, her nails digging into his sleeve.

"He's slipping," Rhosyn hissed, rushing forward to grab Emry's other arm. "And so is Eirin! Pull them back!" Her strength was steady as she strained against the men, her movements deliberate and controlled, but they fought against her, as if the hymn had stolen their will. Sorcha's panic rose.

"Eirin, come back!" Sorcha's voice trembled, a choked gasp escaping her as she gripped his shoulders. Desperation clawed at her, and a blossoming warmth bloomed beneath her skin. Hidden runes beneath her clothes glowed faintly, intricate patterns illuminating her. The air crackled with a light that intensified, igniting the air. The kelpie's song faltered, its eyes flaring like lanterns. Light danced on the water like the sun's glare on the dark waves. The creature recoiled, its smooth body shuddering, the hymn's melody fractured into a raw, guttural cry.

"Sorcha..." Eirin murmured, stumbling as the trance shattered. His eyes flicked to hers, wide with confusion.

Emry's movements stilled as the kelpie let out a final, piercing wail before vanishing beneath the waves. The silence it left behind was almost deafening.

"Emry," Riona whispered, her grip still tight on his arm. He blinked, his blue eyes clearing as he turned to her, his breathing unsteady.

"I'm here," he said hoarsely, though his gaze darted to the water, a lingering daze in his expression.

Rhosyn pulled both men farther from the pier, her movements unrelenting. The group stood in stunned silence, the cool night air suddenly feeling heavy, oppressive.

"What the hell just happened?" Riona asked, her voice tight with a mix of fear and anger.

Sorcha's heart pounded as she glanced at Riona, who was staring at her but not at her face, at her hands. The faint glow of the runes was already fading, the warmth dissipating into the night.

Riona's expression flickered but then she turned away, acting as though she hadn't noticed anything. "We need to get out of here," she said curtly.

Sorcha swallowed hard, her gaze drifting back to the water. "It was a kelpie," she mumbled.

Riona's face became cold, almost angry as she looked around the group, her hand still resting on his arm. "What's happening?"

"I don't know," Emry admitted, his voice still raw from the encounter. "But whatever it is... this is just the beginning."

The unsettling feeling lingered, prompting the group to return to the inn quickly. Inside the group tried to settle, but the chilling encounter remained a heavy weight, a reminder of their near loss.

That night, the women vigilantly watched over Eirin and Emry, their caution fueled by the haunting melody and illuminating eyes they had witnessed. During her shift, Sorcha sat by the cool glass, her fingers tracing the cold steel of her dagger as she scanned the harbor, the distant orbs of light seeming to stare back from the black water. Riona paced, her voice a low murmur as she spoke, while Rhosyn remained by Eirin's side, the smooth wood of her bow ready. Although the night passed without further incident, sleep evaded them all.

The next morning, they readied for the long journey home. They sat down, the rough wooden benches cool beneath them, and forced down breakfast. The smell of frying bacon and stale mead hung in the air. Across the room, Circle members from the coast, their sun-kissed skin gleaming, sat a few tables over, eyes fixed. A hushed tension filled the air. A figure rose and approached, exchanging glances, her polished boots echoing on the floor. She was flanked by a wiry younger man, whose sun-streaked hair glinted in the morning light.

"You're Commander Nethran's people, aren't you?" the woman asked.

Sorcha nodded, gesturing for her to sit. "That's right. I'm Sorcha. This is Riona, Rhosyn, Eirin, and Emry. And you?"

"Lieutenant Elenna," the woman replied, glancing back at her companion. "This is Cadet Loran. We're part of the Coastal Circle."

There was a beat of silence before Elenna leaned forward. "I hope I'm not overstepping, but I couldn't help but notice..." She trailed off, searching for the words. "You all look like you got little sleep. Was it the singing?"

Sorcha froze, her grip tightening around her mug. "You've heard it too?"

Elenna nodded grimly. "It's been happening for weeks now. It always happens at night. Fishers say it comes from the deep waters, a mournful sound that carries on the wind. A few men have gone missing, and so have boats."

Riona cut in, her tone on edge. "Why hasn't this been reported? Something like this should've gone straight to the elders."

Loran shifted uncomfortably, avoiding her gaze. "We tried. But the elders dismissed it as nonsense, superstition from tired sailors. We've been handling it on our own, but it's getting worse."

Emry leaned forward, his expression thoughtful, though unease flickered in his blue eyes. "If it's been happening for weeks, have you seen it? Or anything that might explain it?"

Elenna stiffened. "Not directly. But there's been evidence. Drag marks near the water's edge. Fishing nets shredded like paper. And sometimes, when the fog rolls in, you see shapes. Things that shouldn't be there."

A chill ran through the group. Sorcha glanced at Rhosyn, who frowned deeply. "We ran into creatures last night," Sorcha admitted quietly. "Kelpie. It nearly dragged Eirin and Emry into the water."

Her voice trailed off, but Riona picked up where Sorcha left off, her tone tight and low. "It wasn't just Eirin. The kelpie got to Emry, too, just not as quickly. We pulled them back before..." She stopped, her hands curling into fists against the table.

Elenna's expression darkened. "A kelpie? This far inland? I don't like what that implies."

"What does it imply?" Eirin asked, his voice hoarse from the night before.

Elenna hesitated, glancing at Loran before speaking again, her voice quieter. "It means something's driving them from their territories. Powerful enough to disrupt creatures that normally stay far from the shores. If they're targeting people."

"It's not just kelpies," Loran added, his voice barely above a whisper. "We've seen other things. Shadows in the water. Things with too many eyes. The sea isn't safe anymore."

Emry exhaled slowly, his fingers drumming against the edge of the table. "If what you're saying is true, it's more than just a local superstition. This will spread, displacement of creatures like kelpies isn't exactly subtle."

Riona shot him a glare, her voice tight with worry. "You think it's deliberate?"

"I think we'd be foolish not to consider it," Emry replied. His gaze flicked back to Elenna. "Why are you telling us this?"

Elenna's expression was grim. "Because no one else is listening."

Eirin hadn't spoken since the harbor. He sat stiffly, his knuckles white against the mug's handle. Sorcha knew that look. Emry, too, sat more still than usual, his normally animated expression subdued.

Their conversation ended abruptly as another Coastal Circle officer approached, her expression neutral but her eyes moving between the two groups. Elenna straightened, her professional mask slipping back into place. "If you learn anything," she said, her voice carefully measured, "you'll let us know, won't you?"

Sorcha nodded. "You have my word."

As Elenna and Loran rejoined their group, Riona leaned back in her chair. "Well. That's not ominous at all."

The weight of the conversation hung heavy as they finished their meal and prepared to leave Glenn na Mara.

Though the morning sun glittered on the sea, a lingering sense of unease followed them as they rode away from the city, the haunting melody of the night before still echoing in Sorcha's mind.

Eirin rode beside her, silent. She wanted to say something. But words felt too small for what had happened. So instead, she nudged her horse closer, close enough that her knee brushed his to let him know he wasn't alone.

# Chapter 18
## SLÁN AGAT

The ride back to Lumora was quiet, almost serene. The steady beat of hooves mixed with the gentle whisper of leaves in the breeze. Autumn had painted the land. The bright greens of summer were fading into golds and oranges, though the change wasn't quite finished. Sorcha rode beside Riona, guiding her horse, Shadow. She tried to find peace in the ride, but her thoughts kept returning to the kelpie. The unsettling song still echoed in her mind, along with the image of Eirin and Emry, both under its spell, drawn toward the water as if they were different people. Trying to shake off the unsettling thoughts, she glanced at her friends and spoke.

"Did we get everything we needed for the festival?" Riona, on Briar ahead of them, turned with a raised eyebrow. "Of course, we did. You think I'd let us come back empty handed?"

Rhosyn, her arms protectively around a bundle of silks and spices tied to her saddle, added, "I double-checked everything before we left. The festival planners will be ecstatic. We have spices, silks, crafted bowls, and more. The town will look amazing."

"And the dresses," Emry chimed in from the back, his voice teasing as he looked at Riona. "Because those were, obviously, essential to the mission."

Riona turned in her saddle and grinned at him. "Don't pretend you weren't admiring them, Emry. I saw you."

"Guilty," Emry admitted, his blue eyes sparkling with amusement. "It's hard not to appreciate art when it's right in front of you."

Sorcha smiled slightly. "Good. I don't think I could face the planners if we'd forgotten something important. They'd send us right back."

Eirin, who had been silent most of the ride, finally spoke, his voice calm but quiet. "You're all worrying too much. The festival will happen, just like every year. Let's focus on that instead of... other things."

Though he didn't say it, Sorcha knew he was trying to put the kelpie out of his mind, just like her. She nodded, glancing at him.

"You're right. Besides, I need to figure out how to upstage Rhosyn in her dress."

Riona laughed, her braid catching the sunlight as she turned in her saddle. "Good luck with that. Did you see the embroidery on mine? You'll need a miracle."

Sorcha grinned, her competitive side emerging. "We'll see about that. Maybe I'll add extra flowers to my hair. Or pearls. You won't know what hit you."

Rhosyn, who'd been silently watching, finally spoke. "You're both fighting a losing battle," she said with a sly smile. "I've already outdone you both."

Sorcha turned to her, raising an eyebrow. "I loved the artwork on your dress. Did you get the orange one?"

"I did. It's burnt orange with green leaves embroidered on the hem and bodice," Rhosyn said, pride in her voice. "And tiny beads sewn into the leaves. They shimmer just enough to catch the light without being too much."

"It is beautiful," Sorcha conceded, a little envious.

Emry chuckled softly. "For what it's worth, I think you'll all outshine everyone at the festival. And if anyone asks, I'll take the credit for the dresses."

"Oh, you would," Riona said with a playful glare. "Anything to take credit for our success."

Lumora's spires shone gold in the fading light, the city buzzing with festival preparations. The air thrummed with music, the scent of spiced wine thick in the air. As they passed through the gates, Sorcha exhaled, realizing she'd been holding her breath.

Home.

The familiar sights and sounds of Lumora welcomed them, a comforting wave. Though the kelpie's haunting song still echoed in her mind, the city's energy and the festival preparations were a welcome distraction.

# Chapter 19
## Unspoken Truth

Having entered the gates, Eirin and Sorcha proceeded directly to the Druid School, a place where Commander Nethran often spent his time. He could usually be found there if he wasn't out on patrol or stationed at the gates. Unlike the small, quaint elementary school filled with the sounds of children, the Druid School was ornate and richly decorated, like everything else in Lumora connected to the Circle. Its enormous spires, crafted with crystal cut prisms, pierced the skyline, causing the city to glow in rainbow hues during the day. Rhosyn, Riona, and Emry stayed behind at the stables to unload the horses, ensuring the goods were carefully handled and accounted for. Eirin and Sorcha passed through a large, grated courtyard, surrounded by towering iron gates entwined with greenery, which kept prying eyes away. Etched runes further protected those inside. An incantation opened the gates, revealing the courtyard's centerpiece: a gleaming statue of Lugh. The sun god stood in a throwing stance, his spear poised as if ready to strike. A perfect circle of flowers around him mimicked the hues of a sunset. As they climbed the steps to the main hall, familiar sounds filled the air: the clash of swords, instructors shouting movements, the hurried shuffle of feet, and the overlapping buzz of conversations. A faint smile crept across Sorcha's face, stirring memories of her own days there. Her eyes drifted to the tapestries hanging high above, each depicting scenes from the first and second battles of Mag

Tuired. She could still recite the stories of the forgotten gods and creatures shown on the tapestries by heart after many late nights studying them. Brushing her fingers lightly against the pillars, they reached Commander Nethran's office. Inside, the commander sat at his desk, pen scratching against parchment. He glanced up briefly as they entered, then returned to his task.

"At ease," Commander Nethran said, his gaze sweeping over them. "I appreciate your professionalism in this setting." A quick smirk appeared on his face, only to vanish as swiftly as it came. "Did you secure all the necessities for the festival?"

Eirin stood quietly as Sorcha shifted her weight, her nerves flickering in the slight twist of her rings. Rhosyn had prepared them well, and it was her inventory list that Eirin handed to the commander. "Rhosyn provided this, sir," he said. "It's the list of all items purchased, cross referenced with what's needed for the festival. Everything is accounted for."

Commander Nethran nodded as he reviewed the list. "Anything to report? How was the coast?"

Sorcha glanced at Eirin, then took a breath as she stepped forward. "Sir," she began, her voice steady though her hands still twisted nervously. "We encountered something unusual at the harbor. Kelpies surrounded the harbor."

Nethran's pen stilled as he looked up. Sorcha continued, her voice quieter now. "I saw it firsthand, and so did the others. We had a direct encounter. Eirin... he almost walked off the pier into the sea. We heard their song, but Eirin and Emry reacted to it. They were in some sort of trance when we tried to pull them back, but nothing worked until..."

Her voice faltered, and she hesitated, choosing her next words carefully. She wasn't ready to explain what had happened. The runes, the inexplicable heat, or the way the kelpie had recoiled. Not yet. If she did, the commander might order her to step down from active duty during the festival preparations, or worse, the festival itself.

Eirin, sensing her hesitation, stepped in. "Until something frightened them off, Sir. Sorcha and the others held us back long enough for the kelpie to let us go and when we were finally off the pier, we saw them. Commander, there were dozens of eyes staring back at us."

Commander Nethran's expression darkened. His fingers drummed against the desk as he processed the information. "Dozens, you say?"

Eirin nodded. "Yes, sir. They were watching us."

Nethran leaned back in his chair, drumming his fingers on the edge of his desk for a few moments that stretched in the silence.

"I'll look into this. Until then, none of this leaves this room. The last thing we need is panic spreading before the festival. Understood?"

They nodded, their unspoken relief palpable. "Dismissed," Nethran said, his tone firm but not unkind. "And Sorcha, make sure you hand in a detailed report. I want everything documented."

As they left the office, Sorcha exchanged a glance with Eirin, who gave her a reassuring nod. Outside, Rhosyn, Riona, and Emry were waiting near the stables, having finished unloading the goods and checking the horses.

Riona stretched her arms above her head, letting out a long sigh. "Finally back. I don't know about you all, but I'm eager to disappear into my bed."

Sorcha smirked, her stare lingering on Eirin. He looked worn, his usual demeanor dulled by the weight of the kelpie encounter. His shoulders slumped ever so slightly, his hands stuffed into his pockets. "You should head home and rest, Eirin. You've earned it."

Eirin nodded, his voice low. "Yeah... sleep sounds good. I'll see you all tomorrow." He hesitated for a moment, his eyes flicking to Sorcha before he turned on his heel and headed toward the quieter parts of town.

Emry, brushing his horse's flank as he untied the last saddlebag, glanced at Eirin's retreating figure. "I'm not used to seeing him that shaken. Whatever that thing was, it got under his skin."

"It got under all our skins," Sorcha said softly, wrapping her arms around herself as if warding off a chill.

Rhosyn adjusted the bag of festival goods slung over her shoulder. "I'll be heading straight to the festival planners. These materials aren't going to deliver themselves."

Riona rolled her eyes but chuckled softly. "Of course, you're going to work the moment we get back. Fine, I'll come with you. I could use something normal after the last forty eight hours."

"You mean harassing festival planners is normal for you?" Sorcha teased, earning an exaggerated shrug from Riona.

"Keeps life interesting."

Rhosyn smiled warmly. "You're more than welcome to join me, Riona. The company will make the task less tedious." Together, they set off toward the center of the city.

Emry stepped closer to Sorcha, his expression softening. "And what about you? I don't suppose you'll actually get any rest tonight."

Sorcha huffed a soft laugh. "I'll try, but there's a report to finish first."

"Of course there is." Emry's smile was faint, though there was a glimmer of understanding in his blue eyes. "Don't let it keep you up too late."

"I'll do my best."

Emry squeezed her shoulder, offering silent comfort, then turned his horse toward the stables, leaving Sorcha to her thoughts. She stood for a moment, absorbing the familiar scene in Lumora. The Druid School's tall spires gleamed in the fading light, and the excited chatter of townsfolk preparing for the festival drifted on the breeze. Breathing deeply, Sorcha replayed the events of the past two days in her mind. The walk home was quick, her thoughts racing between the kelpie's haunting song and the pressure of her unfinished report. With a sigh, Sorcha opened the front door. After dropping her things, she grabbed her journal and settled into her chair. Dipping her pen in the ink, she began to write, each word drawing her deeper into the memory of the harbor. She wrote every detail: the sound of the song, its effect on Eirin and Emry, and the many eyes that had watched them from the water. "This had better make sense," she muttered, finishing the last line. Satisfied with her account, she closed the journal and set it aside. Tomorrow she would give it to Commander Nethran. But tonight, she would try to rest.

# Chapter 20
## A Night of Terrors

Sorcha settled into bed, her weight melting into the cool, soft sheets. The scent of star flowers mingled with the crisp autumn breeze, beckoning her to sleep. Soon, the familiar dream arrived, and the wisps returned. Though she tried to resist, their call was as alluring as a flame to a moth. Curiosity overwhelmed her, and she followed their whispers, the wisps playfully bouncing ahead, patiently waiting.

This time, the dream returned her to a familiar meadow. The place's name hovered just out of reach in her memory, a tantalizing whisper. Flowers bloomed in every direction, their petals dancing in the breeze. A gentle brook meandered through the landscape, its waters accompanied by the distant chirping of crickets. The wisps flickered across the brook, anticipating Sorcha's arrival, pacing before the woods. A prickling sensation crawled up her neck, making her hesitate. Cautiously, she stepped into the brook, the cool water lapping at her feet, and turned to look back. A chilling image met her gaze.

A Fomorian surged from the water, its twisted form dripping. Its milky white eyes, clouded and filmed like spoiled milk, held her captive. Its long gnarled limbs emerged from the depths, their blackened, webbed fingers clawing at the embankment. She watched in horror as it rose to its full height. Parts of its body looked waterlogged, its skin stretched tight and slick with rot. Where flesh had peeled away, scales gleamed faintly, catching the dim light. The creature looked as if caught between sea and land, life and death. And it was moving at an unnatural speed.

The Fomorian broke into a sprint, closing the distance in just a few steps. Terror seized Sorcha's chest before her body could react. Then finally her body moved. She plunged into the forest, branches clawing at her arms, legs pumping until her lungs burned. Every heartbeat thundered in her ears, echoing the pounding footsteps behind her. Panic began to creep over her again as the wisps darted around, calling her name with urgent whispers. It was impossibly dark and cold, as if she had been sucked into the vacuum of space. As she struggled to see, the little blue orbs illuminated a path deeper into the unknown. With no idea where she was or how far she had run, or what awaited her, it was her only choice. Taking a deep breath, she moved cautiously, each step light as her eyes darted between the trees. Every sound, or the lack of it, frayed her nerves. As she crept along the narrow path, threads of mist clung to her skin while the crack of splintering branches and the crunch of unseen footsteps echoed across the forest floor.

She stiffened, pressing her back against the rough bark of a tree. One trembling hand clamped hard over her mouth. The cold, damp earth bit at her bare feet, numbing her toes, but she didn't dare move, As the footsteps that crept through the forest grew louder. They seemed to come from everywhere at once. A chorus of echoes tangled in the dark.

And then fingers locked around her throat in a vice grip. Cold and merciless, squeezing until spots burst across her vision. She clawed and kicked blindly at the shadow until his face broke through the blur and, in that instant; she stilled.

A twisted grin adorned his face. Eyes blazing like living fire as they locked onto hers. His voice came low and venomous as he hissed, "Found you."

Before Sorcha could react, her head slammed into the tree. The impact ripped the air from her lungs, and in an instant the world went black.

She jolted awake. Her skull cracked against the cold stone floor. She gasped for air as the sheets enveloped her. Twisting around her limbs as she thrashed. Fighting against the invisible terror that had clawed its way out of her dream.

# Chapter 21
## MORNING LIGHT

The night was quiet, unnaturally still, a silence that should have brought peace, but only amplified Eirin's unease. He'd hoped a walk in the cool air might calm the turmoil in his chest, a lingering effect of recent events.

Passing Sorcha's house, however, he froze. Screams carried by the wind pierced the night. His heart hammered, a wave of heat washing over him as he sprinted to her door, pounding on it with desperate force. "Sorcha!" he yelled, but there was no answer. He tried the windows, searching for an opening. The screams continued, frantic and terrifying, sending panic through Eirin. His lungs tightened, fists clenched; he was ready to lash out at anything. Racing around the other side of the house, the screams grew louder. An open window offered an entry point. Without a second thought, he climbed through, landing silently inside. The room was dim, moonlight barely illuminating Sorcha, tangled in her sheets, thrashing wildly. Terror fueled her screams as she punched and kicked at the twisted bedding, her movements wild and uncoordinated.

"Sorcha," Eirin called softly, approaching her carefully. "Sorcha, it's okay. It's Eirin."

She didn't hear him at first. Her fists were still swinging as she screamed. Eirin knelt beside her, gently gripping her shoulders.

"Sorcha, it's me. It's Eirin," he said again. "You're okay. You're safe."

Her movements slowed as her wide eyes she finally saw him. For a moment, she stared at him as if he were a stranger, her chest heaving, her breaths coming in quick gasps.

"Eirin?" she whispered, her voice trembling.

Confusion and terror rippled across her face. She pressed a shaking hand to her temple. "How?" She rubbed her eyes and then her head. "How did you get in here?"

Eirin's gaze flicked to her hand as she pulled it away. There in the moonlight, red gleaming droplets spilled over the floor, running down her fingertips as they made contact with the floor.

"You're hurt," he whispered, helping her sit up. "Come on, let's get you cleaned up."

Eirin reached for her, helping her to her feet, keeping a steadying hand on her arm as they made their way to the kitchen. Sorcha swayed slightly, still dazed, her fingers brushing her temple as though trying to piece together what had happened.

He guided her to her chair in front of the fire, grabbing a clean cloth, and a bowl of water. Eirin spoke over the bowl, the color pulsing a faint blue as it pulsed for a moment before fading. He dabbed the cloth in water and gently placed it on Sorcha's forehead, wiping away the sweat. He worked his way down her arm and cleaned her hand before carefully washing the blood from her hair.

"I couldn't sleep," he explained quietly as he worked. "I went for a walk and heard you screaming. When you didn't answer the door, I found the open window and came in."

Sorcha winced as the cloth touched her head, but she didn't pull away. "I don't remember," she muttered, her voice distant. "It felt so real, Eirin. Like I was really there."

Eirin finished cleaning the cut and grabbed a small bag of ice, wrapping it in a towel before handing it to her. "Hold this against your head," he instructed.

As she did, Eirin turned on the kettle. He leaned against the counter, watching her carefully, his concern etched onto his face.

"You were sleeping when I found you. It must have been a dream," he said softly, "but whatever it was, it must have been horrible."

Sorcha looked at him, her eyes filled with a mix of gratitude and lingering fear. "It was more than that," she whispered, clutching the ice pack against her head. "It didn't feel like just a dream."

Eirin looked at Sorcha. "I'm haunted by my dreams too."

His gaze now on the teakettle, he poured them each a cup, the gentle clinking of porcelain breaking the silence. Sitting down beside her, he placed a comforting hand on her back.

Sorcha met his gaze, her voice trembling as she spoke. "I'm grateful you arrived when you did..." Her eyes glistened, holding back tears that threatened to spill.

Eirin offered to stay the night, settling into the chair in the living room in front of the hearth, just outside her bedroom. Sorcha kept her door open that night. She felt like a scared child again, afraid of the dark, needing the light and the comforting presence of another person. It brought her a sense of calm knowing he was there, and as she watched him from her bed, sleep eventually claimed her.

Eirin leaned against the doorway, arms crossed. Sorcha's breathing was slow, deep but even in sleep, she tossed and turned. She didn't let herself settle, even now.

He wanted to say something, but would she really listen? Eirin already knew the answer. He shook his head softly and slowly slumped onto the floor, his head resting on the door frame as he sat and watched over her.

When morning broke, the aroma of breakfast filled the air, eggs, toast, jam, and meats. The tantalizing smells beckoned her awake. Sorcha sat up slowly, her head spinning slightly as she rubbed the back of it, feeling the large lump that had formed where she had hit it.

She couldn't distinguish whether the injury came from her fall or the nightmare. Her mind began to race with questions and fragmented memories, but the clinking of dishes and cups pulled her back to the present.

The smell of roasted coffee and crisp bacon hit Sorcha the moment she stepped into the kitchen. Eirin stood at the stove, sleeves rolled up, looking fantastic, even in an apron. He didn't glance up "You drooling, or just impressed?"

She scoffed. "Depends. Did you actually cook all this, or do I need to check for a bribed tavern maid?"

The table was laden with tea, coffee, fresh juice, toast with jam, venison sausages, bacon, and the most perfectly cooked runny eggs she had ever seen sitting alongside some freshly picked flowers. Sorcha paused in amazement, her eyes on Eirin and she wrapped her arms around him in a tight embrace. Eirin, setting down the utensils in his hands, returned the hug without hesitation. His hands caressed her back as he pulled her closer. The hug lingered longer than she had intended, but she didn't pull away. She hadn't realized how much she needed it until then.

When she finally stepped back, "Well, come on, Chef. We can't let this get cold. If I'm being honest, I haven't made anything for breakfast besides toast in so long... I'm way too excited about this."

Eirin chuckled. "I've been told I'm pretty decent in the kitchen," he teased, "And after the nights we've both had, we need something to eat if we're going to survive today. "

"Well, Eirin Oak, I feel pretty privileged to see this side of you," Sorcha said with a smirk.

Eirin was still laughing and shaking his head as he flipped her off playfully before bringing their cups to the table. They sat and had the delicious breakfast he had prepared, laughing and enjoying each other's company, the tension of the previous night melting away.

As they finished eating and tidying up, Eirin stood in the doorway, turning back to face her. "If you need anything, let me know," he said, his tone firm but kind. "I'll let the Commander know you won't be on patrols today. You need some time to yourself. I'll hand in the report."

# Chapter 22
## SEEDS OF DOUBT

Sorcha held Eirin close, her fingertips pushing into the fabric of his shirt. When she finally stepped away they exchanged goodbyes and Sorcha closed the door behind him. Once the latch clicked she sank into her chair again. Letting out a heavy sigh, her thoughts began to swim. Frustration crashing over her, she gripped the armrest of her chair. "Why does it all feel so familiar?" The elusive name hovering just out of reach.

*Meadowrun.*

The name struck her like a blow. The dark growths, the dying flowers... She palmed her forehead. It was a place she'd just been, yet in the dream she couldn't remember it. Letting the thoughts wash over her before reaching for her journal. Flipping to a blank page, she began writing down every detail she could remember, the meadow, the brook, the wisps, and the terrifying chase. She underlined "Meadowrun" twice, the ink digging into the paper; she wanted to remember the place. Time slipped by unnoticed until her stomach grumbled loudly.

She sighed, placing the journal aside as she rose to her feet. Wandering into the kitchen, her stomach twisted with hunger, only to find the cabinets bare. Of course, she thought with a wry smile. She hadn't been home long enough to restock anything, too consumed by patrols, reports, and everything else. Her gaze landed on the food Eirin had brought over, a gesture that had helped more than she'd admitted. Letting out a slightly frustrated grunt, Sorcha grabbed a crumpled set of clothes from the floor, tied her hair into a messy pile atop her head, slung her bag over shoulder, and picked up a basket before heading out to the market.

The market was alive with its usual bustle. The scent of cinnamon and clove wrapped around her as she grabbed a loaf of Barmbrack, its golden crust still warm. She moved quickly, gathering apples, squash, and late season berries and other earthy vegetables. Her stomach growled once again, reminding her to visit the tavern for lunch.

The tavern was quiet at this hour, only a few locals scattered around, sharing muted conversations over teas and ales. Sorcha found a seat by a window and ordered the stew. Settled back and listened to the quiet hum of conversations around her, but one in particular caught her attention.

Sorcha kept her gaze down, tearing at the crust of her bread, but her ears sharpened at the mention of the Hollow.

"The hunters can't find clean meat," one man muttered. "The ones they do kill bleed black and smell foul."

"Yeah," the first man said, shaking his head, "you can't get a word in edgewise with druids. They just repeat the same thing: 'we're looking into it.' Looking into what exactly? Why can't they just tell us if it's a polluted stream, illness or something else?"

"We can speculate all we want but we're here now and we will report it to the Lumora Circle. Maybe someone here in the city can make the Elders and council listen."

"Let's hope so," the first man muttered. "It's hard when everyone back home is struggling."

Sorcha kept the men's conversation in the back of her mind as she ate, their words sitting uneasily with her. Is that why she and Riona been sent out there in the first place? It was supposed to be a routine patrol, a simple task to "keep an eye on things." Commander Nethran had been casual about it, almost too casual. He'd given no indication that the area was of particular concern, yet as she reflected on what they'd encountered he didn't seem surprised. She couldn't help but think that her patrol wasn't about prevention; it was about observation. Had she been sent just to see how bad things had gotten?

The realization left a bitter taste in her mouth. If the Circle knew more than they were letting on, then the people in the towns surrounding the Hollow—Fearnmhar, Fionn na Mist, and Clochar na Mist—needed their help.

Sorcha's fingers brushed against the edge of the table, her runes tingling faintly beneath her skin. Her appetite faded as she pushed her plate aside, her mind a mess of questions. She reached her home just as the last light of day faded into night. Inside she sat in her chair, opened her journal, and began putting her thoughts on paper. The sickness in the Hollow, the Wolves of the Wild Hunt, the kelpie, and, of course, Kyron. What was it about him that kept pulling her attention, no matter how hard she tried to push it away?

She closed the journal and turned her attention to the dress hanging in her wardrobe, a stunning emerald gown embroidered with delicate flowers. Beaded adornments glimmered like dew on the fabric, and the thought of wearing it stirred a mix of excitement and unease. She hadn't allowed herself a moment of joy in so long, and the idea of celebrating felt odd. But as her fingers brushed over the fabric, she resolved to let herself enjoy the festival, even if just for one night.

# Chapter 23
## A Watcher's Duty

Kyron outwardly complied with orders at the Tuatha Court, but his obedience was merely a facade. He performed the required training with the warriors, attended council briefings, and endured the interminable discussions about the spreading sickness. His body was present, yet his mind was elsewhere. He attempted to convince himself that he was fulfilling his duty, that remaining at the Court was the correct course of action, and that observing from a distance was sufficient. However, these thoughts grew increasingly empty with each repetition. Initially, he remained near the borders of Eadartha, rationalizing his presence as mere observation and monitoring of the mortal realm. But his surveillance intensified, and he began to slip past the gates of Lumora, concealed within the city's shadows, watching its inhabitants. He was watching her. Each night, Kyron resolved not to return, but each night he did. One evening, he saw Sorcha arrive with Eirin and the others. From the rooftops, he observed them dismount, their horses weary from the journey. Something about Sorcha had changed; her steps were tense, and her shoulders were tight. Something had clearly affected her, and he needed to understand what. He trailed them through the city's winding, narrow streets, navigating from rooftop to rooftop until they reached the Druid School. Remaining hidden in the shadows, he watched them disappear inside. He then heard their voices emanating from an open window, listening as they recounted the encounter with the kelpie. His fists clenched as his mind raced.

Kyron was haunted by chilling possibilities. What if she had been alone? What if something else had found her?

He remembered the shift in the air, the unsettling restlessness of the land. The weight of his inaction pressed against him, a constant reminder of his failure.

That night, Kyron fled to Lumora, telling himself the departure was temporary, that he would return to the Court once the unrest had subsided. However, each step away from the Tuatha made the lie heavier. The further he walked, the clearer the truth became.

Farmers reported finding livestock dead in their pens, stiff and blackened. Merchants spoke in hushed whispers of the sudden spoiling of their goods, with crates of grain turning sour and fruit rotting overnight. He once found a lifeless hare at the treeline, its eyes clouded and leaking black. The same dread he'd felt after crossing paths with Alenia washed over him. A sickness was moving beneath the surface of the world, and he wanted nothing more than to shield Sorcha from what was coming next. He knew this was just beginning even if the council refused to admit it out loud. He had endured countless council debates that ended without a decision. Words were not enough to hold back what was coming. The Circle wasn't ready, Lumora wasn't safe, and Sorcha was the most vulnerable of all.

When the city gates finally rose into view again, the air hummed with anticipation. The Festival of Light was approaching, and preparations filled the streets. Silks adorned windows, spices perfumed the square, and lanterns shone in careful hands. While most saw cause for celebration, Kyron felt the city's festive atmosphere was a flimsy shield against a gathering storm. He tried to convince himself that he was only fulfilling his duty, that

he stayed for Lumora. Yet, the moment he stepped through the gates, his
eyes searched for her.

# Chapter 24
## GLIMMER BEFORE THE DARK

Lumora transformed as the festival drew near. Streets were dressed in ribbons of gold, and lanterns etched with illuminating runes hung from every post, casting the town in a warm, radiant glow even after night fell. By the time the first night of the festival arrived, Lumora was alive with light and music. As Sorcha stood before her mirror, adjusting her gown, she took a moment to truly see herself. The emerald-green fabric clung to her frame, highlighting her toned figure in a way she hadn't seen in a while. The gown's hollowed out sides exposed just enough to hint at the swirling runes tattoos that danced faintly beneath her skin, their soft glow barely visible through the intricate embroidery of flowers and vines. It was both simple and extraordinary. Her auburn hair was loosely braided and tousled to fall over her shoulders. The firelight kissed her hair, making it shimmer like a crown of autumn leaves. She reached up to fasten a small gold clasp at her neck, shaped like a crescent moon. A gift from Riona after their trip to the coast—when a sudden knock broke her thoughts. Opening the door, Riona, Eirin, and Emry greeted Sorcha.

For a moment, they all froze, taking in her appearance. "By Lugh's light," Riona said first, a sly grin spreading across her face. "If I didn't know better, I'd say you've been holding out on us, Sorcha. You look radiant."

Eirin's gaze lingered a moment too long before he cleared his throat. "Riona's right. You'll have everyone at the festival tripping over themselves."

Emry stood silently at first, his blue eyes softening as he observed her. Then, with his characteristic warmth, he added, "It's perfect. You look like you stepped out of one of the stories we used to read about."

Sorcha flushed, though she quickly masked it with a laugh. "Oh, please. You three look incredible. You're going to outshine me entirely."

Riona stepped forward, giving Sorcha's gown a quick adjustment. "Not a chance. But I'll admit, this suits you."

"It does," Eirin said quietly, his voice carrying an unusual gentleness. Eirin was dressed in a honey-brown tunic, fitted to his body perfectly. Decorated with gold embroidery along the edges, with leaves and blossoms adorning it. A new pair of dark-brown leather pants to top off his ensemble. Handsome and practical, what you'd expect from the weapons expert. Then Sorcha's gaze shifted to Emry and Riona. Standing side by side, the connection between them was impossible to miss, even in the details of their clothing. Riona's silver gown shimmered with frost-like designs and deep blue embroidery. While Emry's navy-blue tunic bore silver embroidery in swirling, constellation like patterns. The contrast of their outfits complemented each other perfectly, like two halves of the same design. Sorcha's lips curved into a faint smile. They didn't even have to say it; the bond between them was as obvious as the stars in the night sky.

"Speaking of perfection, Riona," Emry murmured, his gaze drifting to her with unguarded admiration, "you're breathtaking."

She rolled her eyes, though her lips twitched into a smile. "Flattery will get you nowhere, Emry."

"It's not flattery," he said, his voice earnest. "It's the truth."

Sorcha looked between them both, a teasing grin tugging at her lips. "I don't know what's sweeter, the compliment or Riona pretending she doesn't love it."

Riona huffed but couldn't help the faint blush that crept into her cheeks. "Let's go before this turns into a group confession," she said, grabbing Sorcha's hand. With Eirin offering his arm to Sorcha and Emry walking closely beside Riona, the group stepped into the glowing streets of Lumora. The festival was alive with music, laughter, and conversation, blending into a harmonious buzz that filled the air. Lanterns cast golden hues over the streets, their runes humming faintly, while silk ribbons streamed from posts, creating a dreamlike atmosphere. As they approached the center of the festival, they spotted other Circle members mingling among the crowd, dressed in their best and showcasing the unique styles of their regions. Drystan wore a vibrant green and gold tunic, his hair half up as he soaked in the attention he always seemed to draw. Rhosyn's burnt-orange dress shimmered faintly, embroidered with deep green leaves and adorned with beaded flowers. Mason was dressed in a dark-green tunic with swirls of silver, silver jewelry adorning his neck and arms, black slacks and his hair tousled over his amber eyes. They all looked exquisite.

Sorcha waved to the group, and they greeted each other with warm smiles and easy banter. As Sorcha approached, Drystan plucked a flower from a passing cart, placing it behind his ear. "I'm festival ready. Now who's going to confess their *undying love for me* first?"

Rhosyn glared at Drystan. "Put that back," she replied flatly.

"You know jealousy doesn't suit you," he said, grinning.

She turned looking into the crowd when she caught a familiar figure moving toward them with unhurried confidence. His striking appearance was impossible to ignore. Dressed in black with subtle gold accents, his attire hinted at something otherworldly. He moved with effortless grace, exuding charm and mystery. Though he blended into the crowd, his presence stood apart.

"Good evening," Kyron greeted smoothly, his playful smile growing as he stopped in front of her. "Sorcha."

The casual intimacy of his tone drew immediate attention from her companions. Riona raised an eyebrow, intrigued, while Drystan smirked. Emry's expression tightened almost imperceptibly as he stepped closer to Riona, his hand brushing lightly against hers.

Eirin, however, stiffened, his jaw tightening as he instinctively positioned himself slightly in front of Sorcha. Kyron ignored the silent tension, his eyes focused entirely on Sorcha.

"Aren't you going to introduce me to your friends?" he asked lightly, though he made no effort to wait for her response. "I'm an... acquaintance of Sorcha's," he added, his confidence disarming as his gaze flickered toward Eirin, deliberately testing the waters. Sorcha opened her mouth to respond, but before she could, Kyron stepped closer, placing his hand lightly on the small of her back. With a polite nod toward the others, he said, "I'd like to steal her for a dance."

Eirin's posture tensed further, his knuckles white as his hands clenched at his sides.

Emry, watching the exchange with a quiet intensity, shifted slightly as though ready to intervene. Sorcha glanced at her friends, unsure how to navigate the moment. Kyron's hand, though gentle, was undeniably firm as he guided her toward the dance floor with an ease that left no room for protest.

"What the hell are you doing?" Sorcha hissed as soon as they were out of earshot. Her words cut through the lively music and laughter around them. "You can't just show up here like this."

Kyron smirked, tilting his head as though her frustration entertained him. "Would you rather I appear in the woods again? I thought this might be... less ominous."

Sorcha glared at him, but his gaze softened, his voice dropping to a near whisper. "I wanted to see you, Sorcha. You're impossible to ignore."

The words, spoken so calmly and earnestly, left her momentarily speechless. His movements were smooth, his grip firm but never forceful. Sorcha couldn't help but notice how effortlessly he fit into the rhythm of the festival, as though he belonged there as much as the soft lights and music.

"Kyron—" she began, but before she could finish, a firm hand clamped onto his shoulder.

"Mind if I cut in?" Eirin asked, his tone leaving no room for refusal. His eyes burned with unspoken jealousy as they locked onto Kyron's.

Kyron raised an eyebrow, his smirk returning as he stepped back with a slight bow. "Of course. I wouldn't dream of monopolizing her time." He retreated to the edge of the dance floor, crossing his arms as he watched Eirin pull Sorcha into his arms.

Drystan leaned closer to Riona, his grin wide with mischief. "Think I should go next? Might as well make it a competition."

Riona chuckled, her eyes gleaming. "I think Kyron's face is competition enough."

Kyron stood at a distance, his gaze focused on Sorcha and Eirin as they danced. Though his expression remained calm, the irritation in his eyes was unmistakable. He did little to mask the tension in his jaw or the way his fingers tapped against his arm. On the dance floor, Sorcha's thoughts swirled as she tried to focus on Eirin's steady presence. Yet, in the back of her mind, she couldn't shake the lingering heat of Kyron's touch or the intensity of his gaze that still followed her every move. Eirin's jaw tightened as he noticed her attention drifting toward Kyron, who now stood with other members of the Circle, talking and laughing softly. Sorcha couldn't help but wonder what they were discussing, her curiosity tugging at her despite her best efforts to stay present with Eirin.

"So, Sorcha," Eirin began, his voice cutting through her thoughts, "who's the guy?"

Caught off guard, Sorcha quickly looked at Eirin, stumbling to find the right words. She didn't understand why she felt uneasy talking about Kyron, especially to Eirin. Her feelings were confusing and layered, like a knot she couldn't untangle. After a pause, she finally said, "He's an old friend."

Eirin raised a brow skeptically. "Old friend, huh? And why haven't we met him before?"

Sorcha hesitated, her mind racing for an explanation. "Because... he lives further away, near Ironridge," she said, her voice steady. "We met as kids, and I've only seen him randomly since then."

The lie felt heavy on her tongue, and she hoped Eirin wouldn't notice the slight tension in her voice.

Eirin studied her for a moment, his expression unreadable, before finally nodding. "If you say so. I just wanted to make sure you were okay," he said, his tone softening as his gaze turned warm and reassuring.

The music shifted then, fading into a more upbeat melody, breaking the tension. Sorcha smiled faintly, grateful for the distraction. Eirin offered his arm, and together they walked back toward the group.

At the edge of the crowd, Kyron was chatting away, his voice smooth as he shared his recent exploits. Mason leaned in, his green and sliver tunic catching the light as he grinned. "So, you're telling me you stared down a group of mercenaries and they just... walked away? Sounds like a story to me."

Kyron chuckled, unbothered. "They didn't just walk away, they ran. Sometimes a bit of confidence is all it takes to shift the odds."

Rhosyn smirked as she adjusted the folds of her burnt-orange dress. "Or maybe the odds just favored you this time," she teased.

"Perhaps," Kyron replied, his smile faintly enigmatic.

As Sorcha and Eirin rejoined the group, Kyron's gaze shifted to her immediately, his tone casual but pointed. "And how was the dance?"

"It was fine," Sorcha replied curtly, feeling the weight of Eirin's presence beside her.

Kyron's gaze flicked to Eirin, whose stare was unyielding. Unfazed, Kyron offered him a confident smile before turning back to Sorcha. "I was hoping you'd let me steal you away again, but not for a dance," he said smoothly. "I'd like to walk the festival with you."

Eirin stood beside her again, he didn't try to hide the irritation he felt but his confidence held steady.

Before Sorcha could answer, Drystan broke the tension with a dramatic sigh. "If you don't go with him, Sorcha, I will," he said with a wink. "And honestly, who could blame me?"

The group broke into soft laughter; the tension easing just slightly. Rhosyn rolled her eyes. "You're a little too much, you know that, Drystan?"

"It's part of my charm," he replied.

Kyron's smile widened, his attention fixed solely on Sorcha. "So, what do you say?" he asked, extending his arm.

Sorcha hesitated, glancing at Eirin and then back at Kyron. She could feel the unspoken tension radiating from Eirin, but Kyron's presence was magnetic, and the question hung heavily between them.

"Go," Rhosyn said softly, her voice calm but encouraging. "We'll see you later."

Sorcha finally nodded, taking Kyron's arm. His touch was warm but light, guiding her away from the group with an effortless grace that left no room for hesitation.

Eirin watched them leave, his fists balled tight. Drystan clapped him on the shoulder, his tone teasing but not unkind. "Cheer up, Eirin. There's always tomorrow... or a duel, if it comes to that."

Rhosyn shot Drystan a warning look but said nothing, instead shifting her attention to Emry and Riona, who stood quietly off to the side.

"You two were quiet," Rhosyn said, addressing Emry and Riona.

Emry shrugged, his gaze lingering on Sorcha and Kyron as they disappeared into the crowd.

"Sometimes it's better to observe than interfere," he said simply, though there was a thoughtful edge to his voice.

Riona glanced up at him, her silver gown catching the light as she smiled faintly. "Wise words. Let's just hope Kyron doesn't make us regret it."

As they walked, arms linked, Sorcha asked what he thought of the Light Festival.

Kyron replied with a soft smile, "I've been to this festival many times, and it never ceases to amaze me." He then asked, "Have you been to any of the other festivals in the other realms?"

Sorcha blushed slightly and admitted, "No, I haven't."

Kyron clicked his tongue playfully and shook his head. "That's a shame," he said. "The festivals of Beltane, Imbolc, Yule, and Samhain are some of my favorites. Each has its own magic. You'd love them." His tone was warm, almost teasing.

They made their way toward the Skyfall Waters, where little orbs of light glittered in the air, their glow reflecting off the surface of the water. The magic of runes danced along the currents, adding a soft shimmer to the scene. The falls was a low hum in the background, blending seamlessly with the swaying music and the enticing smells of spices that filled the air. They sat on the fountain wall, admiring the festival when Kyron turned to Sorcha.

"Would you go with me to Samhain this year? It's held in the mountains of Cailleach's Keep?"

Sorcha hesitated, scanning his face for any sign of tricks or deception, but his expression was calm and sincere. She'd never been to the festival herself, though she had always longed to experience it after hearing countless stories. After a moment of deliberation, she nodded.

"Alright, I'll go."

Kyron's lips curled into a satisfied smile. "Perfect. I'll meet you, and we'll ride there together."

He leaned in, his lips just a breath away from hers, his voice a whisper, "I have to talk to you about something"

But as he spoke, a low, harsh growl reverberated through the air, cutting through the sound of the falls. Before Sorcha could process what was happening, icy hands grabbed her waist with an unnatural force. She gasped, but no sound escaped her lips as she was pulled into the fountain. The water swallowed her whole, dragging her under and toward the pounding of the falls.

# Chapter 25

## FESTIVAL

At that moment, screams erupted from the crowd. Twisted grotesque bodies poured from the fountain in cascades, clawing their way across the cobblestones in an unstoppable wave. Their hulking forms were a patchwork of decay, some with barnacle-encrusted flesh, as if dredged from the ocean's abyss. Others bore serpentine heads, their slit pupil eyes gleaming with sinister smiles. Townsfolk ran as talon-webbed fingers curled around rusty swords and sliced the air as others bore bone weapons. Horrifying smiles adorned their faces, revealing blacked fangs jutting from their gaping mouths.

The air reeked of salt and rot as they rushed forward. A crashing wave of destruction, their broken bodies shifting and snapping unnaturally as they descended upon the festival. Blood splattered across the cobblestones as chaos erupted.

Circle leaders engaged in fierce battle, their weapons igniting in arcs of light, while cadets and townspeople fought desperately alongside them. Yet the Fomorians didn't falter. They tore through flesh with merciless precision delighting in the carnage.

Kyron's attention snapped away from the battle to Sorcha. Her blade clashed against claws with such force her sword skittered across the stones. She was losing ground as a Fomorian loomed over her. Its sunken eyes locked onto hers, lips curling into a smile. Her legs kicked wildly, and her fists struck the creature with such force that decayed pieces of its flesh broke away. Yet the creature only smiled a grotesque, mocking grin as he held her under the water.

Kyron's runes flared brightly, casting an eerie glow beneath the water as gray clouds and smoke began to swirl around him. With a fierce lunge, he closed the distance between himself and the Fomorian. Reaching beneath his shirt, he drew a Druidic boline knife sheathed under his arm. The handle was carved from bone, and its curved serrated blade gleamed with deadly precision. With movements as swift and fluid as the falls, Kyron slashed through the Fomorian's neck, severing its head cleanly from its body. The creature's grotesque smile faltered as its body went limp, sinking lifelessly into the water.

Wasting no time, Kyron grabbed Sorcha, pulling her upward. As soon as her head broke the surface, she choked violently, gasping for air before doubling over and retching water. Kyron held her steady as he kept her above the swirling chaos of the fountain.

Sorcha's breaths came ragged as her fingers brushed against her throat where the Fomorian had pinned her down.

Barely above a whisper, she murmured, "Thank you."

Before Kyron could respond, the screams reached her ears. The clash of swords biting into flesh, the shouts of her friends, the whistling of arrows loosed into the fray. Her eyes widened as she took in the chaos unfolding around her. Her drenched dress clung to her frame, heavy and restrictive as she stumbled forward, determined to reach the battle.

Kyron moved swiftly, intercepting her before she could trip again. Dropping to his knees, he pulled out his blade and, with a single decisive motion, he cut her dress to knee length, allowing her to move freely. Sorcha kicked off her soaked shoes, her bare feet hitting the wet stone with resolve.

Kyron held out his daggers, and she took them without hesitation, her grip tightening as she ran toward the fight.

The battle raged on, chaos swirling through the glowing streets. The golden ribbons and lanterns of the festival were tattered and burned, their once brilliant light dimmed by the smoke and blood soaking the air. Fomorians surged unrelenting and merciless. Bodies littered the streets like fallen autumn leaves, their twisted forms sprawled in unnatural poses. Crimson stained the ground, pooling beneath the lifeless shapes, their limbs bent and contorted like the jagged edges of winter.

The sight ignited a fire within Sorcha. She fought with everything she had, her blades a blur as she cut through the creatures, her runes flaring with every strike. To her left, Rhosyn's runes flared. Vines of thorns whipping with the force of a hurricane, each one striking true. Drystan wielded his twin swords in fluid arcs, his movements both brutal and elegant as garnet sprayed the air. Sorcha sliced her way through the creatures, Kyron trailing her, casting mist to conceal them. Each step felt heavier as the chaos around her enveloped them.

In the fray she caught sight of Commander Nethran. His powerful form staggered as six Fomorians circled him, their claws slashing his skin. Blood poured from his wounds, soaking his uniform as he struggled to fend them off. His movements slowed as his breath labored. A fury broke through Sorcha, boiling her blood like molten gold and suddenly she was burning.

A brilliant blue fire erupted over her skin, engulfing her in an inferno that neither charred nor consumed her. Sorcha watched in terror as the flames crackled with a sound like a star splitting open, licking at the air as if drawn from the sun itself. This power was like nothing she'd felt before. It wasn't the quiet nature of the land's magic she had trained in for years. This was older, untethered from the rules that bound the others. She turned her hands over, touching her body to make sure it was real, her eyes searching for Kyron but they landed on the Fomorians and the rage built inside her, her magic consuming her.

The Fomorians turned their attention to her, but it was too late. Sorcha slashed through the circle, igniting each creature on contact. Flames leapt from her blades, consuming the creatures in agonized screams as they crumbled to ash. One lunged at her, its claws barely grazing her arm before it too was consumed by fire. The last creature fell, its decayed body collapsing into ashes.

As the final Fomorians disintegrated, the brilliant glow of Sorcha's runes dimmed, leaving her trembling and breaths became gasps as she stood among the ash and blood, the heat of her magic still pulsing faintly beneath her skin.

She fell to her knees beside Commander Nethran, her hands moving instinctively to cradle his head as he slumped forward. His bloodied face was pale, his breathing shallow.

"Commander," she whispered, her voice breaking. His eyes fluttered open briefly, locking onto hers.

Gratitude flickered in his gaze, but before he could speak, his body gave out. Sorcha held him tightly, tears mixing with the blood and ash staining her face as the echoes of battle raged on around them. She screamed to Kyron, who was fending off the creatures, preventing more from reaching her. Her cry tore through the chaos, loud and desperate.

Kyron turned at the sound, his gaze locking onto the tears in her eyes. He unleashed a deadly force. With renewed ferocity, he began slicing through the creatures, each strike more vicious than the last. Within moments, he was at her side. Sorcha's voice trembled as she looked at him. "Help me move him inside that house," she said, pointing to a small building nearby.

Without hesitation, Kyron lifted Commander Nethran, throwing him over his shoulder as if he weighed nothing. He kicked in the door, his boot splintering the wood, and carried the commander inside. Gently, he laid him down on the ground, the Commander let out a weak groan.

Sorcha knelt beside the commander, her voice soft and trembling as she whispered, "Stay with us." For a moment, her hand lingered against his bloodied face before she forced herself to stand.

Without another word, Sorcha turned back to the battle outside. From the center of the fray came a roar, and Sorcha turned just in time to see Eirin charging into battle. His eyes were splattered with ruby as his brown tunic was streaked with more crimson then honey, the golden accents glinting as he swung a massive cleave with deadly precision. The weapon cleared through the thick hide of a Fomorian, its jagged edges slicing effortlessly. His movements were calculated, the weight of the weapon seemingly nothing in his hands as he cut a path toward her.

Nearby, Emry and Riona fought back to back, their movements synchronized as if they had trained together their whole lives. His navy-blue tunic was slashed and bloodied, the silver embroidery dulled by grime, but his strikes were swift. Riona's silver gown was torn as well and bloodied, her blade flashing as she tried to shield him from the creatures closing in around them.

"Emry, stay close!" Riona shouted, her voice ringing with urgency.

"I'm not going anywhere," he called back, a faint smile flickering across his face despite the chaos. "You'd miss me too much."

Riona's gaze darted to him, her lips parting as if to respond, but her words were cut off by the scream of another Fomorian charging toward them. She moved instinctively, slicing through its throat before it could reach Emry.

For a brief moment their movements were perfectly in sync. But the tide shifted as a hulking Fomorian, larger than the others, emerged from the smoke. Its jagged claws gleamed like obsidian, and its glowing red eyes locked onto Riona with terrifying intent.

"Riona!" Emry yelled, his voice breaking through the roar of the battle.

She turned just in time to see the creature leap. Emry shoved her aside, taking the full force of the Fomorians blow. The creature's claws tore into his chest, the sickening sound of flesh ripping filling the air.

Riona fell to her knees beside him, her hands trembling as she pressed against his wounds, trying to stop the flow of blood. "No, no, no. Emry, stay with me!" she begged, her voice breaking.

His gaze found hers, the usual spark of mischief in his eyes now soft and fading. "Riona," he rasped, his voice barely audible. "You always... looked beautiful in silver."

Tears spilled down her cheeks as she shook her head. "Don't you dare. Don't you dare leave me!"

Emry's bloodied hand reached up, brushing lightly against her face. His lips curved into the faintest smile before his eyes closed, his hand falling limp in hers.

No!" Riona screamed, her voice raw as she held him tightly. The world around her blurred, the sounds of the battle fading beneath the weight of her grief.

"Riona, move!" Eirin's shout snapped her back.

He towered above her, his glaive dripping with blood as he fought off another wave of creatures. "We have to go now!"

Sorcha arrived moments later, the sight before her came like a blow to the face. Riona held Emry's lifeless body, her silver gown stained red.

"Riona…" Sorcha whispered, stepping closer. "Don't!" Riona snapped, her tear streaked face twisting with fury. "You should have been here! You should have stopped this!"

Kyron looked at Sorcha, his gaze softening as he saw the anguish etched on her face. Riona's words had cut deeper than anything Sorcha had just endured. The world seemed to stop around her. In that moment, all she could hear and see was Riona's agony, the sheer, all-consuming pain that tore through her as she cradled Emry's broken body. The weight of Riona's accusation pressing down on her, suffocating her. *"You should have been here. You should have stopped this."*

The words echoed endlessly, swirling through her mind, choking the air from her lungs. It all moved in slow motion, the chaos of the battlefield muted against the crushing grief. Riona clinging to Emry, her trembling hands stained with his blood, her sobs silent to Sorcha's ears. The others fought desperately to finish off the remaining Fomorians, their weapons glinting with flashes of blood swirling around her. Kyron looked to Sorcha and began moving through the fray. His eyes lit like bottled lightning as he wielded the mist with deadly force, choking the life from the creatures that remained. He called for more as the mist grew, skeleton-like hands snapped necks like twigs while others suffocated on gray matter that crept into their mouths.

As the last body fell, Kyron collapsed to the ground, the exhaustion of his efforts overtaking him. Sorcha began to sprint toward Kyron but he raised a hand and shook his head as he pointed to Riona.

Sorcha's gaze drifted back to Riona, whose lips moved in frantic, anguished words. Sorcha could see her speaking, could feel the weight of her grief and fury, but she couldn't hear her.

The battlefield blurred, yet one image remained seared into her mind Riona's tear-streaked face, bent over Emry's still form, the light in his eyes extinguished forever.

Sorcha fell to her knees beside Riona, her hands trembling as she reached out. Her voice was raw, breaking with every word. "Riona, I'm so sorry... I tried. I tried with everything I had to find you, to fight—"

Riona cut her off sharply, her voice trembling with fury and despair. "He's gone, Sorcha. He's gone. The only person in this world who loved me and he's gone."

Her words struck Sorcha again, stealing the breath from her lungs. Riona's hands trembled as she cupped Emry's face, pressing her forehead to his. Her lips brushed against his blood-streaked brow, her tears falling onto his lifeless skin. She rocked gently, murmuring words only he could hear, her grief too profound for anyone else to touch. The group circled around them, their eyes heavy with tears, their sobs muffled by the weight of the moment. Eirin stepped forward, his deep voice steady but laced with sorrow. "Riona," he said gently, "we can't leave him here. He has to be moved. Let us carry him to the medical ward."

Riona shook her head violently, her body curling protectively around Emry. "No," she said, her voice cracking. "No one touches him. No one."

Sorcha's throat tightened as she forced herself to speak, her voice quiet, pleading. "Riona... Eirin's right. We can't leave him here. Please. We'll take care of him. I swear it."

Riona's head snapped up, her tear streaked face twisted with anguish. "No! No one touches him!" she cried, her voice raw with desperation.

Eirin knelt beside her, his expression solemn, his honey-colored eyes glistening with unshed tears. Rhosyn and Drystan joined him, their movements slow and deliberate, their faces etched with understanding and grief.

Eirin placed a hand gently on Riona's shoulder, his voice soft but firm. "We'll carry him. All of us.

Together. I promise you, Riona, we'll honor him."

For a moment, Riona said nothing, her body trembling as she clung to Emry. Then, her sobs broke free, wracking her frame as she lowered her head to his chest. The group stayed with her, silent and unwavering, their shared sorrow binding them together in the darkest of hours.

Riona kissed Emry one last time, her lips trembling against his cold skin. She whispered something meant only for him, her voice breaking as the words fell softly between them. Gently, she placed his head down, her fingers lingering for a moment before she stepped back. She stood trembling, her entire body shaking as she looked at him, lifeless and still. The sight broke her all over again. The scream filled the air and seemed to shred the world to pieces.

Leaders from other Circles, townspeople, cadets, and officers alike turned their gaze to her, their expressions heavy with shared understanding. They stood amid the battlefield, now a mass graveyard, their grief palpable in the quiet that followed. Eirin, Drystan, and Mason knelt beside Emry, their movements slow and deliberate as they lifted his body with great care. Sorcha moved to help, her hands trembling as she reached for him, her face streaked with tears.

Behind them, Riona stood motionless, her shoulders heaving with silent sobs. Rhosyn placed a steadying hand on her back, standing with her. Once at the medical ward, Sorcha remembered that Commander Nethran was dying, and panic seized her. She turned to the others, her words tumbling out in a rush as she explained that she needed to find a healer immediately.

Without waiting for a response, she bolted through the ward, her voice echoing as she screamed for a healer. A young woman, barely sixteen, appeared in her path. Sorcha didn't have time to ask questions or assess her qualifications, only if she practiced healing. The urgency of the situation left no room for doubt.

The healer understood immediately, disappearing behind a door and returning with a pack filled with supplies. She spoke calmly but firmly, her tone leaving no room for argument. "Lead the way quickly."

# Chapter 26
## THE WEIGHT OF LOSS

Sorcha watched in awe as the young healer knelt beside Commander Nethran, her movements purposeful and precise. She placed the runes in a careful circle around him, murmuring softly. The runes responded to her voice, emitting a gentle hum as their light grew brighter. Swirling patterns of glowing energy appeared above each rune, weaving an ethereal glow over the scene. Sorcha felt a flicker of hope. The healer's calm demeanor and deliberate actions gave her confidence that the Commander was in good hands. As much as she wanted to stay, Sorcha's attention shifted to Kyron. His body had given way after the battle, making sure to give his distance from the others, as to not intrude. Sorcha glanced at the healer one last time before stepping outside to check on him. The scent of strong earthy herbs lingered in the air as the healer continued her work.

Sorcha found Kyron leaning against the side of the building, his face pale and drawn but his eyes scanned the remnants of the battlefield. He straightened when she approached, placing a firm yet reassuring hand on her shoulder. "He's going to recover," Kyron said, his voice low and filled with conviction. "I can feel it."

The certainty in his tone left no room for doubt.

Sorcha nodded.

Kyron's gaze softened as he looked at her. "Your friends need you," he said quietly.

The words hit Sorcha harder than she expected as the air left her lungs when her thoughts turned to Emry. She forced herself to turn toward the town square, steeling herself for what she knew awaited.

As she walked the memories of Emry and Riona surged forward painting vivid and painfully clear pictures. Huddled together at the outpost where their hands brushed so subtly that anyone else might have missed it. She'd seen the way Riona's eyes softened when she looked at him, the way Emry's guarded smile broke free so easily when Riona was near. All the assignments together, school study sessions and sparing, they always pretended they weren't together but she had known for a long time they were in love. Everyone did. But she never pressed Riona about it. Riona was private, and Sorcha respected that. It had been enough to witness the quiet moments they shared, like the time she stumbled upon them in the meadow. She could still see it now: the way Riona's head rested against Emry's shoulder, his hand tracing lazy patterns along her arm, their laughter mingling with the hum of summer crickets.

By the time she reached the town square, the sight that unfolded was shattering. The city she knew felt like a faraway dream now. The streets were littered with bodies; people and creatures alike all twisted and broken. The scent of blood hung thick in the air, mingling with the sound of muffled sobs that came from all directions. Sorcha stood silent where Emry had fallen, unable to look away from the spot where his blood still stained the cobblestones.

Riona stood there too unmoving, staring at the same place. Her eyes were bloodshot, brimming with tears that refused to fall.

"Riona..." Sorcha's voice cracked as she stepped closer. She hesitated, her hand faltering mid reach, unsure what comfort she could possibly offer.

Riona didn't speak. Instead, she turned her head slightly, her tear-streaked face twisting in anguish.

With trembling hands, Sorcha reached out again, this time placing her hand over Riona's. "He loved you," she whispered, her voice barely audible. "You know that, don't you? He loved you more than anything."

Riona let out a soft, broken sound, her head bowing as she crumpled further. Sorcha moved closer, wrapping her arms around her friend, holding her as tightly as she could.

At a distance, Kyron stood silently, his gaze fixed on them. He gave her a single nod of understanding before turning and heading back inside to check on the Commander.

# Chapter 27

## THE CITY

Sorcha spent the night after Emry's passing with Riona, their shared grief stretching into the early hours. After that night, Sorcha made it a point to visit her friend daily, though her efforts felt increasingly futile. Riona, usually so sharp and vibrant, had become a shadow of herself. Three days after Emry's death, the city came together to hold a memorial for all who had been lost in the attack. Mourning faces trickled in as silent cries and flickering candles filled the square. Each name that passed the elders lips sent a wave of grief through the crowd. Sorcha and her comrades stood with tears streaming as Riona stood on the farthest edge of town.

That same evening, Emry was laid to rest beneath the towering boughs of a great oak, surrounded by his friends, family, and Riona. Riona lingered by his grave well into the evening hours, her usually pale skin now sickly and frail. Sorcha watched from a distance, her heart breaking as she saw her friend's grief consume her. She knew Riona hadn't eaten in days, and no matter how hard Sorcha tried, she couldn't coax her into taking even a bite. Riona had become like a ghost, withdrawing further into herself with each passing day. Attempts from others to visit her were met with silence, and even Sorcha's gentle persistence failed to reach her.

In the days that followed, Kyron remained in Lumora working closely with Sorcha. An inn near the town square offered him a room as long as he wanted it. Many a night he spent walking the city with Sorcha, helping the townsfolk clean up the ravaged city, lending his strength to repair efforts, or meeting with the others to offer relief for patrols. He also took it upon himself to check in on Commander Nethran's recovery, easing Sorcha's burden when she was too preoccupied to do so herself.

Two weeks passed, and the Circle fell under the temporary leadership of the Druid elders. The city worked tirelessly to heal its wounds. Circle members and volunteers cleaned the streets, disposed of the twisted bodies of the creatures, purged the tainted waters, and provided solace to grieving families. Sorcha threw herself into the work, checking on the families of the fallen, visiting Commander Nethran, and helping wherever she could. Yet, even amid all the efforts to restore order, the weight of loss lingered heavily over them all.

Two weeks turned into a month under the Druid elders' direction. Leaders from the other regions came and went, attending meetings with the elders to discuss the growing challenges and strategies for recovery. It helped put Sorcha's growing concern for the Hollow towns at ease, hearing that they were addressing it.

While others arrived bearing supplies—materials, food, medicine, and clothing, each contribution a small effort to ease the suffering and rebuild the shattered city—Sorcha, Kyron, and the others except for Riona, who had requested to be reassigned to the remote woodland post, were finishing up the last of the city repairs. They spotted Commander Nethran walking toward them in civilian clothes. The sight made them pause, tools forgotten, as Sorcha broke into a run. She threw her arms around him without hesitation, catching him off guard, but he returned the hug with a warm smile.

The others followed behind, their faces lighting up as they expressed their relief and happiness to see him up and about, looking more like himself. Commander Nethran greeted them with a nod, his eyes scanning the group with a mixture of pride and sadness. "Thank you," he said, his voice steady but soft. "You've all done more than I could have asked during these past few weeks. I'm proud of each of you."

A shadow crossed his expression as he added, "I'm deeply saddened by Emry's loss. He was one of our best. I know his absence will be felt for a long time to come."

The group nodded solemnly, the weight of the commander's words pressing on their hearts.

"But," Nethran continued, straightening slightly, "we must honor him by continuing to protect this city and its people. I'll be returning to my duties by the end of the week."

The group exchanged glances, a spark of hope flickering in their expressions. It wasn't much, but having their commander back felt like the first step toward finding balance again. Sorcha continued her duties as directed by the elders; cleaning, rebuilding, and supporting the city. She only caught fleeting glimpses of Riona at the beginning and end of shifts. Her friend had grown distant, retreating into the woodland post, and Sorcha respected her need for space, though it left an ache in her heart. Kyron, on the other hand, had stayed by Sorcha's side through it all, offering a kindness that she hadn't expected. She wasn't sure what to make of him. Here was a man who had appeared one day in the woods, warning her away from danger and speaking cryptically about her not being like everyone else. He had seen her engulfed in the blaze during the battle, yet he never mentioned it, never pressed her for an explanation. If anything, he acted as though nothing had happened. Instead, Kyron integrated himself into her world. He made friends with her friends, lending a hand where he could, and stood beside her during some of their darkest moments. She had grown to like him; more than like him. His presence had become a steady, reassuring force in her life. She pushed all those thoughts aside and worked tirelessly alongside her friends till the end of the week arrived, a day the Circle was anxious for.

When Commander Nethran finally returned to active duty, The Circle greeted him with respect and admiration and he returned it. Of course it was short lived, and he got right back to work, sending members to their assignments. He turned to Sorcha. "But you, Sorcha, I need to speak with you in private"; his expression was serious but not unkind. He waited for the other members to dispatch before speaking. "You did well while I was recovering," he began, his tone steady. "The city owes you a great debt."

Sorcha nodded, unsure where the conversation was heading. Nethran's eyes met hers, and there was curiosity in his gaze. "I've been thinking about the battle," he said slowly. "It must've been the blood loss, or maybe the exhaustion, but I could've sworn..." he rubbed the back of neck as he spoke. "Sorcha, it looked like you were on fire. That you saved me."

Sorcha froze; she hadn't expected him to bring it up, and for a moment, she considered lying. But Nethran's expression held no judgment, only curiosity and a quiet respect. She took a deep breath and told him the truth.

When she finished, he simply nodded. "I thought as much," he said softly. "Thank you. For everything." He paused, a small smile playing on his lips. "Your secret is safe with me."

Relief washed over her, but before she could respond, Nethran spoke again.

"Now, about Kyron," he said, folding his arms. "I'm not sure what to make of him or the circumstances that brought him here." Nethran shifted his weight "We're down an officer, and that isn't meant to sound insensitive. I know it does." He turned to look toward the Druid School and for a moment he seemed lost in thought. "We need more fighters now than ever. He fought alongside us, stayed to help rebuild, and hasn't asked for anything in return. I have my questions and concerns about him but as my lead, what do you think of him?"

The question caught Sorcha off guard. She hesitated, her thoughts racing. Images of Kyron flashed through her mind, his smirk as he teased her, his unwavering focus in battle, the way he had stayed close through every hardship.

"I think…" she began, choosing her words carefully. "He's a mystery but he's proven himself. I think he's dependable, and I trust him for now."

Nethran nodded thoughtfully. "Good. That's what I needed to know before I approach him."

As he walked away, Sorcha couldn't help but wonder what the commander had in mind for Kyron and for her.

# Chapter 28
## A New Member

Sorcha had gone about her daily duties, clearing the last of the rubble, checking the town's borders, and visiting families of the fallen. It was a service she took on herself, making sure those left behind of the fallen had what they needed. Supplies. Comfort. Presence. It was the only thing she could think to do in the face of so much loss. She stood now before a weathered wooden door, its trim painted with curling pastel leaves. A small basket of fruit and vegetables rested on her hip, bright reds and greens against woven straw. It wasn't much, but it came from nearby towns offering aid. Enough to help quietly, without drawing notice. She raised her hand and knocked.

The door creaked open as lilac-colored eyes blinked up at her from the crack.

"Hey there. It's Sorcha from the Circle."

A tiny hand tugged the door wider. A girl stood framed in the light, straw-colored hair loose from a tired ponytail.

"Hi," the girl said softly.

"Is your mom around?"

"She's still sleeping." The girl's voice was barely above a whisper.

Sorcha glanced up; the sun was high now, midday. "Can I come in, Hazel?"

The girl nodded. Inside, the home was quiet and cluttered, dishes stacked, clothes scattered across the floor and piled near the door beside a pair of boots where hunting gear sat untouched.

Sorcha's gaze swept the room and landed on the girl again. She knew this story: during the attack, the family had lost their father while he'd fought alongside the Circle. She set the basket on the counter and gave Hazel a smile.

"You know what? I've got some free time today," she said, reaching for a broom. "Let's play pick up."

Hazel giggled as Sorcha began sweeping with exaggerated flair, twirling and dancing clothes across the floor. The girl jumped in, mimicking her moves by picking up a large shirt and dancing with it cross the floor. Laughter filled the small space between chores. Sorcha washed the dishes, tossed spoiled food, straightened piles but left the boots where they were. Some things weren't hers to touch.

As they finished the last chore, Sorcha hears Hazel's stomach rumble.

"I'm starving," Sorcha said, brushing her hands off. "Want to come to market? Maybe we can grab a few things for home?"

Hazel's face lit up as she bounded for the door barefoot.

"Your shoes!" Sorcha called after her, laughing.

Hazel skidded to a stop, turned, and ran back inside. She returned seconds later, feet covered this time.

On the way to the market, Sorcha let Hazel lead the way. Hazel stopped to sniff flowers, many times, giggling as she went by the fountain when droplets splashed her cheeks. Vendors smiled and waved; most refused coin when they saw who Sorcha was with. Hazel ventured the market, venison was roasting over an open fire and Sorcha couldn't resist. She dug her hands into her pockets, offering coin for venison and barley bread. An older gentlemen who wore a grief-stricken smile reached his rough hands to Sorcha and slowly closed her hand as he shook his head and handed her the food. Smiling back, Sorcha mouthed the words "Thank you" and turned toward a stone bench where they shared lunch. Hazel devoured hers quickly, Sorcha nibbling at hers, lost in thought.

At a nearby stall, a small wooden bear caught her eye. Next to it, a lilac scarf, the same soft shade as Hazel's eyes.

She bought both.

The walk back was much the same as the way they came, frequent stops by flowers and even tracking a chipmunk that skittered across Hazel's path. Eventually they made it back to the house where Sorcha unpacked the supplies.

"Here's dinner for you and your mom, okay? And this..." She held out the scarf and bear. "This is for you."

Hazel squealed, wrapping the scarf around her neck, already dancing with excitement with the bear. "I love them! Thank you!"

"You're welcome." Sorcha tousled her hair gently turning to the door, she paused. "If you ever need me, just ask anyone in the Circle."

Hazel nodded. "Bye, Sorcha."

She waved goodbye, her heart lighter than it had been in days.

After the last of the rounds of the day, Sorcha met with Kyron and the others at the tavern after their shifts. The day had given way to a quiet night, with only a sliver of the moon visible in the sky. Lanterns and stars provided the only light, casting a soft glow over the bustling streets. Inside, the tavern was warm and lively, filled with the hum of conversation and the clinking of pints.

Rhosyn, Drystan, Mason, and Eirin were already seated around a table, their drinks in hand, when Sorcha arrived. Kyron hadn't yet joined them, which gave her the opportunity she'd been looking for. She slid into a chair between Rhosyn and Eirin, ordering a tea already. "So," she began, her voice low, "what do you all think of Kyron?"

Drystan leaned back in his chair with a theatrical sigh. "Dreamy. Absolutely dreamy." Mason rolled his eyes, his shoulders stiffening. "He's... alright. I'll give him this... he's been a big help with the rebuilding, and he fought hard for us. I can't really say anything bad."

Rhosyn added thoughtfully, "He's knowledgeable, more than most, honestly. He knows a lot about the history of the realms, runes, herbs. And he's been nothing but kind to everyone."

Eirin shrugged, taking a slow sip from his tea. "Useful enough. Why do you ask?"

Sorcha hesitated, her eyes tracking her friends.

Her palms felt sweaty, as she tapped a foot under the table. She didn't want her friends to believe she was replacing Emry in some way but it was inevitable. Finally, she said, "Commander Nethran has asked that he join our ranks."

The table went silent. Eirin, who had been lounging casually next to her, sipping his tea, sat upright, his face darkening with disbelief. "It's only been... what? Five weeks now since Emry passed. And you're seriously telling me that someone who hasn't gone through training and isn't even from here, is being placed in the Circle? This soon?"

The concern on Eirin's face spread to the others. Rhosyn and Mason exchanged uneasy glances, and even Drystan's playful demeanor faltered. Sorcha held her ground, her voice steady but firm. "He's grown to be a friend to all of us," she countered. "As you said, he fought just as well if not better than any of us. And we need the help. Someone was going to be placed in Emry's absence... why not him?"

Slowly, reluctant nods passed around the table though Eirin's jaw remained tight. It was then that Kyron appeared, his confident stride drawing the attention of the entire group. He looked around the table, noting the sudden shift in energy.

Drystan, ever the instigator, chimed in with a grin. "Well, hello there, handsome. We were just talking about you. Welcome to the Circle of Light."

Sorcha froze, mortified. Kyron stopped short, confusion flickering across his face as he looked around at the awkward expressions and muffled laughter.

Mason elbowed Drystan hard in the ribs and hissed, "No."

Drystan winced, rubbing his side, while Rhosyn and Eirin dissolved into laughter. Sorcha buried her face in her hands, groaning softly.

Kyron's smile grew wider as he pulled out a chair. "Well," he said smoothly, his voice laced with amusement, "I'm not sure what I've just walked into, but consider me intrigued."

Sorcha peeked out from behind her hands, muttering under her breath, "I'm going to kill Drystan."

Kyron leaned closer, his smirk mischievous. "Should I be flattered or concerned?"

Drystan, ignoring the glare from Mason, raised his glass with a wink. "A little bit of both, I'd say."

The tension at the table eased as laughter broke out, though Mason's frown lingered. Sorcha, however, couldn't shake the flutter of nerves.

Sorcha turned to Kyron, her voice steady but cautious. "Commander Nethran wants to enlist you into the Circle. He asked for my opinion, and I gave it. If you accept, it would mean finding a place to live within the city walls and working alongside us."

Kyron looked at Sorcha, his expression softening as he said, "I'd be honored."

Rhosyn turned to Drystan with a sly grin. "Alright, now you can say it, Drystan." Sorcha crossed her arms, glancing between the others. Kyron's acceptance wasn't a surprise, but the unease in the room was unmistakable.

Eirin, finally spoke. His voice was level, but firm.

"Since you've made your decision, we need to go over the rules. The Circle isn't a group of hunters who charge in looking for glory. We don't kill for sport, and we don't engage unless we're forced to."

Kyron's smirk faded slightly as he studied the faces around him.

Sorcha leaned forward, fingers tapping against her cup. "That means if something comes through the Veil, we don't touch it unless it's a direct threat." Sorcha made sure his eyes were on her before speaking again "We don't know if it's Fae, a god, or something worse. And if we attack first? That blood is on our hands."

Kyron tilted his head. "So what, we just let them roam free?"

Rhosyn calmly answered. "No. We monitor, we track and we watch. But we don't act unless we have to. If you want to pick a fight, you better be damn sure it's one you can win and one you're willing to die for."

Mason folded his arms. "And if you break that rule, you'll wish whatever you fought had killed you first."

Eirin nodded. "Everything that crosses the Veil is part of this world now, Kyron. Whether it's Fae, beast, or something we can't name, it belongs to the earth as much as we do." Eirin leaned back in his chair. "It's not our job to decide what's good or bad. It's our job to protect the balance. That's the purpose of the Circle."

Sorcha held Kyron's gaze, her voice quieter now, but no less certain. "Think of the land itself. The seasons shift, plants bloom and wither, storms rage, rivers carve through stone. Destruction isn't unnatural, it's part of the cycle. Sometimes, what comes through the Veil is just another turn of that wheel. We don't exist to stop it. We exist to make sure the wheel keeps turning the way it should."

Kyron tilted his head. "So, you track them. You watch. You wait. But if you never act first?"

Eirin's stare was unflinching. "Control isn't the goal. Balance is."

Kyron's lips curled slightly, just enough to suggest he wasn't entirely convinced. "And if they decide to act first?"

Drystan answered smoothly, but there was steel in his tone. "Then we finish it."

A slow, thoughtful hum left Kyron's throat. He studied each of them in turn, his gaze lingering on Sorcha. "Interesting," he murmured.

Sorcha stiffened slightly, but before she could ask what he meant, Eirin cut in.

"Restraint is what keeps us alive," he said firmly. "It's what keeps this world from turning into a battlefield."

Kyron exhaled, his gaze flicking to the others before settling back on Sorcha. Finally, he nodded once.

"Understood."

Drystan stood and headed for the bar. A moment later, he returned with a bottle and a stack of glasses. He spun the bottle once in his hand, then flicked it into the air with a grin. It turned midair, caught the tavern light, and landed in his grip clean as a practiced trick. He poured with flair, glass by glass, letting each stream fall just short of overflowing. With a dramatic bow, he dropped into his seat.

Mason whistled, then clapped twice. "Show off," Eirin muttered with a laugh.

The rest of the group joined in, clapping and calling out as Drystan soaked it all in.

"Thank you, thank you. You're all too kind," he said, raising his glass. "Let's make it official."

Sorcha and the others raised theirs.

"Alright, Kyron—on three, we tap the glass and drink as fast as you can."

"It's tradition," Rhosyn said, grinning. "You're one of us now. That means no mercy."

Mason chuckled, shaking his head. "Can't wait to see what kind of drunk you are."

Eirin gave Kyron a quiet look. "Let's get this show on the road."

Sorcha nudged him with her elbow. "Ready?"

Kyron laughed. "I think you're all in for a surprise."

"That's the spirit, lover boy!" Drystan called. "One... two... three!"

Glasses slammed against the table. Laughter burst from every corner, and the night carried them deep into the early hours.

# Chapter 29
## THE ELK

The next morning, Sorcha and the others reported under Skyfall as usual. To her surprise, Kyron was already there with the group, dressed in a gray and brown shirt with the Circle's insignia embroidered on the sleeves. He was talking and laughing with the others when she approached, greeting them all with a cheerful, "Good morning."

Commander Nethran stood nearby, he had slight limp in his step and as he addressed the group he kept a hand on his side.

"I'm sure you've all figured out by now that Kyron has officially joined our Circle. I know there's much we'd like to discuss about what happened at the festival, and as much as I'd like to give you answers, I don't have them yet." His tone was measured but firm.

"What I can tell you," he continued, "is that in the coming weeks, we will be careful and vigilant about everything that happens. I want every single detail accounted for."

The group exchanged glances, a mixture of determination and unease passing through them. Sorcha's eyes met Kyron's briefly, and she saw in his expression the same resolve she felt. Commander Nethran divided the group for patrols:

- Rhosyn and Kyron

- Drystan and Mason

● Eirin and Sorcha

As they split up, Sorcha felt a hand grip her arm, she turned around standing nose to nose with Kyron. She felt heat rush to her cheeks when she realized his lips were only a breath away. Kyron took a step back. "I want you to promise me you won't do anything reckless." Sorcha's eyebrow curled up, as if to say "what?"

"You have a habit of finding yourself in precarious situations."

She sighed, annoyance creeping its way onto her face. "I swear it."

Kyron nodded then turned and strode toward Rhosyn who was watching in quiet amusement. Eirin was similar standing off in the distance looking just as amused as Rhosyn.

"Wipe that smirk off your face," Sorcha shot out when in striking distance of Eirin.

Eirin's smile widened as he gave her a salute. "Sir, yes sir."

Sorcha rolled her eyes as they began towards the woods north of Lumora. Each step away from Lumora brought a gray veil over the world, darkening as they went. The stillness was heavy, broken only by the crunch of leaves beneath their boots. Finally, Sorcha spoke, breaking the quiet.

"Have you spoken to Riona at all?"

Eirin shook his head, his expression somber. "I've tried. I've talked, but she just kept walking; she didn't even acknowledge me."

Sorcha frowned, the weight of his words sinking in. "She's hurting," she whispered, though it felt like an understatement. "It'll take some time, Eirin. Maybe more time than we think."

Eirin sighed, glancing at the surrounding forest.

Crows cawed in the treetops above. "I know she's grieving, we all are, but it's hard to stand by and feel like there's nothing we can do."

Sorcha placed a hand on his arm, her voice wavering. "She's strong, Eirin. Stronger than any of us. We just have to give her space to figure it out." Sorcha blinked hard, and the first tear slipped free as she tried to sound sure, but the ache behind her words betrayed her. One after another, they fell. Eirin said nothing as he reached for Sorcha's face, his warm hands cutting through the chill in the air as he wiped away the tears.

Eirin moved in closer, his boots scraping across the dirt beneath their feet. Sorcha buried her head in his chest as he held her. He placed his head atop hers and he held her until she broke away. "Thank you for being such a good friend, Eirin."

"Always."

They fell into step together, the woods alive with soft sounds, the last traces of green fading into ash. Fall was preparing for winter. The grass, once lush, now dulled to yellow and brown. The leaves clung weakly to the branches, the scattered bare limbs breaking the canopy in patches. But deeper in the woods Sorcha knew too well, something else stirred, like most of the woods she'd encountered lately. The trees grew twisted and burnt. The wind whipped with a voice caught in a scream. Limbs bent and coiled, wrapping around figures half formed as if struggling to escape. Once or twice, Sorcha thought she saw movement. Eirin slowed near one of the warped trunks. A gnarled limb reached outward, and beneath it outlined a Fae face. Its pointed ears, barely visible, were swallowed by the roots. The tree bled dark crimson from its bark. He reached his fingertips to touch the outstretched limb when the tree shivered and a blood-curdling cry tore through the air, sending Eirin stumbling backwards. That's when Eirin and Sorcha saw a massive elk lying on its side just beyond the tree. Its powerful legs kicked weakly at the air as it choked on its own blood. The sound was wrenching, a mix of gargled cries and labored breathing.

As they approached cautiously, the scene became more horrifying. The blood pooling beneath the creature was an unnatural black, seeping from its eyes and mouth like an inky curse. Sorcha crouched beside the elk, her voice catching in her throat. "What could have done this?" she whispered, her voice trembling as she placed a hand on the creature's side, feeling the faint quiver of life still present. Eirin stood frozen for a moment, as he watched the mighty creature's suffering. Unable to bear it any longer, he drew his blade. "We can't leave it like this," he said, his voice heavy with regret.

He knelt beside the elk, his powerful hand steadying its heaving body as he positioned the blade over its heart. With a swift and deliberate thrust, he pierced the creature heart. Its movements stilled instantly.

Sorcha wiped a tear from her cheek, her hand resting gently on the elk's fur. "The blood... it's poisoned," she said, her voice barely above a whisper.

Eirin wiped his blade clean on a nearby patch of moss, his brow furrowed in thought. "Whatever's out here, it's getting worse." He glanced down at the black ink staining the ground. Suddenly, loud snaps echoed from the elk's lifeless body. Sorcha stood wide eyed as the sound grew louder, reverberating through the stillness of the forest. Eirin turned just in time to see unnatural movement stirring within the elk's remains. Black flowers began to shoot out of the elk's rib cage, tearing open the carcass as their petals glistened with blood and tar. They careened around the elk's body and jutted outward, their roots consuming everything in their path. Sorcha's hand flew to her mouth as the once vibrant ground around the elk began to wither.

"Run," Eirin said, his voice low and urgent.

When Sorcha didn't move, transfixed by the grotesque sight, Eirin grabbed her arm with force, pulling her away. "Now!" he shouted, breaking her trance.

They sprinted through the forest, their breaths ragged and hearts pounding as they fled the spreading darkness. Sorcha glanced over her shoulder and let out a gasp of horror. The black flowers were expanding rapidly, curling and overtaking everything in their path. The once thriving forest was now a graveyard of decay, its vibrant greens replaced by deathly grays and blacks.

Eirin pulled her faster, his grip firm as they leapt over roots and ducked under low-hanging branches. After putting a safe distance between them and the bloom, they stopped, their chests heaving as they struggled to catch their breath. Eirin turned to look back, his face pale with disbelief.

The black bloom had devoured everything within its radius, leaving a wasteland of destruction. Trees stood stripped of leaves, their bark cracking and rotting. The ground was slick with a dark, viscous substance, and the air around the bloom felt heavy and suffocating.

"What is that?" Sorcha stammered, her voice trembling.

"I don't know," Eirin said grimly, his hand still gripping her arm as if afraid to let go. "It's just like the last one we saw, but that was on the other side of the city... it's spreading."

Sorcha's mind raced as she stared at the spreading darkness. She turned to Eirin, her resolve hardening. "We need to get back. Nethran has to see this. He has to know."

Eirin nodded, his jaw clenched. "Agreed. Let's go before it catches up with us."

Without another word, they turned and bolted through the forest, the haunting sight of the black bloom etched into their memories, a grim reminder of the growing sickness threatening their world.

# Chapter 30
## A COUNCIL OF FOOLS

Eirin and Sorcha raced to Nethran's office within the Druid School, sweat pouring down their faces and breath ragged gasps as they burst through the doors. The commander, looking concerned, studied them as they tried to catch their breath. He waited patiently, his gaze shifting between the two as they began speaking at once, voices overlapping in a chaotic jumble. Unable to decipher their words, Commander Nethran raised a hand. "Alright, alright, settle down! One at a time, officers."

Sorcha glanced at Eirin. Eirin, still catching his breath, said, "There was a very sick great elk in the forest. It was dying... black blood pouring from its eyes and mouth. It was struggling so much. I couldn't watch it suffer any longer, so I ended its misery."

He paused still breathing heavily. "But as soon as I did, something... happened. Black vines started pouring out of the elk's body, spreading rapidly. We ran as fast as we could."

Commander Nethran remained outwardly calm, but the concern—possibly even fear—etched into his expression was unmistakable. His voice was steady but firm as he spoke. "I need the two of you to head to the library immediately. I'm sending for the others and the elders."

Sorcha and Eirin exchanged uneasy glances. Before they could say anything further, Commander Nethran's voice thundered through the room, "NOW!"

The sharpness of his tone startled them both, leaving no room for hesitation. Without another word, Sorcha and Eirin turned and made their way out of the office, the urgency in his command pushing them toward the library without delay. Once inside the library, the two began pacing. Eirin spoke first, his voice taut with frustration as the words spilled out. "This started three months ago here with that bloom we found after those rogue creature attacked the village's livestock and you. Other regions have encounter this too and the elders keep insisting these are isolated events.

Eirin ran his hands through his hair, his tension etched across the tight line of his lips, the furrow of his brows. "What really pisses me off is how the elders keep brushing it off. Saying the bloom might be part of nature's cycle, that life and death are balanced. As if that explains the decay spreading faster than anything natural. And now, after everything we've seen, they still refuse to admit what's in front of them. The Fomorians have returned; everyone saw them. We've tossed their bodies to the fires."

"People are suffering, and they're being left to deal with it alone. They've come to us as a last resort, and even then, no one listened." Sorcha began fiddling with her dagger hilt, adjusting and readjusting her belt.

Eirin's frustration grew as he rubbed the back of his neck as he continued to pace. Both lost in thought as they pieced together the threads.

Sorcha's voice broke the stillness. "It's all connected, isn't it? Every single thing. The bloom, the wolves, the horse, the kelpie, Meadowrun, the festival... and now that elk. It's spreading."

They stood outside the Grand Mirror waiting for the others to arrive. As the others arrived they filed into the space. Sorcha, Eirin, Riona, Drystan, Rhosyn, Mason, Kyron and Commander Nethran stood together, facing the Elders seated at the far end of the chamber. Despite the weight of recent events, the Elders' expressions remained calm, almost detached.

Commander Nethran opened the discussion. "We've gathered to address the escalating threats in Lumora and beyond. The Circle has faced these events firsthand, and I believe their accounts demand immediate attention."

Elder Caerwyn was the first to speak, her voice composed. "Before we leap to conclusions, we must remember that nature operates in cycles. Life, decay, and renewal are inevitable parts of our world. The black blooms could simply signify a natural shift, unpleasant but not unprecedented." Riona stiffened beside Sorcha, her pale hands curling into fists.

Her voice broke through the room like a blade. "Cycles don't tear people apart. They don't destroy entire regions. What we're seeing isn't some natural shift; it's devastation. It's death. And you're sitting here trying to rationalize it."

The room fell silent as all eyes turned to Riona. Her grief radiated through every word, but her tone was controlled. Sorcha placed a steadying hand on her arm, but Riona didn't waver.

Eirin stepped forward. "We've seen the signs for months now; the bloom started in the forest." His voice grew louder, his hands balling into fists. Sorcha could see his snake rune moving at the edge of his shirt glowing ever so slightly. "These aren't isolated incidents. This is the Fomorians returning, and you're still sitting here debating!"

Elder Orlan's tone turned bitter. "Mind your tongue. We are not dismissing these events, but caution is paramount. Acting rashly could worsen an already precarious balance."

Sorcha spoke up. "We've all seen signs. If we wait any longer, there won't be a city to protect."

Kyron, standing beside Sorcha, finally broke his silence. His deep voice a low warning as he spoke. "The Fomorians have returned. Call it what you like, but you can't deny what's in front of you. If the Elders won't act, eventually the people will." His eyes locked on the elders, daring them to challenge him.

Elder Caerwyn hesitated, her calm facade slipping just slightly. "Are you threatening the council? Commander Nethran, get your officers under control or we will be forced to."

Riona let out a bitter laugh, shaking her head. "People are dying. Emry is dead. What more needs to happen?"

Commander Nethran raised his hand, silencing the room with a booming "Enough." His eyes swept across his Circle before looking back to the elders. "I urge the elders and the council to consider this seriously. We've seen enough to know that this is only the beginning."

The elders exchanged uneasy glances, their grip on the situation loosening. Elder Caerwyn finally sighed, lowering her voice. "We will deliberate and determine our next steps. But understand this: whatever the decision, it will be final."

Riona said nothing, but the cold fury in her eyes conveyed everything. Sorcha gently squeezed her arm, offering silent reassurance, but Riona pulled away and as the meeting adjourned, the Circle gathered near the door.

Kyron leaned toward Sorcha, speaking in a low voice. "They'll deliberate until it's too late. We need to be prepared to act on our own."

Sorcha nodded and looked to the others, who, rightfully so, wore mixed expressions of frustration, anger and even sadness. Riona was already heading out of the main doors of the library without so much as a word. The sight hurt Sorcha more than she wanted to let on.

Commander Nethran spoke only after the elders had left. "What the hells what that?"

Eirin opened his mouth to speak but Commander Nethran cut him off.

"That was a rhetorical question. You think that threatening the council will make them move any faster? Once you begin to threaten them, they stop listening. All you've done is make our case harder to prove and shows that I have no control of my officers," he barked out, fury burning in his eyes. He gaze fell over them again and his expression softened as he exhaled. "For now we need to scout the areas around the town, particularly where the hunters and the gatherers go. Inform the people at the market and the vendors that there are sick animals in the forest and that these particular areas are off limits until further notice. All of you are to take a rope with you and mark the areas far enough out that the townsfolk won't encounter the growth and understand it's unsafe."

Rhosyn tilted her slightly. "Wait, are you saying we should lie to the people of Lumora?"

Nethran's gaze hardened, his voice filled with exhaustion and irritation. "What I'm asking for is your discretion. One thing the elders have right is this: if we alarm the public without solid answers, things will spiral out of control. Hysteria will set in, and chaos will follow. The best thing we can do right now is to keep the people of Lumora safe by keeping them away from danger." He paused, letting his words settle in as tension filled the air. He scanned each of their faces, his tone softening slightly. "Think of it this way: if we tell them there's a threat, Fomorian, sickness, decay, whatever it is but can't provide them with solutions or protection, we'll only breed fear. Fear leads to mistakes. Mistakes will lead to more lives lost. We need to tread cautiously for now."

Sorcha stepped forward. "But what about the hunters and the gatherers who rely on the forest? How long can we realistically keep them out without offering answers? Rumors will spread, Nethran, whether we want them to."

Nethran nodded, acknowledging her point. "You're right, Sorcha. We can't keep this hidden forever, but until we have a clear picture of what we're doing, I'm asking all of you to use your best judgment. Rope off the areas, warn the locals of sickness and the animals, and advise them to avoid those parts of the forest for now. It's not a lie. It's the truth so far. As we gather more information, we'll adjust."

Rhosyn crossed her arms. "What if it's not enough? What if the threat grows beyond what we can handle?"

"That's exactly why we exist. We are among the best minds and fighters in the realm. Whatever is coming, our responsibility is not just to Lumora, but to the entire realm."

Eirin, who had been uncharacteristically quiet, finally spoke. "All right, Commander, we'll do it, but we're going to need more than rope and warning signs."

Nethran's eyes softened, a flicker of weariness breaking through his composure. "I know, Eirin. That's why every one of you matters. I'm counting on you to help protect this city with what resources we have until we can face this head on with help."

Kyron gave Sorcha a reassuring nod, his hand brushing gently against the back of her arm.

# Chapter 31
## THE TRUTH

The Circle dispersed toward the outposts to gather supplies. Each officer selected a section of forest to survey and rope off or to speak with the townsfolk. Their hurried footsteps echoed on the stone walkways as they split up. Sorcha paused, taking in the late afternoon light, a wash of yellow melting into pink and orange hues reminiscent of ruby fruit—a wild citrus that grew in the woods surrounding the city. Its peel was a vibrant red, but the flesh within held shades of pink, the taste a blend of lemon and raspberries. Lumora and the others faded into the background as she entered the woods, branches swaying in the breeze as her boots sank into the emerald moss. Trees danced in the wind, a whistling sound carried through the air when she narrowed her eyes at movement in her periphery, whirling around. Something weaved between the trees.

Sorcha spun in circles, trying to catch sight of it when searing pain erupted in her right arm, then her left, then her right again. Small slashes appeared on her skin, droplets of red flowing from the cuts. Her runes flared, glimmering, when a tiny figure, about two feet tall, emerged from the trees. He wore a red cap and had a twisted grin as he jumped onto a large rock and sat, watching Sorcha before licking the blood from his nails. He howled with laughter at her confusion.

"What burns hotter than the sun, yet dies the moment it's born?"

"What?" Sorcha spat, wiping blood from her wounds.

The little man leaned back, holding his stomach, laughing. "Why, you, silly girl."

Suddenly, he was in front of her, towering, his face twisted, features melting together as he smiled wider, exposing needle-sharp teeth with pieces of flesh caught between them. Sorcha's runes flared, and she began to ignite, fire slowly rippling across her skin. The twisted figure stepped back and screamed, charging at her, only to vanish before reaching her. Laughter had broken out all around, only to vanish instantly. Sorcha's chest heaved as the fiery ripples faded away. She stood there, anticipating the Far Darrig's return. She knew the creature relished its tricks and riddles at mortals' expense, though she'd never witnessed it firsthand. The stories, however, were familiar. As the sun dipped low, casting long shadows, she hurried toward the bloom.

Sorcha finished securing the last of her rope, brushing off her hands. The bloom hadn't spread as far as they'd feared, but even a mile into the forest was too close for comfort. It pulsed softly in the fading light, an unsettling presence. Kyron emerged from the woods, carrying another coil of rope as if he knew she was running out.

"This should finish the last section," he said, handing it to her. "The bloom seems to have stopped spreading."

"How'd you know I needed more rope?" Sorcha asked, knotting the post with practiced ease.

Kyron just smiled. "I had a hunch, and it was getting late." His eyes lowered to the dried blood on her arms. "Everything okay?"

"Yeah, just some branches caught me on my way through." She rubbed her arms as she spoke. "Anyway, as the Commander said, we just need to finish this up."

Kyron stood beside her, following her gaze through the trees.

"It's late. Let me walk you back."

Sorcha hesitated, then nodded. "Alright. Thanks."

The walk back to the village was silent, the streets lit by a handful of soft lights. Sorcha glanced at Kyron, her brow furrowing. "Have you seen Riona?"

Kyron shook his head. "No. I asked Eirin yesterday, and he said she hasn't been at her post much. She's keeping to herself."

Sorcha sighed, shoulders slumping. "I've tried everything. I've gone to her post, knocked on her door, left notes. It's like I'm invisible to her now."

Kyron slowed his pace, his tone careful. "You know how grief can be. She might just need time." Sorcha clenched her fists, frustration bubbling to the surface.

"I know she's hurting, but—" She stopped herself, exhaling sharply. "It feels like she's shutting me out completely."

Kyron reached out, his hand brushing her arm. "You've done what you can. Sometimes people need space to process. Pushing her might only push her further away."

She nodded reluctantly, her lips pressed into a thin line. "You're right. I just... I hate feeling like I can't help her."

They walked in silence for a few moments before Kyron broke it. "Samhain is coming up," he said, his tone lighter trying to change the subject. "I was wondering if you're still interested in going. I know things have changed, but..."

Sorcha glanced at him, surprised by the question. "Samhain?" She hesitated, considering it. "Honestly, I think I need it now more than ever. I need something to take my mind off all this."

Kyron gave her a small smile. "Good. It'll be a chance to step away, even if it's just for a little while.

And," he added with a raised brow, "maybe we'll get a better sense of what's happening in Cailleach's Keep."

Her smile faltered slightly, the weight of everything crashing back down. "Let's just hope it's nothing like here," she murmured.

Kyron didn't reply, but the way his gaze lingered on her spoke volumes. As they reached her door, Sorcha paused on the threshold.

"Thanks for walking me back."

Sorcha started to step through the doorway when Kyron gently grabbed her arm. "Sorcha," he said softly.

She turned, surprised by the unexpected nervousness in his voice. "What is it?"

Kyron ran a hand through his hair, hesitating for a moment as if searching for the right words. "I need you to hear me out," he said, his voice quiet but serious. He muttered almost to himself, "I can't believe I'm saying this."

"What's going on?" she asked, concerned.

He gaze was on ground, kicking the dirt gently as he avoided her gaze. Sorcha studied him for a long moment, sensing the weight of whatever he was about to say. Finally, she nodded.

"Okay," Kyron exhaled, bracing himself. "I'm sorry for the way we met in the woods," he began. "But it wasn't by chance that we met. I was there because of you."

"Because of me?" Sorcha asked, confused.

"Why?"

"Because..." he paused, raising his eyes to meet hers. "I'm part of the Tuatha Dé Danann. For generations, part of my family has lived in the Otherworld, but we've always watched over the mortal realm. Not just the realm itself, but people... people born with special gifts or abilities, like you... demigods."

Sorcha blinked. "Wait... are you telling me the Tuatha Dé Danann are still here?" Then she added, "A demigod?" Her voice trailed off trying to process what he just told her.

"Yes," Kyron said simply, his voice steady. "The mist you've seen me use, it's not just an ability. It's a bridge, a way to transport between worlds. Each of us is gifted with it. I couldn't tell you sooner because of my orders. I know just showing up in the woods wasn't enough to make you trust me, but I was trying to keep you safe."

Sorcha's thoughts swirled as she tried to make sense of it all. "So... the mist is your connection to the Otherworld? And you're here because of me?"

He nodded. "Yes. When I came to the festival, I wanted to talk to you, to explain everything. Then the Fomorians attacked and afterwards wasn't the right time.

The more time I spent with you, the more I realized I didn't want to leave you."

Sorcha's breath caught in her throat as Kyron took a step closer, his voice softening. "You may have started out as my duty, Sorcha," he said, his gaze unwavering. "But you're more than that now. I need you to know my feelings for you go beyond what they should. I stayed here when I shouldn't have, because I care about you."

His words hung in the air between them, Sorcha's heart raced, her mind reeling from the weight of his confession. She didn't know what to say, but she couldn't look away from him, caught in the depths of those swirling waves of his.

"There's more I have to tell you," Kyron said, his voice heavy with hesitation. "And what I'm about to say isn't easy to hear. I need you to understand there's never been a good time to tell you any of this. But it's about who you are and what happened to your parents."

She shook her head, a wave of denial washing over her.

"No," she said firmly, her voice trembling. "I know what happened to my parents. I know who they were." Her eyes searched his face, a mix of terror, sorrow and frustration clouding her expression. "I can't. Not right now. It's too much. This is all too much." She began to back away when Kyron spoke.

His expression softened, a flicker of pain evident in his eyes, but he nodded. "I get it," he said gently. "But if you ever want to know the truth, when you're ready, I'll be here. I'll tell you everything."

Sorcha's eyes lingered on his for a moment longer.

He stepped closer, gently placing his hand over hers. "When you're ready, Sorcha." His voice was barely above a whisper.

Then, before she could respond, he leaned in and pressed a tender kiss to her forehead. The warmth of it lingered even as he pulled away. Without another word, he turned and walked into the night, disappearing into the shadows, leaving Sorcha standing alone in the darkness.

She stood there for a long moment, the weight of his words settling heavily on her chest, her mind spinning with questions she wasn't sure she wanted the answers to.

# Chapter 32
## An Unlikely Companion

Sorcha stood at her door for what felt like an eternity, still trying to process what had just happened. She was too stunned to move, her mind swirling in confusion as she tried to wrap her head around... well, everything. Kyron just laid out more information than she could handle, and then there was the kiss.

Finally, she stepped back inside her home, shutting the door with trembling hands. The dwindling fire in the hearth caught her eye, and she crossed the room, grabbing a few more logs from the basket to feed the flames. The fire awoke with a roar and crackle that let her know she could sit and enjoy its warmth. There in her chair, she sank. Watching the flames twist, rise and fall, consumed her thoughts.

*It was too much. All of it.*

Her journal sat on the table in its usual place, a silent companion in all this chaos, and as she always did, she reached for it. The pages soon spilled over with notes and scribbles, small sketches and scattered thoughts throughout. On those pages, she tried to piece together the picture it was creating, and all she did was connect that somehow she was in the middle of it all. And then there was Kyron.

Her pen stopped as she thought of him. Damn him. *Damn him for complicating everything.* For saying he had feeling for her, for admitting he was here for her. Why did he have to complicate things more than they were? That kiss, the tender kiss he placed upon her forehead...

She slammed the journal and leaned back in her chair, closing her eyes. Her thoughts lingered on Kyron's last words.

*What did he mean about my parents? What could he possibly say?*

*Nothing he said would bring them back, nothing could change what had already happened... could it?*

*How would it break me?*

She tried to push the thoughts aside, to think of anything else, but the question burrowed deep, refusing to let go. The memories of her parents, the moments before they disappeared, the loneliness after—it all surfaced. She scanned her mind for something, anything, that could give her the answers, but all she found was heartache. It hurt deeply, as if it had happened just yesterday. The pain of missing them, wishing they were still here, shredded her all over again. She told Kyron she couldn't hear it not yet. In that moment, it had felt like the right choice. But now, sitting alone in the stillness of home, regret crept in. Whatever it was, it had to be better than spending the night imagining every outcome, tormenting herself with "what if?".

She could no longer bear to be home, so she headed for a forest walk to clear her thoughts. The woods is where she felt most at peace and while walking at night wasn't ideal, she promised herself not to venture too deep. She needed grounding, just to feel the cool earth beneath her. The smell of autumn was heavy in the air, crispy leaves crunched under her feet, the faint babbling of brooks and streams nearby. This was where she felt alive. As she wandered, she stumbled on a perfectly arranged circle made of stone and flowers. It was odd, obviously man made. Nature was never this precise; its edges and patterns always held a kind of chaos. But here, everything was deliberate. Curious, Sorcha moved closer, kneeling to inspect the circle in the moonlight. She bent down, peering at its odd symmetry, when a sudden unexpected *meow* startled her. She yelped, falling backward onto a tree stump with enough force to make her tailbone hurt. "By the Morrigan!" she cursed, rubbing her back. From within the circle, pair of silver eyes glowed in the dark, staring directly at her. Slowly, a sleek form emerged. A cat, though it was unlike any she'd ever seen. It was large, somewhere between a wildcat and small dog. Its fur was dark as night, shimmering almost, the only marking were small white spots on its chest, like stars scattered against the night. The cat padded toward her with an almost amused air, sitting just in front of her as if waiting for acknowledgment.

Sorcha blinked. "You scared the life out of me, you know that?" The cat tilted its head, its silver eyes scanning her, almost as though it understood everything she was saying.

"You're a beautiful cat," she admitted cautiously.

The cat stretched before circling her legs, sitting under them.

"Oooh no. No, no no." Sorcha muttered pushing herself up. "I'm leaving. You can go back to sleep now." She slowly began to retreat backwards. "You just... stay right there, alright? Good kitty, stay here."

The cat didn't move; it only watched her retreat with the same amused glint in its eyes. But no sooner had she turned, she heard the soft pitter patter of paws.

"You've got to be kidding me," she groaned, walking faster.

The cat didn't care, it followed her like a shadow.

Sorcha tripped over a root, landing hard in the meadow with a thud. She grumbled, only for the cat to leap into her lap and curl up.

"No. No. you can't come with me. I don't have pets for a reason," she insisted, trying to push the animal off but it dug in stubbornly.

"Go home and not with me," she pleaded.

She struggled to push the cat off her and stand up, only to have the cat trip her, again, and again and again.

She sat in the meadow and admitted defeat as the cat jumped into her lap once more.

"You know, you really are something," she groaned. "If you come with me I can't promise I'll remember to feed you or give you water, and so help me, if you poop in my house, I'll throw you into the fountain. Got it?"

She narrowed her eyes at the cat, who, to her shock, gave her a nod.

Sorcha froze. "I must be losing my mind. I'm talking to a cat." She stood and began walking again, the cat beside her, its silver eyes glinting in the moonlight.

As Sorcha opened the door to her home, she turned to the cat.

"This is home," she announced.

Before she could fully swing the door open, the cat sauntered in, promptly making itself comfortable in the chair by the fire. Rolling her eyes, Sorcha stepped inside, closed the door behind her, and fixed her gaze on the cat.

"Sure, make yourself at home," she told the cat as she put the kettle on, planning to bathe after her adventure in the woods.

The cat had certainly taken her mind off things for a bit, and it was nice to not feel so alone for a change.

Sorcha eased into the crystal tub, the warm water like a comforting embrace. Just as she began to let her tensions melt away, a distinct meow pierced the tranquility. Opening her eyes, she saw the cat stationed on the washroom floor, its gaze fixed intently on her.

The cat remained perfectly still, except for a slow, thoughtful swish of its tail. Sorcha couldn't resist a smile.

"What is it now?" she asked. In response, the cat tilted its head, giving her a look that seemed suspiciously like a nod.

"Can you actually understand me?" Sorcha asked, with a mixture of amusement and disbelief. The cat blinked slowly, then, unmistakably, nodded once more.

Sorcha let out a soft laugh, the sound echoing slightly off the walls.

"Well, that's settled then. This is probably one of the least odd of things that's happened to me." She settled back against the cool surface of the tub. The cat's eyes never wavered from her. She felt an unusual sense of security.

A few moments later, Sorcha emerged from the tub, with the cat trailing behind as she made her way to the kitchen, where the kettle was whistling. She made herself a cup of tea. With tea in hand, and the cat still following, she settled into her chair by the fire and sighed deeply. As she did, the cat sat in front of her, watching her intently. Sorcha looked down at the cat, and it tilted its head toward her lap.

"Are you asking if you can come up?" The cat nodded.

"Alright, come on up."

With that, the cat jumped into her lap and circled a few times before curling up. As she sat there, the things she had been trying to forget slowly began to creep back, making her heart race unevenly, heavy with sorrow. The cat seemed to notice and started purring on her lap, its gaze locked on hers. It sat up and nuzzled its face against hers. Sorcha took a deep breath as tears streamed down her face.

The cat didn't move but kept itself there, nestled against her as she hugged the animal. Her eyes grew heavy, and she slowly drifted off to sleep with the cat on her lap. That night, no nightmares plagued her, and for the first time in a long time, she slept deeply.

# Chapter 33
## A Terrible Influence

S orcha awoke to the soft crackle of the fire and sunlight streaming through the windows. She didn't remember falling asleep. Looking down, she saw the cat still perched on her lap.

*I guess it wasn't a dream*, she thought, staring at the creature, its fur bright as stars.

She felt a twinge of guilt about moving and waking it, but she needed to get ready for patrols. As Sorcha dressed, the cat darted around the house, circling too many times for her to keep track. She frowned, wondering what it was up to. It acted as though it were impatient, waiting for her. When she finally emerged from the bedroom and headed for the door, the cat was already there, sitting expectantly.

"And what do you think you're doing?" she asked, raising an eyebrow at the feline.

The cat simply stared back, unmoving. She shook her head and opened the door. The cat followed her out, then sat down, watching her close it behind her.

"I'm heading to work," she told the cat firmly. "You can't come with me."

She started walking, but the sound of tiny paws padding behind her made her glance over her shoulder. Sure enough, the cat was trailing her. She sighed and tried to ignore it, but the cat stuck to her like a shadow all the way to the circle. When she arrived, Commander Nethran tilted his head, confusion plain on his face as he eyed both Sorcha and the odd-looking feline at her side. Sorcha noticed the mixed expressions on everyone's faces, too. Most looked amused, but Kyron's reaction stood out; his gaze was fixed on the cat, his face a mix of shock and unease. He clearly didn't like it, though he tried and failed to hide it. Sorcha noticed, and so did the cat.

Commander Nethran finally broke the silence. "Why is there an animal with you, Sorcha?"

Sorcha shifted uncomfortably. "Sir, this cat followed me home last night. I guess it's mine now... It won't leave alone."

The commander blinked, baffled. "And that means it has to be *here*?"

Sorcha nodded awkwardly. The cat, surprisingly, nodded too. Commander Nethran sighed, muttering under his breath before approaching the cat. He reached out to pick it up, but the cat sprang onto his head in one swift leap, clinging there stubbornly.

What followed was chaos. The commander flailed, grabbing at the cat from every possible angle, but the creature dodged every attempt with ease, only to land back on him each time.

The circle erupted with laughter, and Sorcha's face flushed with embarrassment as the commander bellowed, "Sorcha, get this damn thing off me—NOW!

Mortified, Sorcha rushed forward, already trying to wrangle the cat.

"Please stop," she begged under her breath.

To her relief, the cat finally leapt down, landing gracefully on the cobblestones before sitting at attention, staring the commander down.

Commander Nethran, red faced and fuming, took a deep breath and composed himself as best he could.

Without another word about the incident, he quickly assigned patrol routes and stormed off toward the Druid School.

As the laughter died down, Sorcha turned to face the circle. Her friends were still staring at her, and at the strange cat by her side.

Drystan walked over, chuckling as he knelt down to face the cat at eye level.

"Nice work, buddy. I've never seen the commander that shade of red before," he said, patting the cat's head. He glanced up at Sorcha with a grin.

"So, Sorcha, you're taking in strays now?"

Before Sorcha could respond, Eirin appeared behind him. "No, Drystan, she's not taking *you* in."

Drystan shot him a mock glare before looking back at Sorcha. "Really, Sorcha? A cat? I didn't take you for cat person."

Sorcha laughed softly, her cheeks still flushed with embarrassment.

"I'm not, but this little guy didn't really give me a choice. So... yeah, I guess I'm a cat person now."

The three of them laughed as Rhosyn and Eirin approached. Rhosyn leaned down to pet the feline, her expression warm.

"Does your cat have a name?" she asked. Sorcha shook her head. "No name yet, just 'Cat' for now until we figure that out."

Eirin chuckled. "It's practical, and you definitely won't forget it."

The group began to break up into teams, but Sorcha noticed that Kyron hadn't joined them yet, and Riona was still nowhere to be seen. Kyron, standing at a distance, looked uneasy. Sorcha caught his eye, and he hesitated before finally making his way over.

"Where did you find that cat?" he asked, his tone uncharacteristically stern.

Sorcha raised an eyebrow. "I found him in the woods. I stumbled on him sleeping in this flower and stone bed."

Kyron's expression turned cold, his face pale as if he'd seen a ghost. He leaned in closer, his voice dropping to a harsh whisper.

"You found a cat in a *fairy circle*? And you *brought it home*?"

"Fairy circle?" Sorcha repeated, frowning. "Kyron, it's just a cat."

"Is it?" Kyron's tone was tight, his usual calm edged with alarm. "Do you even know what that means?"

Sorcha folded her arms. "It means it was a bunch of flowers and stones in a weirdly perfect shape. It wasn't a fairy circle."

Kyron ran a hand over his face. "It means something was already living there, Sorcha. A being. A Fae."

Sorcha turned to the cat, who, as if on cue, tilted its head in mock innocence, then yawned.

"Oh, please," she scoffed. "It's not like I stole an enchanted artifact. I took in a stray—"

The cat's silver eyes glinted as it stretched, its tail flicking in slow, deliberate amusement.

Kyron stiffened. "Sorcha, it's nodding at you."

"Yeah, it does that," she said dismissively.

"That's not normal," Kyron hissed.

The cat let out a low, pleased purr.

"Okay, fine. Well, I'm glad to see you this morning. How about I walk you home tonight? Meet at the tavern?"

Sorcha smiled. "I'd like that."

As Kyron walked away, Sorcha and Cat made their way through the streets of Lumora. They stopped briefly to grab a loaf of bread and a jar of jam, which she shoved into her bag before continuing on. Their patrol assignment was at the outpost where Riona had specifically requested to be stationed alone. The thought made Sorcha uneasy, and she was anxious to see her.

When they arrived at the outpost, Sorcha was greeted by a few young cadets finishing their rotation. She asked them if they'd seen Riona, but they shook their heads. With a nod, she dismissed them and started walking the grounds.

Sorcha and Cat moved through the outpost, her eyes scanning the tree line as she completed the routine checks. Everything seemed quiet. Satisfied for the moment, she returned to the small building at the center of the outpost. Inside, a worn wooden table and a single chair awaited her. She sat down, pulled out the loaf of bread, and spread a generous amount of jam across a thick slice before taking a bite.

Cat sat beside her, watching intently. Sorcha couldn't help but feel guilty about eating without sharing, so she tore off small pieces of bread with jam and placed them on the floor in front of him. Cat ate them without hesitation but, moments later, caught a mouse. He seemed to enjoy his impromptu second course even more. They spent the day monitoring the decay, keeping detailed records of the perimeters to track its spread; how much and how fast. Hourly, Sorcha checked, though Cat didn't seem to mind; he was happily preoccupied chasing small critters. The hours passed slowly, stretching well into the evening. By the time the moon had settled high into the sky, the cadets arrived to relieve her of her rotation. She gave the orders and called Cat, making her way back into town.

Kyron was waiting at the tavern, just as he said he would be. He seemed to have finished a drink and was now casually eyeing the door. Meeting her gaze, he waved the bartender over and exchanged some coins before walking toward her.

"Long day?" he asked.

Sorcha nodded, letting out a groan. "I spent every hour checking, measuring, and time stamping. Hour after hour, on the hour, for the entire shift." She rolled her shoulders, the monotony still clinging to her.

Kyron smirked, his eyes glinting with amusement. "Ouch, that sounds tedious."

"Agonizingly boring," she corrected, though her tone carried more weariness than bite. "But it's important, even if it feels like torture."

"It is important," he said, his voice softening.

He placed a hand on her arm, the warmth of his touch steadying her for a moment.

They walked side by side, their conversation drifting between what Eirin and Sorcha had discussed in the library, the growing decay, and the druids' increasingly strained efforts to understand it. Eventually, Sorcha hesitated, her steps slowing slightly as she shifted the conversation to what Kyron had said the night before.

She didn't want to bring it up, not really but the questions clawed at her, demanding answers. Even if she feared what the truth might reveal, she couldn't let it go.

Kyron shifted slightly and told her it was best to wait until they were somewhere more private. It was probably better he told her at home or somewhere else she was comfortable. Sorcha agreed they could talk at her home. The rest of the walk was quiet.

Once inside, Sorcha offered Kyron a seat at the breakfast nook where she sat across from him. The tension in the air was a mix of discomfort and anxiety between the two. Kyron looked at Sorcha.

"What did you want to talk about first?" he asked, his gaze meeting hers.

# Chapter 34
## THE FULL STORY

Sorcha tried to speak, but her throat tightened, her heartbeat erratic. A sense of panic began to flood her system, making it hard to breathe. Cat, sensing her distress, leapt into her lap, meowing twice to catch her attention. His purring and warmth grounded her just enough for her to take a deep, shuddering breath.

"I want to know everything," she finally said, her voice trembling. "I just don't know where to start. I'm still trying to understand what you told me last night. Tell me everything from the beginning. I need to know about my parents. All of it." Tears welled in her eyes, threatening to spill.

Kyron's expression softened, his sadness almost tangible. He sighed heavily, as if the weight of what he was

about to say had been pressing on him for years. "All right," he said quietly. "Let's start at the beginning."

He began to explain, his voice laden with heaviness. He spoke of the Second Battle of Mag Tuired, of the god Lugh, part of the Tuatha, and of Bres, the dishonored king, who had allied with Balor of the Fomorians.

Then Kyron turned to her. "Your father was the god, Lugh. Your mother was mortal, and though they loved each other, she knew she could never be part of the Tuatha. They chose to stay in the mortal realm and took you to Lumora, a city built in the image of your father; the god of the sun. It's no coincidence you have remarkable aim, no matter the difficulty or distance.

Your runes, they were a gift from your father. He hoped that, one day, you would join him in the Otherworld."

Sorcha's vision began to blur, the sound of Kyron's voice growing louder in her ears.

His tone darkened slightly as he continued. "Bres had a child as well. Vaelric. Like you, he was born of mortal blood, but Bres took him from his mother and raised him himself, filling the boy's heart with poison and hatred from the moment he could understand words. Kyron paused a moment, placing on hand on Sorcha's. "Vaelric was told he was a king, that his birthright was stolen from him, and that he could only claim it by uniting the Fomorians and gaining power. Bres convinced him that if he could learn the druids' dark magic by using the forbidden books, then he could gather strength from the children of gods left in the mortal realm."

As Kyron spoke, Sorcha's thoughts drifted to her memories of her parents. She saw her father's warm smile as he told bedtime stories by the fire, his laughter as they lay in the meadow under the stars. She remembered the times he disappeared for days, and how her mother would say he was on patrols, hunting, or scouting. But now, in hindsight, she recognized the sadness in her mother's eyes every time she spoke. She thought of the Light Festival, how her father had twirled her through the streets, music and laughter filling the air. Those moments had felt so vibrant, so pure. How could they have hidden something so dark?

Kyron's touch pulled her back as his grip tightened. His eyes were glossy with tears. "Your father heard whispers of what Bres was planning, what he planned to do to you. When he confirmed it, he knew you wouldn't be safe. He warned the Tuatha and begged us to protect you. Your parents told you they were going hunting in the woods, but they never planned to return. They wanted to lead Bres and Vaelric as far away from you as possible."

Kyron cleared his throat, his voice thick with remorse. "Fate had other plans. Vaelric found them years later. He drained what power he could from your father and turned them into creatures, cursed to roam the woods."

The realization hit her like a physical blow, knocking the air from her lungs.

"No, you're lying," she shouted. She thought of the creatures she'd encountered in the forest; the way their eyes had seemed almost human, filled with pain, refusing to fight back. Now, she understood.

Kyron's voice softened. "Sorcha, you couldn't have known. None of this is your fault."

But his words felt distant, drowned beneath the tidal wave of emotions crashing over her. Her chest tightened as if someone knocked the wind out of her, her stomach churned, and she stumbled to her feet, the nausea rising uncontrollably. She barely made it a few steps before doubling over, her body convulsing violently as she retched. Tears streamed down her face, mingling with the cold sweat on her skin.

Kyron stepped closer, his voice low almost a whisper. "I'm so sorry, Sorcha. I wasn't able to get to you in time, to them in time. But I swear to you I'll keep you safe. I made that promise before, and I intend to keep it. We'll find a way to stop Vaelric."

Her body trembled as she tried to stand, her legs weak beneath her. She knew, deep down, that everything Kyron said was true. The pieces all fit together, forming a picture too painful to bear. Her mind swirled with regret, guilt, anger, and sadness, each emotion crashing into her like waves, threatening to drown her. She heaved again so violently that blood speckled the ground. She gasped for air, her throat raw, her body trembling as the truth clawed its way to the surface. The face from her nightmares flashed in her mind, twisted, cruel, and unforgiving.

Vaelric. The one who had stolen her parents, twisted their lives into something monstrous. And worse... it had been her hands that ended them. Because of him.

# Chapter 35
## HARD TRUTHS

Kyron knelt beside Sorcha, her body curled in on itself, her sobs so deep and raw that no sound escaped her lips, as Cat lay pressed against her, refusing to leave her side.

Kyron reached for her and hesitated, his hand hovering just above her shoulder. He wanted to comfort her, but his guilt rooted him in place. The weight of his own failures and regrets clawed at him, threatening to crush him. Memories surged unbidden and unforgiving as he thought back to when he was sent to track Lugh and his wife. The sickness Vaelric had unleashed twisted them beyond recognition, resembling Fomorians in a way, grotesque, monstrous and yet there had been a glimmer of something human buried deep beneath their cursed forms. He had spent months chasing whispers, tracking signs, holding on to the faintest hope that they might still be alive. But he had been too late.

When Sorcha's arrow struck them, it had already been too late. Now seeing Sorcha in this state, he wondered if he had failed her too. If all he'd done had been enough.

He opened his mouth to speak but words stuck in his throat and his eyes burned from the tears he was holding back. In the faint glow of the firelight, he could see the brokenness in Sorcha's shattered heart and knew that anything he could say would fall short. Instead, he kept his thoughts to himself and sat beside her, his arms falling by his side as he silently offered his presence. He would stay with her for as long as she needed, until she told him otherwise.

Beside him, Sorcha's mind and body were locked in a battle to accept the unchangeable. The hard truths she had no choice but to face. Vaelric's twisted smile flashed in her thoughts again and again, his hideous, void-like eyes burning into her memory.

It wasn't her fault, it couldn't be. It was his. He had taken everything from her, stolen any chance of a future with her parents, any hope of peace. He haunted her in both sleep and waking hours, and he was the reason the realm was crumbling. All of it, every bit of it, was his fault.

She curled into herself the tears spilling until she had none left to weep, till the sobs fell silent and her body ached. Lying there on the cold floor, Sorcha shuttered and her runes flickered, reverberating onto the floor, causing a reaction with the runes etched into the stones to answer as warmth slowly emanated from them, warming her bones. The early morning light began to chase away the shadows casting threads of light into her eyes causing her to stir.

She slowly rose to her feet, her chest throbbing and head pounding but careful not to disturb Kyron and Cat, both fast asleep on the floor beside her. Kyron's breath was steady, and Cat cracked one eye open, watching her with quiet curiosity before settling back down. Sorcha stepped over them carefully as she made her way to the bathroom.

Inside, she began to wash herself, scrubbing at her skin as though she could wash away the guilt and tears that clung to her. The water was warm, but it didn't quite reach the cold ache that had settled deep in her heart. Still, she scrubbed, as if cleansing her body could somehow cleanse her soul. After her bath, she stood before the mirror, staring at her reflection. She'd grieved them once, years ago, when they hadn't come back. But there had always been a thread of hope, frayed and foolish though it was. It hadn't broken her. Not in the way people expected.

She turned everything off, because what else could she do? This wasn't the kind of life that allowed for breaking down, not when people were watching. Not when people were counting on her to lead. The person she had been before, before she knew the truth... she was gone. A resolve hardened in her as she lifted her chin. She let tears fall down her; she let herself feel the losses of her family and friends. Standing there, her heart broke wide open once more. Tears struck the sink below as she leaned over it, the only thing keeping her upright was the white-knuckled grip on its edge. She cried until there was nothing left to give—until the ache inside her emptied.

Her thoughts circled around Vaelric. She would be the one to stop him. No matter the cost, no matter the blood, she would make certain no one else suffered as she had. He would not haunt another soul.

Wiping her face with a towel, she dressed quietly. The simple rhythm of smoothing fabric and pulling sleeves straight steadied her hands. By the time she moved to make tea and a light breakfast, her face was calm again, though the quiet inside her felt heavier than before.

When everything was ready, she walked over to Kyron, who was still sprawled on the floor, and gently shook his shoulders. "Kyron. Kyron, it's morning."

He cracked open one eye, his expression groggy. "What?" He blinked slowly, glancing around the room. "Is it really morning already?"

Sorcha's lips curved into a soft smile. "Come get something to eat."

At that, Cat stretched lazily and waltzed over to the table, hopping onto a chair and sitting upright, as if he were expecting a formal invitation to breakfast. The sight made Sorcha's smile widen. She grabbed some scraps and placed them into a small bowl for Cat, who purred contentedly as he began to eat.

Kyron groaned as he pushed himself up off the floor, clearly stiff from sleeping on the hard surface. He rolled his shoulders and stretched, muttering about needing a proper bed. Sorcha couldn't help but chuckle quietly as she set a plate on the table for him. Kyron met her gaze, his eyes heavy with grief, mirroring her own. Sorcha felt a rising urge within her, a need to tell him what she'd come to understand. It wasn't his fault. He carried so much guilt, and she could see it etched into every line of his face, in the way he held himself.

She didn't need saving. She needed someone who saw the fire in her soul and chose to burn beside her, Kyron had chosen just that. The pain of everything they'd endured wouldn't fade overnight; she knew that. It might not even fade in years. Perhaps it would always linger, a dull ache in the background of their lives. But what she was certain he needed to hear that none of it was his fault. And none of it was hers, either.

She leaned forward slightly, her voice quiet. "Kyron," she began, her tone steady despite the storm raging inside her. "You made me a promise. We'll stop Vaelric, together."

For a moment, Kyron didn't speak, his gaze fixed on hers. Slowly, his posture shifted shoulders straightening just enough to lift the weight that had been pressing him down for so long. It wasn't much, but it was enough. His eyes, heavy with grief held hers, and for the first time in what felt like forever, there was a flicker of something else: hope. Or perhaps determination.

He nodded. "Together."

It wasn't a grand gesture, but it was enough.

Enough to remind her that they weren't alone in this fight. Enough to give her a sliver of strength to hold on to. They had no guarantees, no easy path forward, but they had each other and for now, that was enough.

# Chapter 36
## SILENT SORROW

The forest was quiet except for the occasional wind through the leaves rustling around the forest floor. Riona sat atop a moss-covered boulder at the top of Aonach, arms wrapped tightly around her knees. From here, she could see the city of Lumora, the outposts and the meadows, things that once brought her comfort. But not today, not anymore.

Especially not after the meeting in the library, she wanted nothing to do with any of it.

She closed her eyes, digging her nails into her palms, drawing the slightest bit of blood. Emry's face flashed in her mind—his soft smile, the way he'd look at her, the tender kisses they'd shared. Then, that final moment: his limp body in her arms, the light gone from his eyes.

And Sorcha. The thought of her made Riona's stomach turn with a mix of anger and resentment. Her fists clenched tighter against her legs. She hadn't wanted to feel this way. Not about her best friend, not about Sorcha. But she couldn't stop the thoughts from creeping in.

*If she hadn't gone to save the commander first, if she'd come to us instead, maybe Emry would still be alive.*

The thought hit her like a punch to the chest. She hated it. Hated herself for even thinking it. But it was there, and it wouldn't leave; it was a wraith haunting the dark corners of her mind.

Her thoughts drifted back to the night of the festival. She had been fighting desperately, trying to protect their people. Then Sorcha appeared in a blaze of light and fire, tearing through the enemy as if the world bent to her will. If she could do that, why didn't she do it sooner? Why did she save the commander and not them?

"She should have chosen us," Riona whispered, her voice shaking. "She should have chosen Emry."

She hated how much she missed him. She hated the hollow ache in her chest. She hated that Sorcha was still here, still breathing, still with Kyron at her side.

*Kyron.*

His name was bitter in her mouth as she bit the inside of her cheek. It flooded with the taste of metal as her fingernails bit deeper into her skin, drawing a steady flow of blood that she didn't seem to notice. She had seen the way he looked at Sorcha, the way he stayed close to her. He was too much like Emry and too much like what they had, of what she'd lost. And now Kyron was part of *their* circle, standing where Emry should have been.

*They did not even ask me,* she thought. *Maybe it was my fault for keeping my distance, but how could they?*

The anger and grief becoming an entangled mess of threads that seemed impossible to tell where one ended and the other began. The ache in her chest burning so deeply she thought she might stop breathing as the thoughts crashed into her.

*She gets to be the hero. She gets to save Lumora.*

*And I'm the one left behind. The one they stare at and whisper about, the one they walk on glass around. Poor Riona, she couldn't save him.*

Their pity was like reopening a wound and she couldn't heal when being struck in the same place time and again. Her vision blurred as the tear fell, dropping her head to her knees, she rocked. Letting herself weep for all her that she lost, all the parts of her that left with him. She didn't know how to let go of this anger, this hatred that burned inside her like a poison.

But then a thought came: *Maybe I don't have to let it go. Maybe I just need somewhere familiar yet new; to the mountains I'll go, home.*

Riona had made up her mind in that moment. She would leave in silence and even though the thought stung, it was easier than explaining, and the goodbye would hurt far less.

She inhaled deeply, the scent of late blossoms and pine trees itching at her nose as her eyes fell heavy on Lumora. The place she called home. Her gaze swept over the golden spires jutting out toward the clouds. She listened to the sounds of laughter and the roar of the falls echoing off the hills, and then her eyes landed on the oak tree overlooking Emry's grave. A pang of regret and sadness clawed its way back into her chest.

It was time to leave this all behind and take the parts of Emry she held dearly with her to someplace new. Somewhere she could start again. Her legs felt weak and her knees made a popping sound as she stood, wiping her mossy hands on her pants as she straightened. The wind whipped at her face, her hair a rope in the wind as she leapt from the boulder onto the ground below and began her trek toward town.

Commander Nethran met her near the barracks, his brows drawn tight as he listened. The sap lamps swayed overhead, casting soft, golden light across her face.

"I'm heading home to Cailleach's Keep," she had told him. "I need time and if the circle there will have me, I'll join them."

Nethran studied her, searching for even a flicker of emotion. She gave him none and finally after a long moment, he nodded, his expression shadowed with understanding and sorrow.

"The Keep's circle will be lucky to have you," he said finally. "Take care, Riona."

As she walked away from their conversation, home became a clear vision in her mind. The towering, snowcapped mountains of Cailleach's Keep, harsh and unyielding, but they were home. The chill of the air, the frost-bitten trees, and the gleaming peaks had always been home.

If anything could make me strong again, it's those mountains, she thought. She longed for familiar faces, yet craved distance from everything that reminded her of Emry. The streets of Lumora. The other members of the circle. The forest paths they once walked together. Everything here was haunted by his memory, by the life they would never have.

It was the cruelest punishment she had ever known. To love, and then be left to live with the ghost of what could have been.

Riona adjusted the pack on her shoulder as she approached the northern gate. With one last look at the fading lights of Lumora, she mounted her horse. Tears streaked her cheeks as she turned toward the path leading north, her heart heavy but certain.

# Chapter 37
## A Desperate Plan

Kyron sat alongside Sorcha with Cat, as they ate their breakfast in the quiet morning hours. Sorcha's heart thundered in her chest. She wanted to scream, to throw things, to shatter the world, crush the floors beneath her feet just so the silence would give way because in that silence were her thoughts and in those thoughts a crushing ache.

Her breaths became shallow as her gaze fixed on her breakfast, the edges of her vision blurring slightly as her heart continued its rapid pace. The fork in her hand shook slightly as she pushed her food around her plate when a warm hand pressed on her shoulder. Kyron was staring at her with concern pressed against his lips.

Finally, Sorcha broke the stillness, grounding herself with his touch. "So there are more people out there like me? People with abilities? People who were left behind?"

Kyron nodded slowly as he finished chewing on a piece of fruit before answering. "There are. The Tuatha assigned each of us a person or a region to look after, but they never told us how many there were, nor did they give us all the information. I think they did that to protect them so that if we were ever interrogated, we wouldn't know all the locations. The only ones who know everything are the Tuatha." Kyron shifted in his seat, his expression tense.

"The Tuatha never abandoned mortals completely," he continued. "They just couldn't take responsibility for all of humanity. It was too much to bear. That's why the Circles were created, why Druids have the magic and power they do. It's why, when you enter the Circle, you're given rune-etched weapons and why runes are tattooed or etched into your skin to help you combat whatever you might face."

Sorcha took a long moment to think, her eyes settling on Cat as he lapped at some milk. The feline glanced back at her, almost as if he agreed with her unspoken thoughts. Finally, she said, "So, we go to the Tuatha."

Kyron choked on his tea, coughing violently as he slammed one hand on the table and another to his chest. "WHAT?!"

Cat stared at him like he'd lost his mind, then meowed a few times short, with longer ones mixed in, as if he were agreeing with Sorcha and scolding Kyron all at once.

Kyron waved him off, his voice frantic. "WE CAN'T JUST WALTZ INTO THE OTHERWORLD! I'm not even supposed to be here! If they find out. Oh gods, if they find out I'll never be allowed to leave again!"

Sorcha didn't react to his outburst because she couldn't. She had to go and she refused to be told otherwise. She sipped her tea, taking a moment to collect her thoughts. If she focused on this, then it would distract her from the grief she felt, and she welcomed the idea with open arms. When she finally spoke again, her tone was calm and measured.

"Then we don't use your mist to get there. From everything I've studied and from all my work in the Circle, the Veil is thinnest during Samhain. If we go to the festival and cross through the Veil in Cailleach's Keep, they can't say it was your fault. I could have gone through on my own, and you, being my protector, just followed me through. Problem solved."

Cat nodded.

Kyron stared at both of them with wide, incredulous eyes. "You do realize that if we just jump into the Otherworld, we have no idea where we'll land, right? None. When I use the mist, it's precise, like walking through a direct door. But just jumping in? We could end up in the Forgotten Woods, an upside-down castle, or on the Bridge of the Lost! Do you even understand how dangerous that is?"

Sorcha shrugged, her expression nonchalant. "We'll just make sure we're well prepared. I'll bring a pack full of supplies."

Kyron blinked at her, utterly dumbfounded. "Sorcha... let's say we land in Anach Fola, which, by the way, is the Bog of Blood. Do you know what lives there? Sluagh, Bánánach, or the Múiríon! How do you plan on fighting ghosts, wraiths, and, oh, I don't know, essentially water banshees?!"

His arms flailed wildly, gesturing as though trying to physically convey the sheer madness of her suggestion as he laughed under his breath. "And need I remind you—bogs are where the Veil is thinnest! We could end up in any one of them. Do you want to fight whatever horrors lurk in any one of them?!"

Sorcha looked at Cat, her lips quirking in amusement; maybe she had lost her mind. "Well, Cat, it sounds like a lot of danger. I don't really think it's any different than what we're dealing with here. What do you say?"

Cat glanced between Kyron and Sorcha, then hopped off the chair. With deliberate purpose, he sauntered to the door, sat down, and let out a series of meows. As if that wasn't clear enough, he lifted one paw and pointed to the door.

Kyron stared, his mouth falling open like a gaping fish, utterly lost for words. Sorcha chuckled, brushing past him to grab her bag. "Well, that settles that. I guess we're going.

Sorcha turned to Kyron, who was still seated. "We've got patrols to handle, and only a week until Samhain. I'd say we better start brainstorming a plan."

With that, Sorcha opened the door, Cat trotting closely behind her. Kyron jumped up, his chair scraping loudly against the floor as he chased after them. "SORCHA, do you hear yourself?! This is madness! I'm supposed to protect you, not throw you headfirst into danger! This is the opposite of what I should be doing!"

Sorcha spun on her heel, her voice filled with sarcasm. "Well, then PROTECT me, Kyron! Protect me while we actually do something useful for once instead of sitting around waiting for the world to fall apart!"

Kyron threw his hands up in frustration, pointing accusingly at Cat. "And you—you're a TERRIBLE INFLUENCE!"

Cat, entirely unbothered, continued trotting ahead, flicking his tail with purpose. Kyron scrambled after them, his voice rising again. "Well, we can't go alone! How do you expect to explain this to your friends?!"

Sorcha, Kyron, and Cat made their way to Skyfall to meet with the Circle. Before anyone could say anything, Sorcha strode straight to Commander Nethran, stopping abruptly in front of him. She turned to face the Circle, whispered the incantation for the overhead runes, and a flicker of golden light fell around them, drawing everyone's attention.

"Sorcha..." Kyron muttered, his eyes narrowing as he began to piece together her intentions. "Don't! don't do this. I swear, if you—"

Sorcha stood tall, her voice ringing with confidence. "Good morning, everyone. I'd like to tell all of you, my closest and most trusted friends, including you, Commander, that I am the child of a god. The god Lugh."

Kyron froze, his mouth opening and closing like he was gasping for air. Then, like a dam breaking, his words rushed out: "HEY! HEY! I'm talking to you! WHAT are you doing?!"

Sorcha glanced at him, her tone calm but teasing. "Like I was saying..."

"STOP!" Kyron hissed.

Before Sorcha could continue, Cat let out a long, exaggerated sigh and stood up. With a deliberate flick of his tail, he padded over to Kyron, sat right in front of him, and began pawing at his boot in a rhythmic tap tap tap.

Kyron stared down at the cat, irritation spreading across his face as his skin began to flush. "What? What is this? Stop it, you little—"

Tap tap tap.

"Cat, I swear to the gods—"

Tap tap.

"Oh, for the love of—fine!" Kyron threw his arms in the air and stepped back as if surrendering. "Do whatever you want! Apparently, no one listens to me anyway!"

Cat tilted his head, a smug glint in his eyes, and calmly sauntered back to Sorcha. He leapt gracefully onto the fountain's edge beside her, where he sat primly, his tail curling neatly around his paws.

"Thank you, Cat," Sorcha said with a small smirk. "As I was saying..." She turned back to the group, ignoring Kyron's increasingly frantic gestures behind her.

"This is going to be a lot to take in, but it's true.

I'm a demigod, my father is Lugh, because of that I can use the power of the sun. It's why my accuracy is always perfect, no matter the distance. Oh, and Cat can understand us."

At this, Cat let out a short, affirming meow as if to confirm her statement. The Circle stared in stunned expressions, their gazes flicking between Sorcha, Kyron, and the unbothered Cat.

Kyron ran a hand through his hair, walking toward Sorcha. "What she says is true," he said at last, his tone weary. "I would have done this a little differently had it been UP TO ME, but here we are. If anyone has questions, we're open to answering them."

The murmurs of the Circle rose, questions bubbling just beneath the surface, but Kyron turned to Sorcha before they could begin. Leaning close, he whispered, "Have you lost your mind? I'm sorry for everything, but wh—" he paused for a moment before he finished his thought "What is all this?" His eyes searched hers, a mix of concern and exasperation.

Sorcha sighed, her voice steady but firm as she whispered, "Every second we wait is a second Vaelric gets stronger. I'm not sitting around waiting for him to destroy more lives when we can do something about it. We need help, Kyron. We can't afford to waste any more time."

Her gaze was piercing, fixed on Kyron's. For a moment, he held her stare, and then he saw it: the clarity, the unshakable determination that had replaced the doubt she once carried.

He exhaled slowly, his shoulders relaxing as he nodded. "Okay. You're right. I'll follow your lead."

"Commander," she said, her voice steady now, "could you tell them what happened during the battle? They'll need to hear it from you, too, to believe me."

The commander nodded, straightening as he prepared to speak. Clearing his throat, he began, "During the battle at the festival, I was surrounded by Fomorians. They came at me from every side, slashing and attacking. I was bleeding heavily, and my strength was failing." His eyes flickered down for a moment before he continued, "I was close to losing the fight."

He paused, his gaze sweeping over the group. "Then Sorcha came to my rescue. She was fully enveloped in fire. A bright, searing light that burned so hot it killed the Fomorians on contact. If she hadn't been there..." His voice softened. "I might not be here today. If Sorcha says this is true, then I believe her."

Rhosyn stepped forward and pulled Sorcha into a tight hug. "I knew it," she said, grinning. "I knew you always glowed brighter than the rest of us for a reason.

Your runes have always been... twitchy."

Sorcha smiled faintly, the weight of their belief settling over her. Eirin nodded from where he stood. "It makes sense now. None of us could figure out why the kelpie let me go or why they stayed away after. It was you, wasn't it? You drove them off." He held her gaze, his tone filled with certainty. "I had a feeling it was you."

Sorcha nodded, his expression softening as she looked at him.

Drystan let out a chuckle, shaking his head. "Of course one of my friends would turn out to be a demigod. Nothing can ever be simple. If it's not monsters or magic, it only leaves the gods."

Eirin joined in with a laugh. "It's fine, Sorcha. I always knew you had freakishly good aim. You never missed a shot. Not once. Even when the wind turned or the light shifted."

Mason chimed in: "Oh, and those gold strands in your hair? Come on, they literally glow." He walked over and hugged Sorcha before turning to Kyron. "Hey Kyron..." He smirked. "This is going to make a fantastic story one day."

Sorcha scanned the faces of her friends, searching for Riona. Four days—it had been four days since she'd last seen her. Her unease turned into frustration as she turned to Commander Nethran, her voice filled with concern. "Where is Riona? Why isn't she here?"

The commander paused, a flicker of hesitation crossing his face. "Riona left for Cailleach's Keep a few days ago, Sorcha. She's moved back home."

The words hit like an icy blast. She looked to her friends, hoping for some kind of explanation, but their faces mirrored her own shock and confusion. None of them knew.

"She didn't tell any of you either, did she?" Sorcha asked, her voice quieter now, tinged with disbelief.

Her friends shook their heads, exchanging uneasy glances.

Sorcha turned back to Commander Nethran, anger creeping into her voice. "Why didn't you tell us?" Desperation filled her voice as she pointed to herself. "Why didn't you tell me?"

The commander held her gaze, his tone even. "It was strictly between her and me. If Riona wanted to share that information, that was her choice. It's not my place to speak on her behalf, and it's not my job to inform others of her personal decisions."

Sorcha's hands balled into fists at her sides as she tried to make sense of it. Four days. Four days, and Riona had said nothing. No goodbye, no explanation—nothing. Sorcha felt a swell of anger and hurt but forced herself to shake it off. She couldn't afford distractions, not now.

Kyron gave her a soft look, one that said he'd support her without question. She met his gaze briefly before turning back to the commander.

They weren't surprised. Not really. Maybe they'd always known, or maybe they knew something was off about her and just needed her to connect the dots. Whatever the reason, it was enough they believed her.

# Chapter 38
## A Glimpse of the Void

"We'll meet after shifts at the Tavern?" Sorcha asked her fellow Circle members, her hands sweaty as she tugged at the ends of her sleeves.

Eirin nodded. "Of course, we'll see you then." "Wouldn't miss it for the world, princess."

Drystan winked, a devilish grin cracking his lips.

The rest of the Circle nodded, some voices murmuring as they dispatched for the day.

Sorcha exhaled slowly as her eyes closed, a wave of relief washing over. By her feet Cat was circling, amusing himself with sprays of water from the falls. Kyron placed a hand on her shoulders, his hand warm, her eyes fluttered open and her gaze locked with his.

"You ready to go?" he asked, his eyebrow raising. "Yeah, let's get going."

Sorcha and Kyron had been assigned to patrol together, a first since he arrived. Their route was farther south than she'd ever been for a patrol, heading to the woodlands of Na Crainn Fána, where the Fiodh Abhainn River met the ocean. Nestled between the Hollow's towns and Glenn na Mara, far to the eastern edge, it was a half day's ride just to get there.

Sorcha had tried, in vain, to convince Cat to stay behind, but the stubborn creature refused, even going as far as climbing into her bag.

She packed her saddle bags, punching each item into her bag, her brows knitted together as a rose color crept to her cheeks. The thought of carrying Cat in her bag on horseback while patrolling was less than ideal.

"It's going to be a long day," she muttered to herself.

Kyron glanced at her, arching a brow as he noticed Cat poking his head out of the bag slung over her shoulder. "Are you seriously taking Cat with you?"

She shot him a look, pointing at the feline.

"I *tried*, okay? He keeps biting me and follows me everywhere. What would *you* do?"

Kyron rolled his eyes and muttered under his breath.

Then, with a shrug, he offered, "If he's going to be with you all the time, maybe you should get something made for him like a basket attached to the saddle or a bigger saddlebag. Just saying."

Sorcha let out an exasperated sigh.

"I guess I don't have much of a choice. It's been three days, and Cat already runs things."

Kyron chuckled, which only fueled her annoyance.

Without a word, she grabbed the end of her loaf of bread and chucked it at his head.

"Ow! Did you—" Kyron paused, staring down at the hunk of bread at his feet. His expression shifted, caught between disbelief and laughter.

"Did you just THROW bread at me?!" A burst of laughter erupted from him, his voice tinged with exaggerated disbelief.

"Seriously, what's this thing made out of? Gods, maybe we could arm the Circle with it? Our enemies would never see it coming!"

Sorcha doubled over, laughing so hard she could barely catch her breath. Cat, not to be outdone, let out a series of sounds like half growls and half chirps that resembled a warped version of laughter. It sent Sorcha into another fit of giggles.

Kyron shook his head, still chuckling as he rubbed the back of his head.

"Okay, it was funny, but it wasn't *that* funny. Get it together, you two. We have a long ride ahead of us, and at this rate, we'll never get there."

Still grinning, he mounted his horse and waited as Sorcha regained her composure. She stuck her foot into the stirrup and swung her leg over the horse settling into the saddle. Cat meowed loudly as he tousled around in the bag as she began riding. After a few minutes they were through the gates, heading toward the mysterious woodlands of Na Crainn Fána.

The ride was quiet, Sorcha thoughts were loud in the silence. From the evening her blade struck her parents to Emry's death and Riona's words to her, the tears that threatened to break free against the gentle breeze were imminent. They spilled silently but as quickly as they fell she wiped them away with back of her sleeve looking to Cat to avoid Kyron's gaze. Cat seemed to enjoy the wind in his face, lapping at the breeze and basking in the sunlight. But as they approached Na Crainn Fána, the sky began to darken with gathering storm clouds. Sorcha could sense the shift in the air, and it wasn't long before Cat noticed it too. Letting out a comically dramatic whine, he ducked his head into the bag. Sorcha chuckled softly as she closed the top, though Cat still managed to peer out through a small gap at the side.

Kyron gently pulled back the reigns on his horse to ride side by side with Sorcha.

"Something seems to be on your mind, I can tell by the distant look you're wearing."

Sorcha's shoulders dropped as she hunched over slightly, letting out a loud exhale. She didn't want to talk about it all, at least not her parents; that wound was deep and would surely be her undoing today. Riona flickered across her mind again.

"I know you haven't known me for long," Sorcha began, her voice tinged with unease.

"But Riona was my best friend. I mean… she *is*, or maybe she *was*? I don't even know anymore."

She sighed, her vision fixed on the path ahead. "We were so close, we shared everything from the

moment we met at Druid School."

Her voice grew quieter as she continued.

"She didn't even say goodbye. I wanted to give her space, I really did, but every time I tried to be there for her, it was like she was pushing me away."

Sorcha trailed off, lost in her thoughts. Then, after a long pause, she murmured, "I'm sorry. I know I'm ranting"

Kyron glanced at her, choosing his words carefully before speaking.

"It sounds like you feel abandoned," he said gently "Like you deserved an explanation, a reason why. And maybe you did. But have you considered that maybe she just… couldn't give you one? From what you've said, it sounds like her pain might have been too deep, like saying goodbye might have made it worse, not better."

His gaze shifted to the storm clouds ahead, as if searching for the right words midst the rolling gray. "If you two were as close as you say, then there's probably a good reason. Maybe she just didn't have the strength to face you. And who knows? You might see her at Samhain. If you do, I'd approach her gently. Give her the space she needs to explain when she's ready."

Sorcha fell silent, her mind swirling with Kyron's words. She hadn't stopped to consider Riona's perspective, that maybe saying goodbye had been too painful for her.

The thought left Sorcha with a pang of guilt for her earlier resentment. Just as she was about to ask Kyron more about his past, the rain began to fall.

At first, it was a gentle pitter patter, the earthy scent calming as the wind blew softly around them. But as Na Crainn Fána came into view, the wind picked up, swirling violently and causing the trees to sway in what could almost be described as a frantic dance. The rain turned needle-like, stinging Sorcha's face as it pelted her skin. They urged their horses forward, riding faster to find the cover of the trees and some reprieve from the storm. By the time they reached the edge of the woods, the thick canopy broke up the rain, and the wind became less fierce. The river that flowed through the land was raging, its thrashing waters threatening to spill over its banks at any moment.

Kyron and Sorcha decided to leave their horses on higher ground before continuing on foot. The woods felt dark, shadows lurking in the trees. Sorcha's chest tightened as unease crept over her, her nightmares flooding back, visions of the Fomorian that had chased her and the unfamiliar woods that haunted her dreams. There was something... *calling* to her from deep within the trees, it sent shivers through her body. It was like Meadowrun. She turned to Kyron, fear flickering in her eyes. "Kyron, I don't think we should go in. This feels wrong. I can't explain it, but we *can't* go in there," she pleaded.

Kyron's expression grew serious; concern etched across his face. "Sorcha, what's going on? he asked, his tone steady. "We have to go in, we need to know if there's decay here, and if there's anything else, anything dangerous. It's important."

His voice was calm but resolute, and Sorcha searched his eyes for any sign of hesitation or doubt. There was none. She took a shaky breath, trying to push down the rising dread in her chest. Maybe she was letting her nightmares get the best of her, allowing them to cloud her judgment. She couldn't let that happen, not now, not when her work was at stake.

Closing her eyes for a moment, she steadied herself and nodded.

"Okay," she said quietly, her voice firmer this time. "Let's go."

With that, they stepped into the woods, the dense shadows swallowing them as the storm raged on outside. As they entered the woods, nothing seemed ominous at first. The gentle chirping of birds filled the air, accompanied by the soft crunch of fallen leaves underfoot, trees shedding their coats in preparation for winter. The steady rhythm of rain pattering against the canopy and forest floor created an almost peaceful atmosphere. But there was an unusual amount of movement on the forest floor, rustling and scattering in all directions. They froze, listening. The sounds grew louder, animals running... no, stampeding. A massive formation of elk and deer barreled through the trees, their hooves thundering against the earth. The ground seemed to vibrate beneath them.

Kyron looked at Sorcha and screamed, "RUN!" He grabbed her hand and whipped her around, trying to keep ahead of the stampede. They ran as hard and as fast as they could, moving swiftly through the brush, jumping over logs and roots. Sorcha glanced back and, in the distance, she saw it; it was large, cloaked in shadow. She couldn't make out its full form, but she saw its teeth razor sharp and hands like blades. Its head twisted unnaturally to the side as it followed.

"Kyron!" she yelled, panic thick in her voice. "Something is chasing the elk!"

Kyron risked a glance back, and his expression darkened. Without hesitation, he grabbed Sorcha's arm. "Hold on, we're moving. Whatever you do, don't let go!"

With that, Kyron's free hand began tracing patterns in the air, his movements swift and deliberate. Light flared to life, runes glowing brightly against the darkness. Slowly, they were lifted, gliding forward with incredible speed as the ground blurred beneath them. Within moments, the thunder of hooves and the shadowed creature's presence faded into the distance. They found themselves standing at the edge of a clearing.

Kyron's legs gave out as he slumped to the ground, visibly drained. He leaned forward, hands braced on his knees, his chest heaving as he tried to catch his breath. Sorcha looked around and realized this wasn't a clearing at all, it was a void. The forest was dead. Trees twisted and bent unnaturally, some touching the earth and entangling with others to form a grotesque web across the ground. Black and grey creatures, long since dead, lay scattered, their bodies pierced and overtaken by sprouting black vines and strange, spiny growths. The earth was littered with animal remains, bones protruding like a rocky cliff face.

The smell that followed hit her like a physical blow, a suffocating wave of decay and rot so intense it burned her throat. Sorcha turned to Kyron, whose expression mirrored her own horror, etched into every line of his face. His eyes were wide as he searched the area around them. She looked back at the scene below, where smaller twisted creatures like squirrels and foxes struggled to move across the desolate expanse. Each step seemed to pull them deeper into the blackened earth, as if the ground itself were alive and dragging them under like quicksand.

She wanted to turn away, but she couldn't move. Her breath caught as the tar like water in the center of the barren void rippled in an unnatural pattern. From its surface, a dark slithering form began to rise, its movements slow and deliberate. The creature swiped at the struggling animals with chilling precision, dragging them beneath the surface. A sharp crack broke the stillness. The wet snap of bones was followed by a crunch that made Sorcha's chest tighten.

Then something worse emerged. Its face was disturbingly human, marred by patches of decay that revealed glimpses of bone. Its webbed hands, tipped with claws, twitched and jerked as it pulled itself partway onto the shore, its grotesque frame trembling with each movement. It crouched over its catch, tearing into the lifeless form with feral hunger. It ripped the limbs from the body, eating flesh and bone together. Blood sprayed across its hands as it devoured the small animal, which finally stopped twitching only after the creature bit its head off.

Sorcha's lips parted in shock, her body reacting instinctively to the horror unfolding before her, but before any sound could escape, Kyron's hand clamped over her mouth. His grip was tight and his breath brushed against her ear as he whispered urgently.

"Do not make a sound," he said, his voice barely audible. "Whatever you do, do not even breathe too heavily, Sorcha."

Sorcha looked at him and nodded, her voice barely a whisper. Kyron dropped his hand but stayed pressed against her.

"Can you get us out of here, Kyron? Can you use the mist again? I don't know where we are, and I know you don't either. But with those things down there and whatever was chasing us earlier, we don't stand a chance right now," Sorcha whispered into his chest, her head turned, pressed firmly against him.

Kyron looked down, silent for a long moment.

Sorcha's stomach twisted as she waited for him to answer. Her mind racing to come up with solutions. The quiet stretched until she couldn't bear it, and just as she opened her mouth to speak, Kyron finally responded.

"If I get us out of here using the mist again, it's going to take a lot out of me," he said, his voice heavy. "It's different when it's just me and I know where I'm going. But this is different. Moving us through the forest, searching through all this expanse... it'll take everything I have left. I'll need you to help me ride back. You'll have to make sure nothing follows us."

Sorcha took in his words, the weight of what he was saying, settling heavily on her. She could see the strain in his face, she knew he wasn't exaggerating. Still, they had no other choice. She nodded, her voice steady despite her fear.

"I'll handle it. Just get us out of here."

Kyron forced himself to his feet, his movements slow but steady. They walked back into the woods, away from the clearing, each step feeling heavier than the last. Before he began, Kyron turned to her, his expression serious.

"Whatever you do, don't let go."

She nodded again, and with that, he pulled her close to him by the waist. She hugged him tightly as he raised his hands and began drawing the intricate runes in the air. The swirling clouds arrived almost instantly, wrapping around them like a protective cocoon. It felt different this time; thicker, heavier, and moving slower. As they surged forward, the world blurred around them.

Sorcha could barely make out the shapes of the twisted creatures in the forest. She knew they noticed the movement, their heads snapping toward the sound, but it seemed they couldn't see them. To the creatures, it must have been like watching the wind pass. The journey felt endless, the tension mounting with each passing second. Kyron's breathing grew labored, and Sorcha could feel the strain in the way his body trembled beside her. Just when she thought they might not make it, the mist thinned, and suddenly, they were back on the hill where they had left their horses. Kyron collapsed, his body hitting the ground with a dull thud. Sorcha dropped to her knees beside him, panic coursing through her veins. She scanned their surroundings, her heart pounding in her chest, but they were safe. They had made it out of the woods. Cat poked his head out from the bag strapped to the saddle, his eyes fixed on the two of them, his expression almost unreadable. Sorcha swallowed hard and turned her attention back to Kyron. She gently placed a hand on his shoulder.

"Kyron, can you hear me?" she asked, her voice tight with worry.

Kyron groaned faintly and opened his eyes, though they looked heavy with exhaustion.

"I'm fine," he muttered weakly, though his pale complexion and trembling hands betrayed him.

"No, you're not," Sorcha said firmly, slipping her arm beneath his shoulders. "Lean on me. I need you to try and stand. We've got to get you on the horse."

Kyron nodded sluggishly, his movements loose and unsteady as Sorcha hoisted him upright. His weight sagged heavily against her but she didn't falter. Step by step she guided him toward the horses, practically carrying him. When they reached his mare, she braced herself and pushed him upward. Kyron managed to swing one leg over the saddle, but his upper body slumped forward the moment he landed.

"Hold on," Sorcha muttered, already working. She tied Kyron's horse to hers in a makeshift lead. Then she crouched beside Cat, who sat stiff and alert at her feet.

"Cat, I need you to watch the forest," she whispered, urgency tightening her voice. "Warn us if anything follows."

Cat blinked once, then leapt lightly onto Kyron's horse. He curled along the saddle, eyes fixed on the tree line.Sorcha blew out a slow breath, muscles shaking with exhaustion, and swung up onto her own saddle. When she glanced back one last time, Kyron stirred. His hands found her waist, fingers curling weakly into her belt as he rested his forehead between her shoulder blades. His breath warmed the thin fabric of her tunic.

"Careful," she said softly. "You're slipping."

Kyron made a faint sound that might have been a laugh. "If I fall, you're coming with me." His voice was hoarse, a hint of teasing slipping through as his grip tightened.

"Comforting," she muttered, rolling her eyes as she nudged the horse forward.

They started the slow, cautious trot toward Lumora. Behind them, the woods shrank into deepening darkness. Every snap of a twig made her tense, her gaze flicking over her shoulder as her breath stilled with each sound. Kyron heard it. Felt the way her chest rose and fell beneath him, the moments she held the air captive as he leaned against her.

"You're listening so hard you're forgetting to breathe." His hand slid from her waist to her stomach, steady and warm. "In. Out. Humor me."

She tried to scoff, but the heat of his palm anchored her, the tightness in her chest melting until she could finally draw a full breath again. She followed his rhythm with a long inhale and an even exhale.

"You're in no position to worry about me, Kyron. I'm fine."

"Sorcha." His voice dropped, low and tired. "We're in the clear. Let me help."

Her throat tightened, her voice straining as the words slipped out. "You're always helping me."

A tired laugh escaped him, his forehead dropping to her shoulder again. "Careful. Say things like that and I'll think you enjoy having me this close."

"I don't," she said, immediately cursing how soft it sounded.

"Oh?" His breath brushed her neck, the faintest accidental graze of his lips. "Then tell me to let go."

She didn't. His warmth, the faint clover scent clinging to him, the weight of his arms around her... it told her he was still awake and still with her.

By the time they reached Lumora, the moon hung high and the streets were silent. The horses slowed outside the stables. Kyron stirred, lifting his head with effort and offering a faint smile.

"Kyron, you can let go now. We made it back safely thanks to you," she said softly.

He nodded, sitting up straighter. Sorcha moved to untie the lead rope but before she stepped away, Kyron slid from the saddle. He wavered once, then reached for her and pulled her into a tight embrace.

She froze, breath caught. Kyron held her with a quiet desperation, his face pressed to her hair, his arms tight around her as if the moment kept him standing upright.

"Thank you," he whispered when he finally let her go. Their eyes met for only a heartbeat before he turned and guided his horse into the stables.

# Chapter 39
## An Urgent Plea

Kyron and Sorcha walked side by side through the quiet streets of Lumora. When they reached the outpost at the center of town, Commander Nethran was waiting for them. His eyes scanned them, relief washing over his face, though it didn't soften the deep lines of worry etched across his features.

"You're back," he said, standing from his desk. "Thank the gods. Are you both all right?"

Sorcha and Kyron exchanged a glance before stepping forward. Sorcha's voice was steady, but there was an edge of urgency to it. "Commander, there's something happening in the south... something far worse than we expected."

"Go on," Nethran said, his gaze hardening as he motioned for them to sit.

Sorcha began recounting their patrol at Na Crainn Fána: the eerie scene, the stampede of animals, the decay overtaking the woods, and the creature lurking in the blackened water. Kyron added the details Sorcha had missed, emphasizing the rapid spread of the decay and the dangerous presence they'd sensed within the woods.

Nethran listened intently as the story unfolded.

When they finished, he leaned forward, his elbows resting on the desk. "This isn't what I wanted to hear..." he said grimly. "If the decay is spreading that fast, we could be looking at a full scale collapse of the land. If it reaches the towns—"

"It will," Sorcha interrupted, her tone resolute. "It's only a matter of time. That's why we need to act now."

Nethran's gaze flickered between her and Kyron, his worry deepening. "What are you proposing?"

Sorcha straightened, determination flickering in her eyes. "The Festival of Light was a disaster because we weren't prepared for what could happen. We can't let Samhain become another massacre."

"Samhain?" Nethran asked, confusion crossing his face. "What does Samhain have to do with this?"

Kyron leaned forward. "The Veil between realms will be at its thinnest and Vaelric will take advantage of that..."

"Vaelric?" Nethran asked, the name unfamiliar. "A druid," Sorcha explained carefully, though her

voice carried a weight that hinted at far more. "A powerful one with ill intent. We think he's working with the Fomorians and we believe he's behind the decay too, Commander."

Nethran's expression darkened further. "If what you're saying is true, this changes everything."

"It does," Sorcha said firmly. "That's why we need the Circle. We need them at Samhain to protect the festival, to make sure nothing gets through the Veil unchecked."

Nethran sat back, his expression unreadable as he processed their words. Finally, he spoke. "You're asking for a lot, Sorcha. Rallying the Circle isn't a simple task, and convincing the elders to let them leave the region during this danger..."

"I know," Sorcha said, her voice unwavering. "But it's necessary. We can't afford another disaster like the Festival of Light."

Nethran's gaze lingered on her for a long while, searching her expression. "You're sure about this?"

"Yes," Sorcha said firmly. "If we don't act now, we may not get another chance."

Nethran sighed heavily, running a hand over his face. "I'll start reaching out to the elders. But Sorcha if we do this, there's no turning back."

"There won't be," Sorcha promised.

Nethran nodded, though the weight of their words lingered heavily in the room.

"We'll discuss this more tomorrow."

Kyron and Sorcha exchanged glances and nodded, walking together toward Sorcha's house. Cat remained quiet, nestled in the bag he'd crawled into the moment they'd arrived back in Lumora. Sorcha hadn't given much thought to the fact that Kyron had been walking her home regularly these past few weeks. It had become such a natural occurrence that, when they reached her door, she invited him in without hesitation.

Sorcha pushed the door open and guided Kyron inside, keeping a steady hand on his arm until he dropped heavily into the chair by the hearth. The fire was burning low, the warmth radiating throughout the room.

"I'm putting the kettle on," she said, crossing to the small kitchen. "And I'll find something for us to eat."

Kyron didn't argue. He leaned back, eyes half-lidded, letting the chair swallow him. Cat hopped out of the bag, stretched, and cautiously circled near the edge of the room not too close to Kyron but close enough to enjoy the heat.

Sorcha moved quietly around the kitchen, setting the kettle on and gathering what little she had. A small loaf of bread. A wedge of cheese. A jar of berry jam. A few apples. Nothing remarkable, but enough.

When the kettle began to hum, she poured two cups of tea and arranged the food on a small wooden tray. She carried the tray over first, setting it on the low table beside him.

Kyron blinked at it, surprised. "You didn't have to do all that."

"You need to eat something," she said. "Both of you."

Kyron tore off a small bit of cheese and tossed it toward Cat. Cat sniffed, then took it delicately.

Kyron watched this with a faint tired smirk.

"That was surprisingly," Sorcha said "Maybe he's warming up to you."

"Or he's too tired to be difficult." "Could be both."

She handed Kyron his tea. When he reached for it, his fingers brushed hers. His touch was warm despite how drained he looked, and his thumb grazed her knuckles before he finally let go.

Sorcha sat on the floor across from him, folding her legs beneath her. The crackle of the fire filled the quiet between them.

Kyron took a sip and exhaled softly. "Thank you." "It's nothing," she said, though the warmth in her chest said otherwise.

They ate in comfortable silence as Cat settled near Sorcha but kept one wary eye on Kyron, even as he accepted the next bite of cheese he offered. When they finished, they both stood at the same time, reaching for their cups. Sorcha laughed under her breath when they nearly bumped into each other in the small kitchen. As she stumbled Kyron steadied her by the waist. She watched as his hands lingered, warm and careful as he held her, he didn't remove his hands until she looked up at him.

"Sorry," he mumbled, though his voice held no real regret.

She stepped aside, heart beating too fast. "You should rest," she said.

"Let me help. I can manage a cup."

He set the dishes down slowly, stubbornly steady in spite of his fatigue. Sorcha returned the tray to the counter and felt him step beside her. When she looked up, he was already watching her.

Something in his expression softened. He reached for her face, his thumb brushing the curve of her cheek with a gentleness that contradicted the strength in his calloused fingers. His other hand lifted the stray strands of hair that had fallen forward, tucking them behind her ear with deliberate care.

Her heart fluttered as she met his gaze. Swirling blue tides crashed against the grey stone circles around his irises, the colors deepening in the firelight. His lips were full, carrying the faintest flush of pink, but it was the subtle shift in his breathing that stole her own. His chest rose and fell a little too quickly, and the sight sent heat blooming low in her stomach.

Kyron stepped closer, his body almost brushing hers before he whispered, "You should get some rest."

Sorcha nodded as she broke his gaze.

"You're right, I'll try to rest my eyes for a bit," was all she could manage to say.

Kyron's hand stayed a moment longer on her cheek before his hand dropped to his side.

"Good. I'll sit by the fire a while, if you don't mind."

"I'd like that," she replied as she turned toward her bedroom door.

Sorcha slipped into her room, pushing the door only halfway closed. The soft glow from the hearth spilled through the gap, painting a warm stripe across the floorboards. She changed into something clean and comfortable, the day in the forest tugging at her with every movement.

When she finally crawled beneath the blankets, the mattress dipped around her body. Her muscles ached, her mind buzzed, but the quiet murmur of voices from the main room drifted in and slowly unwound the tightness in her chest.

Kyron's voice came first, low and rough from fatigue, barely above a whisper. She couldn't make out the words, only the cadence steady, soothing, familiar in a way she didn't want to admit.

Cat replied with a soft chirp, followed by the pattering sound of him hopping up onto something, probably the arm of Kyron's chair. There was a pause, then Kyron exhaled a tired breath.

"I suppose you're keeping watch tonight," he muttered.

Another little trill from Cat, this one almost smug.

Sorcha smiled into her pillow.

Kyron's chair creaked softly as he moved, followed by the clink of a kettle finding its place on the stove. Warmth spread through the quiet room. Her eyes drifted shut to the gentle simmer of water and the comforting shuffle of feet and paws settling near the fire.

# Chapter 40
## THE BRIDGE OF THE FORGOTTEN

The air shimmered with an otherworldly glow, mist curling at her feet as her toes touched cool moss, soft and pillow like. The towering trees whispered secrets in the wind, their branches intertwined as if to block out the sky. Their bark shifted in hues, deep blue fading into violet, the change so subtle it was almost like a trick of the light. Sorcha blinked, trying to steady herself, but the surreal quality of the place unsettled her.

A low, familiar meow broke the silence. "Cat?" she called out, her voice trembling.

From the shadows, something massive emerged.

She took in the sight of him, Cat, but transformed. His sleek black fur shimmered faintly with silver, and his molten silver eyes seemed to pierce straight through her. He was larger than any cat she had ever seen, almost the same height as her on all fours, his two tails flicking lazily.

And then he spoke.

"Do you ever have normal dreams?" His voice carried a playful yet knowing edge, his mouth not quite moving like a human's, yet the words were unmistakably his.

Sorcha staggered back, her heart racing. "Cat, you're talking? And what is this?"

He tilted his head, delight flickering across his face. "Talking? Me? Of course I am. How else was I supposed to tell you that you're crossing the Veil every time you have these strange dreams?"

"The Veil?" Her voice was barely a whisper as she stared at him, trying to process the enormity of his words.

"This isn't just a dream," Cat continued, stretching as his tails swayed behind him, thick and powerful. "Dreams, for someone like you? They're doorways. Your soul slips through the cracks." He used his paw to imitate a tiny figure walking and then tumbling into an unseen hole in the ground.

Sorcha swallowed hard. That couldn't be true. She had always thought of her dreams as fragments, fleeting glimpses of nothing, but now. Hadn't she always felt something strange when she woke? A lingering weight, a whisper of something she couldn't quite grasp.

"That's impossible," she muttered, but even as she said it, doubt settled in her chest.

"Is it?" Cat's eyes glimmered with something ancient and unyielding. "You're connected to something or someone is calling to you. It's not a coincidence. The wisps have been trying to lead you there."

Her heart clenched as she remembered the dreams, the glowing wisps always darting ahead, pulling her deeper into the unknown. Her mind raced, and before she could stop herself, she thought of Vaelric. The way his gaze seemed to linger in her memory, the pull she felt toward him she couldn't explain.

"Who's calling me?" she asked, her voice trembling.

Cat flicked his tails, turning his attention to the wisps that had appeared around them, their light flickering like playful fireflies.

"Ah, the pests are back," he muttered, swiping at one with a massive paw. The wisp darted away, glowing even brighter as though in defiance.

"What are they?" Sorcha asked, her eyes following the tiny lights as they danced through the trees.

"Guides," Cat said simply. "Or nuisances, depending on your perspective. They lead you toward what's tied to you, your fate, your answers. Or..." His voice lowered, dripping with ominous weight. "Your end."

Sorcha shivered, unable to look away from the bouncing orbs. She had always followed them before, trusting their guidance, but now she wasn't sure. What if they weren't leading her toward answers but toward something far worse?

"They've led me here before," she admitted, her voice shaky. "But why? What do they want from me?"

"It's not about what they want," Cat said, his tone softening. "It's about what you want, what's pulling you. Your power, your bloodline, it calls out to them. And to others."

The air around them seemed to grow heavier with his words. Sorcha glanced back at Cat. "And you knew this?"

"I had a suspicion," Cat admitted with a shrug, his massive form shifting slightly. "But I had to let you figure it out. You wouldn't have believed me if I'd just told you I was Cait Sidhe. Besides," he added with a smirk, "you've been a little... busy."

Sorcha narrowed her eyes at him, though a faint smile tugged at her lips despite the weight of his words. "You're something else."

"And you're just figuring that out now?" Cat teased, swiping at another wisp and catching it under his paw. He held it for a moment before letting it go, watching as it darted away.

The wisps blinked brighter, drawing Sorcha's attention back to the forest ahead. Their glow seemed to beckon her, tugging her forward. But something inside her hesitated. The sense of dread and anticipation twisted together, making her stomach churn.

"Will you stay with me?"

"Always," he said softly, padding to her side. "But tread carefully, Sorcha. The answers you're looking for might not be the ones you want."

The trees whispered as they walked, their voices slipping through the mist, layered conversations Sorcha couldn't quite grasp. Cat leaped effortlessly onto the wisps, bouncing from one to the next as though they were solid.

He seemed unbothered, but Sorcha couldn't shake the feeling that something was watching. Dark shapes flitted between the trees, their forms barely visible at the edges of her vision. The rustling in the undergrowth was constant now, but whatever was making the noise never stepped forward.

The path beneath them changed. Moss and dirt faded into uneven cobblestones, cracked and worn with age. The air grew colder, heavy with something unseen. The mist thickened, and through it, Sorcha caught glimpses of looming ruins, their jagged edges half swallowed by the creeping forest.

Sorcha slowed her pace, her eyes locking on the blurring images emerging from the fog, she had seen these ruins before, but not like this.

The mist caused the cobblestones to become slick, making their steps less than graceful as the crumbling buildings came to view. The limestone structures stretched toward the sky, their spires broken, doorways gaping like silent mouths. Statues of gods stood in half shadow, their faces worn smooth by time, ivy curled around them, dragging them further into the earth, like the land itself was trying to erase them. Who had these gods been? And what had made them fall? She walked towards them as if in a trance, mesmerized by their beauty, the glint in their eyes, the way they seemed to watch her.

As she moved closer, just ahead stood a circle of nine stones. The air from Sorcha's lungs fled as she began to retreat slowly. "Nine stones, remember this. Thrice three, beware what slumbers beneath. For in its center do thy creatures sleep; make haste, for what breaks earth will devour thee."

The verse played on repeat in her mind as she slowly made her way back toward the cobblestones. She wasn't sure when they had stepped off the path, but the childhood rhyme kept looping in her head. She remembered hearing it in the schoolyard, children singing it as they played.

When she had asked her father about it once, he'd told her, "If there's one thing I know, it's to heed the old stories. As silly as they may sound, every tale holds a bit of truth. It's just that we never truly know which parts."

Since that day Sorcha has always held every story and every song a little bit differently in her heart.

The ground trembled beneath them as circle of stones stirred. Dirt rippled outward. A deep crack split between two pillars and the earth opened up slowly as black smoke began to plume from its maw.

Cat's gaze narrowed. "I don't like this," he muttered, his fur bristling as his eyes darted to the ground. Above them strange creatures clung to the edges of rooftops, their cat-like eyes peering down, watching in eerie silence. They reminded Sorcha of the old stone guardians carved into the high terraces of ancient druid halls. Their massive bodies and hooked claws gripping the edges as if fused to the rock, some with wings folded tight.

With haste they continued down the path toward the sound of rushing water. The roar grew louder, a steady thunder beneath the whispering trees and black smoke that followed them. Sorcha's eyes widened as the mist shifted, revealing an ancient stone bridge stretching across a dark river.

"Sorcha," Cat growled, his voice steady but urgent, "we're on the Bridge of the Forgotten. We need to get off it now."

Before Sorcha could react, skeletal figures began to rise from the stone. Hollow faces twisted in silent screams as clawed hands reached for them.

Cat leaped in front of her, his massive form a shield as he lunged at the creatures. Sorcha scrambled, grabbing a loose rock and swinging with all her strength. Bones cracked under the impact, but more figures emerged, relentless in their approach.

Then she saw movement at the other end of the bridge. A shadowed figure stood waiting, unmoving.

Cat turned, catching sight of it. For the first time, real fear crossed his face.

"Sorcha, you need to wake up!" his voice desperately pleaded.

The figure began moving at an unnatural speed toward her, its form shifting and flickering like rushing water. Sorcha couldn't look away, frozen as dread coiled in her body. Suddenly pain erupted from her side.

She gasped, barely able to process the sensation before something tore into her flesh again as a scream ripped from her throat. Staggering back, she turned just in time to see the creature, its body blackened, twisted, with fangs and hooked talons dripping with blood.

It lunged again, its hollow, hungry eyes locking onto her. Sorcha barely had time to react before it struck again, its claws raking into her once more.

Cat roared, his form surging forward, silver eyes burning with fury. Power rippled through the air, shaking the ground beneath them as he threw himself between Sorcha and the creature. The force of his rage made

the mist churn, shadows twisting wildly as the bridge trembled under their weight.

"Wake up, Sorcha!" he screamed. Darkness swallowed her whole. It felt like she was falling, tumbling backward into an endless void. The cold gripped her as if she were sinking to the bottom of the ocean. The pain hit first, burning like breaking through icy waters. Sorcha's eyes shot open, and as she sat upright an agonizing shriek filled the air.

Her hand pressed to her side, and when she pulled it away, blood smeared her fingers. She gasped for air, her chest heaving, but the world around her still felt off. The walls of her room blurred at the edges, like the mist from the bridge still clung to her.

The creature, its claws, the way it had looked at her, like it had been waiting. Had it been waiting? A shudder crawled down her spine, and for the first time, she let herself wonder, what if she hadn't woken up? A ragged breath escaped her lips. Beside her, Cat let out a low sound, something between a purr and a groan. He was sprawled beside the bed, his black fur matted with a steady stream of red. His silver eyes found hers, his breathing labored. He had fought for her, had bled for her and it was real. It had all been real.

Sorcha tried to sit up again but the pain was white hot and unforgiving, and she collapsed back onto the bed. She heard the thundering of footsteps from the next room, and then Kyron burst through the door. Kyron barely had time to take in the sight before him. The scent of blood and sweat filled the air, thick and cloying. Cat lay sprawled beside the bed, black fur slick with streaks of crimson, his chest rising and falling in uneven breaths. Sorcha wasn't much better. She clutched her side, fingers coated in blood, her face pale and strained with pain. For a moment, he just stood there.

"What happened?" His voice came out harsher than he intended, tight with concern.

Before she could answer, Cat stirred, silver eyes cracking open. He barely lifted his head, his massive form trembling from the effort. When he spoke, his voice was gargled.

"Take care of Sorcha." Kyron stiffened.

The words rang through the room, impossible to ignore. He had just heard a cat speak, but there wasn't time to process it.

Sorcha pressed a hand to her wound, her voice ragged. "Cat first."

Even now, she was trying to take care of someone else.

"You're bleeding all over the place, and that's what you're worried about?" Kyron muttered, but he moved.

Crossing the room in a few strides, he grabbed whatever supplies he could find. Linen, ointments, a carved bowl filled with runes. His hands worked quickly, grinding herbs into a thick paste while his thoughts raced. The blood on Cat's fur looked too dark, almost unnatural. Healing magic worked on people, but whatever Cat was, Kyron wasn't sure if it would do any good.

He had no choice but to try. Pressing a cloth to one of Cat's deeper wounds, he murmured a quiet spell, tracing the runes with careful fingers. The bowl's water shimmered, magic weaving through the liquid, but the glow was weak. Cat let out a low growl, his ears flattening, but he didn't pull away.

Kyron exhaled. "If you're well enough to complain, you'll live."

Sorcha let out a rough laugh from the bed, but when he turned, she wasn't laughing anymore. Her head had lolled back against the pillow, her breathing shallow.

Cat would hold on. Sorcha was another story. He wiped his hands on his tunic and went to her side. "Your turn."

She nodded weakly, peeling her shirt up to reveal the deep gash across her side. Kyron clenched his hands at the sight of it. The wound was ugly, torn flesh inflamed and still bleeding. She had lost so much blood already.

"Hold still," he said, pressing a clean cloth against it. Sorcha barely flinched. That was almost worse. "This is going to hurt," he warned. "I'll have to stitch it before we get you to the healer."

She bit down on the edge of her sleeve and gave the smallest nod. Kyron worked quickly, threading the needle with steady hands. He had done this before, had stitched up wounds far worse than this, but something about it being Sorcha made the task feel heavier. The glow of his runes flickered across her skin, dull compared to what he wished they could do. It would dull the pain, but it wouldn't erase it. Something had done this to her. Something had nearly torn her apart. He wanted to demand answers, to know where she had been and what had attacked her, but now wasn't the time. By the time he finished the last stitch, her breathing was uneven, sweat beading across her brow. He didn't hesitate. Kyron scooped her up, slinging Cat carefully over his shoulder. Sorcha made a weak sound of protest.

"You're going to the healer," he said, walking toward the door.

This time, she didn't argue as her eyes fell heavy and the world blurred out of focus.

They say wisps lead you to your fate... but what if the fates tied the wrong threads...

# Chapter 42
## A Bitter Homecoming

It had taken Riona three hard days of riding to reach Cailleach's Keep. Unlike the commanders or elders, who could use magic to propel their horses faster, never needing to stop for food, water, or rest, her journey was slow and grueling. The steady rhythm of her horse's hooves echoed through the quiet wilderness.

As she approached the northern lands, the transformation into winter was unmistakable. Winter always arrived earlier here, in the sacred lands of the goddess Cailleach. Though it was only October, the trees were nearly bare, their skeletal branches stretching toward the grey sky. A few stubborn leaves clung to the remnants of autumn, but the grass had already dulled, and the once vibrant colors of the land faded into muted tones. Riona entered the city of Frostfire, its name comes from the eternal flame blazing within the mountainside overlooking the town. This flame was said to be a divine gift from the goddess Cailleach herself, and a grand temple and statue had been built around it to honor her. Taking a long breath, Riona felt a wave of nostalgia wash over her it as it had been years since she had last stood here.

The city had an elegance about it, a beauty that was almost impossible to capture in words. Frostfire was nestled in a valley between two towering mountains, its buildings shimmering with diamonds that caught even the faintest light and transformed it into a cascade of brilliance. Delicate silver embroidery adorned the exteriors of the structures, like intricate frost patterns on windowpanes. At the heart of the city stood the grand town hall, the centerpiece of Frostfire's life. It was a place of gathering, hosting meetings, banquets, and lessons, as well as sacred marriages performed under the watchful gaze of Cailleach. And yet, for all its beauty, it was a place Riona, years ago, couldn't wait to leave.

As a child, she had craved the warmth of the sun on her skin, the vibrant meadows in bloom, and the promise of spring and summer lasting longer than the harsh northern winters. Her parents had often visited Lumora for the Festival of light, taking her with them often. The moment she first saw Lumora, she dreamed of one day living there but that wasn't the only reason she left. Her father was a cold man, harsh and unyielding. He rarely minced words and even more rarely showed affection unless public eyes were upon them. She knew those displays of affection were all for show, a performance to maintain an image. Behind closed doors, he was a man of ruthless and relentless discipline, the kind that was met with fists more times than words, but the words he did speak were venomous.

The way his quiet judgment weighed upon her, he was always expecting more, always demanding more. The moment she saw her chance, she took it and never looked back. These days no one outside of Frostfire knew who she really was, Riona had refused to use her family name when she arrived in Lumora. Instead, she adopted a different one, far removed from the shadow of her father's legacy. She wanted to be seen for her own worth, not as the daughter of the Commander General Byrne.

# Chapter 43
## New Beginnings

The town of Frostfire was just beginning to wake and a silent cold hush hugged her limbs. She guided Briar toward the inn nestled at the edge of town, her breath visible in the frosty air. Riona hopped off of Briar, leaving him tethered to a post just outside the doors.

"I'll be right back," she murmured, patting Briar's mane.

Smoke curled lazily from the chimney atop the worn greying house. The windowsills were painted silver, matching the shutters, and a young apple tree stood in the small courtyard. Riona pulled on the worn iron handle and slipped inside.

Small conversations hummed in the dining area, the smell of rich stew hanging in the air. A younger woman was collecting trays when her eyes met Riona's.

"Mornin'," the girl called as she waved Riona over to a small counter of oak polished to mirror-like shine despite its chipped appearance. Resting on top was a large book, its engraving worn smooth from time and beside it a pint sized cup of tea.

The girl smiled wide, her eyes shining in the morning light were the color of cinnamon. Riona noticed her freckles scattered across her face and across the bridge of nose when she looked at her and her nose scrunched up.

"What can I do for ye?"

"Do you have a room available for a few days?" She opened the book, scanning the names, dates, times and rooms. After a moment, she brightened.

"You're in luck, a room opened up this morning."

She scribbled down Riona's name and, in exchange Riona, handed over a few coins from her pouch. With a nod, she accepted the key. Riona opened her mouth to thank the woman when a voice called out sharply from the kitchen. She turned quickly as she excused herself and headed toward the voice.

Riona pushed the doors open to leave. The warmth of the inn mixed with the frosty air creating streams of smoke around her as the weight of each step made the stairs groan.

She made her way to the Circle office, there were two. One in the Keep and the other in Frostfire. Kael, the officer in charge of Frostfire when Commander General Byrne wasn't present, was known for his precision and authority. Riona paused for a moment outside the door, anxiety tightening around her. She needed this, needed to work and she knew the Circles were always in need of capable officers. She was good at what she did, and she knew it. But the idea of working under her father twisted her stomach into knots. Taking a deep breath, she straightened her posture and knocked loudly.

"Come in," Kael's voice rang out.

Riona stepped inside, her boots clicking softly on the wooden floor. The office was pristine, every item down to the quill pens precisely in its place. It was a stark contrast to Commander Nethran's chaotic workspace in Lumora, where reports and scrolls were piled high on his desk. Somehow, Nethran always seemed to know exactly where everything was amidst the clutter, but Kael's space reflected the man himself orderly and methodical.

Kael looked up from his desk, his frosty eyes briefly flickering with surprise before settling into a composed expression. "Good morning, officer. To what do I owe the honor of your visit?"

Riona met his gaze, unwavering and confident despite the nerves buzzing beneath the surface.

"Good morning, sir. I've come to inquire about a position in your Circle. I'm transitioning from Lumora to the Keep, and while I'm sure Commander Nethran has already sent his recommendation, I wanted to present myself personally."

Kael's eyes scanned her face, and then his gaze shifted to a piece of parchment on his desk. "The Commander did send a recommendation," he said after a pause. "He spoke very highly of you. Respect and admiration, to be exact."

Kael leaned back in his chair, his eyes narrowing slightly as if studying her more closely. "It struck me as odd that a member of Lumora's Circle would travel this far north. But considering the Commander's words and the circumstances of your transfer, I understand."

Riona kept her expression neutral, but she could feel the weight of his scrutiny. His gaze lingered on her.

"Well," he continued, breaking the momentary silence, "we'll find a place for you. With a recommendation like this, it would be foolish to let such talent go to waste."

Relief flickered across her face. "Thank you, sir."

Kael returned to his papers, his tone brisk. "You'll begin within three days. By then, your position, accommodations, and wages will be finalized. That will be all."

Riona nodded, turning on her heel and leaving the office. Once outside, a smirk spread across her face a rare glimmer of pride and relief. But the moment was short lived. The thought of her father crept into her mind, smothering her satisfaction. She had to eventually see them her parents and now was just a good time as any other. Might as well get it over with it, so Riona made her way to her family's estate, her stomach twisting with unease. She wanted to be the one to tell her parents she was back in Frostfire. She wanted to be the one to tell her father she was now part of the Frost Circle. Her nerves were frayed, her heart racing with a mix of dread and defiance. It had been seven years, seven long years, without so much as a word between them. Neither side had reached out, and the silence had been deafening. As the estate came into view, memories crashed over her like a tidal wave. The towering stone walls loomed just as they had in her childhood, but they felt heavier now, suffocating. She could hear echoes of the past, the yelling, the screams, the shattering of furniture. She remembered hiding behind doors, under tables, wherever she could fit. If she tried to stop him, it only made things worse. Her father's words still rang in her ears: *Discipline is what you need. You don't know your place.*

The first time Riona got into a fistfight, it wasn't in the streets or with some rival, it was with her father. She hadn't been big enough to defend herself back then, and she'd paid the price. A black eye, a cracked rib, and a missing tooth. The fights didn't stop as she grew older. Each one was a clash of will and rage, and for years, she lost every time. But she grew stronger, faster and by her teenage years, she could hold her own. And the moment she overpowered him when she stood her ground and didn't back down everything changed. He stopped looking at her like she was his daughter, if he ever did, but now he was looking at her like an enemy. He avoided her altogether after that, treating her as though she didn't exist. And in some twisted way, she knew he hated her more for it because she was no longer his prey. She was an adult now, a grown woman. He didn't have control over her anymore, at least for now. In the Circle? That was a different story.

She had to accept that he would oversee everything here, whether she liked it or not. Hopefully, he'd be too busy with meetings and paperwork to meddle in the Circle's affairs. From what she'd observed so far, it seemed he wasn't as hands off as she'd hoped.

Riona took a few deep breaths, steadying herself as she approached the iron bar gate in front of the stone wall surrounding the estate. Behind those walls stood a house built of brick and stone, its etched crystal roof blending seamlessly with the sky. The vibrant stained-glass window panes caught the light, showing the intricate pictures inside them. Beside the house was a small stable, followed by rows of apple trees, Blood of the Boyne apples, a variety harvested from autumn through winter. It was beautiful on the outside, picturesque even. But it wasn't home, not to her. Not anymore. As she reached the door, she knocked three times. The sound echoed faintly before the door opened to reveal an older woman, short and stocky, her face kind and warm despite her advanced years. Riona frowned slightly. She'd never seen this woman before. In all the years she'd lived here, they'd never had help. It seemed her parents had made some changes in her absence. The woman greeted her with a polite smile. "Welcome to the House of Byrne. How may I help you?"

Riona studied her for a moment before answering, her expression softening despite the weight in her voice. "I'm Riona Byrne, the daughter of Celeste and Odhran Byrne."

The woman's eyes widened in surprise, her smile faltering as confusion set in. "I'm sorry, Lady Riona, but... they've never spoken of having kin." Her face fell, tinged with sadness.

Riona's composure remained steady, her voice calm though her words carried an edge. "I'm not surprised. I wouldn't have expected any different." She gave the woman a small, tight smile.

The woman hesitated, then offered a kind smile in return. "My name is Myrna," she said, stepping aside and motioning for Riona to enter.

# Chapter 44
## UNEASY REUNION

She moved from the grand entryway into the foyer, she waited as Myrna disappeared into the library, where her mother most likely was. She swore she heard something drop and the shuffle of hurried feet before Riona laid eyes on her mother.

Celeste, her mother, was a woman with a small but athletic frame. Although she seemed to have put on some muscle since the last time Riona had seen her. Her long blonde hair, the color of blue steel, was braided and adorned with a black ribbon at the bottom. She was wearing deep violet riding pants and a white top, as though she might have just come from the stables.

Their eyes locked, and her mother's gaze swelled with tears before they fell freely down her face, her trembling hands covering her lips. Riona's heart softened, and for a moment, she forgot the fears that had followed her here.

Celeste ran to Riona, flinging her arms around her in a tight embrace. The feelings that swirled in Riona's heart threatened to crumble her under the weight of it all. She pulled away before the tears could fall. "Hi, Mom."

Her mother's expression was soft, and Riona braced herself for anger, for being away for so long, for never replying to her letters. But nothing had prepared her for this.

"Hello, Riona," her mother said, her voice trembling with emotion. "I'm so happy you're here. I was starting to think I would never see you again." Tears spilled over as her mother cried softly, trying to push them away.

Riona could see how much she'd broken her mother's heart, and the weight of it was almost too much to bear. She held her mother's hands. "I'm so sorry I left you in the dark. I wanted to start my life over..." Her voice caught, the words stumbling out unevenly. "I made the decision to move back to the region. I don't know if I'll stay in Frostfire, but I've enlisted with the Circle."

Her mother's eyes searched hers as if she already knew why Riona was there. Without speaking it aloud, her mother simply nodded. "Riona, I'm just happy you're here. I don't need an explanation. Let's have some food, you look famished."

Her mother's soft smile told her it was okay, at least for now.

Taking her hand, Celeste led Riona into the kitchen. It was both familiar and different, filled with memories but altered by time. A beautiful stone island had been added, where wooden stools sat. The turf stove still stood, fueled by wood fire. Above it hung pots and pans, dried herbs, and edible flowers. A small basket held apples picked from the apple trees outside. Beside it was another basket filled with rolls, glazed with butter and honey.

The scents filled Riona's nostrils, and memories of making those honey rolls flooded her mind. She hadn't realized how much she'd missed her mother until this moment. All the anger, resentment, and sadness she had held onto for so long faded away. In its place, she saw a woman who had been trapped. And instead of hate, she felt pity. Riona picked up a roll and took a bite. The roll was still warm, and the salty sweet glaze melted in her mouth. "Mmm, they're just as good as I remember them being." She looked over at her mother, whose eyes lit up as she let a soft chuckle escape.

"I actually get to eat them now since you're not devouring them all before lunch," Celeste laughed, but the joy in her face wavered. A flicker of sadness crossed her expression, as if she were lost in a memory. She quickly turned to grab plates, her back to Riona.

She placed the plates on the small table in the corner of the kitchen, a cozy nook with large windows in a semi-circle. The light flooded in, warming the wooden surfaces and highlighting the view beyond: rows of apple trees, the courtyard, and the city's rooftops and spires peeking above the stone walls. It was beautiful, a scene Riona hadn't appreciated until now. Celeste went to the pantry, pulling out a jar of jam, some fresh berries, and an assortment of dried meats. She arranged them on the table alongside the rolls and tea, creating a lovely spread for an afternoon meal. Waving Riona over, she sat down, and they made small talk, the kind that danced around the heavier topics they both knew were there.

After a few moments, Celeste brought up her father. "Your father is currently in a meeting in the next town over. He'll be gone most of the day. Would you like to come for dinner tonight?"

Riona shifted uncomfortably, her eyes avoiding Celeste's. "I don't think that would be a good idea."

Celeste studied her for a moment before choosing her next words carefully. "...You'll have to see him eventually, Riona. It might be better to do it at dinner, to be the one to tell him you're working in the Circle."

Riona knew she was right. She hated that she was right. It would be less of an ordeal if she just got it over with. With a resigned sigh, she nodded. "Alright, I'll come."

Celeste met her gaze now, her smile soft and reassuring. "I have to tend to the horses and finish a few things in the apple grove. You can stay as long as you like, or I'll see you at dinner." She finished her tea before kissing the top of Riona's head, and left, leaving Riona alone with her thoughts. Riona finished her tea and began wrapping the leftovers in a clean linen, jam, a few rolls, apples, and some pieces of dried meat before carefully tucking them into her bag. She walked through the halls, her fingers brushing over the cool surfaces of the stone walls. Her steps carried her to the library, where the sight of the familiar space both comforted and unsettled her. The room was grand, with walls lined from floor to ceiling with hundreds of books. Some were so old that their pages looked as though they might crumble into dust at the slightest touch. As she scanned the shelves, one particular book caught her eye. It was hidden behind another, almost obscured, but the light had glinted off its gold binding, drawing her attention.

It was bound in black leather, worn and cracked, with no title etched into its cover. It was obvious it had been opened many times, its edges softened by years of handling. Her fingers grazed the surface, and an inexplicable wave of fear washed over her. A sense of unease prickled at the back of her neck, warning her not to touch it. Something about the book felt wrong, dangerous even. But curiosity got the better of her. She opened it to the middle. The moment her eyes landed on the pages, her stomach churned. The book slipped from her hands, landing with a dull thud as she backed away. The grotesque images etched onto the aged paper were vivid and horrifying detailed instructions for animal sacrifice, complete with intricate diagrams. Surrounding the drawings was text describing rituals for draining life in exchange for spells of power, dark incantations meant to connect to the Otherworld through sacrifice.

Her hands shook as she picked it up, holding it like it might burn her. She placed it on a small chair and bolted to the kitchen, grabbing another linen. Returning to the library, she carefully wrapped the book, trying to touch it as little as possible, and slid it into her bag. As she left, her thoughts began to race. The Dark Books. She remembered fragments of her studies, how the original book of dark magic had been divided centuries ago. There were four of them, each created from the fractured remains of a single ancient tome:

The Book of Sacrifices, a detailed account of rituals demanding blood and life in exchange for raw power.

The Book of Curses was a grimoire filled with spells meant to inflict suffering, to twist and break.

The Book of Demons, a guide to summoning and controlling malevolent spirits from the deepest corners of the Otherworld.

The Book of the Veil, an exploration of the thin boundary between the mortal world and the Otherworld, complete with ways to cross it.

These books were never meant to be read by mortal eyes. They had been divided long ago, their pages kept hidden in secret places, entrusted to powerful families who were charged with ensuring they would never be reunited. Their existence was meant to fade into obscurity.

But this book, the one she now carried, was real. Had her father known what it was? Had he been entrusted with its safekeeping? She couldn't imagine it, he wasn't the type. But her mother? Celeste. That made more sense. Memories surfaced: how her mother would spend hours in the library, how she reorganized the books constantly, sometimes more than once a week. How she always seemed to be around when someone else was in the library.

Did her father even know it was here?

Riona shook her head, forcing the questions aside.

She didn't have time to sit here and unravel the mystery. She needed to leave. Myrna had already walked by twice, her gaze lingering a little too long, as if she were watching her.

Securing the book tightly in her bag, Riona made her way to the court-yard. She waved a quick goodbye to her mother, who was busy tending to the horses, and hurried back to the inn. Her thoughts were a whirlwind as she walked, the weight of the dark book pressing against her side. She recalled fragments of half whispered rumors from her childhood stories about the Dark Books, forbidden texts said to hold unimaginable power. The book tugged at her curiosity, an insistent itch she couldn't quite scratch. *Could it really be one of them?* The question lingered in her mind, a tantalizing mystery. And if it was, what would happen if she opened it? Could reading it carry consequences? Or perhaps just perhaps it could help her.

*Would that be so bad?*

The thought unsettled her. She couldn't stop herself from imagining what secrets it might hold. The temptation gnawed at her, a strange mix of dread and intrigue. The more she tried to push it away, the stronger the pull became. Fear crept into her chest; not just fear of the book, but fear of herself, of the part of her that wanted to know. By the time she reached the room, her hands trembled as she retrieved the book from her bag. She placed it between the mattress, pressing it down as though that might quiet its pull.

"I'll just leave it," she whispered to herself, though the words rang hol-low. Her thoughts refused to settle. The need to distance herself to clear her mind was overwhelming.

She turned quickly, closing the door behind her and stepping into the crisp early evening air. She had a few hours before she was expected for dinner, so she decided to visit the neighboring town. Staying in Frostfire wasn't an option. The idea of running into her father in town was enough to make her chest tighten. She couldn't do it. She wouldn't put herself through that.

Coill Dorcha lay farther north of Frostfire, nestled closest to the woods. It was quiet and pleasant, with a charm that set it apart. Unlike Frostfire's pointed and rigid lines, Coill Dorcha seemed to blend seamlessly with nature. The town reminded her of Meadowrun with its stone houses accented by wood and brick, all connected by winding stone walkways. Lanterns lined the paths, ensuring travelers wouldn't lose their way in the evenings. She liked the way the town flowed, its natural curves and bends following the land rather than reshaping it. It felt calm here, almost like it had been waiting for her. That is where she'd stay. She could walk or ride into Frostfire when duty called, but her life wouldn't be overshadowed by it. She'd speak with Commander Kael and find a place here in Coill Dorcha.

# Chapter 45
## DINNER WITH A MONSTER

Riona arrived at the estate doors and knocked. The door felt heavier this time, more ominous, like it knew who was waiting on the other side. She knew it wasn't the door it was the atmosphere. It always changed when her father was home. Myrna opened the door and greeted her with a practiced, polite smile.

"Good evening. Come in. Your parents are seated in the dining room."

Riona stepped inside, feeling the weight of the doors closing behind her, the sound echoing through the dimly lit hallway with the click of the lock.

Myrna walked alongside her, her shoes tapping against the polished stone floors, each step making the silence louder.

When they reached the dining room, Myrna stopped at the entrance and said, "Mr., Mrs., your guest has arrived," before disappearing down the hall.

Riona stood frozen in the doorway, her heart pounding in her chest. Her mother sat at one end of the long table, smiling softly, though her eyes betrayed a hint of unease. Her father sat at the other end, a wall of unreadable authority. The table between them was massive, seating at least ten people, yet it felt like there wasn't enough space between her and him.

"Riona," her mother said, her tone light but warm. "I'm glad you could make it. Come, sit down."

Riona hesitated before taking the seat closest to her mother. She glanced at her father and forced out, "Good evening, Father. Thank you for inviting me to dinner."

The words came out harsher than she intended, and she immediately regretted them. His cold eyes locked onto hers, and his face stayed still, unreadable. "Hello, Daughter. It's been... what? Seven years? So nice of you to drop in."

Her stomach twisted. "I've decided to move to Coill Dorcha," she said, sitting straighter, though the discomfort under his gaze remained. "I met with Commander Kael to discuss a position in the Circle. I start in three days."

Odhran didn't move, his expression unchanging. After a moment, he waved a hand dismissively. "I am the final say in who joins the Circle."

Riona's jaw clenched. "I met with Commander

Kael—"

Odhran cut her off. "I saw the recommendation come through. What struck me as odd was the name. I knew you'd find your way to Lumora eventually, but the name listed wasn't Byrne. Common, perhaps, but it wasn't a coincidence."

Riona stiffened, heat creeping up her neck, but before she could respond, her mother spoke up, her voice cutting gently through the tension. "So, Riona, tell us, where have you been? How have you been?"

The shift in topic was obvious, but Riona grabbed onto it. She turned to her mother, her tone softening slightly. "I've been with the Circle of Light for about three years now. I've worked my way up from cadet to officer to second lieutenant. Though, we don't usually call ourselves by ranks. It depends on the region or the day, guardian, ranger, officer—it's all the same."

She paused for a moment, glancing at her father before adding, "I thought it was time for a change. It's been too long since I've been home."

Her father let out a small, humorless laugh. "I can see why you'd need a change. That's ridiculous, the ranks, the informality. How do you expect anyone to take the Circle seriously if you can't even keep the structure clear?"

Riona didn't flinch, though her tone turned darker. "It's what makes Lumora, Lumora," she said. "The people there respect us because we don't demand it. We don't punish them for forgetting titles or ranks. Respect is earned."

The table fell silent. Celeste reached over and gently placed her hand on Riona's, giving it a soft squeeze. Her father said nothing, but his cold, piercing gaze lingered on her, like he was trying to figure out a puzzle he didn't want to solve. Odhran continued, "Like I was saying, Riona, why wasn't your last name on the paperwork? Who is Riona MacKenna? Did you marry?" His tone was flat, almost bored, as if the question annoyed him as much as having to ask it.

Her mother wore a look of confusion, her eyes searching Riona for answers. Riona looked at her mother first. "No, I didn't get married..." She turned her eyes to her father. "I didn't use my last name because I didn't want to get into a position because of your last name, your position... I wanted to earn it myself," she said, trying to sound convincing. But the real reason was that she wanted nothing to do with him, and she knew he knew that.

Odhran sat up straight, his face flickering with rage for a moment before he let out a bitter laugh. It wasn't a joyful laugh, but one filled with anger and disbelief. "I suppose it was admirable, Riona. But, daughter, it's also a disgrace. A slap in the face. Do you know how it looks that I have a daughter in the Circle who refused our last name? That you went out of your way to conceal the truth? Do you have any idea how that reflects on me?"

Celeste looked at Odhran, anger flashing in her eyes. "Must we do this right now?! I haven't seen my daughter in seven years! SEVEN YEARS! And you choose to pick a fight the moment you lay eyes on her?!"

Riona felt a sudden wave of shame, heat rising to her cheeks. Her mother's voice, so stern and laced with sadness, cut through her like a blade, making her want to crumble. She turned to her father, nearly choking on the words. "I'm sorry for any disrespect it causes you, and I'll say again to anyone who asks why I chose a different last name. I'll tell them exactly what I told you."

Odhran wasn't buying it. The smug look on his face said he'd been waiting for this moment. "Riona..." His tongue clicked disapprovingly. "Tsk tsk... you know I don't believe a word you just said. Please, don't lie for the sake of this dinner. It's distasteful."

Riona felt her anger flare as she saw her mother ready to lash back. Rising to her feet, she snapped, "That's enough! You're right. I only came here to get this out of the way and to see Mom, not you. I could have done without you here."

Odhran leaned back in his chair, laughing darkly. "There she is." He chuckled again. "Don't worry, daughter. I didn't miss you either. You can leave whenever you'd like."

Riona's fists clenched at her sides. She wanted nothing more than to punch the smug smile off his face, but the sight of her mother—her hurt—had kept her grounded. The rage inside her twisted with sadness. She walked over to her mother, leaned down, and kissed the top of her head. Whispering softly, she said, "Good night, Mom. I'll see you again soon."

Without sparing her father another glance, she turned and walked away, her steps steady, her head held high. She didn't look back.

# Chapter 46
## AT THE CLIFF'S EDGE

She reached the inn in Coill Dorcha, her steps heavy as the cold night air wrapped around her. She had already packed her things and left the inn in Frostfire earlier that evening, and now the streets of this new town were unfamiliar but quiet, offering her the solitude she needed.

The innkeeper gave her a polite nod as she entered, the warmth from the fire momentarily chasing away the chill in her bones. She didn't stop to enjoy it, didn't bother to meet his gaze. She climbed the narrow stairs, her boots scuffing softly against the wood, and pushed open the door to her small room. The space was modest. Just a bed, a rickety desk, and a single window overlooking the dark woods in the distance. She set her bag down on the bed and hesitated, her fingers brushing against the edge of the dark book tucked away inside. Her mind wrestling with the weight of it, before quickly pulling her hand back as if it had burned her.

Without a second thought, she shoved the bag beneath the mattress, as if hiding it from her own mind. But the room felt suffocating, the quiet too loud in her anger.

Grabbing her cloak, she whirled back down the steps and into the night. the chill biting at her face as the wind whipped through the empty streets. Her feet carried her toward the woods without a plan, her thoughts pulling her in too many directions to stay still. The trees loomed tall and dark as she entered the forest, their bare branches twisting against the sky like crooked fingers. The frost crunched under her boots, and the occasional whisper of wind through the trees seemed louder than it should have been. She kept walking, her hands shoved deep into her pockets, the cold seeping through. Her mind the eye of the storm, memories of her father, her mother, Emry, the Circle, and the book all colliding in a mess she couldn't unravel. She tried to keep it down, but it clawed at her, each thought louder than the last, like storm winds swirling. She kept walking, letting the chill numb her fingers and the movement distract her from the weight pressing on her. She hadn't noticed how far she had gone until the trees began to thin and the ground sloped downward. She stumbled to a stop at the edge of a cliff, her breath visible in the icy air. The jagged rocks below were hidden by the shadows of the night, the sound of distant waves crashing faintly against the shore.

The wind howled around her, like the storm brewing inside her, tugging at her cloak and pulling her closer to the edge. She stared down, her thoughts quiet for the first time since she'd stepped into the woods. It would be so easy, she thought, to take one more step. To let the wind decide her fate. Her hand hovered at her side, her fingers brushing against the emptiness, when a firm grip caught her arm. She gasped, spinning around, her fist ready to swing. But she froze when she saw him. The man concealed in shadow.

He let go of her arm, stepping back just enough to give her space. His gaze, however, lingered. Dark swirling eyes pulled at her, as though they could see far beyond her surface. The faint shimmer within them caught the moonlight, flickering like embers barely clinging to life.

Riona's chest tightened as she studied him. His beauty was startling, almost unnerving, with features that felt more sculpted than born. There was an otherworldly grace about him that made her feel small in comparison. The perfume of ash and pine drifting in the air. Yet, for all his sharpness, there was something... familiar.

It struck her then, a subtle similarity to Sorcha. The set of his jaw, his lips, the chin, the tilt of his head, even the way his hair caught the light reminded her of her friend. The realization made her stomach twist, though she couldn't explain why.

"You should be more careful," he said, his voice low and even, cutting through her thoughts.

Riona crossed her arms, trying to mask the unease crawling under her skin. "I don't see how it's your concern," she said coldly, though her tone lacked conviction.

He tilted his head, his lips curving ever so slightly. "Perhaps it isn't," he replied, his tone carrying a faint amusement. "But standing on the edge of a cliff on a night like this? It's... telling."

Her jaw tightened, heat rising to her cheeks. "You don't know me," she bit back, her voice taut with defiance. "You wouldn't understand."

"No," he agreed, his expression darkening ever so slightly. "But I know what it looks like when someone's on the verge of falling—whether it's by accident or by choice." His words landed with the weight of a stone, sinking into the storm swirling inside her. She looked away, her gaze falling to the cliff's edge.

"Why does it matter to you?" she muttered.

He didn't answer right away. When he finally spoke, his voice softened, almost reflective.

"Maybe it doesn't. Or maybe I've seen enough to know when to step in."

The honesty in his tone—or perhaps the weariness in his eye—made her chest ache. She didn't know what to say, didn't know how to handle the way his words cut so close to truths she hadn't dared to confront. "Come on," he said, stepping back toward the shadows of the woods. "It's too cold to stand here all night."

Riona hesitated, her feet rooted to the ground. Part of her wanted to stay, to let the dark and the wind swallow her whole. But there was something about him, something in his voice, his presence, that made her move.

She followed, keeping a careful distance as they entered the forest. "What's your name?" she asked, her voice angrier than she intended.

He glanced at her, his expression unreadable. "Vaelric," he said simply, his name carrying an almost musical cadence that seemed to resonate in the air around them.

She frowned slightly, the name unfamiliar yet strangely fitting. "Vaelric," she whispered to herself.

"Why did you stop me, Vaelric?" she asked, her voice softening as she spoke his name aloud.

Vaelric slowed his pace, glancing over his shoulder. His face, illuminated by the faint light filtering through the trees, was calm but guarded.

"Because I've seen what happens when no one pulls them back."

Riona swallowed hard, her thoughts a tangled mess of confusion.

They traveled further, the crunch of leaves underfoot and the whisper of the wind through the trees the only sounds between them. And yet, the weight of his presence seemed to steady her, if only slightly.

Vaelric walked Riona to the edge of Coill Dorcha. He glanced at her, his voice calm and confident. "I believe this is where you want to be."

She held his gaze. "How'd you know this is where I was staying?"

He shrugged, a faint smirk tugging at his lips. "It's the only town within miles, and I have a hard time believing you walked farther than this." She felt foolish for asking and nodded. "Well... thank you for... you know..." He nodded in acknowledgment. "Goodnight."

He turned and started walking away, but Riona suddenly called after him. "Wait!"

Vaelric stopped, turning to look at her, his dark, swirling eyes fixed on hers. She hesitated for a moment before speaking. "Vaelric... would you like to go for another walk with me? Maybe tomorrow night? I can meet you here?"

Her voice carried a hint of desperation, one she tried and failed to mask. Vaelric caught it, and a small smirk curved his lips. "Yeah, sure. I'll be here at dusk."

And with that, he disappeared into the night.

# Chapter 47
## Dangerous Paths

Back in her room, Riona bathed and stared at the ceiling for hours. Sleep eluded her as her thoughts turned endlessly to Vaelric, then to the book. The book tugged at her, its pull an incessant whisper she couldn't ignore. Curiosity clawed at her, overwhelming and unsatisfied. Covered in sweat and restless, she finally gave in. Rising from the bed, she retrieved the book from where it lay hidden between the mattress and sat back down. She hesitated, the weight of what she was about to do pressing against her chest, but then flipped it open. Her eyes scanned the first paragraph, the ink on the page seeming almost alive:

*"Power is never truly given, it is taken, forged in fire, and in blood. Those who seek its embrace must first offer a piece of themselves. A price as unyielding as the magic they wish to command. Sacrifice is the bridge between the mortal and the infinite. The key to unlocking doors that were never meant to be opened. Yet, beware: the deeper one treads into the currents of power, the more the tides demand. In the end, all who linger too long are swept away."*

A shiver ran through her as she read the words.

The feelings of hopelessness, weakness, and bitterness she carried for so long rose to the surface, she wanted to rid herself of them and so she read on.

Another passage struck a chord, the words ringing so true they seemed to call her forward: *"What is pain but proof of what you are capable of surviving? If you dare to endure, you can master it. Every price has its purpose. Every wound births wisdom.*

The words sank into her, resonating with a part of her she had tried to bury. Here, within these pages, were the answers she craved. Answers that promised she could be more, that she could finally silence the things that haunted her. She read through the night, her determination pushing her past the heaviness that weighed on her eyelids. Sleep begged for her attention, but she ignored it, consumed by the words on the pages. She devoured the book, committing lines and fragments to memory as though they might someday save her. The quiet sounds of a waking town filtered in from outside, marking the arrival of morning. Riona blinked at the soft light spilling through the window and finally conceded to her exhaustion.

She lay down, her mind still swirling with everything she'd read, and let herself drift into an uneasy sleep. When she woke in the late afternoon, the sunlight streaming in had softened to a golden haze. Her stomach growled in protest, and she realized she hadn't eaten since the day before.

Reluctantly, she left her room and made her way to the inn's dining hall. Grabbing something quick to eat, she hurried back upstairs, eager to return to the book. The hours slipped by unnoticed as she read, her fingers turning the pages faster with each revelation. She barely registered the sun starting to set outside, her thoughts preoccupied with the book. She'd almost forgotten she asked Vaelric to meet her tonight. Snapping the book shut, she carefully placed it back in its hiding spot between the mattress and the frame. With a glance over at the dimming sky, she hurried to the forest's edge.

Vaelric was leaning casually against a tree, cleaning his nails with a small dagger, when Riona arrived. The sunlight caught his face, accentuating his striking features. If anything, he looked even more handsome in the golden glow, though her eyes were drawn to a peculiar scar that ran along the side of his face, almost like a birthmark. It didn't detract from his beauty; instead it added a layer of mystery. Was it something he was born with, or had he earned it in some way? And if the latter, how so?

She shook the thoughts away and managed a smile. "I'm sorry I'm late. I got caught up in something."

Vaelric nodded, slipping the dagger into his belt as his eyes lingered on her. "There's something different about you today..." he said, his voice trailing off, thoughtful and almost searching.

Riona stiffened slightly under his gaze, a flicker of unease creeping in. Had the book already left its mark on her in some way? The thought gnawed at her as Vaelric's eyes narrowed, studying her like a puzzle he was determined to solve.

She quickly tried to respond, her voice a bit rushed. "I didn't sleep much. But I'm glad you came. I could use the company, honestly."

Vaelric nodded, his expression softening. "I get it.

And I'm happy to see you not dancing near a cliff." He smirked, but Riona flinched at the memory.

The thought of how close she had been to the edge, both physically and emotionally, sent a cold shiver through her. It felt like that person wasn't her anymore. As if she'd been someone else entirely in that moment. If he hadn't shown up, what would have happened?

Vaelric seemed to notice the flicker of pain in her eyes and quickly changed the subject.

"Hey, listen, let's go for that walk, huh? You lead the way."

Riona pushed the thoughts away, forcing a small smile. "Yeah, let's head to the overlook. It's beautiful at sunset."

The two of them walked through the woods, the air cool and tinged with the earthy scent of fallen leaves. The shadows danced across the forest floor, illuminated by the shimmers of crimson and orange hues cast by the setting sun. Riona took it all in, letting the warmth of the sun seep into her skin before it faded into night.

When they reached the overlook, the view took her breath away. From here, the spires of Frostfire rose high above the town below, everything bathed in the golden and amber hues of twilight. She sank to the ground, settling beside Vaelric. It wasn't an uncomfortable quiet; far from it. It was the kind of silence that felt welcoming, a shared moment of peace as they watched the sun dip below the horizon. Vaelric reached for Riona's hand, his touch warm despite the chill in the air. He didn't hold it, just rested his hand gently over hers and looked at her.

"Real power comes from rising above the things that try to destroy you," he said quietly. "It seems you've chosen to take control of whatever was haunting you."

He pulled his hand back, his gaze shifting to the horizon where the sun was disappearing behind the town. Riona didn't respond right away, her eyes fixed on the growing night sky. A blanket of stars slowly emerged above them, and the moon rose steadily into its full glow, casting a soft silver light over the landscape.

She finally turned to him.

"You said you'd lost everything too. How did you get past it? How did you move on?" Her voice was soft, almost hesitant.

Vaelric didn't look at her as he spoke, his eyes still on the distant horizon. "I took things into my own hands. I found power and learned to use it for myself. I saved myself and got revenge on those who took everything from me."

He paused, his voice heavy with something she couldn't quite place. "But it came at a price."

His hand moved to his face, his fingers tracing the etched scars that marred his otherwise flawless features. She stood, brushing off the dampness from where she'd been sitting, and offered her hand to Vaelric. He took it without hesitation, his grip warm and steady despite the chill that lingered in the air. Together, they walked toward the edge of the woods, the fading light casting long shadows around them.

Just as they reached the tree line, Vaelric stopped and turned to her. "It was nice to see you again, Riona," he said, his voice low and smooth, "I hope you find whatever it is you're searching for."

He didn't wait for her to finish. Without another word, he turned and disappeared into the night, his figure melting into the shadows like a wisp of smoke.

Riona stood there, frozen in place, the weight of his words sinking into her chest.

# Chapter 48
## Unlocking Potential

The days blurred together. Riona rarely left her room at the inn, barely sleeping and picking at her meals. She couldn't put the book down, the words pulling her deeper with each passage. The outside world faded into the background, swallowed by the book's grip. It wasn't until a letter arrived with her morning meal that reality pierced the haze. The summons to patrols was clear; she couldn't delay any longer. Scrambling, Riona bathed, dressed, and left to meet Kael.

Kael stood outside the Circle's outpost, his posture immaculate as ever, the crisp morning air cool against her skin. He handed her a folded parchment, his tone as icy as his movements.

"I've arranged your accommodations," he said. "You made it clear Frostfire and the Keep didn't suit you. There's a cottage in Coill Dorcha. Modest but adequate."

Riona unfolded the parchment and scanned the neat description. A simple, functional cottage, tucked away at the edge of Coill Dorcha. It wasn't much, but the idea of a quiet place, away from the chaos, brought relief.

"Thank you, Commander," she said sincerely.

Kael nodded. "You'll be able to move in after today's patrols and training. It should meet your needs better than the inn."

"It will," she replied, her voice softer now. "I appreciate it."

Kael's gaze lingered on her. "Your father's name is known here. That alone brings certain expectations.

Commander General Byrne set a high standard, and I intend to uphold it."

Riona bristled slightly but nodded. "I wouldn't expect anything less."

His expression softened, though his voice remained formal. "Prove that you belong, and you'll find your place here."

The air seemed charged with tension, as if the proximity to the Veil made every moment feel urgent. The training grounds left her speechless. They stretched farther than she remembered, the sheer scale of the place staggering. Sparring circles filled the space, cadets locked in combat under the watchful eyes of their trainers. Targets floated erratically in the air, glowing faintly with runes, while soldiers hurled spells and arrows with unerring precision. The air buzzed with the energy of magic being wielded, the sounds of swords clashing and the rhythmic thud of fists hitting dummies. At the center of it all stood a towering structure, its stone walls carved with intricate symbols that pulsed faintly. It was a place that radiated strength and resilience.

Kael's voice broke her thoughts. "You've seen this place before, haven't you?"

Riona nodded slowly. "As a child. My father brought me here."

Her memories flickered walking these grounds, her small hand in her father's, his voice explaining the importance of the Circle. She remembered the awe she felt watching the soldiers train, their movements precise and deadly. But those memories were shadowed by others, her father's distant gaze, his cruel words, the growing chasm between them as she grew older. She hadn't stepped foot here in years...

Kael's voice broke her thoughts. "You'll train under three mentors."

Amara stepped forward first. Tall, muscular, and poised, her mahogany skin gleamed under the sun. Wavy hair adorned with small charms swayed as she moved, and her hazel eyes seemed to pierce through Riona. She carried a staff etched with intricate, glowing runes.

"I'm Amara," she said, her tone steady and commanding. "Combat and endurance are my domain.

Next was Zara. Her sleek black braids framed angled eyes that watched Riona with quiet intensity. Her uniform bore patterns unfamiliar to Riona, and her movements were precise and calculated.

"I'm Zara," she said, her tone cool but calm. "Runes, elemental casting, and defensive magic. Here, control is everything."

Last was Niko, his easy grin a stark contrast to the others' intensity. His hair fell messily over his sun-warmed face, and the massive axe strapped to his back glowed faintly.

"Niko," he said simply. "Survival and weapons training. I'll teach you how to use whatever's in your hand to survive."

Riona nodded at each of them, nerves twisting in her stomach. She could feel their eyes assessing her, weighing her worth.

Her training began under the relentless guidance of Amara. She moved like water, her staff an extension of herself. She vaulted over obstacles, struck with precision, and flowed seamlessly between offense and defense. Her movements were graceful but deadly, her eyes never missing a beat. Riona struggled to keep up, her strikes clumsy and her blocks slow. Her muscles burned, her breaths came in ragged gasps, but she refused to stop.

"You've got instincts," Amara said, circling her. "But instincts aren't enough. Trust your body."

As Amara spoke, memories of Emry surged to the forefront of Riona's mind. She could almost hear his voice, teasing but encouraging, during their sparring sessions back in Lumora.

"You're overthinking again," he'd say, knocking her staff out of her hands with infuriating ease.

"I'm the scholar, Riona, this should be easy for you," he'd tease.

The memory made her ache, the loss of him cruel and bitter. She gritted her teeth and threw herself back into the fight, channeling the pain into each strike. By the end of the day, she was exhausted. Her body ached, her muscles trembling with fatigue. But for the first time in days, her mind felt clear. As she walked back to the inn, the sights and sounds of the Keep surrounded her, grounding her in the present. She thought of Lumora, of its quiet streets and warm faces, and the friends she had left behind. She thought of Emry and the way his death had driven her here. And she thought of the book, its pull dark and insidious.

When she reached her room, she began packing her belongings, her movements mechanical as she folded her clothes and tucked them into her bag. Her fingers brushed against something, and her stomach twisted.

The book.

It's plain, unmarked cover stared back at her, the golden trim on its spine catching the dim light. She froze, dread and anger twisting in her chest. Three days. That's all it had been, and already it felt like it owned her. The promises within its pages had consumed her, making her forget why she'd come here in the first place. She sat on the edge of the bed, clutching the book tightly. Her mind raced with thoughts of Emry, of the person he had believed her to be. Reading this book, succumbing to its pull—it was a betrayal of everything he had stood for.

"What am I doing?" she whispered, her voice barely audible. She wanted to throw it away, to rid herself of its weight. But she couldn't. Not yet.

With a shaky breath, she tucked it back into her bag and sealed it shut. Tomorrow, she promised herself. Tomorrow, she would focus on her training. On the Circle. On rebuilding herself. And maybe, just maybe, she could find a way to let it go.

# Chapter 49
## POWER HAS A COST

Riona woke early for her second day with the Keep's Circle, determined to make a good impression. She certainly couldn't show up late; it would give the illusion that her father's rank and title made her privileged. It would make life a living hell if they saw her as special; they would never accept her, and any aspirations of becoming part of the unit would end just as fast as they started. She made sure to eat, bathe, and dress quickly, grabbing a black set of leathers and a long-sleeved white shirt that swirled with frosty patterns along the arms. Pulling on her riding boots, she quickly headed out the door, taking in the quiet before the sounds of the Keep surrounded her.

The Keep was loud: harsh yells from blacksmiths, the ringing clash of hammers and anvils striking steel as coals were thrown into roaring fires, and the crackling of flames whipping the cold air into misty clouds. Officers, cadets, and leaders of all kinds gathered supplies and food, their voices mingling in the streets with the clang of metal. The air was heavy with an overwhelming blend of smells: the metallic tang of steel and iron, so strong it clung to her tongue like blood; the acrid stench of sweat lingering in every corner; and the warm, earthy spices wafting from food carts. The scents collided, thick and pungent, making her stomach churn with nausea. It was a sensory assault she hadn't expected, another reminder that she was far from Lumora and everything familiar. Walking into the large stone building that loomed over the Keep, it stood at its center like a heart, keeping this place alive and beating.

It wasn't quiet in these early hours though there were no sounds of nature here. Instead, the air was filled with the rhythmic pounding of feet hitting the hard ground in a relentless run, commands being shouted over groans, and the occasional retching of someone pushed past their limits. The voices were unyielding, stripped of any warmth. This place felt intimidating, almost oppressive, but in a way that mirrored her father in every sense. She was beginning to understand the man he truly was. The one who commanded this place with the same stern authority it demanded. She shook the thoughts aside. The idea of giving her father any sympathy for the cruel man he was ignited a fire in the pit of her stomach, one that burned so fiercely it climbed into her heart, demanding to be extinguished.

She had another day of training ahead of her, and this time it would be with Zara.

She made her way through the halls, passing classrooms until she found herself standing at the center of a massive room. It wasn't a room. It was something else entirely, looming and sprawling, stretching so high it felt as though the very sky itself had been invited inside. Skylights towered overhead, their glass panes open wide, allowing the crisp air to rush in. The warmth of the sun streaming through, casting a golden glow across the space.

Riona stepped forward, her eyes sweeping over the area in front of her. The space was unlike anything she'd ever seen. Trees stood scattered across the room, their placement seemingly random yet somehow intentional, their roots twisting through patches of dirt and moss covered stones. At its center a large pond shimmered and on either side of the room were wide sandpits, their edges uneven and lined with rough, jagged rocks. Between the trees and sandpits, logs were haphazardly laid out, some balanced precariously on others, while above, narrow rope bridges and suspended platforms crisscrossed the open air like a web. Every detail of the room felt alive, untamed, as if it had been plucked straight from the wilderness and brought here.

The enormity of the space was dizzying. Riona tilted her head back, feeling small under the sheer scale of it all. The skylights stretched so far upward that it felt as though the room didn't end, open to the elements and breathing with life.

Her thoughts were interrupted by the sound of someone clearing their throat. She jumped, spinning around, blood rushing to her ears.

"Gods, you scared the shit out of me!" Riona gasped, clutching at her chest as she turned to see Zara standing calmly behind her. "I didn't even hear you!" she added, her voice still shaky, her eyes wide.

Zara's lips curved into a faint smile, "I'm sorry," she said, her voice as soft as her demeanor. "Light footwork is something of a habit."

Riona chuckled nervously and nodded. "I can see that," she said, trying to compose herself.

Zara stepped further into the room, her back turned to Riona as she spoke. "Are you ready for today? We're going to work on elemental casting. I'm not sure how much you've learned in your studies, but it's an essential skill. Magic isn't something we can afford to neglect, it's as important as breathing. The more you wield it, the more it becomes part of you. And the more magic you master, the higher your rank."

She turned, her gaze locking onto Riona, who shifted uncomfortably under the weight of it. Zara's presence made her feel small, as if every move, every word, was being measured.

"I've learned some," Riona said finally, keeping her voice steady despite her nerves. "Mostly with rune stones... I don't have many elemental runes."

Zara nodded slowly, taking in the response. "I see.

Well, we have a lot of work to do, then." Her tone was matter of fact, but there was no cruelty in it, only an expectation. "I'll be speaking with Kael. You'll need more than just a day with me."

Riona stayed silent, listening intently. "Alright," Zara continued, "we'll start with the

basics of casting. When you joined the ranks, you were imbued with magic, though learning to wield it is another matter entirely. Magic is tied to the nature around us, to the balance of all things." She turned to Riona, asking, "Are you still following along?"

Riona shook her head. "I'm still following..."

Zara turned back and started walking toward the center of the training room. "It will respond to you but only if you listen, focus, and channel your thoughts and emotions into it. Let nature guide you; don't try to control it, but work with it."

Zara moved with a practiced ease, her hands flowing in deliberate patterns as she spoke words that Riona couldn't quite make out. The air around her started to shift, and suddenly, stones from the ground began to rise. One by one, they aligned, forming a walkway that stretched upward into the sky. Zara stepped onto the first stone, then the next, climbing higher and higher as if the very earth had bent to her will.

Riona stared, wide eyed, unable to look away as Zara reached the top. And then, without warning, Zara jumped.

"Zara!" Riona gasped, instinctively starting to run toward the pond below. But before she could take another step, the water surged upward, cradling Zara gently as if it had reached up to catch her. The water rippled, as it lowered Zara back to the ground with impossible grace.

Riona froze in place, her breath catching in her throat. She stared, awe struck, as Zara stepped forward, her composure unshaken.

For a moment, Riona could only watch, unable to speak or move, as Zara continued her lesson.

"You'll notice this training room is unlike any other," Zara said as she smoothed her tunic. "The reason is that, here, you'll learn to use elemental magic in a controlled setting."

Her hands moved quickly, fluid and precise, while she whispered. Suddenly, the sand began to rise, twisting into a swirling tornado that roared to life. In the blink of an eye, it shifted, transforming into the shape of a lion. The creature looked alive, its mane billowing, its powerful roar reverberating through the room as it charged straight toward Riona.

Riona held her ground, refusing to flinch or retreat. The lion dissolved mid stride, collapsing into a cascade of sand that fell in a soft pile at her feet. Before she could speak, Zara raised her head to the skylights. The wind in the room began to howl, building with relentless force. It whipped and tore through the air, lashing at Riona's face and pushing her backward. She struggled to stay on her feet, but the wind was too strong. It drove her across the room until she was pinned against the far wall. She fought against it, every muscle straining, but it was like pushing against an unstoppable tide. It wasn't until Zara lowered her hands and the wind abruptly stilled that Riona collapsed to her knees, her hands catching her fall.

Her voice came hoarse but steady as she lifted her gaze to meet Zara's. "Teach me." The hours passed as Riona and Zara worked tirelessly, focusing on attuning Riona to the world around her. They meditated, trained, and worked through the obstacle course, with Zara pushing Riona to refine her footwork while attempting to conjure the elements. Riona fell, slipped, and collided with nearly everything in her path. She struggled to balance both tasks seamlessly, it was far harder than Zara made it look, and for that, Riona cursed her over and over again under her breath.

By the end of the day, Riona wanted nothing more than to set fire to the entire course out of frustration. The thought itself seemed to manifest, a flame suddenly appearing in her hand. Panicked, Riona flailed, trying to extinguish it, but all she managed to do was fling small bursts of fire in every direction. The flames licked at the logs, igniting them one by one. Her panic deepened as the fire in her hand grew larger, feeding off her rising emotions. Through it all, Zara remained calm, putting out each fire with precision as Riona unintentionally started them. Finally, Zara fixed Riona with a stern, unyielding gaze. "Anger burns fast, Riona. It consumes and then leaves you empty. Use it. Don't let it use you."

The words struck Riona like a cold wind, and to her amazement, the fire in her hand extinguished as if the flames themselves had heard Zara's command. She stared at her hand, stunned to find it unburned. Around her, the chaos had been brought under control, Zara having effortlessly tamed the destruction as though it had never happened. Zara smiled softly as she approached Riona, placing a steady hand on her shoulder. "It's okay," she said gently. "Once you work with elemental magic more, it'll become easier to summon. Remember, everything in nature is balanced. Fire can destroy, but it also brings life. It warms, it cleanses, it protects. What it does depends entirely on the one who wields "

The words sank into Riona, deep and unwavering. It was almost as if Zara could see straight through her, the meaning behind the words reaching far beyond today's training. The realization left her feeling uneasy in Zara's presence.

Riona nodded, and Zara turned and walked away from the training course, disappearing as she rounded a corner.

Riona stood there a moment longer before heading out of the Keep's halls and back to Briar. She mounted her horse and rode toward her new home.

The house felt empty. She wasn't sure if it was the lack of furniture or the absence of the one person she wished was there. Her heart tightened painfully at the thought of Emry. She shuddered, her gaze drifting to the hearth, which was filled with ash and dust. The place had been neglected for some time, she realized, noticing the cobwebs, the dirt, and the grime that covered every corner.

Riona opened the windows in the small kitchen and living area, letting in the cold air, and propped the front door open. She grabbed a broom and began sweeping the dirt out of the house. She cleaned the hearth first, making quick work of the remnants there, then moved to the floors, counters, and every dusty inch she could find. When she paused to catch her breath, she noticed the swirls of cold air kissing her warm exhales, creating little clouds. She knew she needed to gather firewood before the sun faded. Closing the doors and windows, she grabbed a large basket for wood, slipped a small axe into it, and headed for the forest of Coill Dorcha.

It was getting colder by the day, the ache in Riona's hands a reminder of the biting wind. She searched for fallen trees. The ones that weren't damp or rotting, hoping to make light work of gathering wood. But nothing seemed untouched by the elements. Her eyes caught something strange: patches of rot had taken over the woods, twisting the trees into grotesque shapes. The decay was expansive, right in the middle of the forest. Wilted grass, blackened roots, and frost intertwined in stark contrast, painting the landscape in a haunting mix of black and white. Riona pushed her way through the tangled limbs, the branches tugging at her clothing. She wanted to know how far the decay stretched and was determined to find its edge when a familiar voice stopped her in her tracks.

"Riona?" The sound of her name dripped with honey. "Funny how I keep finding you in such precarious situations."

She turned to see Vaelric casually standing against a tree, his elbow resting on the bark and his hand propped against his cheek. A smirk curved across his lips as he took in the scene before him.

Riona stiffened, realizing how ridiculous she must have looked, headfirst into tree limbs, her clothes snagged and her hair a disheveled mess. Her cheeks burned with embarrassment as she stumbled, trying to free herself. In her haste, she ripped her shirt sleeve. She finally stopped moving, attempting to compose herself and act like none of it had happened.

Standing upright, she locked eyes with him. "I'm just collecting firewood and doing a little exploring," she said with a forced smile, quickly tucking stray hair behind her ear.

Vaelric chuckled softly. "I'm not trying to say anything here, but you look like you could use some help," he teased, his ember-like eyes glowing in the fading sunlight. They locked onto hers, and for a moment, it was like she forgot how to breathe. She shook it off quickly.

"No, really, I'm fine," she said, tugging at the small branches tangled in her clothes. "I'm just collecting kindling," she added, breaking the twigs around her, though her voice lacked conviction.

Vaelric leaned back against the tree, clearly enjoying the view. "I'll just hang around in case you change your mind."

Riona's frustration bubbled to the surface. She shot him a fake smile before turning back to free herself. Her mind cursed her for not carrying the axe, it would've made this mess avoidable.

"Are you looking for the axe?" Vaelric asked casually, still leaning against the tree.

"Yes, actually," she said sharply. "Do you see it?"

He pointed to a far corner where the brambles and thorns wove together into a chaotic web. "It's over there. Looks like you dropped it, though I'm not sure how or why," he added, his smirk widening.

Riona rolled her eyes. "Thanks for the observation. Think you could grab it for me?"

Vaelric raised a brow, his grin growing.

"Are you asking me for help?"

She muttered a curse under her breath and seriously considered lighting the entire mess, herself included on fire, just to end the humiliation.

"Nope, I've got it. Thanks, though," she huffed, clawing her way through the twisted branches.

For nearly half an hour, Riona struggled. Small cuts covered her arms and face, her clothes were torn, and her hair was tangled with twigs. Finally, she dropped to the ground, admitting defeat.

"Vaelric," she called out, exasperated. "Yes?" he drawled, his tone laced with amusement.

"Can you get me out of here?" she pleaded.

In moments, Vaelric was at her side, pulling her free with one hand while holding her axe in the other. Her basket hung neatly over his arm. He smiled at her, his expression softening. "It's the least I could do. Though, I won't lie, that was the most amusing thing I've seen in a long time."

Riona couldn't help it, she laughed, and Vaelric joined in. The tension broke, and for a moment, the awkwardness faded.

She noticed the basket was now filled with firewood. "You didn't have to do that," she said, glancing at it in surprise.

"Well, you had enough going on without having to worry about this," he said, still chuckling softly.

Riona smiled, feeling her earlier frustration melt away. Before she could speak, Vaelric offered, "Can I walk you home? I'll carry this—you look like you could use some company."

She hesitated for only a moment before nodding. "Yes... I'd like that."

They made small talk as they walked, the conversation easy, unhurried. Then Vaelric cleared his throat.

"You know... I understand what it's like to have a father who's never satisfied with anything." He paused, as if weighing his next words. "My father..." his voice trailed off, deep in thought. "He saw everything I did as failure. I was never good enough, and he made sure I knew it. He beat it into me. Every. Damn. Day. He had a bad day? I was the target. He was sad? I was the target. Never a moment's rest in that fucking house."

He shook his head, looking at Riona, anger flickering behind his eyes. Riona nodded slowly, She didn't question how he knew of her father. She assumed that everyone knew who she was by now, it was hard to miss the daughter of the commanding general, and she was sure that he made sure everyone knew who she was. "I'm sorry. Some people were never meant to be parents."

Without thinking, she reached for his hand, holding it gently. The weight of the moment settled between them, but the conversation flowed easily again, shifting back to lighter things as they walked.

By the time they reached her front door, a slight smile tugged at Riona's lips. "This is me," she said, swaying lightly on her feet. "If you'd like to come in for some tea... I don't have much right now. I just moved in."

Vaelric responded almost instantly. "It would be a pleasure."

They stepped inside, and Riona went into the kitchen to find a kettle, rinsing it and filling it with water. Meanwhile, Vaelric examined the small space. His eyes lingered on the empty hearth before he began bundling small pieces of parchment and broken wood. With a fluid motion of his hands, the fire sprang to life, flames licking at the cold air until they crackled and roared, filling the room with warmth. By the time Riona returned with two cups, Vaelric had fed the flames into a steady blaze. She glanced at the small side table and its matching chair, both worn with time. The green and gold paint swirled across them, faded in places where they'd been well loved. Riona sighed. "I suppose we'll sit on the floor," she said, setting the cups down before lowering herself in front of the fire.

Vaelric joined her. "Thank you for the tea," he said, his voice soft as he took in the room. The glow of the fire caught the gold and fiery hues in his eyes, and Riona couldn't help but stare, losing herself in their swirling depths.

Vaelric noticed her gaze, his own desire growing as he took her in. She was beautiful and powerful, yet there was a vulnerability that tugged at him. But then something else caught his attention, the faint glimmer of gold trim sticking out from Riona's bag. The firelight reflected off it, and Vaelric's eyes narrowed ever so slightly.

Riona followed his gaze; it was on the book. She had forgotten about it, forgotten it just long enough for it to make itself known again. Her body tensed, and she shot to her feet. "It's getting late, and I have training in the morning. Thank you again for everything," she said, moving toward the door.

Vaelric nodded and rose, setting his empty teacup on the table before meeting her at the threshold. His eyes held hers, and he leaned forward, pressing a gentle kiss to the top of her head.

"Thanks again for the tea. Goodnight, Riona," he whispered gently before stepping into the shadows and vanishing into the night.

# Chapter 50
## THE FALL

The training grounds were nearly empty when Riona finally stumbled off the course breathless and aching. The sky had turned to deep violet as the last light of day clung stubbornly to the horizon but she hardly noticed. Sweat dripped from her brow, her muscles trembling with exhaustion.

*Another failure.*

Zara had pushed her harder than ever demanding more, expecting more, and Riona had given everything she had. But it still wasn't enough. It never felt like enough.

Kael had told her she needed this, needed more time with Zara. "You have the potential, Riona. You just need to unlock it."

*Unlock it. What a joke.*

Riona groaned, rubbing at her sore arms. The course had been brutal. Every time she found her footing, Zara changed the game. Fire. Water. Shifting ground beneath her feet. Illusions twisting the terrain. She had barely managed to counter any of it. She'd tripped, stumbled, hesitated too long and just didn't have endurance. She bit her lip in frustration the anger growing hotter by the second.

The fire in the hearth had burned low by the time Riona returned. She let the door fall shut behind her, barely registering the cold creeping into the room by the dying embers. Her legs carried her to the small desk by the window, her body moving before her mind could catch up. The book was still there tucked away in her satchel. She dropped into the chair, her hands running through her hair as she exhaled, trying to shake the day's failures from her mind. But they clung to her like ghosts.

*You'll never be strong enough. Not for them. Not for the Circle. Not even for the people you love.*

Her fingers twitched as she slowly she reached for the book. The leather was cool beneath her fingertips, the edges of the pages worn but sturdy. Her hands began to tremble with its weight in her hands. No, not just the weight, but with the decision she had made. If she had been stronger, she could have saved Emry. If she had been better, she could have fought harder, moved faster, done anything to stop him from leaving her. Riona traced the cover, her breaths hiccuping. Her heart began to sputter as she began to lose control of the tears building. Each tear felt like losing a piece of Emry. The room blurred and became hazy.

She would never lose another person again. If she could use the book for good, if she could wield whatever power it held for the sake of the Circle, for the realm, for the people who still lived... then wasn't that worth it? Wasn't that the kind of sacrifice a warrior was meant to make if it was for the greater good? Magic demanded a price and she needed to pay the cost, no matter the price. Riona grabbed her satchel and tucked the book inside while also strapping her daggers; then she opened the door and stepped into the night.

The dark stretched wide and endless, the trees arching their skeletal branches toward the moonlight. The cold bit at her skin, but she paid no mind. As a child, Riona walked these woods many times, possibly hundreds of times. She spent long nights tracking in the thick of winter, waiting for the perfect moment to strike. This was just another hunt she reminder herself but doubt crept in. A sinking feeling that this was wrong. Her fingers tightened around the hilt of her dagger, as she exhaled slow and steady.

Her eyes froze on a shimmering light. Just beyond the tree line was a large deer with antlers similar to tree adorning its head like a crown. It was as white as fresh fallen snow and it was watching her. The way its glacier touched eyes locked onto hers, sent a strange chill through her. It didn't run, not so much as a twitch as it stood there. Her hands were trembling slightly now as sweat loosened her grip. She approached the deer as it watched her. Then to her shock, it laid down, exposing its chest to her. Riona raised the dagger and paused. The magnificent creature was beyond beautiful. It was as if it was dipped in starlight, its antlers looked as old as the ancient yew trees in Lumora. A single tear dropped onto the deer fur as she whispered, "I'm sorry." The blade found its mark driving deep into its heart. The deer exhaled a soft shuddering sound as it left the world. She sank to her knees, fumbling for the book as she flipped it open, its pages illuminated beneath the glow of the moon. The words twisted and shifted, reshaping themselves into words she could understand. Her breath came fast and shallow as she quickly moved. She pressed her bloodstained fingers to the parchment and spoke the words. The air crackled as the clearing darkened, shadows stretching unnaturally, creeping closer, curling around her wrists, her ankles, her throat. Power slammed into her. Cold fire pouring into her veins, filling every corner of her being. She screamed as her runes twisted and changed. A faint, pulsing red spread through the markings on her skin, curling around her arms, her hands, her collarbone.

The pain dulled and a sensation took over that was intoxicating, unlike anything she had ever felt. Fluttering of wings struggling against the cold air, the whisper of voices, fires crackling. So many sounds all at once, so clear, overloaded her senses. She could smell iron in the air mix with spices and flowers from the town miles behind her. It was all overwhelming.

Riona rolled her shoulders as she stood, flexing her fingers as the power settled beneath her skin. Everything was loud and intense but the wave has passed just as quickly as it came. She heard the soft crunch of snow and whirled around for her eyes to meet fire.

Vaelric watched from the tree line, his figure carved from shadow, as if he had always belonged to the dark. The space between them melted away, each step drawing her deeper into his gaze.

Riona hadn't noticed she crossed the final stretch of distance between them before she stood in front of him, her body pressing against his. Calloused fingertips grabbed her chin as his thumb caressed her jaw, lifting her gaze to his. It was her undoing. Her lips trailing down the curve of his neck, nipping at the skin just above his collarbone before dragging her mouth back up.

Vaelric inhaled, his body tensing beneath her touch. She felt the shift, the subtle change in his breath. The way his grip on her waist tightened for a moment before relaxing again, she took that as an invitation and bit his lip hard. Hard enough to break skin. She watched as single drop of crimson welled up and slid down the curve of his mouth. The red stark against the pale glow of his skin beneath the moonlight. Riona stood still as she watched it, watched the way it caught the silver light, how it stood out like ink against his lips. Vaelric's eyes burned into hers. But it wasn't pain or anger, it was hunger.

Slowly he lifted a hand and ran his fingers along his lower lip, smearing the blood before licking it away. Riona's stomach fluttered.

She didn't know what she had expected, surprise, hesitation, even the possibility that he'd pull away. But he didn't, instead he matched her, his lips curling into a smile.

"Careful, Riona." His voice was deep, smooth as silk, dark as the night pressing in around them. "You might start something you're not ready to finish."

The magic burned too hot, and standing there, staring at him, she felt alive.

A thrill shot through her, wicked and delightful, as she smirked, running a hand up his chest.

"I never start something I don't intend to finish," she whispered.

Vaelric's eyes sparked red, his head tilting slightly.

The tension between them was suffocating and when he finally spoke, his voice was barely more than a whisper.

"Then finish it."

The world around them blurred. The trees, the silver streaked sky, the ground beneath their feet, it all faded into nothing but heat and the tension crackling between them. Riona barely noticed how Vaelric moved, how he twisted them with effortless strength. One moment, she had him caged against the tree. The next, he had her. Her back hit the bark, rough and unyielding, the shock of it sending a shiver down her spine. She gasped, her fingers tightening against his tunic, her body arching instinctively. The pressure of him was everywhere, his weight, his heat, the solid press of his hips against hers, pinning her in place.

His dark eyes flickered over her face, taking her in. His hand tangled in her hair, Riona shuddered as he pulled her head back, exposing her throat to him. A soft, desperate sound left her lips, swallowed instantly by his mouth crashing into hers again, stealing the breath from her lungs.

She felt it all. The scrape of bark biting into her skin. The contrast of his lips, hot and demanding against the cool night air. The slow grind of his hips against hers, leaving her lightheaded and wanting more.

She should stop and think but she couldn't focus on anything except the freedom this moment held. In the quiet, out slipped a moan echoing into the night and, in that moment, Riona let go.

# Chapter 51
# MEANWHILE IN LUMORA

The towering spires of the Druid School glinted faintly under the early morning light, and Kyron's voice echoed through the halls as he called for help. The weight of Sorcha and Cat didn't slow him, his steps purposeful and his tone commanding.

"Help! We need a healer!"

Doors creaked open as startled figures emerged, but it was Commander Nethran who appeared first, his gaze taking in the scene in an instant.

"Sorcha?" he said, his voice tight with concern as he approached. "What happened?"

"She's hurt," Kyron said shortly, adjusting Sorcha in his arms. "And so is the damn cat. They need a healer now."

Nethran didn't waste time. "Follow me," he said, turning sharply and leading them toward the medical unit. Once inside, Kyron gently laid Sorcha on one of the cots while Nethran called for the healers. Cat slipped from Kyron's grip, landing awkwardly on his feet but managing to limp to Sorcha's side. The healers arrived quickly, working on Sorcha and Cat with practiced precision.

Nethran stood off to the side, his arms crossed as he watched the scene unfold, his jaw tight with unspoken questions.

As the healers worked, Cat's silver eyes flicked to Nethran, and he spoke. "You're wondering what's happening," he said evenly. Nethran's eyes narrowed. "You could say that. So, you're not just a cat… Cait Sídhe. It's been a long time since I've heard the stories." His gaze bore into Cat, scrutinizing every inch of the creature.

Cat looked amused by the statement, tilting his head with an air of mock offense. "I was… intrigued.

Sorcha reeked of magic, and that kind of scent is hard to ignore. But in a short time, I've grown to like her," he confessed.

His eyes glimmered like crashing waves, their tides of light and shadow pulling at the room's attention. "She is mine, and I am hers. There's no place she can go that I can't follow."

The words hung in the air, weighted with meaning. Cat turned his gaze to Nethran, who stared back unblinking for a long time. The commander wasn't sure he could trust the Fae. He knew too well the stories of their kind, creatures of habit, cunning, and contradiction. The Cait Sídhe could guide souls or steal them, and it was impossible to know which path they might choose at any given moment. But tonight, there wasn't much choice. After a beat, Nethran nodded slowly.

"I suppose it's no surprise, with Samhain being so close, that she found you when she did," he said. "So then, do you have any idea what happened to the two of you tonight?"

Cat, who had been casually licking his wounds, paused to glance up, his expression irritated at the interruption. "Well, Commander," he began, "Sorcha, for reasons beyond my comprehension, decided to take us to the Bridge of the Forgotten."

He straightened, his voice dropping slightly as his eyes scanned the room, ensuring he had everyone's attention. "For those of you who don't know, the Bridge of the Forgotten is a death trap. All who walk across it if they aren't already dead soon will be. It's haunted by souls whose lives ended unnaturally: by force, by tragedy, or by betrayal. These spirits wander the bridge endlessly, damning anyone foolish enough to cross. Anyway, in doing so," Cat continued, his tone laced with dry exasperation, "she managed to draw the attention of every skeleton, walking dead, banshee, wraith, and just about any other creature in the area."

He let out a heavy sigh, his tail twitching.

Suddenly, it split into two, the newly formed tails whipping through the air with almost deliberate nonchalance. Nethran's eyes flicked around the room. Kyron stood off to the side, his expression unimpressed, a flicker of annoyance in his gaze as he crossed his arms tightly over his chest. The healers, however, were transfixed, one of them letting out a soft gasp at the sight of Cat's transformation. Sorcha lay motionless on the cot, her breaths shallow but steady, oblivious to the growing tension. Nethran's gaze snapped back to Cat, his patience visibly thinning. The Cait Sídhe seemed entirely unbothered, tending to his wounds as though he had all the time in the world.

"Oh!" Cat suddenly exclaimed sarcasm dripping off every word like venom. "I almost forgot to mention the near-death experience at the hands of her impeccable sense of direction." He glanced at Sorcha. "Really, Commander, she nearly got us killed. It was impressive, in a catastrophic sort of way."

Kyron, muttered what sounded suspiciously like,

*"unbelievable."*

Commander Nethran cleared his throat loudly, his tone edged with irritation. "And was there anything else?"

Kyron turned his glare on Cat, shaking his head. "You know, for someone who *almost died,* it's great to see you walked away completely unbothered. Maybe just get to the point and tell us what happened, since you're feeling so chatty."

Cat froze mid lick, his tails flicking menacingly behind him. "I *knew* you didn't like me," he said, narrowing his eyes at Kyron.

Kyron shot back a pointed glare, raising an eyebrow. "I know an Otherworldly being when I see one, Cat. I was suspicious of your motives from the start. Your kind has a *reputation*."

Cat's lips curled into a sly grin. "Hmm. So is *that* why you've been hanging around Sorcha all this time? Or could it be there's a little *more* to it, Kyron?"

Before Kyron could retort, Commander Nethran's voice thundered through the room, silencing them both. "*That is ENOUGH!*" he barked, his tone cutting through the tension like a blade. "I need to know what happened to my ranger, and I need to know now. If you two have finished your bickering, someone explain things to me."

Cat tilted his head toward Nethran, his expression suddenly calm and serious.

"I am telling you, Commander. Sorcha has been dream walking into the Otherworld, and it's a miracle she hasn't died yet. She's crossing the Veil without any understanding of what she's walking into or how dangerous it is. She's been doing this long before I arrived." He paused, his voice dropping lower. "And now her powers have begun to emerge. That magic makes her a beacon for everything that walks, crawls, flies, and slithers in both planes. And worse, someone is actively hunting her."

Nethran's brow furrowed. "Hunting her?"

"Yes," Cat said bluntly. "Whoever or whatever it is, they are tied to her by fate. The wisps are leading her to it, this thing cloaked in shadows. She can't outrun it, Commander. She can't hide from it. Whatever is happening is bound to her, and she plays a key role in all of it."

The room fell silent, the weight of Cat's words pressing heavily on them.

Finally, Cat let out an exhaustive sigh. "Anything else you'd like me to explain? Oh, yes—the bridge. A wraith sliced her side open while I stood in front of her, protecting her with my life. That vermin managed to get past me while I was busy fighting the masses of undead and the shadow figure that was chasing us across the bridge."

Kyron looked at Cat, regret flickering across his face. He opened his mouth to speak, but Cat cut him off with a raised paw. "Now, now, no need to get sentimental, Kyron. Keep that away from me before I start to like you too." Kyron felt a smile tug at the corner of his lips.

Commander Nethran stepped closer to Sorcha, turning to Cat with a stern expression.

"How do we know she's not there right now? How do we know she's safe?"

Cat, unbothered as always, flicked one of his tails lazily. "If she wasn't safe, I wouldn't be here talking to you."

Nethran considered this for a moment, then nodded. He turned to Kyron, his tone brisk.

"I need to think this through, get some things in order, and prepare the Circle and cadets for the day. Kyron, you'll stay here and keep watch over both of them."

Kyron straightened, his reply immediate. "Yes, Commander."

With that, Nethran walked out the door, leaving Kyron alone with Cat and Sorcha. Kyron and Cat settled into the quiet room. The bells of the Druid School rang softly in the distance, marking the passage of time. The clash of swords and muffled commands of training drills filtered faintly through the walls, but in the medical unit, all was still.

Kyron sat in a chair near Sorcha's cot, his gaze flicking between her and Cat, who lay curled at her feet. The Cait Sídhe's eyes would close briefly, only to snap open again as he drifted in and out of consciousness.

Eventually, the sun began its slow descent, flooding the room with warm, golden light. The rays seemed to be drawn to Sorcha, enveloping her in their glow as her runes absorbed the light, flickering bright and then dim. Her hair shimmered, curling slightly and twisting in the light, as though it were alive and reaching toward the sun. For a moment, Kyron was caught off guard by the sight of her. In the stillness, she looked more like a goddess than a mortal.

Then her eyes fluttered open, and she blinked slowly, her gaze sweeping the room. Her voice, raspy and strained, broke the quiet.

"Kyron... Are we at the medical unit?"

Kyron leaned forward, his features softening as his dark eyes met hers. Her green eyes, now swirling faintly with liquid gold, glowing in the sunlight.

"Yes," he said gently. "You needed more help than I could give."

Cat stirred, his eyes flicking up to meet Sorcha's. "You're safe now," he said, his tone uncharacteristically soft.

Sorcha's gaze lingered on him, her expression caught in disbelief. Even now, it was hard to process the reality that Cat could speak—that he was so much more than she had imagined.

She tried to push herself up, but a sharp pain in her side stopped her, drawing a hiss from her lips. The sudden jolt grounded her. It was all real. The drowning weight in her returned, and with it, the image of his face, the one she had seen every time she dreamed.

Vaelric. He had been there again. Watching her. Chasing her. Sorcha shifted uncomfortably on the cot, her eyes flicking to Cat, who sat perched at her feet.

"Did you see him?" she asked quietly, her voice edged with unease.

"On the bridge. Did you see who it was?"

Cat paused mid lick, his silver eyes lifting to meet hers. His expression was unreadable, his twin tails twitching erratically.

"I saw someone," he said at last, his tone low. "But the shadows were thick. I couldn't see his face."

"It's him," Sorcha whispered, her voice trembling. "It's the same person who's been after me whenever the wisps appear. Vaelric, the Dark Druid."

At the mention of the name, Cat hissed, his ears flattening as his tails lashed violently. His silver eyes flared, and a string of curses in a language she didn't recognize escaped his mouth. He recoiled slightly, his gaze snapping to Kyron, who stood stiffly by Sorcha.

"What's going on?" Sorcha asked, her brows furrowing as she looked between them.

"Why are you reacting like that? What aren't you telling me?"

Cat's silver gaze shifted back to her, his frustration barely restrained. "Vaelric," he said, spitting the name like a poison.

"Of course, I've heard it. Everyone in the Otherworld has."

Sorcha's chest tightened. "Why?"

Cat's voice grew tighter, laced with anger. "He's draining magic, Sorcha. Sacred beings, the gods forgotten children, creatures tied to the Veil itself. He's ripping life from them, twisting them into husks, all to fuel his own power."

Her breath caught, and her hands tightened on the blanket draped over her legs. "Kyron told me he was stealing power from the half gods...And my parents? Is that why he turned them?"

Cat's glare snapped to Kyron, his silver eyes narrowing dangerously. "What has he told you?" he snapped, his twin tails whipping through the air.

"Enough," Kyron said, his voice steady but defensive. "She knows what happened to her parents. She knows Vaelric drained them and turned them into those monsters... that she had to kill. She knows that he's stealing power Cat. That I'm from the Tuatha, I'm here to protect her. But I didn't know about the rest, not the sacred creatures or the children. I told her what I could confirm."

Cat let out a bitter laugh. "Didn't know? You can't protect her by keeping her in the dark, Kyron. You've only made it worse."

Kyron's jaw tightened, his blue eyes darkening. "I wasn't keeping anything from her. I told her what I knew, what I could prove. It sounded like whispers, not truth."

"They aren't whispers," Cat hissed, his voice low and dangerous. "Vaelric isn't just building power. I'm telling you, he must be building an army. He's not satisfied with draining sacred creatures or the gods and anything else tied to the Veil. He's using that power he takes to strengthen himself and the Fomorians, to take back what he thinks was stolen from them by the Tuatha Dé Danann."

Sorcha's stomach churned, her mind racing. "Why? What does he want?"

"To destroy the Tuatha, to destroy and conquer everything. Both realms," Cat replied bluntly. "He's willing to poison both the mortal realm and the Otherworld to achieve his goal. He's already amassing an army,

Sorcha. Every creature you've seen crossing into this world they're either running from him or fighting for him."

Her heart twisted, the weight of his words pressing heavily on her chest. "But why me?" she asked, her voice breaking.

"Why is he after me?"

Cat's gaze softened, but his frustration still lingered. "Because of who you are, because of your bloodline, Sorcha. Your magic makes you a beacon, and he knows you're one of the few who could stand against him. Your father was the one to defeat Balor in the last battle. If you rise to the occasion, then you could stand to defeat him. Bres and Vaelric need to see that you don't raise an army. You must fall."

Sorcha shook her head, tears stinging her eyes. "You knew this, and you didn't tell me?" she snapped, her voice rising as she turned to Kyron.

Kyron stepped forward, his expression hard. "I didn't know this," he said firmly. "I suspected, yes, but I didn't have proof."

Cat scoffed, his tails flicking in irritation. "Your feelings for her clouded your judgment, Kyron. You should have told her everything, proof or not."

"STOP IT!" Sorcha snapped, cutting them both off. She turned to Cat, her voice trembling but forceful.

"What are the creatures in the Otherworld saying?"

Cat's anger simmered down slightly as he met her gaze. "Bres and Vaelric have been traveling between realms. The sacred lands are being poisoned, and the creatures tied to them are disappearing, drained or twisted into monsters. Old gods have started reappearing, and now creatures of the Veil have started crossing into the mortal world, hoping to escape him, but there's nowhere to run. Vaelric's power is growing, and with Samhain approaching, he'll use the thinning Veil to expand his reach. Create away for the creatures in the Veil to cross over. The more he taints the Otherworld, the more he thins the Veil between these worlds. Soon this world will be crawling with creatures."

Sorcha's hands trembled as she clenched the blanket tighter, her mind spinning with the enormity of what she'd just learned.

She swung her feet over the cot, planting them on the cold stone floor. Pressing her weight into her legs, she stood slowly, the sharp pain in her side making her wince. "Shit, that hurts," she muttered through clenched teeth.

Taking a few unsteady steps, she began gathering her belongings.

Kyron and Cat exchanged uneasy glances, prepared to step in. Sorcha caught their looks and shot them both a death glare.

"I'm going home now."

Kyron opened his mouth to protest, but Cat beat him to it.

"You can't just leave not in that state... can you?" His head tilted as he eyed her with faint disbelief.

"Watch me," Sorcha snapped, brushing past them.

Blood trickled faintly behind her as she walked out the door, ignoring the burning ache in her side. She made her way home without stopping, though much of the journey passed in a blur of sound and movement. Her thoughts spun endlessly, replaying everything Cat had revealed and everything Kyron hadn't. The weight of what lay ahead pressed down on her, and the looming reality of Samhain keeping her focused. When she reached her home, she threw the door open and slammed it shut behind her, leaning her entire body against it as she slid to the floor. Her head thudded back against the wood, her eyes slipping closed. She wasn't sure how long she stayed like, lost in the storm of her mind until she stirred, rubbing at her temples and blinking at the dim light of the room.

The hearth was cold, the embers long dead.

Outside, the sun was sinking low, casting warm streaks of orange and red through the windows. She groaned, her muscles aching as she shifted against the door.

*Gods, how long did I just sit here? My head is killing me.*

Using the door to push herself to her feet, she winced as the pain in her side flared again.

*This is going to leave one ugly scar.*

She glanced down at the faint traces of blood seeping through her bandages and caught the stench of sweat clinging to her skin.

*Manannán's breath, I need a bath. What else could possibly—*

The door slammed into the back of her head, cutting her thoughts short as she stumbled forward, cursing loudly.

"What in DAMNATION, Cat?!" she snarled, spinning to glare at the feline as he casually strolled inside.

Cat stopped mid stride, wrinkling his nose in exaggerated disgust. "Have you thought to bathe, dear? You smell horrid."

Sorcha opened her mouth to retort, but her side throbbed, cutting her off as fresh blood seeped through the bandages. She groaned and pressed a hand against it, muttering under her breath.

*I don't have time for this. I need to fix this wound first then I'll deal with everything else.*

Moving to her vanity, she unwrapped the bandages carefully and used her runes to cleanse and patch the wound as best as she could. The magic numbed the pain slightly, enough to give her some relief, but she still needed to clean herself properly. Grabbing fresh clothes, she headed toward the bath. The first sting of the hot water meeting her raw skin made her gasp, but the pain ebbed as she sank deeper into the tub. Finally, for the first time all day, the tension in her shoulders began to ease. She let out a soft sigh, leaning her head back against the rim of the tub, closing her eyes.

"MEEOOW"

Her eyes snapped open to find Cat perched smugly on the edge of the tub.

"Cat, for the love of—what are you doing in here?"

"Checking on you," Cat replied, his voice innocent, but the smirk tugging at his lips said otherwise.

"Cat. Privacy," as she pointed to the door.

"Privacy?" Cat said, cocking his head. "I'm not looking at your body! By the Gods Woman, I'm concerned about your mental state."

Sorcha groaned, sinking further into the water until it lapped at her chin. *Of all the creatures to be cursed with...* She resisted the urge to scream and instead fixed him with a death glare. "Please. Get. Out."

Cat sat there, unmoving, his tail swishing. "Is this better?" he asked, turning to face the door but remaining firmly planted on the tub's edge. "This is just ridiculous, you know?"

Her face burned red, equal parts mortified and enraged. "NOW, CAT!" she yelled, pointing furiously at the door.

With an exaggerated sigh, Cat hopped down and padded toward the door. The door closed behind him and Sorcha exhaled deeply, her hands coming up to rub her face. For a brief, blissful moment, the silence returned, and she let herself sink deeper into the warmth of the water. In this moment things felt normal, even if it was only a moment, she was grateful for it. As she emerged from the tub, sleep beckoned her, as terrifying as sleep felt. She looked to Cat "Will you stay with me tonight?"

Cat whispered, "Always, Sorcha." He padded over to her bed and waited for her to finish dressing before settling in beside her. "Goodnight, Sorcha," he murmured softly.

# Chapter 52
## THE MOMENT RUINED

Sorcha's eyelashes fluttered as she blinked awake, the morning light prying her from the restless, dreadful sleep she'd endured. She had spent the night tossing and turning, the ache in her side a constant reminder of her injury.Groaning softly, she turned her head and spotted Cat, still curled up and sleeping soundly.

"At least one of us slept well," she mumbled Carefully or so she thought, she tried to slide off

the bed without waking him, but her groggy limbs had other plans. She winced as a sudden twinge of pain shot through her side as her foot snagged on the tangled mess of clothes she'd discarded on the floor.

With all the grace of a drunken sparrow, she stumbled forward, catching herself on the corner of a chair with a muffled yelp. Her hair fell in a wild mess across her face as she froze, glancing over her shoulder at Cat, who remained blissfully undisturbed.

Her relief was short lived as she groaned and rubbed her side, muttering under her breath, "So much for a quiet exit."

Sorcha walked to the washroom, quietly closing the door behind her. She lifted her shirt and, as much as it hurt, removed the dressing. To her surprise, the cut had already healed. Sorcha had always healed quickly, but she had never really thought about it until now.

*Maybe it's because of my powers.*

The thought lingered as she recalled all the times she had been hurt—every cut, scrape, and bruise. But she couldn't think of many. Her hand moved to her head and arm, touching her most recent injuries. Both had healed so fast that she had nearly forgotten about them. Now, as her fingers brushed over her side, only a thin sliver of a scar and some bruising remained, hidden among her runes.

She changed her clothes, brushed her hair, and tied it back with a ribbon at the nape of her neck, leaving a few strands to frame her face. Emerging from the washroom, she found Cat still lying on her bed, now watching her as she moved around the room.

Cat lazily stretched. "Good morning, Sunshine.

Oh, I like *Sunshine*, it works."

Sorcha rolled her eyes. "And I suppose I should continue to call you *Cat*...?"

Cat, now leaping off the bed, padded toward her. "Cat works just fine. I'm not really a cat, and Cait Sídhe have many names. Mine is *Maelan*, but I'd rather not have others know my name... Cat is perfect."

Sorcha tilted her head, considering the name.

*Maelan.* She nodded. "Alright, *Cat*. It'll be our secret."

Cat was already making his way toward the kitchen when he turned back. "Thank you, *Sunshine*."

"Sorcha! It's *Sorcha—MAELAN*!" she called after him, a grin spreading across her face.

But Cat just kept walking, calling over his shoulder, "We have work to do, *Sunshine*! We have to find Kyron and the Commander and get your powers under control. We can't have you exploding fire or blinding half of us, now can we?"

Sorcha exhaled, shaking her head. She knew she didn't have much time. Samhain was only four days away, and she would have to work harder than ever to figure it all out.

She followed Cat into the living room when a steady thud... thud... thuddd... thud... thud echoed in rhythm against the door. Kyron stepped inside, greeting them with a wide smile and a wave, holding up a bag as if it were a peace offering, as though he expected an ambush the moment he entered.

"I brought food!" he announced in a singsong voice before stepping fully inside.

The rich smell of cinnamon, sugar, spices, and freshly baked bread filled the air. Sorcha's stomach rumbled in response, and even Cat was no better, licking his lips.

Kyron set the food on the table before walking over to Sorcha, his expression softer, more hesitant. "Are you alright? I didn't dare come by last night after the way you walked off. I know you're mad at me, and I'm sorry, Sorcha."

He took her hand, his touch warm, steady. With his free hand, he brushed a few stray strands of hair behind her ear, his fingers lingering for a moment. His gaze met hers, deep and unwavering.

"I care about you, Sorcha," he said, his voice low and sweet. "I'm sorry that in my desire to protect you, I ended up hurting you. I can't change that now, but I promise you I won't hide anything from you again. Even if I don't have all the answers myself."

He meant it. She could see it in the way he looked at her, the way he leaned in, mere inches from her lips. She could feel the warmth of his breath against her skin, as heat crept up her cheeks. Sorcha's breath caught in her throat. The warmth of his touch sent a ripple through her.

A loud, choking sound shattered the moment.

Followed by gagging. Then what could only be described as someone drowning in their own disgust.

"Please, for the love of the gods and all things Otherworldly, STOP IT!" Cat hacked violently, his body convulsing. "That was just... disgusting. Kyron, that was the best you had?"

Kyron barely had time to react before Cat dramatically gagged again, this time coughing up an actual hairball. He spat it onto the floor and glared at them.

"SEE? YOU MAKE ME SICK!"

Kyron turned a shade of red so deep it could rival the autumn leaves. Sorcha, on the other hand, lost all composure, doubling over with laughter.

"I'm sorry, Kyron—" she gasped between wheezes, clutching her stomach. "It's Cat!"

Kyron groaned, rubbing a hand over his flushed face while Cat smugly licked his paw, looking far too pleased with himself.

Still grinning, Sorcha took a deep breath, finally regaining control. "I accept your apology, Kyron. Now, let's eat."

They sat to eat, giving Cat his own small mound of food of his choosing, before diving into a discussion about Commander Nethran, the Circle, and everything Sorcha needed to know before entering the Veil. The conversation was heavy, but Cat kept it from becoming too serious with his snarky remarks and ever growing confidence in giving unsolicited advice. Eventually, their talk boiled down to three key points:

- Sorcha needed to gain better control of her power, working with someone who could teach her how to harness and manipulate it properly.

- They needed to convince some of her friends to follow her to Samhain, she would need protection during their descent into the Veil.

- They had to prepare to survive in the Otherworld... somehow

Once they finished eating, they all filed out the door and made their way to Commander Nethran's office at the Druid School. Nethran looked fatigued, deep shadows bruising the skin beneath his eyes, exhaustion etched into every line of his face. It was clear he hadn't slept. He hovered over stacks of books and scrolls, looking older than the building itself. His bloodshot gaze lifted when Sorcha entered, and he leaned back in his chair, rubbing his temples before exhaling heavily.

"Glad to see your encounter hasn't slowed you down," he said, his eyes flickering briefly to her side before returning to her face. "I know we need to talk, but I need coffee and some food." He stood abruptly, already heading for the door. "Wait here. Read through these scrolls. I'll be back soon." Without another word, he shut the door behind him.

Sorcha turned to Kyron. "That was weird, right?" Kyron nodded, his gaze drifting over the disaster that was Nethran's desk. Papers were scattered everywhere, as if a small tornado had torn through the room.

"I'm not sure what that was about," Kyron muttered, stepping closer to the mess, "but it looks like he was doing some serious research... maybe he found something."

Sorcha and Cat lingered by the door, watching as Kyron sifted through the documents. Then, something caught Cat's attention. In the corner of Nethran's desk lay an ornate scroll, its edges gold and green, covered in a script Sorcha didn't recognize. But Kyron and Cat did. With incredible grace, Cat leaped onto the desk, landing as softly as a feather, not disturb-ing a single page. He walked over delicately, his silver eyes flickering as he pawed at the scroll, rolling out the parchment. His gaze widened. The silver in his irises churned violently as he read. He suddenly stopped and looked at Sorcha.

"I have a good idea why he needed a break." Kyron and Sorcha ex-changed glances before turning back to Cat, who seemed... tense. "This," Cat continued, his voice unusually serious, "is a recorded account of the Veil. A detailed list of creatures, gods, the Tuatha Dé Danann, even a map." He flicked his tail, his eyes scanning the words again. "And this was written by a Fae."

Sorcha stiffened.

"This is Fae script. It's old. And this was not shared easily..." Cat's voice dropped lower, the weight of his words settling into the room. "There isn't a creature in existence that would willingly give up this information... unless..." His silver eyes darkened, his expression distant, lost in thought. "Unless it was trapped." A cold prickle ran down Sorcha's spine. "It would have taken someone very clever to bind a Fae," Cat murmured. "By bar-gain, iron." His voice faltered. His eyes darted to Sorcha. "Or by name."

"There are many secrets to trapping the Fae," Cat continued. "Luckily, this doesn't list all of them. But it gives you enough, Sorcha. Enough to know what we're up against. Enough to guide you."

He pawed the scroll completely open, revealing a parchment inscribed with a map generalized, yet marked with specific locations to avoid. It also detailed how to fight the wraiths, witches, and fairies they would encounter.

Cat read aloud the materials they would need for protection: "Iron, holy water, blessed objects, rowan wood, red thread, salt, and fire."

His voice was clear and deliberate, Sorcha wasted no time scribbling it all down. She then took another piece of parchment, tracing the map while carefully. noting every detail, name, and area of importance.

Once done, Cat gently rolled the scroll back up and set it precisely where it had been. Just as if he had planned it, Commander Nethran returned. Sorcha turned, prepared to ask him about the scroll, but before she could, he abruptly cut her off, speaking loudly.

"That is an ancient text, not meant for anyone other than the Elder Druids or the High Council. I'm not sure how it ended up here, but I'm certain it was an accident. I will be returning it to the library archives immediately."

His gaze darting between them. A slow, careful nod followed, his expression telling them everything they needed to know they were being watched.

Sorcha caught the message and responded accordingly. "Yes, sir. Of course."

At that moment, the sound of heavy footsteps echoed outside the door, pacing back and forth. Whoever was out there was waiting for the Commander.

Kyron met Nethran's gaze before speaking. "Apologies for disturbing you, sir. We'll speak another time."

As Sorcha, Kyron, and Cat turned to leave, the heavy sound of footsteps echoed beyond the door were deliberate and unhurried. Whoever was there had been waiting and listening. The moment the door swung open, they were met with the piercing gazes of two elder druids standing just outside.

Their robes, dark and heavy with embroidered symbols of rank, seemed to add to the weight of their presence. Lines of worry creased their faces, their expressions carved from stone, somber, unwavering. One druid, an older man with silver streaked hair and deep set eyes, studied them with the quiet intensity of someone who already knew too much. The other, a woman with sharp cheekbones and a stern mouth. She crossed her arms over her chest, her fingers tapping against the worn leather of her sleeves restrained frustration barely concealed.

Sorcha's throat tightened, but she forced herself to hold their gaze, to keep her expression neutral. Kyron stiffened beside her, his shoulders squared, while Cat flicked his tail, eyes darting between them and the commander.

Commander Nethran, to his credit, remained unreadable. He stepped forward, his expression a mask of calm authority. "Elders," he greeted them smoothly, though Sorcha didn't miss the slight tension in his voice.

Neither druid immediately responded. Instead, they exchanged a glance silent. After a few moments, the older one spoke, his voice stern and slow.

"We need to speak. Now."

It wasn't a request. Sorcha swallowed hard. Whatever was happening here, they didn't want to be involved in it.

Exiting Commander Nethran's office, Sorcha pulled her cloak tighter against the crisp autumn air. The sun hung high in the sky, casting golden light over the rooftops, but the chill of late October lingered, biting at her skin. A thin mist clung to the cobbled streets, curling around doorsteps, and the scent of damp earth and distant wood smoke filled the air.

The plan had been simple track everyone down, one by one, and tell them to meet at the tavern that evening. They weren't going to pull them from their posts. Tonight, they would finally lay it all out: the Veil, Vaelric, the creatures stirring on the other side, and the war creeping ever closer.

Sorcha sighed, her breath visible in the cold.

Kyron, walking beside her, smirked. "You keep doing that. You know, sighing dramatically isn't a strategy."

Sorcha shot him a look. "It is if I do it enough times and the problem disappears."

Kyron chuckled. "Let me know how that works out for you."

They were making their way toward the post when a loud burst of laughter cut through the market square Drystan's, unmistakable and full of mischief.

Her gut twisted at the sound. It had been a long time since she'd heard such an easy, carefree laugh. A time when Emry would have been right there beside him, adding his own wry remarks, making her roll her eyes even as she smiled. The absence of his voice stung, settling into a familiar ache in her chest.

Kyron glanced at her but said nothing, giving her the space to process.

Then, as if reading her mind, he jerked his chin toward the tavern. "Might as well just go for it."

Sorcha exhaled slowly. "Let's get this over with."

Pushing open the heavy wooden door, they were met with the comforting warmth of the tavern. The scent of spiced cider and roasting meat filled the air, mingling with the crackling fire in the hearth. Lanterns flickered overhead, casting a golden glow over the room.

And there, gathered near the center, was nearly everyone they had been looking for.

Drystan, leaning back in his chair with a grin, was in the middle of telling some exaggerated story, arms waving dramatically. Eirin sat across from him, arms crossed, shaking his head at whatever nonsense was spilling from Drystan's mouth. Mason, half listening, his attention more on the plate of food in front of him, while Rhosyn and a few others were lost in quiet conversation at the nearby table.

This wasn't a coincidence.

Nethran must have known this conversation had to happen, had likely worked it out in his head that Sorcha would track them down or they'd find him first. And since he was tied up in his own meeting at the Druid School, he had given them the space to start this on their own.

Kyron leaned in slightly, lowering his voice. "Well, that saves us some time."

Sorcha swallowed, her fingers curling into the edge of her cloak. She had been dreading this moment, not just because of what they had to discuss, but because she had barely spoken to any of them since her abrupt announcement about who she was. Especially Eirin.

Eirin... his gaze locked onto hers the moment she stepped inside. Sorcha's breath hitched, her pulse skipping, but she forced herself to keep walking. To pretend she didn't feel the warmth of every moment they had shared pressing against her like a ghost.

She had come here to tell them the plan. To prepare for what was coming. But as she stepped further into the room, she realized she wasn't sure if she was ready to face Eirin, or what came next.

She could feel the weight of that avoidance settle over her now, pressing into the space between them. She had feelings for him there was no denying that but she also had feelings for Kyron, and the confusion of it all had kept her distant. And then there was Emry, the guilt that gnawed at her for failing him, and the sting of Riona's absence, now somewhere far in the north.

She met Eirin's gaze briefly before looking at the others, her fingers tightening into fists at her sides.

"I need to tell you all the truth about what's coming."

Drystan, who had been mid sip of his drink, set his mug down slowly. Rhosyn leaned in slightly, her gaze locked onto Sorcha. Even Mason straightened in his chair.

Sorcha exhaled. "We know who's behind the decay and monsters... It's Bres, the ex-king of The Tuatha and Fomorians, and his son Vaelric... he isn't just gathering power, he's hunting others like me. Other children born with gifts. He's raising an army, But he's not looking to recruit them. He's looking to drain them. He takes their power for his own..."

A few of them stiffened. Eirin's eyes locked into hers. Sorcha forced herself to keep going. "He's twisting them. If he succeeds, they won't just be fighting alongside the Fomorians they'll become something far worse." She let that sink in before continuing. "I need to find them first. To warn them, to tell them what's coming. Maybe some of them will join me. Maybe some of them won't. But they deserve to know."

The silence stretched.

"Gods," Drystan muttered, running a hand through his hair. "So you're telling us we either fight these half gods or save them?"

"Save them," Sorcha corrected firmly. "If I can reach them in time."

Rhosyn frowned. "And if you can't?"

Sorcha clenched her fists, hating the answer she had to give. "Then we fight."

A heavy tension settled over them.

"And what about your power?" Eirin asked, his voice quiet but steady. "You still don't have control."

Sorcha met his gaze, her throat tightening. "I know. That's why I need to train. I need to learn how to use it, to wield it before it wields me. If I go into this blind, I'll be just as dangerous as the things we're fighting."

Kyron crossed his arms, his expression unreadable. "And how exactly do you plan to do that?"

She hesitated before looking down at Cat. "With help."

Cat let out a long suffering sigh. "Finally, she admits she needs me."

Drystan snorted, but the humor didn't reach his eyes. "So let me get this straight. We go to Samhain, you cross the Veil, and while you're off speaking to the Tuatha Dé Danann, we're stuck dealing with creatures, Fomorians, and possibly a handful of kids that Vaelric is turning into monsters?"

Sorcha lifted her chin. "That's the plan." Drystan exhaled. "You're lucky I love chaos."

Eirin still hadn't looked away from her, his expression unreadable. "You'll need someone to watch your back."

Sorcha's stomach tightened. "I know."

Eirin nodded once. "Then I'm going."

Kyron's gaze flickered between them before he sighed, running a hand through his hair.

Rhosyn smirked. "Well, someone has to make sure you don't all die."

Eirin, still unreadable, simply nodded.

Sorcha let out a breath she hadn't realized she was holding. "Thank you."

Drystan clapped his hands together, grinning. "Well, this should be interesting."

Eirin's gaze lingered on her for a moment longer. Sorcha swallowed hard, trying to ignore the way her heart was beating too fast.

Mason leaned forward "I'll pick the cadets to stay behind and watch over Lumora. We need the strongest, the smartest, the ones who won't hesitate if trouble comes."

Drystan stretched out in his chair with an easy grin. "That leaves me and Eirin to build targets for Sorcha's training. We'll make sure they can actually withstand her magic."

Eirin grunted in agreement. "And reinforce them properly so she doesn't bring the whole damn training grounds down."

Rhosyn leaned in, her eyes settling on Sorcha. "And I'll help you control that power. You need precision, not just strength. If you want to wield it properly, you'll have to learn how to manipulate it, not just let it explode."

Sorcha turned to Cat, narrowing her eyes. "And you didn't think to mention that you could help earlier because...?"

Cat stretched lazily, flicking his tail. "Where's the fun in that?" His silver eyes gleamed with mischief. "Besides, nothing like a little pressure to bring out the best in you."

Sorcha exhaled loudly. "You're impossible."

"And yet, you keep me around."

Eirin drummed his fingers against the table. "The commander will enhance the horses, so we can make it to Samhain in a day's ride, but that still only gives us three days to prepare. If we're doing this, we do it right."

Sorcha's chest tightened as she looked at them, at the weight they had taken on without hesitation.

She took a breath and nodded. "Then we start now."

# Chapter 53
## TRAINING

The field stretched wide, golden grass swaying in the late afternoon October breeze. At the far edge of town, where an old patrol tower stood unoccupied, Sorcha rolled her shoulders, trying to ignore the nervous energy humming in her chest. She had spent the past few days avoiding her emotions, but now, standing opposite Rhosyn, there was no more time to run from what she was.

"You need to stop thinking so much," Rhosyn said, crossing her arms, her eyes studying Sorcha like a puzzle she intended to solve. "Magic isn't just power, it's the connection. It's no different than using our runes. You're not wielding a weapon. You're commanding a part of yourself. You need to feel it, not force it."

Sorcha exhaled slowly. "Alright. So, what? I just... tell it what to do? It doesn't work like the runes or Druid magic, it does what it wants."

"Not tell. Listen. Listen to your body Sorcha." Rhosyn's voice softened. She knelt down, pressing her hands to the ground. "Your Magic is alive. The world responds when you understand how to ask. Watch."

At her touch, the earth shifted. Green tendrils of vine slithered from the soil, weaving together in intricate, writhing knots. Then, with barely a flick of her wrist, the vines snapped forward, wrapping around Sorcha's arms and legs. Before she could react, she was yanked into the air.

"Rhosyn!" Sorcha yelped, struggling as the vines held her aloft, suspending her midair.

Rhosyn only grinned. "See? The vines listen. They trust me."

She made a small motion with her fingers, and the vines twisted again, gently lowering Sorcha before setting her on her feet.

Sorcha glared at her. "I had no idea how powerful you are! You could've warned me."

"Why else would I be head of magic? I've been doing this awhile, the more you cast it, the better you'll get" She smirked "Oh, and you could've stopped that attack, you've been slacking on your rune training," Rhosyn countered, raising a brow. "That's what we're here for.

With a flick of her hand, she gestured toward the towering trees surrounding the field. At her silent call, the branches groaned as they twisted downward, the limbs stretching unnaturally before whipping out violently, striking at the air.

"You're part of this world, Sorcha but also the otherworld. You have to feel that other part of you, locked away somewhere, hidden. Find it." Rhosyn stepped closer, lowering her voice. "Close your eyes."

Sorcha hesitated, then obeyed.

"Breathe deep. Feel the sun on your skin, the ground beneath your feet. What does your magic do when the light touches them?"

Sorcha's body slowed. She felt the warmth of the sun filtering through her skin, igniting deep within her, she thought of the battle, Commander Nethran, the Fomorians, Emry. Her runes tingled, no, they burned, with a steady rhythm that matched her own heartbeat. She reached for that feeling, let herself sink into it.

Then, light erupted from her.

A brilliant white blast flared across the field, blinding but not painful. Rhosyn turned her face away from the sheer intensity of it. When the light dimmed enough for her to see, she gasped. Sorcha stood at the center of it all, transformed.

Her runes, once a faint glow, now shone like molten starlight, white hot against her skin. Her hair shimmered with fiery gold, catching the light in restless flickers. Her eyes, no longer green, had turned to swirling liquid gold, flecked with large specks of emerald.

Sorcha stared at her hands, her fingers trembling. The runes along her arms glowed faintly, still radiating soft tendrils of white light.

Rhosyn's lips parted in awe before she stepped forward and pulled Sorcha into a fierce hug. "You did it," she murmured, pride thick in her voice. "You finally let go."

But Sorcha barely heard her. The power still buzzed beneath her skin, demanding more. She stepped back, lifting her hands again, and this time, she willed the light to bend.

Threads of light spun from her fingertips, coiling and twisting like sun threads. She shaped them, wove them into something tangible. The air crackled with power as the threads took form. A creature slithered into existence.

It emerged from the golden strands, a serpentine in shape, glowing like a creature born from the heart of the sun. It coiled, its shimmering body pulsing with raw energy, rows of gleaming, translucent fangs lining its mouth. Its eyes flickered like embers, and when it opened its mouth fire roared to life within its throat. Sorcha's gasped. The fire grew, surging forward aimed straight at Rhosyn.

Before she could react, a blur of movement cut between them.

Cat.

But not as he was before. Where the small feline had stood now loomed a massive, jaguar-like beast, nearly the size of a human on all fours. His sleek black fur shimmered, the silver markings along his body pulsing with an ancient power. His tails, long and whip like lashed through the air as he let out a thunderous roar that shook the ground. The force of it shattered the construct.

Sorcha's creation exploded into embers, threads of light dissolving into nothing. The fire that had threatened Rhosyn vanished in an instant.

Cat shifted his enormous form back into a house cat. With a final flick of his tail, he sat primly at Sorcha's feet, licking his paw as though nothing had happened. Sorcha wide eyed and stunned looked at Rhosyn and Cat.

Sorcha opened her mouth and began to apologize "I'm sor— "

"I really shouldn't have to save you from yourself," he interrupted, his tone exasperated. "Honestly, Sunshine, I thought we were past the accidental murder stage."

Sorcha let out a breathless laugh, shaking her head in disbelief. "I didn't know that was your true form, I thought it was just part of the dream…You didn't tell me?"

Cat smirked, eyes flashing silver. "I didn't think you'd all handle it well if I started the journey by being the size of a horse. Humans tend to panic."

"Panic?" Rhosyn scoffed. "I watched a serpent made of pure light nearly incinerate me, only for you to explode into a gods damned shadow beast and roar it out of existence. I think I'm entitled to a bit of panic."

Well," he mused, "it was dramatic. Another second and you would've become the next verse of my favorite nursery rhyme."

Sorcha's breath was still ragged as she stared at him. "What?"

His silver eyes gleamed as his voice dipped into a lilting sing song. "Ashes, ashes, we all fall down."

Rhosyn stifled a breath, brushing soot from her sleeve. "Charming."

"You're welcome, by the way," Cat added, flashing a lazy grin before stepping back. Sorcha swallowed, still feeling the remnants of her magic buzzing beneath her skin. She turned to Cat, her voice quieter. "Why didn't you tell me?"

Cat tilted his head, as if genuinely considering. "I could have," he mused. "But where's the fun in that?"

Sorcha gave him a deadpan look. "Fun? I nearly burned Rhosyn alive."

"Yes, and it was terrifying. You should be proud," he said smoothly, then yawned. "Besides, I did stop you. So technically, no harm done."

Rhosyn, who still looked a little winded, eyed Cat again. "So that is what you are. A Cait Sídhe. And a powerful one, if I had to guess."

Cat's eyes gleamed. "*The* Cait Sídhe, darling," he corrected smoothly, his voice silk and shadow. "And you haven't even seen the half of it."

None of them had ever truly questioned what Cat was capable of. He had always been clever and knowing. But this?

Cat stretched, flicking his tail, and turned away. his usual casual demeanor sliding back into place like a well-worn mask.

Rhosyn exhaled, rubbing her temples. "Right. Well. That was horrifying. But also... effective."

She turned back to Sorcha. "Your power is raw, but I can teach you to control it. No more accidental summoning of light serpents with a god complex, alright?"

Sorcha huffed a laugh, shaking off her lingering unease. "No promises."

Rhosyn rolled her eyes. "God's help us all."

Training had been relentless. Morning until night, Sorcha had been pushed to her limits, her body aching in ways she hadn't thought possible.

The weight of their mission loomed over them But tonight, for just a moment, they could breathe.

The tavern was warm, filled with the low hum of conversation, the clatter of tankards meeting wood, and the occasional burst of laughter from Drystan, who seemed to be regaling Eirin with some wild tale. The fire crackled in the hearth, casting flickering light over their faces as the group nursed their drinks.

Eirin was the first to leave, stretching as he pushed back from the table. "I've got some things to take care of," he said, his tone unreadable. His gaze lingered on Sorcha for a second longer than necessary before he turned and disappeared into the night.

Cat followed soon after, yawning dramatically. "Well, this has been delightful, but I think I'll go exploring. Perhaps I'll find something interesting... or pretty to borrow." His eyes gleamed with mischief. He flicked his tail lazily before adding, "Goodnight, Sunshine."

And then it was just her and Kyron. Sorcha exhaled, the tavern suddenly feeling smaller, warmer. Kyron leaned back in his chair, watching her.

"Come on," he said finally, pushing to his feet. "Let me walk you home."

She nodded as slight grin reached her lips.

The streets were quiet, the night crisp. Their boots crunched against the cobblestone, mist curling around the edges of the lantern lit path.

She was exhausted, but not too exhausted to feel the way his presence wrapped around her, steady and warm despite the chill.

When they reached her door, she turned to thank him but before she could, Kyron stepped closer, invading the space between them.

"Sorcha." His voice was low, rough around the edges.

She swallowed hard. "Yes?"

His fingers brushed against her wrist light and her pulse fluttered.

Kyron inhaled loudly as if waging some internal battle but then gave in. The space between them disappeared. His lips crashed against hers. Sorcha gasped into the kiss, fingers tangling in his shirt, pulling him closer instead of pushing him away. His hands found her waist, anchoring her. It was a messy, breathless tangle of limbs and heat that it made her head spin.

They stumbled inside, barely making it past the threshold before Kyron's hands were on her again, his body pressing her back against the door as his mouth claimed hers. She wasn't sure who pulled who first, but suddenly they were moving, tripping over each other, lost in the haze of it. Somehow, they ended up in front of the hearth.

Kyron lowered her onto the rug, his body hovering over hers, the firelight casting golden embers across his face. She wanted this, she wanted him. He kissed a slow trail down her throat, his mouth lingering where her pulse beat just beneath the skin. His tongue tracing the line of her collarbone, tasting salt and the faint earthy tang of magic that always clung to her.

He moved lower, his mouth charting a path down her body. Between kisses, his tongue swirled against her skin, teasing the spaces between. When he reached the hollow between her breasts she curled her fingers into his hair, holding him there just for a moment longer as he lifted her shirt. Cool air slid over her exposed skin, chasing the heat his mouth left behind. He continued to kiss her stomach slow, each press of his lips torching a fire inside her. When he reached her navel, he paused. His breath skated over her skin, and the heat of it sent more shivers through her. He dipped lower, lips grazing just above the band of her pants. His tongue traced a single, deliberate line across the sensitive strip of skin that made her stomach tighten.

Then he looked up, his eyes locked on hers as she held his gaze. He kissed her again, deep and slow, his hips rolling against hers as she wrapped her legs around him. He reached for the button of her pants when her hands flattened against his chest.

Kyron froze, breath hitching as he looked down at her. They were tangled together, heat coiling, the air between them charged, but he didn't push.

Her fingers curled into his tunic. "I can't."

Kyron didn't move for a long moment. Then, slowly, he exhaled. "Is everything okay?"

Sorcha bit her lip, forcing the words out even though they tasted bitter. "I don't know what's going to happen after tonight. I don't know if I'll make it out of the Veil."

He bit the inside of cheek and spoke gently.

"You will."

"I might not." She stared into the fire as she spoke. "And I can't... I can't let us get mixed up, not with so much at stake."

Kyron sat up, running a hand over his face.

"I understand." His voice was quiet and she flinched at the softness in it. She wished he would scream, get angry or upset because it would make this whole situation easier to end.

"I don't want to start something I can't finish," she admitted, continuing to try and explain, her voice barely above a whisper. "Not when everything is this uncertain."

Kyron exhaled, his gaze sweeping over her face and body like he was trying to memorize every curve of her.

Finally, after what felt like an eternity, he nodded.

And after another long, heavy silence, he huffed a quiet laugh.

"You're going to ruin me, Sorcha."

She turned to him, blinking back the sting behind her eyes. She smiled softly. "I think that's *a you* problem."

His lips twitched into a slight smile as he reached for her hand. And in the quiet, with the fire burning low, they stayed like that. The silence between them stretched as the fire crackled low in the hearth, casting golden embers over his face once more.

His exhale broke the silence, raking a hand through his hair. "I should go."

She almost told him to stay but instead, she only nodded.

Kyron pushed himself to his feet, grabbing his cloak and heading for the door. He paused as he reached it, his hand resting on the wood for a fraction longer than necessary. For a moment he hesitated, as if he might turn back.

Without another word he pulled the door open and began to step into the night when Cat sauntered in, of course Perfectly timed. Kyron barely had time to react before the Cait Sídhe effortlessly slipped past him, his tail flicking in what was definitely smug amusement.

"Good talk?" Cat purred. He cast a knowing glance at Sorcha, his silver eyes gleaming in the firelight. "Very productive, I see."

Kyron huffed a short, humorless laugh, shaking his head as he stepped fully outside. "You're a menace."

Cat grinned, all sharp teeth and satisfaction. "I know."

Kyron hesitated for only a moment longer before closing the door behind him, leaving Sorcha alone with Cat and the dying embers of the fire. The weight of everything settled over her as she let out a slow breath, pressing her fingers against her temples. *Gods. That was... a lot.*

She turned to Cat, who was already stretching luxuriously on the rug, looking far too pleased with himself.

"What?" she muttered.

Cat merely flicked his tail. "Oh, nothing. Just enjoying the show."

Sorcha groaned, throwing a pillow at him.

Cat dodged it effortlessly, smirking. "A little tense, are we?"

"Cat."

"Yes, Sunshine?"

She sighed, flopping back against the rug.

"Shut up."

Cat purred, utterly unbothered. "Never."

And with that, the fire crackled as the night stretched on, and Sorcha was left with the lingering warmth of what was left unfinished.

# Chapter 54
# A RACE AGAINST TIME

Sorcha spent the next two days training relentlessly. Each sunrise bled into sunset with barely a breath in between. Every morning, she stepped onto the training grounds, and every night, she left more exhausted than the day before. Rhosyn, Commander Nethran, and Cat pushed her harder, making sure she had full control over her abilities or at least enough to keep from burning the place down. She had managed to conjure creatures from sun threads, summon small fireballs, and wield a whip of liquid light that incinerated anything it touched.

Kyron, Eirin, and Drystan had the unfortunate job of being moving targets. Clad in full armor, they held up wooden planks, bracing themselves for whatever Sorcha threw at them. By the end of the second day, most of their time was spent dodging, rolling, and throwing themselves behind cover.

Drystan, in particular, suffered the worst of it. One poorly aimed fireball hit his helmet dead on, leaving nothing but a cloud of embers and an unfortunate consequence; his pants catching fire. What followed was absolute chaos. Drystan tore off his armor, sprinting across the training grounds, flailing and cursing as flames licked up his legs. Cat was doubled over, wheezing with laughter. Rhosyn, between fits of giggles, still managed to summon a wave of water, drenching Drystan from head to toe. He stood there, soaked and miserable, his once pristine tunic dripping onto the dirt. "I'm done," he declared flatly, throwing up his hands. "I'm absolutely done."

For the rest of the day, the remaining guys had to draw sticks to decide who would be next in Sorcha's line of fire. Exhaustion was a permanent weight on Sorcha's limbs. The others fared no better. Drystan had yet to forgive her, Kyron had nearly taken an ember to the face as well and even Eirin was beginning to regret volunteering. But there was no time to slow down. Each session pushed her further, each spell growing stronger, wilder. And still, it wasn't enough. She trained from dawn until long after nightfall, her body moving on pure determination alone. Sleep was scarce. The few hours she managed to steal were restless, her mind too busy memorizing maps and scrawled notes. Every spare moment was spent gathering supplies. Commander Nethran had called upon the High Druids and priests to bless their weapons, gear, and even the clothing they would wear. She packed canteens full of holy water, checked and rechecked their provisions. If she wasn't training, she was preparing. There was no room for hesitation. No room for failure. At the end of the third day, Eirin found her.

She was sitting on the edge of a wooden bench near the forge, rolling the stiffness from her shoulders when he approached. Without a word, he handed her a small box, a deep blue ribbon tied neatly around it.

Sorcha blinked at it, then at him. "What's this?" "Just open it, don't think I forgot your birthday,"

Eirin said, his voice softer than usual.

Sorcha smirked as tugged at the ends of the ribbon, letting it fall away before lifting the lid. Inside, resting on soft cloth, were four intricately carved bracelets made of silver, each one etched with runes of protection.

She traced a finger over the delicate engravings. The weight of them was solid, grounding.

"I wanted you to have something on you at all times that could protect you," Eirin said. "I had two made for each wrist."

She looked up at him. His smile wasn't the usual smirk, nor the warm, easy grin she had grown used to.

There was a sadness behind it. Unspoken words lingered between them. It wasn't until Kyron saw the exchange that a sharp pang of jealousy flared in his chest. The way Eirin looked at her, the way she looked back, it burned through him. He had known from the moment they met that he had feelings for Sorcha. And he knew, perhaps, that Eirin loved her too. But she had feelings for him as well, he was sure of it. He clenched his fists at his sides, heat crawling up his spine. He would prove himself. He would show her that she was meant for him, not Eirin. He just had to make her see it.

Lost in thought, he didn't realize he had been staring until a voice cut through the moment.

Cat cleared his throat. "Cat got your tongue?" Kyron snapped his gaze to him, his glare ice cold.

Cat grinned, unbothered. "Ooooh, I think we've struck a nerve."

The tavern was warm, filled with the scent of spiced cider, roasted meat, and the low hum of conversation. But beneath the comfortable noise, tension curled at the edges of the room like a slow building storm. Sorcha sat at their usual table, absentmindedly running her fingers over the rim of her cup, her mind already miles ahead on the path they would take, on the Veil, on what lay beyond it.

Commander Nethran cleared his throat, breaking the lull in conversation. "Let's go over the plan one last time." His gaze settled on Sorcha. "We ride at dawn. It'll take nearly a full day to reach the outskirts of Cailleach's Keep with the horses imbued with magic. Once you're there, you'll be escorted to the Veil."

Sorcha nodded. "No one else should follow. Kyron and Cat will go with me. The rest of you stay behind."

Eirin, who had been quiet for most of the night, finally spoke. "That's a mistake."

Sorcha sighed. "Eirin—"

"You shouldn't go in with just them," he pressed, leaning forward, his voice edged with frustration. "You'll need another fighter. Someone who can watch your back."

"I can watch my own back."

His teeth clenched. "That's not the point."

Before she could argue, Cat stretched lazily from where he perched on the table, tail flicking like he had been waiting for this moment.

"Oh, Eirin," he purred, silver eyes gleaming. "You're one of Lumora's elite. If anything happens, you're the best chance they have at defending the city. And, more importantly..." He tilted his head toward Sorcha. "You and Kyron don't exactly bring *neutral* energy to the mission, do you?"

Eirin's expression darkened, his fists clenching at his sides.

Sorcha stiffened, but she couldn't argue. Cat wasn't wrong. If Eirin and Kyron went with her, there would be too much *unsaid* lingering between them.

She needed someone who wouldn't complicate things. She swallowed, choosing her words carefully. "If I had to take someone else, it would be Drystan or Rhosyn."

Drystan, who had been listening with mild interest, grinned. "I'm available."

Rhosyn rolled her eyes. "No one asked you."

Sorcha ignored them, looking back at Eirin. "But I won't risk you, or anyone else, for this. You're needed here, we just need some of you to ride with us and make sure we make it across."

Eirin's gaze burned into hers, but he didn't argue.

She didn't know what he wanted to say, what *he would have said* if they weren't in a room full of people but after a long moment, leaned back in his chair.

Kyron, who had been watching all of this with a careful expression, finally spoke. "We need to be focused when we cross. The Veil isn't like anything in this world. It shifts, and if we aren't careful, we could end up somewhere far worse than where we need to be."

Sorcha nodded. "That's why we need Cat. He knows a fairy mound that will take us across with the least resistance. It's our best chance of making it through without immediately running into something we don't want to face."

Commander Nethran's gaze swept over them all. "Then it's settled."

Sorcha barely heard him. She could still feel the tension crackling in the air, Eirin's stare heavy on her skin, Kyron's presence a reason for tension.

Cat, ever observant, tilted his head at her, a knowing smirk playing on his lips.

She ignored him. Tomorrow, they would ride. The streets of Lumora were quiet at this hour, lanterns flickering in their iron sconces, casting soft golden halos over the cobblestone paths. The night was crisp, cool air curling around them as Sorcha and Cat walked in easy silence, the sounds of the tavern fading behind them. The others had stayed behind, lingering over their drinks, laughter still echoing faintly in the distance. But Sorcha had wanted to leave early. Maybe she just needed a moment of peace before everything changed. And Cat, for once, had followed without a quip, padding beside her, his silver eyes reflecting the torchlight like mirrors.

They walked at a slow pace, unhurried, her boots tapping lightly against the worn stone roads. It felt different tonight. The weight of what was coming settled between them. As they reached the heart of town, the Skyfall Fountain shimmered ahead, water vapors rising where the cascade met the basin. Beyond it, the towering cliffs cradled the true falls, water spilling down in torrents of silver, crashing into the depths below.

Sorcha paused at the edge of the square, her eyes drawn to the waterfall.

"There's a story about these falls," she murmured. Cat tilted his head, watching her. "Oh?"

She nodded, wrapping her arms around herself against the night chill. "It's said they come from the Otherworld. That the water flows between realms. That this place is a meeting point, where the Veil is thinner."

Cat was silent for a long moment, his tail flicking lazily as he stared at the rushing water. Then he let out a soft hum. "That would explain a few things."

Sorcha huffed a quiet laugh. "You believe it?" "Would you believe me if I said I've seen stranger

things?" His voice was filled with mischief.

She turned to him then, studying the way the moonlight played across his features, the way his silver eyes caught the glow of the falls

He had given her his name. A gift and she hadn't really said what she needed to.

"I want you to know," she said softly, "I won't betray you, Cat."

His gaze flickered to hers.

She swallowed, holding his stare. "I understand what it means that you trusted me with your name. I know how much that cost you. And I need you to know, I would never use it against you. Never."

His expression shifted. For once, he didn't have some quick witted remark, some playful deflection. Instead, he smiled small, but real. "I know."

Sorcha exhaled and before she could stop herself, she whispered, "I'm scared, Cat."

His ears flicked. "Of what's coming?"

"Of what I might become," she admitted.

"Of what happens if I fail."

Cat studied her for a long moment, then sighed, stepping closer. "Then I guess it's a good thing you have me, isn't it?"

She looked at him, searching. "You're bound to me now, aren't you?"

"I am." He didn't hesitate.

Her throat tightened. "You chose that?"

"I did."

"Why?"

He exhaled, the smirk falling from his face, something gentler taking its place.

"Because you're worth it."

Sorcha blinked, caught off guard by the simple sincerity of it. Before she could speak, Cat stretched, rolling his shoulders as he turned toward the road again. "Now, come on, Sunshine. You need sleep. And so do I, apparently." She let out a quiet laugh, shaking her head, but followed him down the path, casting one last glance at the waterfall.

A meeting place. A threshold between worlds. She only hoped, when the time came, she would find her way back.

# Chapter 55
## SAMHAIN

The morning of Samhain arrived with November's frostbitten kiss waiting on the wind, a silent herald of the season's turn. The smell of wood smoke from Cailleach's Keep curled through the wind, carried far across the realms. It was the time where the realm stood on the cusp of change where the Veil between the living and the dead was at its thinnest.

The wind brushed softly over Sorcha's skin, the fine hairs on her arms prickling. Only then did she realize she had left her window open. The sun was rising, casting a pale glow across the room. Cat had already jumped off the bed, padding toward the hearth to shake the cold from his bones.

She stretched, closing the window before following him into the living area, sinking into the quiet warmth beside him. She sat for a long while, taking in the room, her things, the life she had built here the possibility that she may not come back lingering, unspoken, in the air.

Last night, she had triple checked everything. Her outfit blessed and waiting. Her notes, materials, all secured inside her pack. The cold iron bracelets were already on her wrists, the woven red thread braided carefully into her hair, a final measure of protection. The threads stood starkly now, their color sharper against the hues overtaking the red. She made tea, setting aside a small sachet of herbs and spices, a cup, and a canteen of plain water marked with a ribbon so it wouldn't be mistaken for the blessed water. She ate slowly, toast drizzled with honey and strawberry jam, inhaling the rich scent of her tea star flower, cinnamon, cloves, night root, and morning dew. She savored every sip, every bite, moving deliberately, as if committing each moment to memory.

She sighed as she began to dress, walking past her shelves, fingertips tracing the spines of books, past her vanity pausing. Her reflection. She looked different. Something about her felt foreign, distant, as she took in the changes the way gold had melted into her auburn strands, how her eyes held more ember than green now, the faint speckles the only remnants of what they had once been. The outfit light armor of iron, the worn boots she had loved for years, the faint glow of runes warming against her skin. She had changed, not just physically. She was stronger now, no longer questioning the truth of her heritage, her parents. The truth that she had killed them. But it wasn't her fault. It was his Vaelric. The name felt venomous, leaving a bitter taste in her mouth. She was stronger than she had ever thought. She was different. And she could no longer pretend otherwise. The weight of it settled over her, but she did not shrink from it. She embraced it. Looking once more at her reflection, she turned away. And walked to the door.

She took her time walking the streets of Lumora, the early morning mist creeping along the cobblestones. Merchants stirred, their footsteps shuffling over stone as they began setting up for the day. The soft glow of the rising sun filtered through the trees, casting scattered shadows, while the cold air curled around her and Cat, swirling at their heels. He walked beside her without sarcasm or sharp remarks just quiet understanding. He had read her emotions, and for once, he did not fill the space with words. Instead, he simply walked, matching her pace, embracing what she was going through as if he himself understood. She committed everything to memory even the flowers in the window boxes dusted with frost, others standing resilient against the cold. As she rounded the corner, the horse stables came into view, and there, already waiting, stood Commander Nethran. His hands moved in intricate patterns, his lips murmuring softly as he traced protective runes over the horses. He was careful, deliberate. Gentle.

She watched, saying nothing, as he stroked their manes, whispering to them. One by one, he moved to the next, repeating the ritual until he had blessed them all.

From inside the stables, she could hear the others gathering their supplies the rustle of saddlebags, the clink of buckles, the murmur of quiet voices. She stepped forward.

"Good morning, Commander."

He turned at the sound of her voice. For a moment, he studied her, then nodded, a small, knowing smile crossing his face.

"Good morning, Officer."

They spoke of preparations, of the others, of everything left to do. And then, as the words faded between them, she hesitated before speaking again, her voice quieter now.

"Commander... I just wanted to say thank you." He watched her, listening.

"For taking a chance on me. For always supporting me. For pushing me to be better. I want you to know that I will always be grateful for that."

Her throat tightened. Tears burned at the edges of her vision, but she refused to let them fall.

Nethran's gaze softened.

"Sorcha," he said, steady, certain. "This isn't goodbye. It will never be goodbye. It will always be until I see you next time."

Eirin was the first to emerge from the stable, his expression steady, certain. One by one, the others followed, leading their horses into the cold morning air, loading saddlebags and checking their weapons. Their armor, their supplies, their movements everything mirrored her own preparation. This was it.

Eirin's gaze found Sorcha. He walked toward her, stopping just in front of her, his voice low, almost a whisper.

"Come back in one piece, okay? Try not to cause too much trouble."

A slight grin flickered across his face.

Sorcha held his gaze. "Of course. I would never."

He nodded once, watching as the final preparations wrapped up.

Kyron stood nearby, dressed in iron armor like hers, the morning light catching along the worn edges of the metal. His gaze met hers.

"You ready?"

Sorcha turned to Cat, offering her lap as a seat.

He recoiled instantly, tail flicking in irritation. "Do I look like I have a death wish? I'm not about to sit on iron."

She exhaled, shifting to place him in the side saddlebag, but before she could, Kyron stepped forward, hand resting against a newly fitted saddle on her horse one she hadn't seen before.

"Figured this would be an issue," he said, patting the small, reinforced seat built into the back of the saddle one perfectly sized for Cat. "I told you if he was coming everywhere, you should do something about it. So I did."

Sorcha blinked, stunned for a moment. "You actually—

Kyron shrugged. "Better than him clawing his way out or jumping out mid ride."

Cat narrowed his silver eyes, leaping gracefully into the seat. He sat up, curling his tail around his paws, surveying the setup. "I suppose I can tolerate this."

Sorcha shook her head but couldn't help the small smile that tugged at her lips.

She swung onto her horse, gripping the reins. "Move out," she called.

And with that, they rode. The ride stretched long beneath the shifting autumn sky, the wind brutal with the bite of encroaching winter. Sorcha pulled her cloak tighter, feeling the chill seep through the fabric, creeping beneath her armor like an unwelcome whisper.

The world around them had turned brittle with frost. The trees, once golden with the last remnants of autumn, now stood bare and skeletal, their branches rimmed with ice. Patches of snow clung stubbornly to the earth, spreading in thin sheets where the ground had frozen overnight. With every breath, clouds of warmth curled from the riders' lips, vanishing into the air as they pressed forward. The road to Cailleach's Keep had always been an unsettling one, but under the weight of Samhain and winter's first grip, it felt wholly unnatural.

Mist slithered along the frozen ground, coiling around the horses' legs as they moved. The hooves of their mounts struck against hardened earth, the sound swallowed by the thickening fog that stretched like a second skin over the landscape. Cat let out a slow breath from his perch, his eyes focused at the endless fog.

Mason was the first to speak. "Anyone else notice it's gone eerily quiet?"

As the road curved along a rise, a figure appeared ahead.

A woman stood alone in the path, her dress torn and stiff with frost, her arms hanging limp at her sides. She swayed slightly, as if caught between waking and sleep.

Sorcha slowed her horse. "Hello?"

The woman lifted her head. Her eyes were gone—hollow pits, black liquid spilling down her cheeks. It was the same woman from Meadowrun. Before anyone could move, she screamed and charged. The horses reared, their panic cutting through the screams. Sorcha was thrown from her saddle just as the woman hit her, slamming her into the ground. The impact tore the breath from her lungs.

The woman's hands clawed at her leather, black veins threading down her arms. Her skin was cracked, her mouth full of blood and soil.

"Get off her!" Eirin roared.

He lunged, striking with his blade, but elderly woman twisted with unnatural speed. The sword grazed her shoulder, and she shrieked, thrashing wildly. Sorcha rolled aside, dirt scraping her palms, and gasped for air.

Drystan rushed in, dragging Sorcha to her feet.

Mason took a defensive stance, shield raised. Rhosyn began murmuring an incantation, her hands glowing faintly green.

The woman's movements were erratic, she snapped and bit at the air, nothing about her human. Her head jerked at impossible angles, her body twitching and jerking. She lunged again.

Cat hissed sharply. "Sorcha—your left!"

Sorcha spun just as the woman lunged again. Steel met flesh. The creature's strength was monstrous, forcing Sorcha back step by step until her boots slid on the frozen soil.

The moment the creatures blood touched her skin, Sorcha's runes flared. Erupting light through her leathers. The glow spread, rippling across her skin in waves.

The creature shrieked and stumbled, her body smoking where the glow touched her.

Kyron moved in fast, sword arcing clean through her neck. The body hit the ground with a dull thud, twitching once before falling still.

Then the blood began to move. It bubbled where it touched the soil, hissing, spreading in thin veins that pulsed outward. Black moss burst from the cracks, creeping across the road. The stench that hit them was rot and it was enough to choke them.

Rhosyn took a step back, her voice low. "What is happening?"

"Rhosyn, move back!" Drystan shouted, breath ragged.

"Gods," she whispered.

"Move, now!" Sorcha yelled, Kyron grabbed Sorcha's arm and ran with her to the horses.

The others didn't hesitate. The moss reached for their boots, curling like fingers through the frost. Mason vaulted into the saddle, Drystan right behind him. Rhosyn ran beside them, tunic whipping in the wind, while Cat crouched low on his perch, eyes fixed on the spreading darkness.

They spurred their horses hard. The road behind them writhed as the moss swelled, bubbling, spreading like a living wound.

When they finally reached the ridge, Sorcha looked back. The place where the old woman had fallen was gone, swallowed whole. The earth there pulsed faintly red and black, beating like an open sore.

They rode in silence and it followed them all the way to the shadow of Cailleach's Keep.

The outline of the Keep rose from the frost-laden mist, its blackened walls streaked with veins of ice that caught what little light there was. As they drew closer, the first sounds of the festival began to rise, faint at first, then building like a pulse beneath the wind.

By the time they reached the gates, the quiet of the road had been consumed. Laughter and drums echoed from within the walls, the air thick with the scent of roasting meat and spiced cider. Fires lined the battlements, their glow slipping through the mist and turning it gold and red.

Inside, the courtyards were alive. Bonfires burned high, their light spilling over the faces of those who gathered to celebrate. The Chief Druid stood near the central pyre, preparing to light the sacred fire of Tlachtga. The ritual marked the turning of the year and honored Lugh, whose blessing was said to guard the realm through the dark months ahead. The fire itself took its name from Tlachtga, Daughter of the Druid Mug Ruith, who legend claimed died upon the hill after giving birth to triplets. Her death had seeded the first flame, a fire that was said to bridge the world of the living and the dead.

Every year the flame at Tlachtga was lit anew, its light visible from the heights of the Keep. Tonight, it burned once more, mirrored by the countless fires within the courtyard. The torches along the walls dripped wax like melted bone, the heat and frost colliding until the air shimmered and wavered before her eyes

People filled the courtyards and winding halls, moving in a restless tide of color and sound. Some wore masks of delicate filigree and fine metalwork, their faces hidden beneath painted porcelain. Others wore grotesque visages, twisted wood and carved bone, teeth filed into sharp, wicked points. Some masks were beautiful. Others were not.

Pumpkins, gourds, and hollowed turnips lined the paths, their carved faces glowing in the firelight. Each one was meant to ward away the spirits said to roam free on this night. Just as the masks hid the living, these small, grinning sentinels were meant to keep the dead at bay. Sorcha watched the crowd and wondered how many among them were truly still human.

Dancers moved around the fires, their silhouettes wild and fluid, cloaks flaring as they spun. Their feet barely touched the frost slick stone, as if they danced just beyond the reach of the mortal world. Voices rose in haunting songs, old as the stones beneath their feet, threading through the smoke.

At the base of the great statue of Cailleach Offerings were piled at her feet: coins, flowers, carved stones, and vials filled with something dark and glimmering that caught the light of the flames. The air was thick with burning herbs and spiced wine, but beneath it lingered a scent of metal, faint and wrong.

A hand brushed hers. Kyron.

She glanced at him, finding his gaze fixed on the revelry before them. He said nothing, but she could feel it too, that ripple of unease beneath the beauty. Samhain had turned Cailleach's Keep into something both sacred and unholy, a place where joy and dread mingled until they were indistinguishable.

They wove through the crowd together. The deeper they went, the thinner the noise became. Laughter faded to murmurs, the music dimmed, and the firelight weakened. Smoke hung in the air, curling around them in soft grey ribbons.

Cat shifted in his saddle and spoke quietly. "The fairy mound is in the woods beyond," he said.

At the edge of the festival, Eirin, Kyron, and the others tied their horses to the wooden posts just before the forest. As they moved toward the tree line Sorcha caught movement, just at the edge of her vision. A figure, cloaked in shadow.

It was barely more than a flicker, blending into the shifting dark. The group ahead pressed forward, but Sorcha hesitated, eyes narrowing. The shadows were outfitted in Circle uniforms from the Keep. And that's when she saw her. Riona. Only it wasn't her.

Riona had always been vibrant, untouchable in her strength. But now, she looked as if something had hollowed her out. She was wrong, wrong in the way you would describe a reflection in murky waters. She was thinner, but not fragile. Her white hair, always striking, now looked dull and pale. Her eyes the color of ice had dimmed, a red ring outlined the cold blue. Sorcha's pulse thundered in her ears, and for the briefest moment, their gazes met. But Riona turned and walked away. There was no recognition or hesitation. Just silence.

# Chapter 56
## HOME

Sorcha shook it off and ran ahead to catch up as the group pressed deeper into the woods. The trees growing denser, their gnarled branches reaching overhead.

The festival's warmth had faded behind them, swallowed by the creeping dark. Eirin had the foresight to mark their path, carving small notches into the bark as they went. It was the only proof they had traveled this way at all. The forest ahead felt untouched, as if no one had set foot here in centuries.

Without a sound, a stark white rabbit landed directly in their path. Its silver eyes gleamed in the unnatural stillness. "Not again," Sorcha muttered to herself.

The first time it had appeared, she had been on patrol near Lumora, a warning. The second, in Meadowrun,

another warning. Both times, something had lurked in the shadows, watching. And now, it was here. Its small body remained unnervingly still, but its gaze flicked toward the trees ahead.

"Don't move." Sorcha's voice was barely above a whisper.

Rhosyn, sensing the shift, lifted a hand. Flowers bloomed beneath them, their petals unfurling in a soft, fluorescent glow. The light pulsed gently, casting waves of shifting color across the forest floor.

"It's trying to tell us something," Cat murmured, stepping closer. "Or lure us in."

Eirin gripped his glaive tighter, shifting into a defensive stance. Drystan, Mason, and Rhosyn instinctively moved into formation, backs to each other, scanning the shadows.

The rabbit twitched. A violent shudder ran through its small frame. Then another. Sorcha barely had time to react before the sound of cracking bones split the air. Its body contorted, stretching and twisting as flesh rippled like unraveling thread, limbs elongating, fur darkening. A low sound rumbled from deep within as the creature rose, towering over them. What had been a rabbit now stood a black horse, its mane flowing like liquid shadow. Its ghostly eyes burned as it reared back, hooves pawing the air. The pooka hesitated only for a moment before it bolted into the trees.

The sound of fabric whipping in the wind had reached their ears and from the shadows, a figure stepped forward. She was draped in flowing white gown, its edges torn, hood pulled low, she moved with unnatural grace.

At her side, a black boar trotted, its beady eyes gleaming in the dying glow of Rhosyn's flowers. The air turned colder and the flowers began curling inward as their light withered and died. When the woman spoke her voice was soft, desperate, laced with sorrow.

"I've lost my way," she murmured. "I cannot find my way home. Will you help me?"

Sorcha's runes blazed, their light flaring bright as the sun. She then focused and conjured a flame of light to chase away night. The shadows recoiled, and as the light touched the woman's face, it was missing. Rhosyn whispered to the others "I think that's Lady Gwyn. She only walks on Samhain, looking for lost wanderers in the woods."

Above, the apple trees swayed. Then, abruptly, they stilled. Everything was still and the air became stale.

Then, Cat growled. "Run."

The woman's scream tore through the clearing, raw and unearthly. The boar charged, hooves tearing up the frozen earth. Drystan loosed an arrow, aiming for her head. It struck passing straight through. The hood tore away, revealing the truth. She had no head. Her scream came again, closer this time, shaking the ground beneath them. Sorcha staggered back as the boar lunged. Its tusks gleamed red in the fading light. Kyron drew his sword but Sorcha raised her arms first, her runes blazing like wildfire. The air cracked, her power colliding with the creature mid charge.

The world exploded with light.

When Sorcha's vision cleared, the boar's body was falling apart, its skin unraveling into black smoke.

Laughter erupted in the air. As the headless woman slammed into an invisible force. She stood laughing for a moment before she called to the boar that reappeared beside her. She turned toward Sorcha. "Daughter of Lugh," she hissed, her voice seething with anger as she melted into the night.

Before them, stretching across the forest, was a wall of rippling energy. It shimmered like water beneath the moonlight, only visible when the light struck it at the right angle. Shades of purple and blue undulated across its surface, their glow like deep ocean currents. At its edges, a smoldering ember colored light curled and flared, firelight swallowed by the tide. Sorcha shuddered. She had seen that color before. Drystan stepped forward before anyone could stop him, reaching out. His fingers disappeared the moment they met the surface. He yanked his hand back, staring at it, flexing his fingers. Nothing felt different. Nothing looked wrong. But the sensation of the Veil pulling at him beckoning sent a shiver down his spine.

Then Eirin's voice shattered the moment. "What do you think you're doing?!" Eirin

snapped, his voice low but furious. "What if something on the other side had ripped your hand off?"

Drystan swallowed hard, taking an uneasy step back.

Cat, watching from the side, looked nothing but amused. He prowled along the Veil, scanning it before finally stopping at a spot where the air thickened where the boundary was weakest. "The Veil is always here," Cat muttered, looking around. "Samhain just allows us to see it." Just then a mound rose before them, covered in tangled wildflowers. Without warning, he changed.

The small, sleek creature they had come to know stretched into the massive, powerful creature in the field. His shadow elongated, form shifting into the ferocious, otherworldly feline they recently met. He roared and the ground trembled beneath them, the air humming with energy and then the land split open. An entrance yawned before them, dark and waiting.

Cat turned back to the group, his voice smooth but final. "This is our way in. We part ways here."

The words settled like stone in Sorcha's chest.

She had known this was coming. She had prepared for it. But still—it was different, standing at the threshold.

Eirin said nothing. Just stood there, staring at her.

Their goodbye had already been said at the stables. And yet, it still didn't feel like enough.

She swallowed, turning to the others. "Thank you.

For everything. Please protect the realm. And be safe."

A silence stretched between them. Then, slowly, they nodded, the sadness in their faces unmistakable. But beneath it pride. One by one, they stepped back and Sorcha turned toward the Veil. They did not look back. Not Kyron. Not Sorcha. Not Cat. They stepped forward, into the dark, the entrance yawning like the mouth of an ancient tree and waiting.

The smell of earth was the first thing to envelop them damp, rich, untouched. The walls around them closed in, the tunnel winding downward in a slow descent, wrapping them in silence. Their boots pressed into soft dirt, the weight of the world above shifting with every step. And then the change began. A mist curled in from nowhere. Soft, glowing purple vapor that swirled like breath on a cold morning, rolling over the ground, wrapping around their ankles. Tiny, flickering insects appeared within the haze, their bodies pulsing like tiny bolts of lightning, casting brief flashes of white blue light in the darkness. The air changed. The scent of earth was drowned by something new, flowers. Sweet, sharp, overwhelming in its intensity.

Then the ground beneath them shifted. The packed dirt was gone. In its place, smooth marble stretched beneath their feet, cold and gleaming in the dim light. Their boots echoed against it, the sound jarring after so much silence. A path formed, leading them deeper. And ahead stairs. They were carved from pristine marble, twisted with veins of gold dust, shimmering as if lit from within. It was breathtaking. They ascended in silence. And when they reached the top, the cave mouth opened. The first thing Sorcha saw was the sky.

It was not the sky of her world.

It stretched wide and endless, painted in shades of purple and pink, like a sunset caught in its most perfect moment, never fading. Clouds hung soft and full, pristine white puffs against the dream like expanse. Above them, dragons soared.

Not menacing or monstrous but swift, soft, gliding through the air with an effortless grace. Their wings caught the light, reflecting iridescent colors that shimmered as they passed. Among them, birds of all kinds darted and wheeled, their feathers flashing in shades Sorcha had never seen before. Then her gaze lowered and she saw the castle. It hung in the air, upside down, as if the sky itself had claimed it. Intricate, beautiful, its towers stretching downward, defying gravity. A waterfall ran from its highest spire backward, upward rushing into the sky instead of falling to the earth. The land beneath them was vibrant, more alive than anything she had ever seen. The trees were not green but bold, luminous shades of blue, crimson, gold. Some leaves seemed to glow, their veins pulsing with soft light. A flicker of movement caught her eye. In the distance, a great white stag stood, watching them. Its antlers were massive, its eyes dark and endless. Around it, small creatures flitted through the wilderness, some familiar, some impossibly strange. In the distant was a darkness sprawling with bridges that stretched across the vast landscape, leading to places she could not yet name.

And there coiled upon itself, massive enough to block out entire portions of the horizon, was a snake. A serpent larger than the Druid School, its body twisting upon itself, still and waiting.

Beside her, Cat exhaled. And then, almost to himself, he sighed. "Home."